PENGUIN BOOKS

Your Word or Mine

Lia Middleton is a barrister who specialises in crime and prison law, and lives with her husband and two young children in Buckinghamshire. You can find her on Twitter @liamiddletOn and on Instagram @liamiddletonauthor.

By the same author

When They Find Her

Your Word or Mine

LIA MIDDLETON

PENGUIN BOOKS

PENGUIN BOOKS

UK | USA | Canada | Ireland | Australia
India | New Zealand | South Africa

Penguin Books is part of the Penguin Random House group of companies
whose addresses can be found at global.penguinrandomhouse.com.

First published 2022
001

Copyright © Lia Middleton, 2022

The moral right of the author has been asserted

Set in 13.5/16pt Garamond MT Std
Typeset by Jouve (UK), Milton Keynes
Printed and bound in Great Britain by Clays Ltd, Elcograf S.p.A.

The authorized representative in the EEA is Penguin Random House Ireland,
Morrison Chambers, 32 Nassau Street, Dublin D02 YH68

A CIP catalogue record for this book is available from the British Library

ISBN: 978–1–405–94823–4

www.greenpenguin.co.uk

Penguin Random House is committed to a
sustainable future for our business, our readers
and our planet. This book is made from Forest
Stewardship Council® certified paper.

To Dan – for everything.

We both watch as the jury file in. They each take up their places, just as they have for the past ten days, but something in their faces has changed.

They've made a decision.

Do they believe him?

Or me?

My eyes flash to the dock. He is pristine as always, his suit pressed, his dark brown hair slicked to one side, his face cleanly shaved.

'Anabelle, don't look at him,' Mum whispers.

My body jolts at her voice – a gunshot in the quiet courtroom.

'It's okay, sweetheart,' Dad says, his eyes shining with emotion. 'No matter what happens – it'll be okay.'

'Don't say that,' Mum mutters. 'They're going to find him guilty.'

'Can the foreman please stand,' the man who sits in front of the judge says, his voice ringing through the large room and up into the expanse of the vaulted ceiling. I tear my gaze from Dad and look back towards the jury.

The lady who's sitting in the front row, the one who has been taking notes for the whole trial, the one who wears glasses at the bottom of her nose while she's writing, her greying hair tucked behind her ears, stands.

'Have you reached a verdict upon which you are all agreed?'

The lady coughs, clearing her throat. 'Yes,' she said.

'On the count of rape – what is your verdict?'

She looks down at her hands. I inhale sharply, my breath crackling in my lungs as I wait for her to speak.

Guilty. Please let them find him guilty. Please let me put this all behind me.

Her voice breaks and she stammers, but the verdict spills from her lips and ripples through the air.

'N-not guilty.'

ONE

To spare the guilty is to injure the innocent.

Publilius Syrus

1. Ava

Eighteen years later

'You bitch.'

The defendant's rage leaves globules of spit on the glass separating the dock from the rest of the courtroom. His fists are clenched, even in their restraints – a pair of shining silver handcuffs fastened to contain his unpredictable anger. They aren't usually restrained in the dock, but Justin Anderson has a reputation. He is violent: often dangerously so. And his mouth is always full of bitter, hateful words. In his mind it is my fault that the judge has decided to withhold his bail. It is my fault that he will have to stay in prison until his trial. He seeks a victim on which to hang the blame – someone, anyone. Anyone except him. And the prosecutor is always the easiest target.

The guards yank Anderson to his feet and he stands, his shoulders slumped as he turns to leave the dock. 'Bitch,' he shouts over his shoulder in one final attempt to rile me. The door clangs loudly as he is taken down to the cells.

'Thank you, Ms Knight,' the judge says. 'Miss Jones.'

He stands and the defence barrister and I follow his movement like shadows, bowing our heads, just a fraction, as he nods to us and leaves.

The defence sighs as she begins stacking her belongings on top of one another, her hands shaking. She is new. I could tell, even before her reaction to her client's profanities gave her away: the pristine state of her robes, the bright whiteness of her wig. A baby barrister, newly born into this life of prosecution and defence where justice falls like an axe whose blade has become blunt and dull over time. She isn't used to it – not yet anyway.

'Try not to be too hard on yourself,' I say as I reach up to pull my wig from my head, tucking my short hair behind my ears. 'Some people just can't be saved.'

She sighs, her expression pained. She looks so young. So naïve. But soon she'll learn, as we all do. Even the best of people aren't truly innocent.

I push my way out of the courtroom into the long corridor, walking past the short rows of seats where family members sit in small huddles, whispering in hushed voices, whilst the defendant's gaze sits somewhere in the middle-space, their head lowered, their words stroppy or sullen or scared. I've become used to the way their eyes veer towards me as I pass, drawn to the long, black robes – a bull to red cloth.

My phone vibrates and I glance down at the screen. Message received: Will.

What time will you be home tonight? I have to leave for my dinner by 7. Are you going to your mum's first? Love you x

I met Will during pupillage. I remember seeing him that first day, sneaking a look as we stood next to each other, almost shoulder to shoulder. That evening he asked if I wanted to go for a drink. I took in his warm eyes and truly beautiful face. His kind voice. I said no, like I always did when men tried to approach me – shrinking away from the glare of their attention. But over time I learned to trust him. Over time he became my friend. And last month he proposed, quietly in our flat, just the two of us.

I reach the dark wooden door and balance my phone on

6

top of my file, but as I punch in the key code to enter, the door swings open.

'Here she is,' Caroline, the advocacy manager, says, stepping out of the room reserved for the Crown Prosecution Service. 'How was Anderson?'

'As charming as always.'

'Silver tongue, that one.' She laughs but then reaches for my arm, her eyes shifting away from my face. 'Ava . . .'

'Is something wrong?'

'There's a first hearing for a Grievous Bodily Harm with Intent in Court One,' she says.

'Okay . . .'

'Jonah was meant to be covering it but he's been pulled into some urgent police briefing at the office –'

'So you want me to do it?'

'Please?'

'Caroline, you know I want to help you but I'm so busy already. I've still got the list in Court Three and I really can't finish late today. I have to go and see my mum and –'

'Come on, the hearing shouldn't take long. They'll just take her not guilty plea and set a date for the trial. And it's in front of your favourite.'

'Gilbert?'

She smiles. 'Gilbert.'

I glance down at my watch – 10:45 a.m. If I get to Court Three by half eleven, maybe I can still make it . . .

'Fine,' I whisper. 'But you owe me.'

'I know.'

'When's it going on?'

'I told Gilbert's usher that I'd grab you and you'd come straightaway.'

'Okay.' I turn away from the CPS room and we begin to

walk, Caroline trotting beside me. 'Quickly give me a summary . . . What's the defendant's name?'

'Lily Hawthorne,' Caroline whispers, her eyes darting around for anyone who might be able to hear. 'She's only fifteen.'

'Fifteen?' I mutter. 'The youth court sent her here?'

'Yep, she's very young. Long history of convictions.'

'Is she in custody?'

'No, she's in local authority accommodation with a tag. We asked for a remand to custody but the judge went soft. And the children's home she was in before agreed to have her. I was surprised.'

'And what was the GBH?'

'Stabbing.'

'Why?'

'Something of a teenage crush. He rejected her and she lost her temper.'

'How many times did she stab him?'

'Just once. But to the torso from behind.'

I nod. 'Okay. DNA evidence?'

'Yes. When she was arrested, she was covered in his blood and the knife had her prints on it.'

'Did she talk in her interview?'

'No. She went no-comment but we're expecting her to claim self-defence.'

I slow as we reach the door to the courtroom and glance at the large metal 'One' fixed to the wall.

'Okay . . . And the victim?'

'Forty-three-year-old photographer and entrepreneur. Runs a chain of hotels. She was at his house when she attacked him and –'

A rush of air interrupts Caroline as the door to the courtroom opens outwards.

'Oh good,' Charlie – Judge Gilbert's usher – says. 'You're

here.' He tugs his robe onto his shoulder. 'He's waiting to start.'

'See you soon,' I say, flashing a wide smile at Caroline.

'Good luck,' she says.

Charlie opens the door and I step inside, the courtroom expanding in all directions before me. Dark beams support the high ceiling and the walls are windowless, the room lit by artificial light even in the height of summer.

I glance to my left to where the judge usually sits, but he isn't there. He must have returned to his chambers. And the dock is empty too. I walk forward, towards the front where prosecution and defence share a bench. But as I do so I glance to my left, to the public gallery. Three of the seats in the front row are occupied: journalists – I recognize their faces. And just behind them a man is sitting, his head lowered, but he glances up, his gaze briefly dancing over me.

I freeze.

He is staring down at his lap again now, no longer looking my way, his focus drawn to his phone. But . . . that face. Those eyes.

I rush towards my place on the front row and slam my notebook down, opening my laptop. The screen glows. I navigate quickly to the court files, my fingers flying over the keys as I type her name – Lily Hawthorne. The casefile loads and I quickly move the mouse to the summary tab, hesitating just for a moment.

It can't be him.

I click. My eyes quickly scan over the police summary, my brain automatically acting on years of experience, years of having to quickly ascertain key pieces of information –

There it is. The name of the victim.

My stomach plummets.

Michael Osborne.

He has never truly left me. His name has lingered, refusing to fade even after I stripped myself of my own. The last time I saw him, Ava Knight didn't exist. I was a different person with a different name.

I was Anabelle King.

2. Belle

Eighteen years earlier

'Not guilty.'

The words vibrate and the courtroom sways violently, my ears ringing, like I've been punched. I glance down to the benches to where Sergeant Cavanaugh is sitting behind the prosecutor and, as if he can feel my gaze burning into him, he turns and looks at me, his eyes wide.

'What?' Mum shouts.

'Darling, don't . . . .think of Anabelle,' Dad whispers.

'No,' Mum shouts again as she thrusts his hand from her shoulder. 'I don't understand –'

'Mum, please,' I cry, my cheeks stinging with tears. Everyone is looking at me. They don't believe me . . . Why don't they believe me?

'She's just a young girl! She didn't make this up –'

'No one is alleging that she made this up, Mrs King,' the judge says, his tone kind but tinged with authority. 'I need you to refrain from speaking out or I'll have to ask you to leave my courtroom.'

'We're leaving anyway. This is disgraceful! Come on, Belle.' Mum tugs on my arm, pulling me to my feet like a ragdoll.

Dad stands too but nods to the judge respectfully, his eyes downcast.

My lip quivers as I stare across at the jury, taking in their embarrassed, solemn faces. I rush out of the courtroom, through the narrow rows of the public gallery, flanked by my parents on either side. But I don't feel protected. I am completely exposed. Everyone can see me, everyone can see right through me, all the way down to my core, to my soul. And they don't like what they see.

They didn't believe me.

Dad opens the door, but I throw one final glance over my shoulder, drawn to him like a magnet.

Michael Osborne.

Not guilty.

A cry bursts out of me and I run through the open door into the cavernous hall, out through the exit and back into the world, my parents calling my name as their footsteps thunder behind me. I need to get away from everyone, from everything.

'Belle, wait,' Dad calls out to me as I reach the road.

I stop, breathless, my feet poised at the edge of the pavement, cars flying past me, just inches away.

All it would take is one step. One step forward, and I can make all of it go away.

Just do it —

'Belle!' Dad's strong hands grip my shoulders, and he tugs me away from the road. 'What are you doing?'

I look up at his astonished face, his eyes full of love and sadness and anger, and collapse forwards, my head pressed sideways against his chest. I sob, crying like I never have before. Not when I was cross-examined and his barrister claimed I was mistaken, her eyebrows raised as she looked at the jury, her insinuation that I was making it all up ringing as high and clear as a bell. Not when I had to tell the police what he had done to me. Not when I had to strip, taking off the clothes that I had been wearing when it happened.

Not even when he did it.

'Mr and Mrs King! Belle!' a voice shouts.

Sergeant Cavanaugh is sprinting towards us. He comes to a stop, pulling his tie away from his neck.

'Belle, I'm so sorry,' he whispers.

'I –'

'How dare you,' Mum interrupts, her face screwed up in anger. 'If it wasn't for PC Hart, they would have found him guilty.'

PC Hart. I wish I didn't know that name. I wish he was just another cog in the police machine, another of the many faces I've come across. But no. He is the officer who mishandled the dress I was wearing, accidentally cross-contaminating it with evidence from another case, making it useless. The man who took away the strongest piece of proof we had. Without it, my word wasn't enough.

'We don't know that for sure,' Sergeant Cavanaugh says.

'But she identified him! It was you lot who found him based on her description –'

'Yes, and I said that in my evidence. You heard me.'

'You didn't do enough –'

'I told them that based on her description we recognized Michael Osborne from a warning he had received, and Belle then identified him from a line-up. But the jury clearly didn't think that was enough –'

'But it would have been enough if the jury were allowed to know about the DNA! You put Michael Osborne in that line-up and out of all those men, she knew it was him. And his DNA was on her clothes! She did everything right. She told us and we came to you straightaway. She didn't shower, she told you everything she knows. But PC Hart doesn't do his job properly and poof! – the most important piece of evidence is gone! How is that fair? How is he going to get away with this?'

I close my eyes, blocking out Mum's wild movements and Sergeant Cavanaugh's excuses, focusing instead on the rise and fall of Dad's chest, the faint drumbeat of his heart.

'PC Hart has been suspended and is under investigation.' Sergeant Cavanaugh's words creep into my thoughts. 'I know that doesn't seem like any consolation, but we're trying our best –'

'Your best has left my daughter like this. Look at her! Look at what you've –'

'Penny, that's enough.' Dad's voice thunders over Mum's exclamations, his words rumbling through me. 'Arguing like this isn't helping Belle. It's over. All we can do now is move on.'

'Move on?' Mum's voice trembles as she meets Dad's eyes. 'How can we move on?'

I crane my neck to look up at Dad, desperately searching his face for reassurance. But he says nothing, his mouth falling open as an answer fails to form.

Mum sighs angrily and leaves, her anger propelling her away.

'Sergeant Cavanaugh,' Dad says, 'I know you did everything you could. You've been there since the beginning – I know you wanted this as badly as we did. But that mistake . . .' His arms tense around me, his body rigid. 'That mistake has destroyed our lives. It's destroyed Belle.'

'I really am so sorry,' Sergeant Cavanaugh responds, bowing his head.

Dad squeezes my shoulder and leads me away, his hand tight on my upper arm.

'Wait,' I say. I walk quickly back towards Sergeant Cavanaugh, but I suddenly find that I'm unable to speak, the words I want to say faltering. Instead, I rush towards him, throwing my arms around his torso. He stands awkwardly, his hands dangling by his sides.

'I . . . it wasn't your fault,' I whisper. 'Thank you for believing me.'

I turn swiftly away and rush back towards Dad, my cheeks flushing, but I can't help but glance back. Sergeant Cavanaugh's shoulders are slumped over, his face almost grey. He looks exhausted, weighed down – an intense investigation, suddenly over. He was the officer in charge of my case, he was closer to it than anyone else. Soon enough though, he'll forget me. Another case will take over and I'll leave his mind. But I'll still be trapped.

And they did this to me: PC Hart by ruining my best chance; Mum by telling me that they would still believe me, even without the DNA. Him . . .

And them.

The jury.

They let him go.

3. Ava

I stare at his name on the laptop, my fingers frozen on the mouse.

Michael Osborne.

I should have known it was him. I should have realized as soon as Caroline described the victim: a forty-something-year-old entrepreneur who runs a chain of hotels ... I've spent year after year having to force down nausea whenever I'm faced with a tower or boutique hotel bearing the Osborne name. And he hasn't changed either. Other than the way his hair has greyed, his once almost-black hair now speckled with white, and the lines that have etched into his skin, around his eyes and mouth – he is the same. His skin is still pale, his face still chiselled: high cheekbones and a strong jaw, the same mole near his ear. His eyes still the same shocking blue.

Did he recognize me?

Panic unfurls in my chest then quickly tightens, screws turning on a vice as I glance at him again. But he is paying me no attention – none at all. He has moved on, frowning as he looks down at his phone.

I let out a slow breath through rounded lips. He doesn't know who I am. I've changed so much after all – no longer the skinny teenager in loose pastel clothes and trainers, face partially shrouded by thick-framed glasses, long blonde hair and cheeks filled out with the roundness of childhood. My hair is now jet-black, sharp and blunt at my chin. I wear contacts. My face is angular, my body curved. The passing years have changed me: inside and out. Evidently, much more than they have changed him. He looks the same, just older. But the last time I saw him, he was already a man: fully grown. I was just a child.

How has this happened? How, after all these years, are we in the same place at the same time?

I turn back to my laptop, clicking quickly on the witness form. And there at the top of the list are his name, his number . . . and his address. I reach for my phone and open the map. With trembling fingers, I tap in his postcode.

A pinpoint appears, highlighting a private road – Meadow Gardens.

I pinch my fingers against the screen, and the map zooms outwards. Meadow Gardens is in a town just outside the suburbs of north-west London, so this is the closest Crown Court to where the offence took place . . .

A tingle runs down my spine: I spend my days flitting across the courts of London, travelling from mine and Will's flat south of the river to the courts dotted around the city. And today of all days, I am here. If I had been scheduled to be at Isleworth, or Southwark, or the Old Bailey, I wouldn't have seen him. This day would have passed, like any other, with Michael Osborne being just a bad memory, forced into the furthest corners of my mind.

'Tut-tut, Ava,' a familiar voice whispers to my right. I jump, my mind racing, and turn to face my opponent. But her smile sends a rush of comfort washing over me.

'Marissa,' I say with a sigh. 'I'm so happy you're here.'

'Is something wrong?' she asks, frowning.

'No, no . . . just . . . one of those mornings.'

Marissa and I went to bar school together, studied side by side for every exam, pushed each other through the unrelenting pursuit for a pupillage. She sat down next to me in

17

that first class on criminal advocacy and nodded approvingly after she watched my cross-examination. 'Expertly done,' she had whispered. 'I hope I never have to face you in a courtroom.'

'As opposing counsel or as a defendant?' I smirked.

'Well . . . I guess we'll have to see how well bar school goes.'

But we have faced each other – time and time again. The criminal bar is a small world. Forever shrinking.

'Where's your client?' I ask, steadying my voice, my back tingling as I turn it away from the gallery. Marissa cocks her head backwards, towards the door.

'She's outside. Eleanor, her social worker, is with her . . . I think Charlie's gone to get them now.'

'What special measures are there?'

'None – Lily didn't want any. I spoke to her about it again today but she says that she's still in court even if we take off our "lame costumes".' She shrugs, shaking her head.

'And open court . . . the complainant is here?' I lean my head back towards the gallery. Don't look at him.

'I argued for a closed courtroom but Lily didn't help matters by saying she didn't care. And the reviewing lawyer from the CPS opposed. They said that her anonymity is enough to protect her, and that court should be open. "The interests of open justice" and all that –'

A cough interrupts her and Marissa glances towards the police officer who is sitting directly behind me. He is there in my peripheral vision, leaning forward on his forearms, his eyes burning holes into the back of my head.

'I'd better . . .'

Marissa nods then looks back down at her screen. I stand and walk around the bench, meeting the officer's confused gaze.

'Apologies for the circumstances in which we're meeting, but I'm Ava Knight,' I say as I hold out my hand. 'I'm a Crown Advocate for the CPS.'

'Hi . . .' he says and reaches forward. I shake his hand firmly. 'Where's Jonah?'

'Unfortunately, he's stuck in the office –'

'Ah.' He frowns. 'Sorry, no issues with you, it's just that he's worked on this case since we charged it.'

'I know, but . . .' I shrug. 'You know how it is – sadly this happens all the time. And it's just the plea, it's fine.'

He nods. His face is blotchy, as a rash spreads up his neck and onto his jawline.

'I'm sorry, but I didn't catch your name?'

'I'm DC Hewitt.

'Nice to meet you.' I pause. 'Do you . . . do you know why the complainant's here?'

His eyes dart sideways to the gallery. 'He wanted to hear her plea.'

'It's quite unusual, isn't it?'

'Yes, I suppose, but –'

'All rise.'

The voice of the judge's clerk rings out through the court-room. I dash back to my place and lower my head – a brief mark of respect.

'Good morning again, everyone,' Judge Gilbert says, his voice quiet but commanding. 'Please be seated.'

I stay standing and wait for the collective noise of the courtroom to die down. I pull at the shoulder of my gown which is already slipping backwards but pause as my fingers touch the stiff, rough fabric – when I first put it on, wearing it had felt triumphant. I had worked so hard, for so long, to get there. Now, it feels heavy. Now, it is my armour.

But I don't need protection. All I have to do is hear her

not guilty plea. All I have to do is get through this one appearance – just a few minutes long – and I'll never have to hear his name again.

Gilbert's eyes fall on me, his eyebrows raising in recognition.

'Ah, Ms Knight. Are you here to save the day as usual?'

Marissa scoffs next to me then tries to cover it with a cough, but Gilbert looks over at her with disapproval.

'Beg your pardon, Your Honour,' she says.

'I can but try, Your Honour,' I smile widely.

He smiles at me then lowers his half-moon glasses to the end of his nose and looks at Marissa from above the rim. 'Ms Levey?'

'Yes, Your Honour?'

'Your client?'

'Apologies, Your Honour, and apologies to my learned friend,' she says in a rush, 'I believe your usher went to find her. Might I quickly go and –'

She stops speaking as the door to the courtroom creaks open.

There she is.

Lily Hawthorne.

I balk, taking in her long blonde hair, her small frame. She looks just like I did.

'Lily, if you could please return to the dock,' Judge Gilbert says.

She nods hesitantly, glancing sideways at her social worker beside her before walking slowly behind the rows of benches to the back of the court, where a security guard is waiting by the open door of the dock. She is wearing a black dress, more like an oversized T-shirt, which hangs loosely on her, and Converse, scuffed and greying. Her hair is loose and falls to the middle of her back. She is pretty, her eyes wide and framed by thick, dark lashes. She is the picture of innocence.

But she plunged a knife into a man.

And not just any man.

Michael Osborne.

Why would she do this? Why would she attack someone so brutally? Did she lose her temper that easily? Or was it something else?

'Lily,' Gilbert says, fixing her with his commanding stare, 'my clerk will now read out the charge against you and ask you how you plead. Do you understand?'

'Yes,' she says, her voice cracking, her eyes searching once again for her social worker who has taken a seat on the back bench.

The clerk stands. 'Lily Hawthorne, you are charged with Grievous Bodily Harm with Intent under Section Eighteen of the Offences Against the Person Act 1861.'

We all turn in our seats to look at Lily. Everyone except Marissa, who is staring down at her notebook. I frown, then fix my eyes on the child in the dock. Her eyes are bloodshot and swollen, her jaw clenched, her full lower lip set in a pout.

What did he do to her?

Soon enough, she'll have to give her defence. And when she speaks out at the trial, maybe this time the world will see Michael Osborne for what he really is. Maybe she'll be believed. I can feel it: this girl in front of me is innocent. But she's alone. Nobody by her side except a social worker. Where are her parents? How has her young life led her here?

'How do you plead?' the clerk continues.

In the dock, Lily steps forward, her fingers pressing against the glass, and clears her throat, the corners of her mouth turning downwards.

'Guilty,' she whispers.

4. Lily

Six months before the attack

Smoke hits the back of my throat and I cough, my eyes stinging. I rub them with the back of my hand before starting my slow march past the houses. I scan the numbers hammered to wonky gates and shingle-covered walls, searching for two figures. Five and two. Five and two. Five and –

There it is: 52 Vereland Road.

I knew my new children's home was close by, but I had failed to piece it together. I hadn't realized that on my walk to school I would stumble across the last place where I truly belonged: the place before the short-term foster placements and care. The place where I lived with her. With Mum.

The red door is even more scuffed with age, the paint largely chipped away. Black mould surrounds the door frame and the window to the living room is broken – a jagged hole in the glass, boarded from the inside.

I pull my coat closer around me and stare upwards to the window at the top of the house which looks out on to the road. The net curtains are drawn, and the inside is dark.

The cigarette drops from my fingers, the tip glowing on the tarmac.

That's where I was when they arrived. The police. Social services. I saw them out of that window. I watched as they got out of the car and knocked at the door.

'Don't answer it,' Mum shouted.

I stared down at them, my view obscured by grime, smiley faces and hearts drawn by small fingers in the dirt. Part of me wanted to stay silent, to never be found so that I could stay with her forever. She was my mum. The only mum I would ever know. But the other part, the part screaming deep down inside of me, wanted to pound my fists, fling open the window and cry out. Help. Help me.

I climbed into the back of the car, the social worker whispering that everything would be okay. I stared back at the house, searching for Mum.

But she wasn't there. She didn't even watch as I was taken away.

A tear streams down my cheek but I quickly swipe it away, the tip of my finger coated in thick black mascara. I place my shoe on the still gently smoking cigarette and push down, pressing my weight into the ground, starving it of oxygen.

I shouldn't have come here.

The sound of chatting voices floats down from the main road. But my gaze is drawn to the left, to the bottom of the hill where Vereland Road meets a long dual carriageway.

I can circle back to school. It's my first day – they'll understand if I'm late. But I just need to see it.

My feet carry me quickly downwards, and as the road flattens my pace quickens until I'm jogging briskly, turning right on to the adjacent road, which unfolds itself, long and empty.

Just a bit further and it should be there.

The top of the small row of terraced houses slowly appears, like the sun from beyond the horizon.

I stop outside the railings which are rusting with age. Reaching forward, I lace my fingers through the metal and the hairs on my arms stand on end. It isn't the gentle wind sending shivers across my skin, but the memory of this place as it pulls me back in time: I can still feel the gravel of the path up to the house as it scuffed under my trainers, the clammy grip of Mum's hand. Graffiti that was once colourful, is faded and dull.

She brought me here all the time – whenever her stash ran low. She used to take me to other places too, run-down flats and bedsits, but this was her favourite haunt. Once a week, sometimes twice.

But maybe people don't come here any more.

I squint and stand on my tiptoes, trying to see through one of the darkened windows into the building beyond. The curtains are drawn, but through the gap, there is movement. And a light flashes, deep inside.

5. Ava

Guilty?

Everyone turns away from Lily, their focus reverting to the front of the room, awaiting Gilbert's indication that we should continue. But my gaze remains fixed to the dock.

She's pleading guilty?

I can't stop looking at her. I can't stop looking at this girl, and her blonde hair, and her sadness: the sadness pouring out of her. It could have been me standing there in a dock if I'd chosen to fight back. If I'd stood up for myself. If I'd been within reach of a weapon.

It could have been me.

But she isn't claiming self-defence. She isn't defending herself at all. But . . . he must have done something to make her do this. What did he do to her?

'Ms Knight?'

Judge Gilbert's voice is dull – a droning buzz, his words struggling to morph into something I can understand. I can't hear anything. I can't see anything. All I can see is her.

All I can see is me.

'Ms Knight?'

He barks my name and the world becomes clear. Judge Gilbert is staring at me, his white, thin eyebrows raised in a question. Marissa is watching me too, perplexed.

'Apologies, Your Honour. I –'

'Ms Knight, I am minded not to sentence Lily today and instead adjourn for two weeks for pre-sentence reports.

Given Lily's age and vulnerability, I'd like to have full details from the youth offending team before I sentence her. Does the Crown have any objections?'

I hold my breath as relief flurries in my stomach. If he adjourns for sentencing, then Jonah will take the case back and I'll never have to think about this again. I don't want to read the detail. I don't want to speak this case into existence, to utter the word 'victim' and his name in the same sentence. I shouldn't even be doing this hearing, let alone the sentencing. I should have realized who he was as soon as Caroline mentioned the hotels – I could have backed out. If anybody discovered our connection . . . would I be suspended?

'No objections from the Crown, Your Honour.'

'Thank you.'

I sit down but my eyes fly up to the rows of seats in the gallery. Michael is staring at the dock, leaning forward, his chin resting on his clenched fist.

'Any other submissions, Ms Levey?'

I purposefully turn my body towards Marissa, my back to the gallery.

I will never look at him again.

'Your Honour,' Marissa says, 'I'd ask that Lily isn't remanded into custody until sentencing but instead is remanded back to Franklin House – the children's home she has been in since before she was charged.'

'Thoughts, Ms Knight?' Judge Gilbert says as he pushes his glasses on to the bridge of his nose.

I stand, clasping my still trembling hands behind my back. 'No views from the Crown, Your Honour. Until now, Lily has abided by the curfew and all other conditions of her remand to the local authority.'

'Very well.' He looks to the dock, fixing Lily with his piercing gaze. 'Lily, can you stand, please.'

She gets to her feet, her face so close to the divide that her breath is visible as it pools against the glass.

'You will be remanded back to Franklin House until this time in two weeks when you will be sentenced. You are required to continue with the conditions of your remand and to abide by the curfew requiring you to remain within Franklin House between the hours of seven p.m. and seven a.m. Do you understand?'

'Yes,' she says.

Judge Gilbert stands, nodding briefly before turning to exit through the door to his chambers.

'Case of R against Hawthorne adjourned until Friday the twenty-eighth of May, not before ten a.m.'

The door to the dock clangs open. I glance over my shoulder as Lily steps back out into the world. She walks quickly towards the exit, peering briefly across at the gallery before diverting her gaze. She reaches her social worker and lowers her head, raising her hands to cover her face.

She's crying. Is it guilt that she's feeling? Embarrassment? Fear? There're only two weeks until she is sentenced: fourteen days more of freedom – that's all she has left. She's pleading guilty to GBH, she'll be sentenced to detention, there's no doubt about that. And once she's disappeared into that system . . .

I shake my head. I need to get out of here.

'Marissa, I'll speak to you soon, okay?'

'Sure. See you on Sunday,' she says, sliding out of the bench and making her way to speak to Lily.

'Thank you, DC Hewitt,' I say, nodding at the officer.

The door to the CPS room crashes closed behind me, a sanctuary sealing shut. Caroline turns her head at the loud noise and smiles as she sees me collapse into my chair.

'That bad, was it?' she says with a chuckle.

I pull my wig off and fling it on to my desk. It lands on a pile of books, lopsided, and I slump down as Lily's face flashes before my eyes.

She's just a girl. Afraid. Alone. Just like I was.

'Ava,' Caroline says, still facing her computer. 'I'm going to put you down for the sentencing in two weeks. No point handing it back to Jonah.'

My eyes sting, my stomach turning violently as a tight hand of panic begins to crush my chest.

'Caroline, I need to talk to you about –'

The door bursts open and a flustered usher, the new girl, steps inside.

'Ms Knight?'

'Yes?'

'We've been calling you on the tannoy –'

'I was called into Court One –'

'Well, the judge wants to know how long you'll be for Court Three.'

'I'll be five minutes, I just need to go to the loo,' I say, grabbing my phone and rushing towards the door. She steps awkwardly aside.

I turn out into the main expanse of building and on my right the courtrooms stretch out, one after the other. My eyes fixate on the door at the end, and my heels click as my feet begin moving faster and faster, my breath fast and shallow, my heart thrumming out its frantic beat.

I rush into a stall and quickly unlock my phone, tapping quickly on George's name. The dial-tone blares.

Please pick up. Please.

'Answer the phone, George!'

The ringing stops abruptly.

'This is George Cavanaugh. If you want me to get back to you, leave a message –'

I cancel the call.

Just breathe, Ava.

It's okay – I'll see George later tonight for dinner. I can speak to him then.

I hang my head to look down at the floor which is swaying beneath my feet. But Michael's face appears, not as it was in the courtroom, but younger, his eyes staring at me blankly. Empty.

Don't think about that night. Don't do it. Don't. Don't. Don't –

The party.

It was Dean's birthday – the boy my best friend Rachel liked. I couldn't stand him. He and his friends were the only people in our year that I didn't like – I was friends with everyone, popular, even. But I couldn't find anything to like about those boys. And Finn wasn't going to the party, he'd made up a lie about being grounded. But Rachel begged me.

So, I went.

Only an hour in, I wanted to leave. I was tired from athletics training, and tired of watching Dean and his stupid friends down drinks and guffaw at each other's stupid jokes. I just wanted to go home.

That's where I made my mistake.

The walk.

I decided to walk.

That was the moment. The moment my world changed. If I had left earlier, or later, or asked one of the upper years for a lift, it wouldn't have happened. Or it would have happened to someone else.

Ten minutes from my house, I stopped by the river and looked up at the stars as the sound of a passing train rushed behind me. It was so beautiful, the moon on the water, the stars shining down on me.

And then . . .

I've tried to forget but –

Hands over my mouth. Strong arms pushing down against my chest. My legs kicking. His blue eyes. My dress being pulled upwards. Hands on the inside of my thighs. Pressure. Fear. Stillness.

A sky full of stars.

A shaky breath whistles through my clenched teeth, but I stand and walk out of the stall, out of the toilets, and back into the hall. I can't stay there, locked in the past – I have a job to do. For years I have pushed these feelings away, and I can do it again. I can do it now.

I shake my hands out at my sides, fingertips tingling with adrenalin, my feet guiding me towards Court Three. My lip trembles as I reach the door, but I pause and close my eyes, forcing my face into a neutral expression, my downturned mouth curling upwards, the creases in my forehead ironing themselves out as I push my emotion down, holding my breath until it all drains away.

I blink slowly and then open the door, stepping into the courtroom.

'Ah, Ms Knight,' Judge Falconer calls from his bench. 'Good morning.'

'Good morning, Your Honour,' I say with a smile. As if nothing has happened.

Nothing at all.

6. Ava

'Mum?'

Closing the front door behind me, I shout out, hoping I'll hear her respond, her voice cheerful. Or at least neutral. But I am greeted by silence.

'Mum? Where are you?'

Nothing.

I walk through the narrow hallway, the gift-bag dangling from my fingers, my eyes darting into the small living room at the front, before heading to the kitchen. But she isn't there.

I stride back into the hallway. 'Mum?'

'I'm upstairs, Ava,' her voice calls out, floating down the stairs.

I run up them two at a time, my dress riding upwards, and dash past the room at the front – my old bedroom – coming to a sudden stop in front of her door. I push with my finger-tips, and it swings open slowly, a sigh escaping my lips as the room reveals itself.

Mum is sitting on her bed, a large glass of red wine in her hand, a half-empty bottle on the bedside table next to her.

'Hi, Mum . . . what are you doing up here?'

'I was just getting ready for dinner.'

She looks at me with a half-smile and pats the space beside her. I clamber on, like I used to when we first moved here, occupying the side of the bed that would have been Dad's. She would wrap her arms around me and tell me it was going to be okay. That we would be okay on our own – we'd get there.

'Happy birthday, Mum,' I say, leaning across to kiss her on the cheek.

'Thanks . . . did you come here straight from work?' Her words are tinged with the slightest of slurs. I nod, my eyes fixed on her hand as she lifts the glass to her mouth and gulps. 'When did you last see your dad?'

I look down at my hands and begin to pick at the loose skin around my thumb. Speaking to her about Dad is like tiptoeing towards a dangerous animal – one that could hurt you at any moment. But avoiding the conversation can be just as dangerous.

'I visited at the weekend. Saturday . . .' I glance at her sideways, but she is staring into space, her eyes glazed over. 'When did you last speak to him?'

'This morning. Just . . . just for a minute or two. You know I can't stand to think of him there. He's a good man. He doesn't belong in prison.'

Prison. She said it: the word that so often sends her catapulting into a rage or bursting into tears. It's been eighteen years, and it's never changed or become better. It's just become worse. And she blames me.

I blame myself.

'I know, Mum.' I sniff, my mind racing as I try to think of something else, anything else, to say.

'Well, I came to give you your birthday present.' I nudge my knee against her leg. 'Do you want to open it now?' I lift the bag and place it on her lap.

I freeze, my breath shallow as she removes the tissue paper and pulls out the leather-bound sketchbook and watercolours. What if this was a mistake? What if this present sends her into a spiral? She might think I'm forcing her to remember our past, the hours she would spend in our old house, facing out to the bottom of our garden, painting the trees and the birds. The river.

'Mum, if you don't like it, I can –'

'No, don't be silly. I love it.'

'I just thought it might be a nice thing for you to do, and I –'

'Ava, seriously,' she says. She reaches across to where my hands are clasped together on my lap, and covers them with her own, her fingers warm, like always. 'I love it.'

She meets my eye but hers are bloodshot, glazed with tears, and as she sniffs, a few fall down her face.

'Oh Mum, I'm sorry. I shouldn't have –'

'It's not that. I really do love it, it's just . . . Painting always reminds me of your dad.'

I nod. 'He always loved your paintings.'

'Even my terrible ones.'

'None of them were terrible, Mum.'

'Yes, they were. Remember that one of you that he put above the fireplace in the lounge? It was horrid.'

I snort, the violent laugh dispelling the cry that had been threatening to emerge. 'Yes, that wasn't great, was it?'

'No,' she whispers, smiling sadly. 'But he loved it. I painted that just before . . . everything. You were even wearing your bracelet –'

I wince – the mention of my bracelet sending me reeling back to that moment: the grip of Michael's hands around my wrists, the silver charms digging into my flesh. But it snapped off and was never found. Just like so many pieces of me, it was irretrievable. Lost.

Mum stops speaking abruptly, her eyes reproachful, as if she has stung me.

'Sorry, I know you don't like to talk about it.'

'Neither do you.'

'No.'

Our conversation turns to silence again, the mere hint of what happened sending us away from our old relationship, one of ease and comfort and love, and back into the present: stilted conversations, awkwardness, fear of saying something wrong.

Michael Osborne's face flickers at the forefront of my mind – a picture that for years has been grainy and faded, like an old photograph, but now is clearly defined.

He did this to us.

'What would you do if you saw him again?' I whisper.

I turn my head to look at Mum, my face pressing against the musty, hardened headboard. Her eyebrows lower as she considers the question, shocked by its directness.

'Who?'

'Michael Osborne.'

Her mouth falls open at the sound of his name. We don't talk about him. Ever. The sound of his name within these walls is like a stranger wandering through the rooms. 'Why would you ask that?'

'I saw . . .' My words trail away. 'I had a case earlier today and it just made me think about what happened.'

'Don't think about it. Never think about it. It happened, he walked away, that's that.'

'But if you saw him today. Say he walked right past you in the street. What would you do?'

'What could I do? The past needs to be left in the past. Look at your dad. If he'd been able to leave it behind, he would still be here with us. But he isn't.' She shakes her head, her mouth set in a stern line. 'If I saw that man walking past me in the street, I'd walk right on by.'

I roll my eyes. *The past needs to be left in the past . . .* That's easy for her to say – whenever she is confronted with the past, she drowns it out, submerging it, until it can't be seen or heard or felt.

And in my own way, I've done the same. I've buried what happened deep down inside me, and refused to let it emerge for air, even for a second. I've set my focus on one thing: become a prosecutor, make sure guilty people are charged. Make sure guilty people are punished. And don't think about Michael Osborne.

'Are you sure you don't want me to stay with you?' I say, staring into the blank space before me.

'No, I'm going out with friends from work.'

'I could come with you –'

'No, Ava, you get on home.' She avoids my eye. 'Thank you for bringing me my present.'

I swing my legs sideways and push myself off the bed. I pull my dress back down to my knees and walk around the edge of the bed to lean down and kiss her on the cheek.

'Bye, Mum. Enjoy the rest of your birthday.'

'Thanks,' she whispers. She doesn't move, making no motion to get up from the bed, to follow me downstairs and wave from the door.

When I finished school, it took so much for me to leave her. I was desperate to escape but terrified that if I left, I would lose her completely. But George encouraged me to go. *Go to London and start your life again,* he said. *She's only an hour away. You deserve to have your own life. You deserve to not be trapped by what happened forever . . .* So, I went. I went to law school, I met Will, I built a career. I constructed myself a new life, brick by brick. But every time she doesn't answer the phone, every time I push my key into the lock and am greeted by silence, I wonder if the state of our relationship is my fault too.

I take a final look at her, then walk out, leaving her door open behind me. But I pause at the top of the stairs and stare inside my bedroom. It's just an empty box – no life, no personality – so different to my bedroom before it all happened. That one was covered in photos of my friends, running medals hung over the headboard and my ceiling was covered with glow-in-the-dark stars. But after Dad was arrested, Mum and I moved in with Grandma and then here. Mum changed her name too. It had been the plan that we all would once we moved away, even Dad, but he remained a King – he wanted to keep as much distance as possible between my new name and his conviction. We were living the new life he had planned for us, away from the whispers at school and the stares in town, but we had to do it without him. It wasn't the same. And then I left.

But now, standing here, just one degree away from Michael Osborne, it feels like the girl I was is here again, resurrected, after all this time.

And as I leave the house behind – imagining Mum sitting on her bed, gulping from the dregs of wine left in her glass – my young voice echoes in my ears.

Don't let him get away again.

7. Ava

The door swings away from me before I have a chance to push my key into the lock.

'Hello, gorgeous,' Will says, standing in the doorway. He is dressed in a pale blue suit, his white shirt open at the collar, bright against his dark skin.

'I thought I'd missed you,' I say, a smile spreading across my face.

He holds out his arms and I step into them, breathing in his familiar scent.

'How was your mum?' he whispers.

'You know . . . The same.'

'I'm sorry, sweetheart.'

I step backwards, taking comfort in the sight of Will's broad frame, his eyes wrinkled with concern.

'I know. Me too.'

His hand moves to the small of my back and we both retreat into our apartment. We've lived here for four years, our lives blended, our routines inextricably entwined. We've outgrown the flat: our belongings are scattered around it, an extra wardrobe tucked into the corner of the living room, and the ceiling in the bathroom is speckled with damp. We've been saving to buy somewhere better but now we're saving for the wedding instead. A criminal barrister and the owner of a brand-new start-up do not make a money-flush pair, especially in London. But a move can wait – there's some comfort in this home that has become a part of us, stitched into the fabric of our relationship.

I take off my blazer and then kick off my heels, sinking down several inches so that my head now barely grazes his shoulder. I shuffle barefoot, crossing the short distance to flop down on to the sofa.

'Hard day?'

'Long day.'

'Do you want to talk about it?'

He stands above me, and my heart swells as I take in his warm, beautiful face. But it abruptly sinks under the weight of my secret. For so long I have found countless ways to convince myself that it isn't a betrayal of our relationship to not tell Will what happened. He hardly knows Mum. And he doesn't know about Dad. He thinks Dad moved away. I've told myself that it's my past and it's my decision whether to reveal it to anyone – that it's my choice. But each time I give myself this reassurance, I know that the right thing to do would be to tell Will the truth.

'I –'

I stop – the still open door, and the space beyond it, catching my eye. If I tell him what happened, after so many years of lies – could he walk out and never come back?

'No, it's fine,' I say, smiling. 'Go to your dinner. Jamal will kill me if I make you late.'

Will and his business partner have been wooing a new investor – their biggest yet. I tried to talk Will out of leaving the Bar: only one year into practice he decided it wasn't for him. But once Jamal had told him about his idea – a new type of virtual-reality for businesses – Will made the leap. And he hasn't looked back.

He rests his hand on the arm of the sofa and leans down to kiss me, his other hand on my cheek.

'I love you,' he whispers.

'You too.'

'I won't be too late.'

'No worries, I'll be working. Good luck.'

'Bye, sweetheart.'

The thud of the door closing vibrates in my chest.

'Bye,' I whisper as loneliness swiftly fills the room. It's been a strong presence ever since that night, a figure that hovers in corners, consuming the energy of any other person, fading their outline so that it might as well be that they're not even there. The only time it ever truly disappears is when I'm with Will. In his company it shrinks, unnoticeable. But as soon as he leaves, it comes back in varying degrees. The feeling of being completely alone, nobody understanding – nobody believing. Sometimes, in a crowded courtroom, I wonder: if I screamed now, would anyone hear me? Can anyone see me?

After Michael Osborne was acquitted, I sought what little comfort I could in reassuring myself that it couldn't get any worse. But I was wrong . . . And so, Ava emerged. Ava – the Ava that everyone sees – isn't real. Not really. She's what I became to get by, to claw myself upwards and put as much distance as I could between who I wanted to be and who I had become. Now, everyone sees Ava Knight, the advocate who speaks her mind and is straight to the point. Confident.

But she's a lie.

Inside, I'm still Belle. Sad. Alone. Angry.

I throw my arm over my face and inhale deeply. I just need to forget today. I need to forget that this ever happened and get on with my life. I glance at my watch. George will be here in forty minutes.

I push myself off the sofa and stride to our bedroom. I peel off my fitted dress and toss it on to the bed, then squeeze around the small gap between the bed and the wall to reach my wardrobe. I pull on leggings and a top, then head to the front door and shove my feet into well-worn trainers. A quick run will help me forget today.

I follow my usual route, the same playlist as always blaring through my headphones, expecting the mindless monotony of placing one foot in front of the other, over and over again, to quiet my mind, to take me away from work, away from the courtroom, like it always does. But his name rings in my ears, drowning out the music.

Michael Osborne, Michael Osborne, Michael Osborne.

I throw myself back through the door of the apartment, my jaw clenched. I was fine this morning – I can't let one glimpse of him take me back eighteen years. I rush to the shower and quickly wash, and just as I'm pulling on a hoodie and jogging bottoms, a familiar rhythm of knocks raps on the door.

I open it and George's face beams back at me, a bottle of wine tucked under his arm, a paper bag held out in front of him, the smell of Chinese food wafting into the apartment.

'Hi, George,' I say.

When I first arrived at the police station, I sat down with my dad on a row of chairs by the entrance, while Mum spoke to someone at the front desk. I stared down at my lap, my fingers grazing the hem of my ripped dress. Mum had told me not to take it off – the police would need it. After a few minutes, we were taken into a small room, just behind the front office, and questions were rattled off quickly: what had happened, when, where . . . Who? Then I was taken to a hospital unit – a Haven, as they called them – to be examined. My dress and socks were taken from me, my shoes, my body swabbed for evidence, and a doctor with sad eyes and a quiet voice pulled on gloves and told me to lie still. That she would be as quick as possible.

The following day I returned to the station. A female officer led me through the seemingly infinite corridors, my parents following behind, until we reached the room. A room that looked different to what I had imagined, different to what I had seen on television and in films. So different to the sterile white rooms of the Haven. Calming blue adorned the walls and a large sofa sat on one side, two armchairs opposite. There was a coffee table in the middle, with a jug of water and several glasses. If I hadn't been led through the police station, past officers dressed in uniform, every muscle in my body aching with exhaustion and discomfort and shame, we could have been in a stranger's living room. But as I sat down, a camera hanging in the far-right corner of the room caught my eye. Its lens was fixed on the sofa – an imposing reminder of what had happened, what I was there to do. I was reporting a crime. I was the unwitting girl who was in the wrong place at the wrong time. I was a victim. I would always be a victim.

'Anabelle King?'

I nodded at the man who entered the room – a middle-aged officer with greying blond hair and stubble.

'I'm Detective Sergeant Cavanaugh. But you can call me, George. Okay?'

'Yes,' I whispered, shrinking away from him, my eyes darting to the woman who was still sitting at my side.

'Do you like to be called Anabelle?'

'Belle,' I whispered.

George touches my arm. I jump, jolting back to the present.

'Ava? Are you okay?'

'Yes – sorry,' I say, focusing on his now aged face, my cheeks flushing. 'I went somewhere else for a moment there.'

'Sorry I missed your call earlier. I did try to call you back –'

'No, it's fine, don't worry. Come in, come in.'

41

He smiles and steps inside, hugging me tightly. I rest my trembling chin on his shoulder, fending off a wave of emotion. My fingers press into his back, holding on to him briefly before he releases me to take off his coat and hang it up by the door.

When we first met, I was scared of him. Frightened of the man who seemed to hold justice in his hands. But he didn't speak to me like a victim – his eyes weren't filled with sadness or sympathy. He listened. All he wanted was to hear my story and I told him everything, just as I remembered it. He tried. He did everything he could. And after everything happened, he kept helping me. He made sure that I was okay.

Without George . . . I'm not sure I would have survived.

'Ava?'

His voice, weathered and deep, breaks into my thoughts.

'Yes?'

'Do you want wine? Or have you stopped for the marathon?'

'The marathon isn't until next April!' I laugh. 'I think a glass of wine is okay.'

The wine glugs into the glass, and I take it from him gratefully, smiling as we both take our first sip.

'Shall we eat?' he asks.

We place our glasses on the table and unpack the Chinese: always the same order. We've had dinner together every week for years. Sometimes alone, sometimes with Will sitting beside us, both of us more careful with our words. Our joint history our well-kept secret.

'How's Will?' George asks as he loads beef and black bean on to his plate.

I glance down as I load a forkful of sweet and sour into my mouth. 'He's good. He's got a really important meeting tonight – a big potential new client.'

'That's exciting.'

'He's doing really well.'

'And you?' he says gently, looking up from his plate. 'How's your mum?'

My fork scrapes across my plate as I poke it through my food. 'The same. You know . . .'

He nods, his eyes dancing down to his plate. 'How is she feeling about your dad's parole review? It's coming up soon —'

'You know we can't talk about stuff like that, George. She's spent all these years mourning him, like he's died . . . I don't know how she'll react when he's released.'

He catches my gaze, a strange look in his eye.

'What?' I ask.

'What are you going to tell Will? When your dad's released . . . what will you tell him?'

My mouth drops slightly. 'I . . . I'll tell him that Dad has moved back —'

'After eighteen years?'

'George, I . . . I don't know.'

'You could tell him the truth. He'd understand.'

'Maybe . . .' I shake my head. 'How's retirement?'

George smiles, knowing me too well to resist the change of subject. 'Boring.'

'Really?'

'Mm. Who knew?'

'You could always go back . . .'

'I'm an old man now, Ava. That's definitely behind me.' He sighs. 'And your work? Anything interesting this week?'

I look up from my plate. He is watching me, waiting for a standard answer to what would normally be a standard question. I continue to play with my food, and then reach for my glass, drinking steadily, sip after sip. A trick barristers use in court to bide time.

'George . . .'

43

He pauses, his fork raised halfway to his mouth. 'What is it?'

'I got thrown into a PCMH this morning. Last minute. A fifteen-year-old girl who stabbed someone.'

'GBH?

I nod. 'She pleaded guilty.'

'God, how awful.' He sighs. 'Another child lost.'

'The victim . . . the person she stabbed . . .' I pause, my heart racing as the words poise themselves on my lips, begging to be said. 'The person she stabbed was Michael Osborne.'

He freezes, blinking rapidly. His upper lip twitches as he frowns, trying to make sense of what I've said.

'That's why I called you . . .' I continue, my words fumbling over each other. 'I was panicking.'

George lifts his hand to pinch the bridge of his nose, his brows knitted together. 'The victim was Michael Osborne?'

'Don't call him that.'

'Okay . . . you're telling me that the person who was stabbed by this girl, was Michael Osborne?'

'Yes,' I whisper.

'Fuck.'

I stare at him. I don't know what to say. All I can do is watch as he processes the sudden shift into the past, the unwelcome presence of the ghost we have both tried to forget for so long.

'Ava . . . Jesus. And you did the hearing?'

'Everything was so rushed, you know what it's like, I just –'

'You should have told them straightaway –'

'I only realized who he was once I was actually in the courtroom!'

'You could have asked for a quick adjournment and told Caroline that you knew the victim –'

44

'Stop calling him a victim!' Tears fill my eyes as frustration swells in my chest.

'If this girl stabbed him, Ava, then that's what he is!'

I slam down my fork. 'Stop it!'

George watches me silently, but I look away, my breathing fast, my temper rearing – a horse ready to bolt.

'Ava, I'm sorry. I just . . . I can't believe you did that.'

I swallow then take in a deep breath. 'I know,' I mutter, finally meeting his worried gaze. 'Neither can I. And I knew I had to back out but I just . . . couldn't.'

'When's the sentencing?'

'Two weeks today. They've expedited reports and Caroline has assigned it to me.'

'But you won't do that, right? You'll come up with an excuse –'

'Yes, of course.'

'Good.'

Silence fills the room, awkward and unnerving. So different to the atmosphere that usually surrounds us. George is like family.

'He was there,' I whisper.

'At court?' George asks, his eyes wide.

'Hmm. Sitting in the gallery. That's how I realized.'

'Did he see you?'

'Yes. But he didn't recognize me. He wouldn't . . . Would he?'

'I –'

'Would you if you were seeing me again for the first time now?'

He falters, his face changing as he considers my words, as if my transformation is happening all over again, right before his eyes. 'No, I suppose not. I forget how much you've changed. Your face . . . everything about you. You're so different now.'

'I'm nothing like I was then. And I was in my wig and gown. Also, my name . . . he doesn't know it.'

He nods, reassured. 'How did you feel? Are you okay?'

'Sick. I felt sick. Seeing him there . . .' I shake my head. 'But I'll be fine. I just need to forget it ever happened. He's a memory. That's all.'

George reaches across the table, over our still-full plates of food, gesturing for my hand. 'You know I'm always here for you, right?'

I squeeze his fingers. 'I know. Thanks, George.'

We spend the next couple of hours eating and drinking, and slowly we revert to our usual comfort, the same warm conversation, a blanket on a cool evening.

He leaves and I climb into bed. I try to do what I said I would – I try to forget. But even though it is midnight and the room has fallen into darkness, my mind is consumed with bursts of the past, with imaginings of the present. With Michael.

What is he doing?

Does he ever think about me? About what he did?

Maybe once he was acquitted, I disappeared from his conscience completely – the jury's proclamation of his innocence making it so that it had never happened at all. But that's what most people don't understand . . .

Not guilty does not equal innocent.

What if there've been other girls? How long did it take him to work up the nerve to attack someone again? Has there been one? More? How many? If I had done something different, would he have been locked away, unable to do them harm?

And how, if I stand by and do nothing, will I ever live with myself?

8. Ava

The number of the house is marked on the brick column, a large thirteen in metal – modern and cold.

Number 13, Meadow Gardens.

I woke up this morning, early as usual, and tried to put him from my mind. My eyes still bleary, I tiptoed out into the living room, careful not to wake Will. But I couldn't stop thinking about Michael Osborne. And now I'm here, staring up at his home, just half an hour out of the city. Less than an hour from my home and the life I built to escape him. I've often thought about where he might be, but I never expected this – the unnerving closeness makes my skin crawl, as if I'm being watched. As if I've been watched all these years.

The house is large and double-fronted, the cream arch of the doorway covered in ivy, the black front door shining in the sun. It is beautiful, so different to our cramped flat above a row of shops, the smell of kebabs and noise of late-night revellers floating up through the floor. But he didn't make this life for himself. Everyone knows the Osborne name, even if they don't know who it belongs to. This life was given to him, on a platter, and even what he did to me never came close to being able to take it away. His future – this present – was always mapped out.

I lean back in my seat, my neck falling back against the headrest, and close my eyes. My head is thrumming, the ache of anxiety starting to twist at the temples. I should just drive away. No one needs to know that I came here. I could drive to see Mum – the lie I've told Will can transform into the truth – and I can pretend that I never climbed into my car and drove the twenty miles to the leafy suburbs.

But curiosity is clawing at the back of my skull, like an itch that you can't quite reach to scratch. Like searching for toxic friends or ex-lovers on social media, picking at the healed scar just to satiate the need to know what they're doing. And now that I've seen him again, this feeling won't go away – not until I've seen him. Just one more time.

A sudden slam of a door echoes out over the low grumble of the engine and my eyes fly open.

He is there. Standing on his doorstep. Dressed in a long tan coat, a white shirt peeking out from beneath, black shoes shining in the light. My breathing slows as he begins to walk away from the house, my mind unable to process seeing him like this, going about his everyday life.

I shrink down in my seat. He's paused, standing still in the middle of the drive. He's waiting . . . But what for? Another slam sounds out and my stomach rises upwards slowly, that moment at the top of a rollercoaster: the split second before the drop.

A young girl is stepping out into the sunshine, running down the drive. As she reaches him, he pulls her closely to his side, his arm clasping her shoulders, and they begin to walk. He is limping slightly on his left side, his movements slow and awkward.

My face is pressed to the window as they reach the gates, my eyes unblinking as I take in every detail. She is small, barely reaching his chest, and she is shrinking away from his grip as he presses a kiss to the side of her head, her shoulders rising up towards her ears.

I'm plummeting, my stomach turning over and over. She's just a child . . . but she must have stayed with him last night.

What did she tell her parents? Where did she tell them she was staying?

They step out on to the pavement and he removes his arm from her shoulders. He is careful now. No longer reckless. And his victims are no longer randomly selected. Unlucky. Now they are chosen.

I turn off the engine and climb out of my car, closing the door carefully, making sure that it doesn't make any noise. I click the keys. The headlights flash.

I'll follow them for a few minutes, just to see where he is taking her.

They're walking in silence but every so often he looks down at her, the side of his face stretched in a smile. I slow as they reach a small parade of shops, and they enter a busy cafe, the bell jingling jauntily as they enter.

My feet move quickly underneath me, and I dart across the road. I approach the large window of the cafe, its frontage painted sky blue. It is busy, almost every table occupied, full of families and teenagers, and couples having brunch. I scan the tables, searching for them –

There he is – setting up his laptop at a table near the far window. But the girl has disappeared from his side.

Where is she?

I move closer to the door. If I went in, would he see me? Would he even notice me? I could go inside and observe them up close, maybe even catch a few words from their conversation. Just for a few minutes. If he has another victim with him, another girl who has fallen into his grasp, I need to help her.

My fingers tremble as I reach for the door, withdrawing as they brush against the smooth metal handle.

I can't.

I can't do this. I need to leave right now.

Guilt surges inside me as I quickly walk away. I left her there. Alone. With him.

'Ms Knight?'

The guilt dissipates, instantly replaced by panic, and I freeze.

It's him. His voice, just as I remember it, just as it has sounded in my mind, in my nightmares.

I should keep walking, pretend I haven't heard him, but my legs won't move, and my heart is hammering away in my chest, blood rushing in my ears. Fight or flight. The basic human responses. But people forget that there is a third response to fear . . .

Freeze. Complete shut-down. Be polite. Don't reject. Don't say no.

Just like before.

Close your eyes and pray for it to be over.

I turn to face him.

'Ah, it is you,' he says, standing just outside the door of the cafe. 'I thought I recognized you . . . I wasn't sure. You look different without your wig.'

'I'm sorry, do I . . .' I say, arching an eyebrow, feigning ignorance.

'No, it's my fault. I recognize you from court yesterday. I'm Michael Osborne. From Lily Hawthorne's case.'

'Oh, right. Nice to meet you, Mr Osborne,' I say, coughing loudly to disguise the break in my voice, the tremor at the end of his name.

He holds out his hand. 'Please, call me Michael.'

I reach out slowly, the taste of sick stinging the back of my throat as his fingers close around mine.

'Michael. I'm . . . Ava,' I say, forcing a smile, trying to focus on anything except his eyes on my face, the grip of his hand.

'What a small world,' he says, laughing as he lets go. 'Do you live around here?'

'No, I . . . I stayed at a friend's house . . . She lives just around the corner.'

'What a coincidence – I live just down the road.'

I smile. 'Well, I really should –'

The bell sings out its happy tune as the door opens behind him.

'Dad, did you get me my juice? I need to go.'

The girl has appeared behind him, no longer smiling, her face now contorted into a scowl. But her image blurs, softening into no more than an outline as her words ring loudly in my ears. One word.

Dad.

9. Lily

Five months before the attack

Shadows fall over me, blocking the sun that has been warming my face against the winter chill.

'You're still here then?'

Kacey, an older girl from Franklin House, stands over me, her silhouette darkened by the sun. But I can make out her features, her voice, cruel and cold. Her friends linger behind her, the three of them huddled together, like witches around a cauldron.

'Yes,' I say, placing my book on my bended knees. 'Am I meant to be somewhere else?'

'I looked for you when I got here.' False concern stretches her pout into a smile. 'You left just after me but when I arrived at the gate you weren't here.' Her eyes narrow, her smile falling away. 'Where'd you go?'

'Nowhere,' I mutter, imagining the small bottle of pills buried at the bottom of my bag.

'Nowhere?' She laughs, and her friends all cackle in response. 'Really?'

'What's your problem?'

She steps forward, the point of her shoes knocking into my shin.

I resist the urge to stand up. If I stand up, I won't be able to stop my temper. And I can't get in trouble again. Franklin House said: no trouble.

'You're my problem,' she mutters, crouching down, her

face close to mine. 'I could tell as soon as you arrived that you were going to cause issues. We've got a good thing going at home and I'm not letting some drug-addled little crack-baby come in and ruin it.'

I bite down on my back teeth.

Don't react.

Reaching into my jacket, I pull out my cigarettes.

'You can't smoke on the field,' Kacey says, her mouth twisted into a snarl. Her friends laugh again, but this time it is tinged with unease.

I don't look away. My fingers instinctively open the box and slide out a cigarette, tapping it twice on top of the carton. I hold it between my lips and click my lighter. The tip of the cigarette glows.

I inhale deeply, my mouth filling, and then exhale, long and slow, my mouth shaped like an 'O', the smoke billowing into Kacey's face.

I smile.

'Don't call me a crack-baby again,' I whisper.

Her nostrils flare, her lips wavering, her cheeks puffing, as she struggles not to cough. 'Let's go,' she says, standing. She links arms with one of the girls, all of them watching, mouths open. They turn and walk away, stalking across the field, their heads occasionally craning over their shoulders to stare me down.

I remove the cigarette from my mouth and push it into the ground. It sizzles gently as it meets the damp dirt.

'Are you okay?' a voice says from behind me.

It's a girl from my form class. I've not spoken to her before but I've noticed her – her dark hair and black nails, just like mine. But hers aren't bitten down, they're perfectly painted and smooth. She smiled at me, once. But I let go of the urge that I had to speak to her and instead let her disappear into the crowd. It's easier that way. Another potential friend lost to the tide.

'I'm okay.'

She walks a few paces forward and stops directly in front of me.

'Can I sit down?'

I shrug. 'Sure.'

She folds her legs beneath her, tucking them out to one side elegantly, her oversized jumper sloping off her shoulder. She is very thin, her limbs long and lean. She reminds me of a baby bird, like she might break at any moment.

'I'm sorry she said that to you. That was really cruel.'

I shrug again, looking down at my hands which I twist in the grass in front of me. 'It's okay.'

'But it isn't. It isn't okay.'

'I've been called worse.'

'But it isn't fair to call someone names like that. You should say something.'

'No . . . no. I have to live with her, I can't do that. Seriously, it's not a problem . . . Sorry, what's your name?'

'Orla.'

'Orla,' I repeat, and she nods, smiling.

'And you're Lily, right?'

I nod.

'Where in London have you come from?'

'East. I was in a . . . I lived in Hackney.'

She scrunches up her nose, grinning. 'Must feel weird coming to live out in the suburbs.'

'Well, I grew up here actually. Lived not far from here until I was ten.'

'Really?'

I nod. 'Yeah. But then . . . I moved away.' I cough, clearing my throat. 'How about you? Have you always lived around here?'

'Yes, I . . . my parents got divorced last year so I split time between them now.'

'Oh, I'm sorry.'

'Thanks. They fought all the time. It was . . . horrible.'

'Do you live with your mum or dad more?'

'It's pretty even. But a bit more with Mum. Our house is on Hersham Way – do you know it?'

'Yeah. And your dad?'

'He's in Meadow Gardens.'

My eyebrows raise involuntarily. 'Wow,' I whisper.

Meadow Gardens. When Mum was with Phil, the three of us would walk from our side of town over to Meadow Gardens and stare up at the houses. We used to play a game, imagining the people who got to live there. Creating lives for them. Lives that we would never get to lead or ever understand.

Orla blushes. 'That's where I grew up. But Mum moved out when they separated.'

'Is your dad famous or something?'

'I guess. He's a photographer. And he has famous hotels.'

'That's cool.'

She shrugs. 'He used to go away a lot.'

'Is that why they separated?'

'I . . . Maybe. I don't know. They just . . . didn't get on. Not any more. I actually think they only got married because Mum got pregnant with me. And he . . . they didn't want to be together any more.'

I look down and begin to pluck blades of grass free from the dirt, the roots clinging on.

Please don't ask about my parents. Please.

'I heard that girl in form-room ask you about Franklin House,' she says.

My face flushes, scarlet shame tingling my cheeks.

'How long have you been there?'

'Not long. Just a couple of weeks.'

'What's it like?'

I search her face. There is no air of judgement, she just wants to know. No one has ever been interested in my life. They've found me interesting in the way an animal in a zoo is interesting. But they've never *been interested*. There's a difference. I can feel it in the way they ask questions, in the way they look at me: a pitying fascination.

But she is different.

'It's okay. Being there isn't bad. I've got my own room and . . . It's the moving around that's bad.'

'Why do they move you around?'

My fingers pull at the grass again, this time in clumps.

I can't tell her, this first semblance of a friend, that I'm moved around because homes can't handle me any more. Because of the police knocking at the door. Because of things I do that aren't acceptable. Things like fights. And the bottle of pills in my bag.

'I don't know. Just the way the system works,' I say instead.

'That's sad,' she whispers.

'That's life.'

She shuffles closer, her folded knees nearly touching mine. 'What happened to your parents?'

The ground tilts in front of me, jolted by the innocence of her question. My hands turn clammy, the tips of my fingers stinging.

'Sorry. You don't have to answer that if you don't want to.' She is biting her lip, her eyes full of sadness.

'Do you mind?'

56

'Of course not,' she whispers.

I exhale and she smiles, nodding in understanding.

We fall into silence. I blink rapidly, sitting with the awkwardness, even though it buzzes so strongly under my skin that I want to scream.

Please, Orla. Please say something.

'What are you reading?' she asks, pointing at the book that is still resting face-down in my lap.

I sigh, the silence evaporating up into the sky. '*Carrie*. Do you know it?'

'Oh wow, yes – I read that in the summer. You know that . . .'

I watch her face move as she continues to speak, so passionate and bright. The sun peeks out from behind the clouds, warming my face again. And as her words spill out, wave after comforting wave, I listen, and the anxiety eases, the tingling in the tips of my fingers disappearing completely.

10. Ava

He has a daughter.

Michael Osborne has a daughter.

'Yes, here it is, darling,' he says, handing her the large bottle-green juice. 'Orla, this is Ava Knight. She was the prosecutor yesterday . . . when Lily pleaded.'

Her head jolts in my direction, only now taking in my presence, but her face transforms: her sullen frown of mild annoyance falling away, her eyes growing round and sad.

'Hi,' I say, but her gaze falls to the ground.

She doesn't respond.

'Orla . . .' Michael lifts a hand to shield his eyes from the sun, leaning forward to peer at her. 'Sorry,' he says, turning to me. 'They were best friends – you understand.'

They were best friends. Lily was best friends with Michael's daughter.

'Of course,' I say. 'It's nice to meet you, Orla.'

'You too,' she mumbles, her voice fading away.

'Orla's doing a model-UN competition today . . . Looks good on the CV,' Michael says, his face filling with pride.

She lifts her head. 'Actually, I really need to go, I don't want to be late. Dad, I'll see you next week.' She glances at me. 'It was nice to meet you.'

'You too,' I say.

'See you, darling,' Michael says, leaning down to kiss her on the cheek. 'Good luck.'

She nods but doesn't say anything in return, just hurries away.

I stare at her back as she leaves, her figure slowly shrinking into the distance.

Michael Osborne has a daughter. A living, breathing child who likes green juice and does competitions for the model-UN on Saturdays. A daughter who was best friends with the girl who stabbed him.

I was so sure that Orla was another victim, my image of him tarring everything in his life, even his innocent daughter. I can only see him through ever-increasing shades of darkness.

But that same sadness was there. The sadness that had been emanating from Lily as she stood in the dock. It was there in Orla's eyes, in the way she stood. A strange awkwardness lingering between her and her father.

'Do you want to have a coffee with me? Or do you need to run?'

I glance away from where Orla has long disappeared and back at his expectant face.

'Um, I should really go,' I say, beginning to back away. Just one small step. I need to get back to my car and not look back.

'Are you sure?' he asks. 'Come on, one quick coffee won't hurt.'

'We shouldn't . . . having coffee with a victim of a case I'm working on is –'

'Oh, come on, who's going to tell? No one in there knows who you are. You could just be my friend –'

'No, really –'

He smiles, dimples appearing in his cheeks, a charming glint in his eye. 'I insist.'

I glance after his daughter, her back just a small dot at the far end of the road. I want to leave, to insist that I shouldn't even be talking to him, but –

No.

I'm here – so close to the man who ruined everything. Men like him don't change. They need to be stopped. I just need to find a way: an avenue into his life.

'Okay, fine,' I say, the words falling quickly from my lips.

He nods, satisfied, and turns away to walk back towards the cafe.

I follow and he props the door open with his foot then leads me to a table by the window, where his coffee – a steaming black americano – is waiting for him.

'What would you like?'

'I can get it –'

'No, it's my treat,' he says, smiling coyly, his eyes warm.

'An almond milk latte, please.'

'Coming right up.'

I sit down in the chair facing the window but watch over my shoulder as Michael approaches the counter and beams at the girl behind it, all lightness and charm. He carries on talking to her as she rings in my order and turns to the coffee machines behind her to make the drink. They chat easily – he must be a regular here. A waitress says hello as she passes him, and he responds, calling her by name. 'See you soon,' the girl behind the counter says, her voice a singsong as she places my coffee down, smiling at him as he says thank you once again.

I search for something to say as he walks back towards me, but my mind is completely blank. He sits down, but as he bends forward, he winces sharply.

'Are . . . are you okay?' I ask.

He gestures to his back then grips his side, his eyes squeezed shut. 'I'm fine. It's still quite painful, that's all.'

'It must have been a very difficult time for you. And your daughter –'

'Yes,' he says, the word clipped, his eyes now cold. 'I'm

sorry,' he sighs, allowing his features to soften, 'but it's hard to talk about. And . . . I suppose we are crossing a line right now. Aren't we?'

His eyes pierce mine and my jaw tightens, my throat thick with anxiety. 'We are.' I slide my chair back slightly, my heart racing.

'Don't leave,' he says quickly, an apologetic smile spreading across his face. 'Sorry, I didn't mean to make it awkward. At least drink your coffee.'

I pause, my eyes fixed on the exit.

'Okay.' I look down at the steam rising from my mug, avoiding his doleful gaze. He sips slowly, and even though I'm staring at the table, I can feel him looking at me. He swallows loudly.

I clear my throat and force myself to smile. 'So . . . do you come here often?'

'I haven't heard that line in a while,' he responds quickly, one eyebrow raised.

My face flushes, my cheeks hot. 'I –'

'Don't worry, I'm teasing. Sorry.' He sits back in his chair, his coffee cradled in his hands. 'I come here a lot for coffee or brunch. And my daughter loves it too.'

'She's a lovely girl,' I say, lifting my cup to my lips, glad that he's brought her back into the conversation. But I need to bide my time.

'She is,' he says with a proud nod, before sipping from his own wide-brimmed mug. 'And so ambitious. She wants to be a lawyer. She's got work experience starting Monday at a solicitor's firm.'

A sudden thrill rushes through me. *It's perfect.*

'I'd love to spend more time with her,' Michael continues, 'but I'm so busy, and she lives with her mum a lot of the time.'

'You aren't together?'

'No . . . We separated a few years ago.'

'I-I'm sorry.'

'Don't be. It was for the best. For everyone. I'd just love to spend more time with my daughter.'

'How often is she with you?'

'Three days a week, but it's very ad hoc.'

I look down, take another sip, my nerves burning as he watches me closely.

'Are you married?'

'No.'

'Boyfriend?'

Will's smiling face appears in my mind.

'No,' I say quickly. I don't want to talk about Will. I don't want Michael to even know his name.

'A career girl,' he responds. My body winces – I want to squirm, his use of the word 'girl' sending a repulsed shiver down my spine, but I resort to pinching the skin between my thumb and index finger, hard.

'Evidently.'

'I can imagine it was hard work to get to where you are now?'

I should say something about his daughter: it's the perfect opportunity. But my stomach flips. 'Yes, it was difficult,' I say instead, clasping my hands in frustration. 'But I love my job. I can't imagine doing anything else.'

'Your parents must be very proud.'

'Uh . . . Yes. My mum . . . my mum is proud of me.'

'And your dad? He must be over the moon – I'd be beside myself if Orla became a barrister.'

'My dad is dead.' The lie falls out of my mouth, a bitter-tasting concoction I need to spit out. I could have said that I don't know my dad, that he left when I was little or some other story, but death brings a certain finality to conversations. It scares people.

'Oh, I'm sorry . . . I didn't mean to –'

'It's fine,' I say, shaking my head.

He taps his finger against his china cup. 'My dad died about ten years ago. So . . . I understand.'

We fall silent but he doesn't look away from me. His gaze is unflinching. I meet his eye, maintaining contact for a couple of moments longer than feels comfortable, then glance down at my lap.

'I –'

'I'm just going to go to the toilet,' he interrupts. 'Do you mind watching my laptop?'

'No, of course not.'

'Cheers.'

He stands and squeezes through the small gap between our table and the one next to us, and his body brushes against me. I shiver.

Once he's gone, I release a shaky breath and lean forward on the table, but freeze suddenly as a low buzz rumbles on the table.

His phone.

He left his phone here, lying innocuously beside his closed laptop, the screen now alight with a new message.

Leave it.

I peer over my shoulder. Michael is waiting outside the closed toilet door. He meets my eyes and flashes a smile. I smile back but he steps to one side as the door opens, then disappears inside.

I turn back to stare at his phone, my hands twisting together, my legs restless.

It buzzes again.

I snatch it up quickly and place it in my lap.

Two messages are waiting. They're from an unlisted number, just the first few words of each message visible. I swipe upwards but the series of numbers and empty circles appear, waiting for a passcode.

My finger skims the screen and it lights up with the incomplete messages.

I've done what you said –
Please leave me –

The door creaks behind me.

'Michael,' a voice says. 'It's so lovely to see you!'

I quickly press the side button and the screen grows dark. I put the phone down, pushing it across the table in one swift movement. Turning to look over my shoulder, I sigh with relief – Michael is standing with his back to me at another table talking to a middle-aged man, both laughing conspiratorially.

I turn away and wait.

Who is messaging him? Is it Lily? Please leave me . . . ? Please leave me alone? Is that the end of the message? It must be. What other possible conclusion could that sentence have?

But if that is what the message says . . . why isn't he leaving her alone? And she's done what he said? Done what?

'Sorry I took so long,' his voice says suddenly, and my body flinches. 'I just saw someone I know from work.'

'Not a problem,' I say, the phone fixed in my peripheral vision.

'Would you like another coffee?' he asks, returning to his seat carefully, the same wince briefly passing across his face. 'Something to eat?'

'No, I'd really better go. I'm meeting some friends back at home.'

'Are you sure you wouldn't like something to eat?'

'Yes, but thank you.'

'No worries. Have a lovely time.'

'Thank you. Before I go, though . . .' I pause, nerves thrumming through me. Once I do this, I can't turn back. But this is my only chance: my one chance to get closer. 'If your daughter wants to come and spend a day with me during her work experience,' I say quickly, 'I'd love to have her.'

'Really?'

'Sure.'

'She'd love that,' he says, beaming.

He reaches inside his jacket, then pulls out a small white rectangle, embossed black letters on its smooth surface.

I bite down on the inside of my cheek, reach out and take it.

'I'll message you to let you know which day is best?'

'Great,' he says, smiling. I stand and he sips his coffee, peering up at me over the rim. 'It was lovely to meet you. Properly. Without the wig.'

'You too.'

The bell rings as I step out into the street. My pace is fast as I walk away, my heart quickening at the feeling of his card between my fingers, adrenalin buzzing through me with a strange sort of triumph.

11. Ava

I pull off my trainers and sit back down at our small table, my laptop still open. I woke early, with daylight slowly filtering in through the darkness, night giving way to day. I couldn't stop thinking about Michael. Or about Orla – her reaction to Lily's name. And the messages . . . *I've done what you said. Please leave me . . .*

As the sun rose, I consumed the casefile, going over every word of the witness statements, the police summaries, the forensic reports, their phone records – the phone calls made that night. Lily's police interview, the detective asking question after question, her doggedly replying, 'No comment'. The only piece of evidence that made me pause was a phone call to an unknown number, just fifteen minutes before the emergency services were called.

Michael's statement is clear and detailed. Lily arrived at his house after a fight at the children's home. He told her that Orla was not there. She asked if she could stay anyway. He let her in as he didn't want to turn her away: she had become so important to his daughter. She tried to kiss him. He pushed her away. And that's when it happened.

After I'd pored over every detail, I went for a run, trying to quiet my thoughts, but I couldn't stop the barrage of questions. If those messages were from Lily, why is he contacting her? It's against her remand conditions. And why would he do that? There's no reason for it unless . . .

Unless he's trying to keep her quiet.

I pull his business card from my pocket and look down at it, my fingers tracing the embossed lettering.

'You were up early.'

I jump. Will has emerged from our bedroom, his pyjama bottoms slung low over his hips, his short curls ruffled. He rubs his dark eyes with his fist.

'Not that early,' I say, smiling at him, sliding the business card into the pocket of my hoodie.

'It was half-five, Ava. On a Sunday. That's not normal.' He laughs and crosses the room to stand behind me.

I peer up at him, my head tilted back against his stomach. 'I wanted to get some work done.'

He leans forward and kisses me, his lips gentle, upside down.

'Coffee?' he asks, giving my shoulder a squeeze before making his way past the sofa to the kitchen. He clicks on the kettle.

'Yes, please.'

'What case are you looking at?'

'The GBH.'

'The fifteen-year-old?'

'Hmm.'

'But there's nothing for you to do on that, is there? Isn't it just sentencing now?'

'Yes, but it's in less than two weeks and I won't get a chance to look at it before then,' I say, lying smoothly. 'So, I just needed to look at the summary.'

He smiles, deep dimples forming in his cheeks. 'You work too hard.'

I watch as he potters around the kitchen and try to focus on his movements, on his small, inconsequential actions. He spoons coffee into the cafetiere, pulls four pieces of bread out of the bag and puts them in the toaster, pushing the lever

67

down as he simultaneously pours hot water with the other hand, the ground beans flurrying behind the glass. Just simple acts . . . he is so beautiful. So good. But I can feel myself being drawn back to my now dormant screen. Dragged back into the world of crime and violence and guilt. Pulled back to Michael.

He joins me at the table, placing my favourite mug in front of me. He tilts the screen of the laptop closed.

'Just while we eat,' he whispers.

I smile, screwing my face up affectionately. 'I'm done anyway.'

He pours coffee into my mug, and I lift a piece of toast to my mouth. Butter drips down my chin. Will scoffs, his eyes bright and happy.

'So why did she do it?'

My brief contentment shrinks away, disappearing like sunshine behind a cloud.

'She . . . She had developed feelings for her friend's dad. She tried to do something about it and he rejected her. So she lost her temper – attacked him.'

'Just because of that?'

'People have killed for less,' I mutter.

'I know, but . . .' He unscrews the lid of the orange juice, pouring some into our glasses, his brow furrowed. 'She's fifteen. She's just a child.'

Now is my chance to tell him. Tell this man – the man I love, who loves me in return – everything that happened. The truth about me. That I was just a child, too.

But I can't. He doesn't know that person. He doesn't know that girl: angry and outraged. And I don't want to let her in. I can't let her seep into the veins of my relationship, poisoning it from the inside.

I nod, saying nothing.

'It's just unbelievable,' Will continues. 'Someone that young doing something so horrific for no reason at all. But . . .'

'But, what?'

'If she had a defence, she would give it, wouldn't she?'

I shrug, faking nonchalance. 'There are lots of reasons why people stay quiet.'

He nods, the edges of his mouth turned downwards. But as he bites into his toast, he smiles unevenly at me, blinking away the heaviness of our conversation, the weight of his thoughts already lifting.

'Have you decided on what we're watching for movie Monday?' He smiles. 'It's your turn to choose.'

I smile back at him but a creeping sadness has wrapped its fingers around my shoulders, and I can't simply shrug it away.

People remain silent all the time. Keeping the secret truth close to their hearts, away from judging, disbelieving eyes. *The truth will out* is a fallacy. The truth can remain buried forever.

'Ava.'

Hands grip my shoulders, and my hands jolt forward, water spilling over the rim of my glass.

Marissa's face appears in front of me, and I exhale.

'Shit, sorry. I always forget how jumpy you get,' she says, laughing.

'It's okay,' I say.

She leans down to hug me and I wrap my arms around her neck, blinking away tears laced with adrenalin. No matter who I am seeing or where I am – meeting a friend in a crowded bistro, like today – my body never fails to respond to the feeling of hands grabbing me. It's involuntary. Like breathing.

'How are you?' she asks as she sits down, crossing her legs elegantly, tossing her thick, tight curls over her shoulder.

'I'm fine. Just a bit tired.'

'Have you ordered?'

'Yes.' I wiggle my eyebrows at her. 'The usual.'

'Bloody Marys?'

'Of course. And avocado toast.'

'Perfect,' she says, her tongue rolling around the R. She's so expressive in real life, her face and voice made for performance, vivacity running through her veins, but in court she's controlled, measured. 'We'll be getting plenty of those on your hen do! I've started planning and –'

'The hen is ages away! We're not getting married until next year –'

'I know, but let me have my fun, please!' She laughs. 'How's Will?'

'He's great,' I beam. 'He's busy with work, but you know Will. Always so –'

'Chilled?'

I laugh. 'Yes. So unlike me.'

'You're complete opposites,' she agrees. 'It's perfect. I can't wait for the wedding.'

I smile and she nods happily back at me. It was Marissa who pushed me towards Will. They had met a few times, when the pupils at my chambers and hers would gather at the pub late at night, all of us whispering stories about work we were being given and whether we thought we'd be taken on once pupillage was over. But one night, Will and I were tucked into the corner of a worn leather booth, our heads close together to hear each other over the noise of the packed bar, and I glanced across the table to find Marissa watching us, her eyes knowing.

'You like him, don't you?' she had asked as we stood at the sticky bar.

'I –'

'Ava, I know you! And I've never seen you like this around

a guy. You like him. And why on earth would you stay just friends with a man like that? He's perfect for you.'

I had shrugged, laughing it off, unable to tell her that I was scared to let a man too close. That my only experience with a man had been at fourteen years old when it was forced upon me.

But her words wouldn't leave me. And that night, when Will walked me to the station, he hugged me goodbye, as always, but he paused briefly, his face so close to mine, and . . . I didn't move away. He kissed me, gently, his hand lifting to cup my chin.

The waitress arrives at our table, two long glasses balanced on her tray. 'Two Bloody Marys, one spicy?'

'Yes, thank you,' I say. 'Spicy one here.'

She places them down and rushes away, weaving through the tightly packed tables.

'Well, cheers,' Marissa says.

'Cheers,' I say, chinking my glass against hers.

We both sip, and she rolls her eyes backwards. 'Bloody hell, that's delicious.'

'Mmm.' I stir the red liquid with the celery, avoiding her eye. 'That case is crazy, isn't it?'

'The stabbing?'

I nod.

'Yeah, it is. She's . . . in a way I feel really bad for her.'

'Why?' I ask, innocently, sipping from my drink again.

'She's ended up where she is because of her childhood. Parents who didn't care, abuse, the care system . . . She had no chance.'

'I was surprised, if I'm honest.'

She lifts an eyebrow. 'Surprised?'

'At the guilty plea.'

'Why?'

'I don't know . . . I just didn't expect it.'

'I had a conference with her that morning. And she just . . . she just seems like she's given up.'

'On a defence?'

'No, no – she doesn't have a defence. She's given up on life. She doses herself up, she doesn't really have any friends –'

'What does she take?'

'Benzos.'

'Benzodiazepines?' I shuffle forward to the edge of my chair. 'Where does she get them?'

'A few different drug-houses. Her mum used to take her when she was a child. Before she was taken into care.'

'Jesus . . .'

'I know. I think this man, Michael Osborne, was her first ever experience of kindness. Especially from a man. And she read it the wrong way. When he pushed her away, like so many others have done, she broke. Snapped. I'm just glad they didn't charge her with attempted murder.'

I sniff, pressing my lips together. 'Do you think she meant to kill him?'

Marissa smirks, raising her hands mockingly. 'All right, Persecutor.'

'No, Marissa,' I say, shaking my head. 'I'm not asking because I want to increase the charge, I'm just curious.'

'I know.' She sighs. 'I . . . I don't think she knows what she meant to do. She just reacted.'

'Don't you think it's strange that she was at his house? When the daughter wasn't there?'

She shakes her head. 'She said exactly what he said in his statement. She needed help and asked to go inside. There's nothing suspicious about it.'

'Nothing in the evidence that makes you think something sinister was happening? I noticed there was a phone call from

Michael's phone fifteen minutes before the police were called. Do you know why? Have you asked Lily?'

She lowers the celery from her lips, frowning. 'What's going on with you?'

'What do you mean?'

'I mean, I've known you since bar school, we've been against each other more times than I can count, and you never ask questions about a guilty plea. Why so curious about this case?'

My face flushes, heat rising up the back of my neck. 'I'm just interested . . . She seems so innocent.'

'Don't be fooled by that pretty face. I've represented her before on drugs charges, and on a common assault – if she thinks she has a defence, she gives it, even when she's wrong, even against my advice. Otherwise, she pleads.' She shrugs. 'Lily is guilty.'

'Avocado toast?' the waitress says, arriving at the table once more.

'Thank you,' Marissa and I say in unison.

Marissa instantly dives into her food, nodding enthusiastically as she takes her first bite. 'This place is so good.'

I smile, but my plate remains untouched. Marissa's my best friend. She would understand. We could help Lily together –

'Marissa?'

She looks up from her plate, licking avocado from her bottom lip.

But the bravery that briefly washed over me, dissipates instantly. She can't know. No one can know. If I tell her, I'll have to tell Will, I'll have to tell everyone. I'll have to tell them about everything: what Michael did . . . and everything that came after. My whole life will unravel.

'Nothing,' I whisper.

12. Lily

Four months before the attack

The houses in Meadow Gardens are as big as I remember. I thought that it might have been my childish perception that had made them grander than they actually are. That my memory was distorting real life.

But it wasn't. Orla's house is massive. Frost-covered trees line the drive on either side and lead up to the house which is white and pristine. She grew up here. Imagine that.

Orla smiles at my shocked face. But as she reaches into her pockets her grin falls away.

'Shit,' she whispers.

'What's wrong?' I ask.

'I forgot my key again. Dad will kill me.'

'Really?'

'Yeah, I do it all the time. It really pisses him off.' She reaches down behind the large planter that sits to the left of the door. Huffing, she pulls her arm out, her fingers clutching a key.

'I hide a spare just in case . . . Don't tell him.'

'I won't,' I whisper.

She pushes the spare key into the lock and turns. The door clicks open, and she rushes back to the planter, returning the key to its hiding place.

'Come on in,' she says.

My eyes are immediately drawn upwards. The black iron stairs sweep up the left-hand side of the house and circle up one, two, three floors. And suspended at the top is a glass dome, flooding the hallways and the infinite loop of stairs with light.

'It . . . It's beautiful,' I say.

The whole of Mum's old house would fit in this hallway.

'Thanks,' she replies. Her eyes shift away from me to the floor. Is she embarrassed? What is she thinking, knowing that I grew up on Vereland Road and have been shoved from children's home to children's home? Is she embarrassed *for* me? Or *of* me?

'Dad?' she shouts. She walks to the first door on the left and peeks her head inside. 'Dad?' she shouts again. She marches across the hallway to the last door on the left and pushes the door open.

I frown – beyond the door there is nothing but black.

'Dad?' she calls again. 'Maybe he isn't home yet –'

'Hi, Orla,' a deep voice shouts from somewhere beneath us.

'Oh, hi. I didn't think you were back.'

'I'll be up in a minute. Get your friend a drink.'

'Okay.' She pulls the door closed. 'Come on.'

I follow her through double doors at the back of the hallway. An expansive room opens out before me, the kitchen sitting on the left with a dining area and living area spanning the rest of the space.

'Do you want a Coke?' asks Orla.

'Sure.' She opens the fridge and I take one from her out-stretched hand. 'Thanks.'

We crack open the cans, letting out the satisfying fizz.

'What's down there?' I ask, nodding my head back towards the hallway.

'Oh, downstairs? It's Dad's studio. And there's a darkroom down there too.'

I lift the can to my mouth and gulp thirstily.

Orla's eyes narrow and she moves towards me. I pause as she leans in, her face close to mine. She sniffs.

'Shit, you smell like cigarettes.'

'I'm sorry, is it —'

'Dad won't like it. And he'll think I'm smoking too.'

'You didn't say anything at your mum's house.'

'I know, but Mum's different. Um, let me run upstairs and get —'

'I've got body spray?'

'Do you mind?'

I shake my head. Delving inside my bag, I grab the canister and quickly spray myself then grab at strands of my hair and pull my jumper up to my nose, checking for remnants of stale smoke.

'Better?'

She leans in again, pressing her nose to my shoulder.

'All good now.'

I watch as her hands jangle at her sides with nervous energy. 'Is your dad really that strict?'

She crosses her arms. 'He . . . No, he just likes things a certain way.'

A door slams and we both jump.

'You must be Lily,' Orla's dad says, smiling as he strides towards us across the hallway. 'I've heard so much about you.'

I nod, looking at my feet as he stops in front of me.

'Hi, Mr Osborne,' I say. 'Thanks . . . thanks for having me.'

'Not a problem. And please, call me Michael.'

'Michael,' I repeat.

'Now . . .' he says, turning his attention to Orla. 'How was your day? School good?'

I watch him as Orla answers. He leans back against the island, tucking his fingers into the pockets of his black jeans, his loose white T-shirt lifting as he wraps his arm around her

76

shoulder. His eyes are focused on her, but occasionally he glances my way and smiles, trying to include me.

I smile back. He isn't what I expected. I imagined a stern old man, but he isn't like that at all. I have always known that fathers like this exist – attentive, kind, encouraging – but I've never seen one. Not in real life. The fathers in my life, both in blood and by marriage, have been . . . different.

'What are we eating tonight?' he asks. 'Lily, are you happy with pizza?'

'Sure,' I say, finally meeting his gaze.

His eyes are so blue.

'And are you staying over?'

'I –'

'Ooh yes,' Orla says, clapping her hands together. 'Yes, Lily, stay!'

'Um . . . I would have to ask.'

'Call your parents – I'm happy to speak to them if they want.'

'I . . .'

'Dad, Lily's in care,' Orla interrupts, frowning.

'Oh God, I'm so sorry,' he says, reaching out to grip my arm. 'Orla told me and it completely slipped my mind.'

'It's okay,' I say. Orla mouths 'sorry' at me and I shake my head, my cheeks burning, but my eyes are drawn back to Michael's hand still holding my arm.

'Well, if you want to call and ask, I can speak to whoever I need to.'

'Anne. I'll call Anne.'

'Perfect,' he says and smiles.

He lets go.

My skin tingles.

13. Ava

I flop down on the sofa, my eyes blurring as they try to focus on the dark images on the television.

'What are you watching?'

'*The Office*,' Will says.

'Again?' I laugh fondly.

'Always,' he whispers as he holds his arm out, making space for me to shuffle in beside him. I rest my head on his chest, my arm extended to rest across his stomach. My engagement ring catches my eye as it always does – I'm so used to my hands and wrists being bare. I had never loved jewellery, but the bracelet from Dad was so precious to me. After I lost it during the attack, Mum bought me a replacement but the feeling of silver around my wrists felt like the grip of fingers, forcing my hands down. So, I stopped wearing it. I close my eyes, concentrating on the rise and fall of his breaths, his smell, the weight of his hand on my thigh.

But Lily's face appears in the darkness. Her sad eyes. Her defiant scowl.

After I came home from lunch with Marissa, I returned to the casefile, rifling through its contents like a burglar pillaging a room, fact after fact discarded as I searched for some hidden truth, secreted away. But there wasn't anything. All that lay in that file was evidence of guilt. A knife covered in her fingerprints. Her clothes soaked in his blood. And a clear intent to harm.

But then why is he contacting her? Why won't he leave her

alone? I thought it was strange that he was at the hearing – victims don't usually do that. They usually attend court only when absolutely necessary. It's like he's watching her. Is that what's happening? Has he silenced her? And now, is he trying to ensure that her silence continues until it's too late for her to speak?

Maybe I could talk to her myself . . . maybe if I reach out to her and explain who I really am, what happened to me, she might tell me the truth? Maybe –

But no. No, I can't do that. Speaking to the complainant of a case is bad enough, but if anyone found out, I could at least attempt to explain it away. But speaking to the defendant?

And she's a teenage girl. Vulnerable. Unpredictable. She could expose me without thinking twice.

I sigh heavily and shrink out of Will's arms.

'Everything okay?'

'Yes,' I say, pushing myself off the sofa. 'Just need the toilet.'

I run my wrists under cold water, my eyes lingering, as they always do, on the ladder of white scars that run up my forearm. I try to hide them, wearing long sleeves whenever I can, but the first time Will caught sight of them, he asked what had happened. 'Dad left,' I said. 'Just teenage angst, you know.' I laughed it off. I couldn't tell him the truth.

I sigh and turn off the tap, drying my hands on the hand-towel, before tucking them into the pocket of my hoodie. And then I flinch.

His business card.

I've been putting off contacting him, telling myself it would be too risky, too impulsive. But what if I can get close enough to unearth what he really is? He hides behind the Osborne façade – protected by his wealth, bolstered by his charm – but what if I could tear it down?

I pull my phone out of the back pocket of my jeans. Tapping on the address book, I key in his number, hesitating over the blank space meant for his name. My index finger travels over the letters, keying in an additional 'a' – creating another secret.

Michaela.

Hi, it's Ava. We had coffee yesterday at the cafe near Meadow Gardens. I can have your daughter for work experience on Tuesday, if that works?

I press send, chewing on my lip, and the message flies away. Almost immediately a reply appears, his message hanging just below mine.

That's amazing – she'll be so excited. Thank you.

A shaky breath escapes my lips. That's one step closer to him.

But . . . not close enough.

Great. I also really enjoyed chatting with you . . . Fancy it again sometime?

I pause, my breath quickening.

Do it, Ava.

The sound of the message leaving my phone sends a chill down my spine. His face comes to the forefront of my mind, his eyes widening as he opens the text, that signature smirk settling on his face as he finishes reading.

'Are you okay?' Will asks as I sit back down beside him.

'Yeah, fine,' I say, smiling reassuringly.

He narrows his eyes. 'You sure?'

'Promise.'

I settle into my usual space, the perfectly sized nook between his open arm and his chest. But it isn't as comfortable as usual. It feels awkward, too small, not big enough for both me and my guilt.

My phone pings, the innocuous sound filling me with dread. I glance at Will, but he hasn't reacted. Why would he?

Message received: Michaela.

Heat spreads across my chest and I sit up. Will peers over at me, his eyes darting down to my phone in worry.

'Is it your mum?'

'No, no . . . Just a friend from work.' I run my tongue along my top teeth. The lie tastes sour. But his eyes slide away and back to the screen, and he chuckles gently, preempting the joke, his lips subconsciously mouthing the words.

Guilt tingles through me once more as I look away from him and open the message. I expect the familiar nausea of anxiety as I read his words, but a thrill of victory zings in my chest.

Me too. Dinner tomorrow?

14. Belle

Eighteen years earlier

I lie awake, staring up at the ceiling of stars – faint glow-in-the-dark remnants of my childhood. Dad and I painstakingly spent one evening, when I was around ten, sticking the stars to the ceiling and watching in amazement as they began to shine. I loved looking up at them as I fell asleep, those tiny pinpricks of false light glimmering above me, offering me comfort. Hope. But now they offer neither. Now, they are taunting. Their light has faded, and so has mine.

Sighing loudly, I roll on to my side, turning my face away from the stars to look instead at the wall. It's covered in photographs of my friends. Their happy faces beam at me, and mine is there too, smiling along with them. Me and Rachel at the beginning of the summer, sat at the riverside, our legs dangling off the edge. My group of friends in the field behind the school, lying down in the grass, our wrists stacked with friendship bracelets; Finn, sitting in my garden, leaning towards the camera, his cheeks dimpled with laughter.

I wanted to tell them all what happened, but Mum said no. It's bad enough that Rachel knows, she scolded. If she tells just one person, it will spread, Belle. Do you want this to spread? Do you want everyone to know? Do you know what that could do? She said that once he was convicted, the truth could come out. My friends would understand, people would understand. I'd be the victim, not the accuser. But until then,

I was just a girl, accusing a grown man – a respected man from a renowned family – of something terrible.

But he wasn't convicted. And now I will always be the accuser. Worse: I'll always be the liar.

'Are you lying, Belle?'

The voice of the defence barrister echoes suddenly in my ears, and I sit up, the duvet falling away from me, sending a chill down my arms. That day has buried itself in the depths of my mind, emerging without warning: the day where the trial, which seemed so certain, turned upside down.

The room where I waited to give evidence was sweltering. Sweat bled through my blouse and ran in sweeping fingers down my back. We all looked up at the sound of a knock on the door and watched as the prosecutor strode into the room. His walk was as assertive as ever, but his face . . . Something about his face wasn't right. I knew it, even then.

'Is something wrong?' Dad asked.

He didn't respond but grimaced as he lifted a chair from the other side of the room and placed it in front of the sofa where I was sitting in between Mum and Dad.

'How are you all doing?' he said quietly as he sat down, removing his wig and placing it on his lap.

'What's happened?' Mum asked, loud and insistent. 'Are they ready for her yet?'

'Unfortunately not.'

'What? We've been waiting all morning.'

'We've spent this morning in legal argument. There's been an issue with the DNA evidence that had to be resolved.'

'What kind of issue?'

My stomach sank down towards my feet as he paused before answering, sipping water from his bottle, which crackled as he gulped loudly.

'Evidence of any kind has to be handled in a certain way during a criminal investigation. If it isn't, it can end up with the evidence potentially being contaminated which can result in unfairness or miscarriages of justice. And –'

'What has this got to do with Belle?' Mum interrupted, shaking her head.

'There's evidence that Anabelle's dress was mishandled by a police officer before it was sent off for testing. It was accidentally cross-contaminated with clothing from another case. The defence have argued that including the DNA evidence in the trial would be unfair to the defendant –'

'Which police officer?' Mum said, her voice raised.

'Police Constable Hart. He handled the DNA before it was sent to the lab –'

'And? What happened? What has the judge said?' Dad whispered, his usual smiling face creased with anxiety.

'The judge has directed that the evidence is inadmissible. The fact that the defendant's DNA was found on Belle's clothing cannot be put before the jury. In fact, I'm unable to present Belle's clothing as evidence of a rape occurring whatsoever.'

The revelation plunged us into silence, breathless, submerged in deep cold water.

I licked my lips, forcing my voice to remain steady. *Be a brave girl.*

'What's going to –'

'I don't understand how this could happen,' Mum spat, interrupting. 'How the bloody hell –'

'Penny, let Belle speak!' Dad said, his voice raised – a rare show of impatience.

Mum stopped, her chest rising and falling. I glanced around, taking in all of their expectant faces.

'The trial . . . What will happen now?' I whispered.

'It means that there will be more reliance on your evidence and the cross-examination. Physical evidence that he had contact with you has been taken away.'

'Essentially what you're saying is that it will be his word against Belle's,' Dad said.

'Yes.'

'What if Belle doesn't give evidence?'

The barrister inched forwards on his chair. 'Then we would have to offer no evidence and it would be over.'

'I can't . . . I c-can't do this –' I stammered.

'Darling, I know that it's hard, but you know what happened,' Dad whispered, his hand cupping my chin. 'All you have to do is tell the truth.'

'But I'm scared. I can't –'

'You have to, Belle,' Mum said. 'You have to or he'll get away with it. All you have to do is stand up there and tell them what happened.'

'But his barrister . . . His barrister will try to make them believe him. She'll try to make me look like a liar. And without the DNA –'

'They'll believe you. You identified him before there was any DNA evidence. You described him and then identified him from a line-up. We don't need the DNA. They'll still believe you, I promise.' She glanced at the barrister. 'Can't she give evidence over a video-link or something?'

'I'd have to apply for that and we would probably have to adjourn until tomorrow –'

'No,' I interrupted. 'Sorry . . . I'm sorry. I have to do this today.'

When they called my name, I felt as if I was watching myself walk out of the witness room, as if I had been pulled from my body. Surely it wasn't me entering the courtroom, the jury's eyes hot on my face as they followed me to the stand? Surely it wasn't me saying the promise to tell the truth? Just as it had the night of the attack, my brain was shutting everything down – my nerves, my emotions, my senses – so that it wasn't me at all. It was just an image of me, a ghostly girl, and I was simply a spectator. An unwilling voyeur.

But as I finished speaking, I looked away from the clerk and the blurred faces of the jury, my eyes drawn to the back of the room. And just like that, I plummeted back into my body, forced to return by the face staring back at me. His face. Michael Osborne.

I hadn't known his name until after he was charged. When I identified him, all I knew was his face. And now he was there, his eyes boring into mine, waiting for the questions to begin.

'Belle?' the judge said, his glasses pushed down his nose. 'Are you ready to begin?'

I looked around the room. It wasn't just the judge watching me with concern. The prosecutor, who was sitting furthest away on the front row, had stood up, his mouth slightly open as if he was poised to speak. George was sitting behind him, surrounded by stacks of files.

'Are you okay?' he mouthed silently.

My eyes returned to the back of the room – to him – like a magnet drawn to its opposite. He was still watching me, one eyebrow raised. They had asked me weeks before whether I wanted to be shielded from him. They said that they could put screens around the witness box, so that the judge and jury could see me, and the barristers, but not him. *I'll be fine*, I had whispered in response. *It would be good for her to face him*, Mum had said. *She needs to face him*. And I thought she was right – the Michael Osborne in my mind was just as much of a monster as the one behind the glass. They were the same. Hiding him wouldn't change that. I wanted to be brave. To show him that this time, I could fight.

But there we were, face to face, and I didn't feel brave. I wanted to shrink. Shrink down so small that he could no longer see me.

'I'm ready,' I whispered.

'Belle,' the judge said, leaning forward in his chair, making direct eye contact as if he was speaking to me alone. 'The jury have already seen the video interview of your evidence that was conducted by Detective Cavanaugh the day after the events of the twenty-third of November of last year. That will stand as your main evidence, but Ms Greystone, the defendant's barrister, may have some further questions for you. Do you understand?'

'Yes.'

'I would like to remind members of the jury and persons sat in the public gallery,' said the judge, 'that the witness is a child and is subject to an order of anonymity. It is against the law to identify her or describe her in any way that would lead to her identification.'

His stern gaze transformed into a kind smile as he nodded at me, then turned his attention to the defence who stood, placing a notebook on the lectern, a pen laced between her fingers.

'I won't keep you too long, Belle, I promise,' she said, a small smile settling on her lips. 'I've just a few questions for you.'

I waited.

'As we've heard in your evidence, on the night of the twenty-third of November, you were walking home alone when you say you were grabbed from behind and dragged from the riverside.'

She stopped speaking. But I simply stared at her, not understanding. Where was the question?

'Is that correct?'

'Yes,' I whispered, my cheeks flushing red.

'When the attacker grabbed you, he did so from behind.'

'Y-yes.'

'And when he put you down on to the ground, he was on top of you.'

'Yes.'

'But he was masked.'

The barrister's stare was cold and severe. I tried to hold it but I couldn't; everyone was looking at me, their eyes brimming with questions.

'Yes, he was masked but –'

'While he was on top of you, did he ever remove his mask?'

'He removed it later –'

'But while he was on top of you, when you had a clear view, did he ever remove his mask?'

'No.'

The barrister glanced at the jury, her head tilted to the side as she allowed the point to fall. She picked up the glass of water that was placed next to her open file, raised it to her lips and sipped. The silence made my skin crawl.

'You stated in your evidence that it was as he walked away from you that he removed his mask.'

'Yes. He got up and walked off and as he reached the riverside, he pulled off his mask and turned his face.'

'Why would he do that?'

Heat rose up the back of my neck, turning the skin of my chest clammy.

'I . . . don't understand the question.'

'Well, why would someone who had attacked you, raped

you, as you allege, take off his mask as he was walking away? Why give you even the smallest glimpse of who he was?'

I chewed on the inside of my cheek, trying to concentrate on the feeling of physical discomfort rather than the feeling of all those eyes upon me, waiting for an explanation that I could not give. I turned my head and looked up to the public gallery, desperate for just a glimpse of my parents.

Dad caught my eye. He was leaning forward, his hands clasped together. He nodded.

'I think he did it because he was going back on to the riverside. There might have been people there.'

'He had stayed masked throughout. Doesn't it seem strange to you that he would remove his mask before being out of your sight?'

'Yes. But that's what happened.'

'Is it? Because –'

'That's what happened. I'm telling the truth.'

'What I think might have happened, Belle, is that you were worried that if you said your attacker remained masked throughout, he wouldn't be found.'

'No, that's not –'

'So, you gave a generic description of a man in his late twenties – dark hair, blue eyes – and when you were asked to identify the attacker, you chose this defendant. You chose Mr Osborne.'

'That isn't true. I'm not a liar . . . I wouldn't do that.' Tears stung the corners of my eyes. I exhaled slowly, as if I was blowing out candles, blinking rapidly to suppress the emotion. I couldn't cry. Not in front of all these people. Not in front of him. 'I identified him because I saw his face,' I continued, my voice cracking. 'It was him.'

'Now, Belle, if you are correct and the attacker did remove

his mask, he had his back to you when he took it off – that's correct, isn't it?'

'Yes.'

'And you say you saw his face as he glanced back at you.'

'Yes.'

'It was dark.'

'Yes, but I could see him clearly.'

'It was the end of November, past ten at night and he had his back to you, correct?'

'I saw him.'

'If anything, wouldn't it be accurate to say that all you saw of the man who attacked you was a fleeting glance?'

'Rapist.'

The barrister balked, her eyes widening as she looked up at me from her notebook.

'Pardon me?'

'Rapist,' I said, as the tears I had been holding in finally fell down my cheeks. 'You keep on calling him an attacker. But . . . he raped me. He's a rapist.'

'Well, whatever you want to call this person . . . You did not see them clearly and then you identified an innocent man.'

'I didn't,' I cried. 'It was him. I'm certain it was him.'

'Are you lying, Belle?'

I slam my fist sideways into my bedroom wall, violently tugging myself out of the memory. Pain rushes up my hand and into my arm, all the way up to the elbow. There's nothing I could have said in that courtroom that would have made them believe me over him. Not without the DNA. After his defence barrister sat down, the prosecutor asked me more questions and I looked at the jury as I told them that I had described his face in detail, down to the mole on his jawline, near his ear, and then I had identified him by sight *and* by voice. But it wasn't enough.

I swing my legs off the bed and creep across the carpet and down the hall to the bathroom. I inch my fingers around the side of the mirrored cabinet, avoiding the watchful gaze of my lifeless eyes. It swings open, and I allow my eyes to travel over the shelves, until they finally settle on what I need.

The blades for Dad's razor.

If I'd asked for a lift that night, it wouldn't have happened. If I had worn something different, he might have chosen someone else. If I had walked on the main road instead of cutting across the riverside, he wouldn't have seen me.

It was my fault.

I press the edge to the middle of my forearm, readying myself for the heady feeling of release, but Michael Osborne's face appears in violent bursts. I shake my head, biting down on my back teeth.

I would give anything for his face to disappear. For the memory of him to disappear.

I never want to see him again.

15. Ava

I pelt across the road, my head lowered as I try to shield myself from the onslaught of rain that has chosen this moment to fall from the dark grey sky. As I reach the black canopy that overhangs the entrance, the metallic letters that spell out the name glimmer in the light of the streetlamp.

The Osborne.

His hotel. He has asked me to meet him at his hotel.

I try not to think about Will's face when I told him I was having dinner with Marissa and wouldn't make it home for movie Monday. It's his favourite night of the week. A tradition we've had for years now to make sure we spend at least one evening together without distractions. He tried to hide his disappointment, but his face fell, just for a moment.

My phone rumbles in my handbag. I pull it out, smiling quickly at the man dressed in a long black coat, a top hat adorning his head, poised to open the door.

It's George.

> Was emptying some drawers in my office and found this. Can't believe how much time has passed. G x

I tap on the photo attached beneath his text.

It's us, ten years ago. We are sitting on a bench in the pub, my graduation cap balanced wonkily on his head. Both of us laughing, my head flung backwards. I remember that feeling – laughing so hard my stomach hurt. The security of George's arm around my shoulders. Mum had come but she hadn't been present: she was there but not, staring at the seat beside her. And I knew what she was imagining – Dad. Dad should have been there. But George was there in his place.

If George was here now . . . I can imagine his face, the confusion, the reeling disappointment.

I shake my head and push my phone back into my bag then step under the canopy. The door swings open as the man lowers his head and gestures for me to enter.

'Welcome to The Osborne,' he says.

'Thank you,' I answer, walking past him into the bright light of reception. Black and white checkerboard tiles shine under my heels as I stride towards the front desk. My hands are curled into fists, the back of my neck slick with sweat. The hotel is stunning, bright white and dotted with lush green plants, but I feel as though I'm suffocating. Terror hangs in the air, pushing slowly downwards.

I wheel quickly back towards the doors. Why am I doing this to myself? The entrance spins and I blink rapidly, the high vaulted ceiling rocking above me. The doorman frowns.

My vision settles, the world falling into place, and I turn again, back towards reception.

I know why I'm here – to help Lily. To prove what Michael Osborne truly is. And the only way to do that is to move closer, inch by inch, in ever-increasing steps. Tonight is the first. I've been thinking about it all day, rehearsing what I might ask. I need to get him to talk about Lily's plea but I also need to get him to trust me. I'll find something if I can just get close enough. Guilt always leaves a trace.

'Welcome to The Osborne,' the receptionist says. I glance across at the other woman standing a few feet away from her. They are both beautiful – strikingly so. Their hair falls in soft curls down their shoulders, and their make-up is natural but flawless, their lips painted red.

'Thank you,' I say. 'I'm meeting someone for dinner in the restaurant. Can you point me in –'

'Are you Miss Knight?'

'Um . . . yes. Yes, I am.'

'I'll take you through to Mr Osborne.' She emerges from behind the desk. 'Follow me.'

'Thank you.'

She leads me across the foyer and into the small, intimate restaurant, through the tables lit by candlelight towards a table in the corner.

And there he is.

He stands to greet me and I glance away, focusing on the low buzz of conversation humming through the room. There are other people here. Customers. Guests. He can't do anything here. He can't hurt me.

I'm safe.

'Ava,' he says, his voice deep and raspy. His hand rests on the small of my back as he leans in to place a kiss on my cheek. My body shudders.

'Hello, Michael.' I meet his eye, smiling widely. 'Thank you,' I say to the receptionist.

'Yes, thank you, Delilah,' Michael says.

'You're welcome,' she says. 'Enjoy your evening.'

I watch her leave, trying to extend the pause – this brief gap in time – before we are alone.

'Please, Ava, sit,' Michael says, his words imbued with charm. But a command, nonetheless.

I can feel him appraising me as I settle into the velvet chair, crossing one leg over the other. My foot grazes his under the table. I recoil quickly. He smiles.

'I hope you don't think I'm arrogant inviting you to the restaurant at my hotel, but I just . . . it's the best restaurant in town.' He laughs. 'I guess that was quite arrogant.'

I force a laugh. 'No, no . . . it's beautiful. How many hotels do you have?'

'Well, my father opened around twenty before he died, and I've opened a few more since then. But it was his baby. His legacy. I'm just carrying it on.'

I nod politely. I don't know where to put my hands. Normally, I would rest them on the table, but Michael's forearms already reach halfway across – the intimacy of our almost joining hands would be too much. I rest them instead in my lap, searching for something to say.

'And you're a photographer too?'

'Yes – that's my real love. You know, the hotels run themselves. I started in my twenties and built a career for myself. Celebrities, models, you know.'

'Good evening, sir,' a waiter says as he appears at our table, and I exhale slowly, dizzy with relief. 'Can I offer you both some drinks?'

'Um . . . Red wine would be lovely,' I say.

'Perfect,' Michael says. 'A woman after my own heart. Can we have my usual, please, Stephen?'

'Of course, sir.' He turns and walks briskly towards the dark mahogany bar.

Michael clears his throat, shifting slightly in his chair. 'How are you?'

'I'm well, thank you. It's been a busy day but this is definitely a treat for a Monday night.'

'Your boyfriend doesn't take you out for dinner on a Monday night?'

I laugh gently. 'I told you I don't have one of those. It would be quite inappropriate for me to be here if I did, wouldn't it?'

'Would it?' He leans forward, inching closer towards me across the small table, his teeth grazing his bottom lip.

'You don't think so? Dinner with a man I barely know?'

'That would all depend on what you have in mind, Ava.' He raises an eyebrow, his eyes sparkling as he throws his head back and laughs, hearty and full. Nausea sloshes in my stomach.

Tucking my hair behind my ear, I rest my fingers under my chin.

'It would be inappropriate,' I whisper.

'Here is the Querciabella Camartina.'

Stephen has appeared again, one hand behind his back, the other holding a bottle of wine.

'Would you like to try it, madam?'

'No,' I say, looking away from him and across to Michael. 'If Michael says it's a good wine, I trust that it is.'

Michael smiles, showing all of his teeth – a full, satisfied grin. *Bingo*. This is a man who desires praise. A man who relishes being needed. That is a weapon: a sharp blade that I can wield against him.

'It is quite superb,' Stephen says, pouring the dark crimson liquid first into my glass and then into Michael's.

'Thank you, Stephen. To you,' Michael says, raising his glass.

I smile, turning my head coyly to one side, and chink my glass against his, the sound ringing out across the quiet buzz of the restaurant.

We both sip, and his eyes linger on mine.

'Would you like to order, sir?' Stephen asks as Michael places his wine back on the table.

'I haven't even looked at the menu yet, we've been busy chatting,' I say. 'Do you mind just giving me a few more minutes?'

'Yes, of course –'

'I'd highly recommend the steak,' Michael interrupts. 'If you like steak, that is.'

'I . . . Yes, I do like steak.'

'It's the best thing on the menu.'

'Well then, why would I order anything else?' I pause. 'Thank you.'

'How do you want your steak, madam?'

'Medium-rare, please.'

'Perfect. It will be with you shortly.'

'Thank you.'

'Yes, thank you so much, Stephen,' Michael says. 'The usual for me.'

'Straightaway, sir.'

I look around the restaurant, my eyes travelling over the tables filled with people: laughing, eating, enjoying their time together. Completely unaware of what I'm doing. Do I hide it well? Or will a stranger looking in our direction know that something is off? That there is a tension between us that is impossible to ignore. I can feel it, all the time, buzzing incessantly. But can he?

I glance back at Michael – but his eyes have glazed over with a sudden sadness.

'What do you think will happen to Lily?' he asks.

I hesitate, swirling the wine around my glass before taking a prolonged sip. I don't want him to realize I'm keen to talk about Lily, about her plea. He needs to think it's the last thing I want to discuss. Glancing at him from the corner of my eye, I cock my head.

'I'm not sure we should discuss the case. I'm breaking every rule there is by just being here with you.'

'Do you think she'll be sent to custody?'

'Michael –'

'I'm sorry.' He looks down at the table – the first time he has broken eye contact. 'It's just . . . She became very close to my daughter. And it's so sad, so upsetting, to see a child lose herself like that. We still care about her. You understand?'

'Of course,' I mutter. 'It's hard to predict with children. With adults, I can normally tell what the judge will do, but with children, they have to think about so much, including her welfare.'

He nods.

'I . . . I was surprised that she pleaded guilty. I thought she might try to pull a defence out of nowhere.'

He doesn't flinch. 'But she doesn't have one.'

'A lot of people will try anything. Anything they can . . .' I lick my lips, my mouth dry as I poise myself to continue. 'And some innocent people plead guilty.' I watch him closely, scanning his expression for the slightest change, looking for a hitch in his breathing or a fidgeting of fingers.

'I just hope that no matter the outcome, she tries to get help.'

Nothing.

No reaction at all.

'Anyway,' I say, drumming my fingers on the table. 'Let's change the subject. I'd rather not talk about work, if that's okay.'

'Sure. It's not like I asked you here to talk business.'

'No . . . you asked me here to be your friend. Right, Michael?' I raise my eyebrow, my index finger gently grazing the bottom of my lip. I hold his gaze, but inside, it's as though all my organs are shifting, repulsed. By him. And by me, by what I am doing. He stares, watching me closely.

'Don't you want to be my friend, Ava?'

The perfect question. I can tell him the truth but dress it up in seduction and charm. The meaning will transform before his eyes: the truth turning into exactly what he wants to hear.

'No, Michael,' I say softly. 'I don't want to be your friend.'

He grins broadly and shifts forward, but as his fingers graze my knuckles, nausea careens up my throat.

Stephen appears beside us, two plates balanced – one in his hand, and one on his lower forearm. The smell of steak wafts towards me and I taste sick on the back of my tongue, the ghost of his touch still burning my hand.

'Your steak, madam. It is served with pomme fondant, caramelized shallots, and green beans topped with toasted almonds.'

'Thank you.'

He nods at me and turns to Michael, setting his plate before him.

'And yours, sir.'

'Thank you, Stephen. Oh – and some mustard?' Michael says.

'Of course, sir. Right away.'

He lifts his knife and fork. 'Enjoy.'

'I'm sure I will.'

He stabs the meat with his fork and hews a chunk away, lifting it to his mouth, his eyes rolling back in enthused enjoyment.

He seems so sure of himself, so convincing in his sympathy for Lily. His care for her. But as he takes another bite of his steak, all I see is a wolf. Devouring its prey.

The heavy stream of water pounds on top of my head, the droplets stinging against my skin. I tilt my head backwards, glancing briefly at the ceiling before closing my eyes. But his face flashes in the dark.

I rub each eye with the back of my hand and the thick coat of mascara I was wearing smears across my skin. I pour face wash into my hands and scrub furiously at my cheeks and mouth. When I left the hotel, he kissed me goodbye, his lips lingering on the very edge of my cheek, close to my mouth, his hand as low as it could rest on the small of my back. He asked if I wanted to go up to his suite for a drink. *Ninth floor*, he said. *Beautiful views.* I told him no, that I had a busy day tomorrow. I wanted to shrink away from him, to run away, but I locked my feet in position, leaning into him as I said goodbye, whispering that we would see each other again soon.

I hold a trembling hand up to my mouth. I feel sick at the thought of his touch, at my willingness to engage with him. My willingness to entice him.

I lift my face so that the droplets of water splash on to my cheeks.

Hands over my mouth. Strong arms pushing down against my chest. Legs kicking. Blue eyes. My dress pulled upwards. Hands on the inside of my thighs. Pressure. Fear. Stillness.

A loud cry escapes my lips. I rest my forehead against the tiled wall and concentrate on the feeling of water thrumming against my back.

I mustn't think about what he did. I won't. All I should think about is how to prove *what* he is.

Michael Osborne is not an innocent man.

And I can't let him hurt another girl. Never again.

I step out of the shower and wrap myself in a towel, then cross the short distance of the corridor from the bathroom to our bedroom.

Will is propped up in bed but his eyes are closed, his thick-rimmed reading glasses slipping down to the end of his nose as his head lolls sidewards on to his shoulder.

I pull on an oversized T-shirt and towel dry my hair, then climb slowly into bed, trying not to wake him.

'Hello, gorgeous,' he whispers.

'Hi,' I whisper back as I roll on to my side to face him, pulling the thick duvet up under my arms.

He shuffles downwards and moves towards me so that we are face to face, his lips just a ripple of breath away from mine. 'How was Marissa?'

'She was fine . . . Sorry, I know it's usually our night.'

'It's okay.' He reaches across and cups my chin in his hands, kissing me gently. 'I know it's just movie night, but we've both been so busy recently, we hardly get to spend time together . . . I could leave for my trip late on Sunday instead of Saturday –'

'But haven't you made plans with Jamal? You're wining and dining the clients on Saturday, aren't you?'

'Yes, but I could –'

'No, this is so important, Will. I know we need to spend more time together but this is your business. You've worked so hard.'

He lifts his fingers to my face and strokes my cheek. 'Okay . . . We should both get some days off once I'm back from my trip next week and go somewhere together.'

I rest my hand on his chest, focusing on his steady breath. His steady presence. 'That would be lovely.'

His hand snakes around the back of my neck and he strokes my hair, just like always. The first time we slept in the same bed, he moved towards me and I pressed myself against him as he stroked my hair, but I imagined that we would only stay like that for a few minutes before he moved away, finding his own space. But he didn't retreat. At first it was unnerving, and it was me who shifted away, waking up on the opposite side of the bed. But after a while I stopped. And now, I struggle to sleep without him. I search for his touch, my mind aching for the safety that only he can give.

'Night, beautiful,' he whispers. 'I love you.'

'I love you. Night.'

He closes his eyes and guilt shudders through me. But I'm not doing this to him. I'm doing it *for* me. For Lily.

I blink slowly, my eyes fluttering closed. But the dark is swimming with images, my thoughts thrumming ceaselessly. I try to concentrate on the sound of Will's breathing, now slow and steady as he has given way to sleep. But I can't settle, and Michael's face, as he stared at me across the table, refuses to disappear.

I roll away from Will. He shifts in his sleep, his arm searching for me until he falls still, his hand draped across my stomach. I carefully lean sideways, reaching down the side of the bed to where my laptop is laid on the floor.

I prop it on my chest and wait as it whirs to life, reaching across to my bedside for my barely worn reading glasses. I double-tap on the internet and open the search engine – but my fingers hesitate over the keys.

All these years, I've been so careful, never allowing myself to search his name, to re-read these articles, knowing that if I followed that path, I would lose myself forever.

I slowly tap on the keys, and letter by letter the names emerge, tied together.

Michael Osborne + Anabelle King.

A list appears, our names side by side, over and over again, and my eyes quickly settle on a news article from eighteen years ago.

YOUNG PHOTOGRAPHER OF THE YEAR FALSELY ACCUSED OF RAPE

My heart pounds in my chest as I stare at the photograph of a young Michael. And then I ferociously take in each word, unable to look away. The newspapers didn't name me. They weren't allowed. But that didn't make a difference in the end. After they let him go, I thought that everything would die down. I thought that we'd be left to try to recover from the fallout. But it was just the beginning. Like a stone tossed carelessly into a lake, the acquittal created ripples that grew bigger and bigger, each one unexpected, giving no hint that there was yet more to come.

Another article appears:

POLICE INVESTIGATE – LAW BROKEN AS VICTIM'S NAME LEAKED

Police are investigating the publication of the identity of the complainant in a recent rape trial. The trial was widely reported, and the defendant – Michael Osborne, a successful young photographer, and heir to the Osborne empire of hotels – was acquitted. However, restrictions that prevented the complainant's name being reported due to her age have been breached, with her identity and photograph being published on several websites with the title, 'The Girl Who Cried Rape'. The breaches have since been removed from –

I scroll away and as I lift my fingers from the touchpad, the screen keeps on moving downwards, finally coming to a stop in the comments which are still intact.

She was asking for it.
She goes to my school. Knew she was a whore,
it's always the quiet ones.
Why do people feel sorry for her? She lied! What kind of sick girl
makes up something like this? Bitch deserves prison.

I tap quickly on the backspace. The police tried to take everything down, but some stories still linger, like smoke clinging to hair and fabric, impossible to remove. My old name is there, repeated over and over. I close my eyes, inhale deeply –

And click.

16. Lily

Two months before the attack

The tablet bottle rattles in my hand as I slide to the floor. I lean back, tucking myself in the small gap between the bed and the wall, my knees propped up in front of me. I push down on the lid and turn, then tap out two into my hand.

My door flies open, banging against the wall.

'What are you doing, hiding away in here?' Kacey says as she bursts in.

'You're supposed to knock,' I say, not even turning my head to look at her. I slowly slide my hand backwards releasing the pills, and then the bottle, under the bed.

'And you're supposed to join everyone else for dinner.'

I push myself to my feet, glancing down quickly to check that everything is hidden. All clear. I lift my chin to look at Kacey who is standing at the foot of my bed, arms folded, mouth sneering.

'It's too early,' I say. 'I'm not hungry.'

'You never are. You always hide in your room or go off to your posh little friend's house.' She moves closer. 'Is that it? We're not good enough here?'

'I never said that.'

'You didn't have to.' She steps forward again and I stumble backwards, my shoulder hitting the wall.

'Like you ever wanted to be my friend, Kacey. Just fuck off.'

She sneers. 'You want to hit me, don't you? I can see it in your face.'

'No, I –'

'You know, we all know about you. About your temper, your arrests. How you've been kicked out of other homes. The drugs. Is that what you're doing now? Doing drugs?'

'No.' My hands curl at my sides as anger washes over me in a stream of white light, blinding me. 'Please, just leave me alone.'

'But this is fun, no? Seeing how far I can push you?'

'Kacey, seriously –'

'How long does it usually take you to lose it?'

'Kacey –'

'How long until –'

'What's going on in here?' Anne's astonished voice breaks through the noise, silencing Kacey, silencing the thrum of anger, stilling my temper – so taut it was ready to snap. 'Kacey, get away from her.'

'I wasn't doing anything, Anne,' Kacey says. 'I was just trying to speak to her.'

'Don't pull that innocent act, Kacey, I heard what you were saying to her. You were provoking her.'

'I –'

'No, I don't want your excuses. Just stay away from each other. You don't have to be friends, but you do have to live together.'

Kacey closes her mouth, locking away her protestations.

'And if you pull something like that again, I'll have to escalate to Harriet. Understand?'

'Yes.'

'Good. Now, go, and close the door behind you.'

She stomps out of the room, but as she turns to shut the door her eyes capture mine, her scowl full of hate.

Anne sits down at the end of my bed, the old mattress sinking beneath her weight. 'Are you okay, Lily?'

'I'm fine. She . . . she just doesn't like me. And I don't know why.'

'She's always hard on new girls. But if she does that again, you tell me. Okay?'

'Okay.'

She nods decisively and stands.

'Anne?'

'Yes, Lily?' she responds, turning back in the doorway.

'Could I . . . could I go and stay at my friend's house?'

'The one in Meadow Gardens?'

I nod.

'Yes, as long as her father says it's okay.'

Michael's kind, happy face appears in my mind.

I smile.

'Thank you for picking me up, Mr Osborne,' I say, as I clamber into the back of the car.

'Not a problem, at all, Lily,' he says, as he indicates and begins to drive away from Franklin House. 'But please, call me Michael.'

'Sorry,' I say, blushing.

'Nothing to be sorry for.' His eyes flicker to the rear-view mirror. His mouth isn't visible, but I can tell that he's smiling at me. I imagine his lips stretched into a grin, laughter lines appearing. The dimple in his chin.

'What did Kacey do now?' Orla asks, turning in her seat to face me.

'Orla – seatbelt,' Michael says, his voice suddenly stern.

'It's on!' she says, snapping it against her chest.

'Okay, okay.'

'Yeah, what did Kacey do?'

I look out of the window, at the houses flying past, the lights starting to turn on as the sun sets behind the trees, the sky pink and orange. 'She was just trying to intimidate me.'

'She's such a bitch.'

'Orla –' Michael warns.

'Dad, she is. She's so mean to Lily, for no reason at all.'

I look back to the mirror, and his eyes are on me again. But this time they are serious, his dark eyebrows lowered.

'Why doesn't she like you?'

I shrug. 'Just one of those things, I guess.'

'Well, if you ever need anything, you know where we are. Always feel free to come to us for help.'

'Thank you, Mr Osborne.'

'Michael.'

I smile at his reflection. 'Michael.'

We spend the rest of the journey talking and laughing, Orla smiling at me over her shoulder, my attention being pulled constantly towards the mirror. To where his eyes occasionally fall on my face with a secret smile. We eventually turn on to the private road, slowly rolling past various gated houses until we turn into theirs.

'Right, girls,' Michael says as we step inside. 'What do you want to eat tonight? Have you eaten, Lily?'

'No,' I say. 'But I don't mind.'

'Oh, pizza!' Orla says.

'Again?' he says mockingly, rolling his eyes at me. The back of my neck tingles. It's like he shared a secret with me. A look between us, and us alone.

'Please!'

'That's fine. And I've got some work to do, so do you want to eat it upstairs?'

'Oh yeah,' Orla nods enthusiastically.

'You can eat in your room?' I mutter.

She nods. 'Mmhmm.'

'Cool. I'll bring it upstairs when it's here.'

'Thanks, Dad.'

'Thank you, Michael.'

We run upstairs, our feet pounding on the steps as we rush to her room. She jumps on to her bed and I follow, my heart spilling over. I'm slowly becoming used to the feeling of being with Orla, of being here, in this house. It felt alien at first, but now – it feels almost like home. More home than anywhere has ever felt.

'So you weren't ever allowed to eat in your room?'

I scoff. 'No.' I shake my head, my eyes searching her face. 'I was lucky if I ate at all.'

Her eyes widen. 'Really?'

'It wasn't as bad when she was with Phil. But once he . . . was gone . . . she just stopped trying. The cupboards were empty a lot of the time. I just had to make do. I used to eat at school and that was it.'

'Just one meal a day?'

'Yeah. She didn't really want to spend money on food. Or clothes.'

'What did she spend money on?'

I raise my eyebrows.

'Oh,' Orla says, realizing. 'Drugs?'

'Yeah. But after about a year, a neighbour noticed that I was left alone a lot. School noticed that I was skinny . . . Dirty. So social services got involved. And then about a year after that, they came and took me away.'

'What happened to your mum?'

I shrug, my eyes stinging. 'She left. I never saw her again.'

'And . . . is what they say about you true?'

'What who say about me?' I ask, frowning.

'People at school. Kacey and her friends . . . is it true that you take drugs?'

I look away from her, licking my lips. 'Would it bother you if it was true?'

'No, I . . . I just worry about you.'

I want to tell her the truth. I want to be able to tell her anything, to trust her with anything. 'I . . . I used to smoke weed. And I tried some other stuff . . . I didn't like it though. And I got in trouble. But . . . sometimes I take benzos.'

I watch her carefully, my eyes watering as I try to gauge her reaction.

She frowns. 'What are benzos?'

'They're pills. Doctors give them to people with anxiety.'

'So does a doctor give them to you?'

'No . . . Someone else gets them for me.'

She nods, but I can see that she doesn't really understand. That she'll never understand the absolute need to quiet all of the noise. The desperation to make it all fall silent and calm, if just for a little while. When they took away my prescription, the world was chaos. With them, the chaos is still there, but it is blurred, irrelevant.

'But what happened to your step-dad?' she asks, changing the subject. 'Why did he leave?'

I sniff and the tears I've been holding back stream down my cheeks. Orla's face falls and she wraps her arms around my shoulders, hushing me gently, her breath warm on my forehead.

'Oh Lily, I'm sorry, I didn't mean to upset you. I'm so sorry –'

'It's okay,' I whisper. My voice feels tight, trapped, as if someone has placed their hands around my throat, tightening second by second until there is no air left.

'You don't have to tell me, I didn't realize –'

'No.' I sniff, wiping my face with the back of my hand. 'I want to.'

Her arm loosens and I sit up to face her, tucking my legs beneath me.

'I've never told anyone this before,' I say.

'You can trust me. I won't tell anyone. You're my best friend, Lily.'

'I know.' I swallow, inhaling deeply. 'When I was five, Mum met Phil. They got married really quickly and I . . . I don't remember much, but it was really intense. I just remember them always being together. Him never leaving her side. He never left her alone.'

'Okay . . .'

'And then, when I was around seven, he . . . he started to hit me. A lot. All the time. They'd keep me out of school, tell teachers I was ill –'

'They? You mean your mum knew?'

I nod slowly and her mouth drops open. 'Yes, she knew. She knew and she . . . she turned the other way. She protected him.'

She shakes her head, the shock rising from her like a haze of heat off the pavement.

'But one day,' I continue, 'they let me go to school and didn't realize that I still had bruises on me. I showed my teacher and told them what had happened. And Phil was arrested.'

'Did he . . . Did he touch you?'

'No. Not like that.'

'Did he go to prison?'

'Yes. I don't think Mum ever forgave me.'

'So why didn't they take you away from your mum then? Why did they leave you with her?'

'Because I didn't tell them. I told the police, social

services – everyone – that she didn't know. That I'd hidden it from her.'

'But why?'

'Because I thought that no matter how bad it was, being with my mum would be better than being without her. Sometimes, I still think that.'

'Lily, no –'

'It's true. She was my mum. It was horrible and I hated her, but I loved her too. I didn't want her to get into trouble, I didn't want to lose her.' I wipe my face with the back of my hand. 'You have no idea how lucky you are to have a mum and dad like yours.'

She crosses her legs, pulling a pillow on to her lap and hugging it to her.

'Before they separated,' Orla whispers, 'I used to hear them arguing all the time . . . It's been much better since they've been apart.'

'You must miss it, though.'

She nods slowly, her eyes focusing somewhere else, on something else, distant in her mind. 'I do. But I couldn't stand the fighting. And I hardly ever saw Dad, he was always out or away. One night, when I was younger, I heard . . .' She cuts herself off, hesitating, disappearing into a memory.

'You heard what?'

'I . . .' She scans my face, her eyes full of emotion.

'You can trust me,' I whisper.

She nods. 'I heard them arguing about something that happened to my dad when he was younger.'

Her face has transformed, as if she has thought of something and is keeping it restrained within her, like a wild animal bursting to be set free.

'What is it?' I ask.

'He . . . When he was in his twenties he was accused of rape.'

My mouth drops open. 'Really?'

'Yes. But they let him go, he wasn't convicted.'

'Who accused him?'

'A girl. She was just a teenager. I looked it up.'

'But . . . how could someone accuse him of that? Your dad is so kind.'

Michael's warm face shimmers in my mind, his soft smile and softer words. He could never do something like that.

She looks down, twisting her fingers in the duvet. 'I don't know. But I've always wondered if it had something to do with why they separated. I've always wondered if . . .'

'If what?'

Her eyes dart up to meet mine and she snaps her mouth shut, shaking her head. 'Nothing. It's nothing.'

'I told you –'

'No, seriously, it was nothing, Lily. My dad wouldn't like me talking about it and it's just me being stupid.'

I go to speak again but stop myself. I don't want to push her. What if I push her too far and she starts to pull away from me? What if instead of us drawing together, I am suddenly repelled?

'Okay,' I smile. 'Shall we listen to some music?'

She nods, finally meeting my eye again, her face cracking into a hesitant smile.

'Actually, there's something I wanted to give you,' she says.

'Give me?'

'Yeah.' She climbs off the bed and walks to her dresser, her hand dipping into one of the drawers. She pulls out a small white box and hands it to me, smiling.

I stare down at it. 'This is for me?'

'Open it.'

'But what's it for?'

'Just open it,' she says, laughing.

I slowly untie the dusky pink satin bow. But as I remove the lid, I gasp. Inside is a necklace: dainty and silver, a thin disk with my initial and a small green gem hanging from a fine chain.

I look at her with wide eyes, overwhelmed. 'It's just like yours. Orla, I –'

'Do you want to put it on?'

I nod eagerly and she carefully pulls it out of the box. I sweep my hair away from my neck and she stands behind me.

'There,' she says as she lets go and it settles on my chest. 'Beautiful.'

My fingers automatically reach for it. It's the most perfect thing I've ever owned.

'Thank you so much. But I don't know why –'

'Because you're my best friend. And you deserve beautiful things.'

She steps forward and wraps her arms around my neck, her head close to mine.

'Thank you,' I whisper again.

Hours later, after pizza and a film, and countless conversations, our voices leading us into the night, Orla falls asleep, her breathing loud and deep beside me. She is sprawled out, her limbs flying out across the bed, as if she is jumping out of a plane. Falling.

She knows my secrets now. Will she keep them? What if our friendship ends? What will happen then? Will she hold them inside her or will she crack like an egg, spilling them out for the whole world to see?

I slowly get out of bed and open her door, letting a sliver of faint light shine into her room. Walking down the stairs, I concentrate on my footsteps, keeping them quiet. I cross the hall to the kitchen and help myself to some water, draining one glass thirstily before refilling it to take upstairs.

'You're up late.'

I jump at the sound of his voice and water sloshes out of my glass, splashing on to the tiles.

'Sorry,' he laughs, standing up from the sofa and walking towards me. 'I didn't mean to scare you.'

'It's okay,' I say, my hand pressed to my chest, my breaths fast. 'I was thirsty.' My eyes flicker down to the floor, to where the water is reflecting the lights that hang above the island.

'Don't worry about the spill,' he says, reading my mind.

I smile. 'Thanks. I'll . . . I'll go to bed now.'

'Sure. Goodnight, Lily.'

I go to leave, but my eyes are drawn to what Michael is holding – large photographs held against his chest.

'Did you just develop those?'

He glances down. 'Oh, these? Yes.'

'Can I . . . can I see?'

'Of course.'

He spreads them out on the island, six black and white photographs, soft and romantic. A girl stares out of them, so stunning that I almost don't recognize her.

'It's Orla,' I whisper.

'Yes, I took them last weekend. I haven't photographed her in years but she saw some photos I did of a model and loved them so we did something similar for her. Doesn't she look great?'

'Beautiful.'

I look at him out of the corner of my eye and he turns sideways to face me. My face flushes, my cheeks hot, burning under the fire of his attention.

'I could photograph you, if you'd like?'

My stomach flips. 'Really?'

'Sure, if you'd like that. I don't suppose you've ever been photographed . . .'

'No. No, I haven't,' I say, my eyes dancing over the pictures of Orla, imagining my face looking back up at me, transformed. Seen through his lens, his eyes. Maybe I could be beautiful, too. 'I'm not a model, though.'

'Don't be silly,' he says. 'You're gorgeous.'

I slowly step sideways, closer, just a fraction, just an inch. So little that it's barely even noticeable. But my arm rests against his.

'Really?'

'Of course.' He doesn't move his arm away. 'Stunning.'

My stomach flips again.

17. Ava

'Thank you so much for today,' Orla says as she settles into the passenger seat. 'I loved it.'

'It was a pleasure,' I say, smiling.

And it was. Orla was polite and charming, confidently chatting to other barristers, but also disappearing into the background, aware of the need for subtlety. Every so often, I found myself forgetting who she is – buying into my own explanation that she was an old friend's daughter – but then she would tilt her head just so, or smile with her mouth pursed, dimples appearing, and I remembered. In both looks and mannerisms, she's the image of her father.

'Are you sure you don't mind taking me home?' she asks. 'It will take about forty minutes from here –'

'No, of course not. Gives us a chance to chat some more. Am I taking you to your mum's or your dad's house?'

'Dad. I'm with him tonight and then I go back to Mum's for the rest of the week.'

I start the engine and reverse out of my space. She arrived at court this morning, not a minute late. She was pulling at the sleeves of her blazer, her eyes darting around while she was scanned by security, waving nervously when she spotted me waiting for her on the other side. But I didn't get a chance to speak to her. We talked about criminal law and the career, and I explained the intricacies of the trial and the legal arguments, but nothing more. Nothing about her father, or Lily. Nothing that can help me.

'Did you enjoy watching the trial?' I ask after a minute of awkward silence.

'It was really interesting.' She turns slightly in her seat, her seatbelt straining across her shoulders.

'It was a great case for you to watch – gave a good insight into lots of the different challenges we face as barristers. As prosecutors. Unwilling witnesses, hearsay, evidence admissibility . . .'

'Is it always so complicated? So intense?'

A buzz of excitement runs through me. The same buzz I get when a witness perfectly lands their evidence, or a defendant unwittingly gives themselves away: she's opened herself up for questioning without even realizing. People do it all the time, and the sense of satisfaction is always the same: that sense of control, influence. Will rolls his eyes during disagreements, muttering under his breath – *'you're cross-examining me again.'* But now the thrill is tainted with guilt. She is just a child. A child who bears no responsibility for her dad's actions. Or her friend's. But . . . I need to know. I need to know more.

'No, not always. And even when it is, there isn't a job like it. Exciting, interesting, stimulating . . . We make a difference. But sometimes cases are very simple.' I pause, ready to lead her into a conversation she doesn't know is coming. 'Like what happened to your dad. There were no issues: she pleaded guilty and that was that.'

I glance sideways, my eyes scanning her quickly for her reaction. Her head has dropped and she is looking down at her lap, her hands clasped together. But she hasn't turned away from me. She hasn't disengaged – not completely. Not yet.

'I'm so sorry,' I say, reaching out to quickly squeeze her knee. 'I know she was your friend.'

She looks up but her eyes have glazed over with tears. 'It's okay,' she whispers.

'I really am sorry; I didn't mean to upset you.'

'No, it's okay. It's just hard to think about her. She . . . she was my best friend.'

I focus on the road in front of me. I want to dig deeper, go further – but I don't want to push her too far.

'How long had you been friends?'

'Only since December. It was just after my birthday –'

'Are you December? So am I.'

She smiles. 'Yes, the fourth.'

'I'm the fifteenth. So . . . Lily was a new friend?'

'Yes, but . . . Never mind.'

My eyes flicker to her face. 'What is it?'

'I've always had friends, a group of friends, you know, but . . . never a best friend. Not like I wanted. The girls at school are so cliquey. But Lily . . .'

'She wasn't like that?'

'No, not at all,' she says, staring into space, disappearing into another time. 'She wasn't interested in any of the super-ficial stuff. She didn't worry about who was friends with who, or who hated who, or what bag someone had, or what the boys thought. She didn't expect me to . . . to be perfect.'

'Who expects you to be perfect? Your parents?'

'Mum is really laid-back. My dad expects a lot though . . . But all Lily wanted was a friend who would listen to her. Care about her. And she did the same.'

'She sounds like a great friend,' I say, turning to her as I pull the car to a stop at a set of traffic lights.

She nods, staring into the distance, unfocused, almost as if I'm not there at all.

'Orla?'

She blinks quickly, shaking her head. 'She was a great friend up until . . . Until she did what she did.'

I nod. 'Have you spoken to her?'

Her eyes widen, round and fearful.

'You wouldn't be in trouble,' I say quickly. 'I just wondered . . . It must be hard to lose such a close friend so abruptly.'

'I . . .' She stops, her mouth open. 'No. I haven't spoken to her.'

'You can still miss her, though.'

She doesn't say anything. She simply shakes her head and unfolds her legs to face forward. Conversation over.

The lights turn green and I accelerate away. The busy streets begin to disappear and are replaced by rows of houses, parks, as the city gives way to the suburbs. I wait, allowing the silence to settle – to shed its awkwardness and diffuse into stillness. Orla's head is turned away from me as she looks out of the window, but her cheeks are blotchy and red. She sniffs.

'So . . . do you think you enjoyed your first day with the solicitors or your day in court more?'

A small smile plays on her lips but she sighs, rubbing her eyes with the back of her hand.

'You can tell me the truth,' I whisper conspiratorially. 'Being in court is better.'

She laughs suddenly, throwing her head back.

Just like him.

'Definitely being in court.' She moves towards me again, her gratefulness at the change of subject, clear on her face.

I listen to her talk, her demeanour changing as she relaxes again, her hands moving with enthusiasm. But my mind keeps replaying her candid words, her brief confession.

All Lily wanted was a friend who would listen to her. Care for her. And she did the same.

I remember the intensity of teenage friendships. Girls huddled together, whispering secrets long into the night. Friendships that feel more important than anything or anyone else. My best friend when I was younger – when it happened – was the only person who knew besides my mum and dad. And the police. And she never told a soul. She stood by me, defended me at school when it all got out of control. But once I changed my name and we moved away, I let our friendship disappear. As if it was tied to the old me, and to move on, I had to let her go.

There must be things that Orla and Lily told each other that they never told anyone else. Secrets that they will keep locked inside of themselves. Forever.

Even now.

I stop the car outside the front door. The true size of the house becomes clear up close: it towers over us, three floors topped with a glass lantern.

'Thank you, again,' Orla says.

'You're welcome,' I say, yanking up the handbrake. 'And I'm sorry if I upset you.'

She shakes her head. 'No. It's nice to talk to someone.'

'Good.'

She opens the passenger door, but pauses, glancing back at me. 'Would you like to come inside? Dad will be home soon and I'm sure he'd love to have a quick chat, see how it went.'

'Um . . .' I look up again at the house. My breathing slows, almost to the point of stopping completely. 'Sure. Why not.'

'Great,' she says. She turns towards the door but comes to a standstill, throwing her head backwards to look up at the sky. 'Oh shit.'

'Something wrong?'

'Oh shit, sorry – I didn't mean to swear. Sorry!'

I laugh. 'It's fine. You can swear.'

'I . . . I forgot my key again.' She rolls her eyes and leans over a large planter beside the door. When she straightens up, she is holding a key, small and silver, shining in the light.

'Don't tell my dad – he'd kill me if he knew I hid a key out here.'

'I won't say a word.' I mimic locking my lips, throwing away the key.

'Thanks.'

She unlocks the door and the alarm sounds inside, but she waves at me, fluttering her fingers back and forth. 'Come in.'

I nod, glancing quickly over my shoulder, and step inside.

18. Lily

One month before the attack

'We can start with you standing if you like? And then do sitting?' Michael says as I step into the white space in the back corner of his studio. 'Whatever you're comfortable with.'

'That's fine,' I say, my voice shaking with nerves.

'Don't be scared,' he says. 'Remember it's just us here. This is supposed to be fun.'

'And you look freaking gorgeous!' Orla says, her words echoing, bouncing off the concrete walls. 'I did her make-up. Doesn't she look amazing?'

'Yes, she looks great,' he says to Orla. He glances at me, nodding. 'You look great.'

'Thanks,' I say. But my insides feel as though they're burning. As if he has lit the tiniest of flames inside me, and slowly but surely it is growing, turning into a fire. Blazing.

'Perfect, so if you just stand in the centre of the white floor, and we can just snap away, okay?'

'Okay.'

I step on to the white floor, ready to begin. But he turns away, heading to a desk in the back corner. I watch as he retrieves his camera and other things, my hands tugging at the bottom of the top that Orla forced me into. Her face had changed when she saw what I was wearing: my loose black T-shirt and eyes dark with liner. I almost didn't recognize myself when she stood me in front of her full-length mirror.

The perfect skin and wide bright eyes. The white off-the-shoulder top, cropped, my stomach exposed.

'Right,' he says, standing just a couple of feet away from me. 'You ready?'

'She was born ready,' Orla says.

I snort loudly, then cover my eyes as my cheeks flush with heat.

'You girls are mad,' Michael says. 'Right. Just do whatever you like, Lily – however you feel most you.'

I hook my thumbs into the top of my jeans, my ankles rolling outwards, and look straight down the lens.

His camera clicks. The lights surrounding me flash.

'Great,' he says, his voice low.

'I . . . I didn't do anything.'

'You don't need to. You look perfect.' He smiles softly at me. A smile that feels as if it's meant just for me.

I beam back at him, my fingers reaching to hold on to my necklace.

The lights flash again.

'I wasn't even looking at the camera.'

'But look, it's lovely,' he says. He gestures, calling me over to the monitor. My eyes land on the screen and I –

I can't believe that's me. I look so happy. Free. But my eyes aren't looking at the lens. I'm looking at him.

I'm always looking at him.

'See,' he says.

I nod.

'Go on then.'

I nod again and walk back to my place.

Click. Click. Click.

'Great. Okay, now maybe –'

'Hello?' Orla says loudly, her phone to her ear. 'Mum? I can't really hear you –'

'Orla –'

'Mum, I can't hear you –'

'Orla.' Michael pulls the camera away from his face and it hangs down by his side, an extension of his arm. 'Go upstairs to speak to your mum. You're so loud –'

'Sorry, sorry,' she says, rolling her eyes at me. 'I'll whisper –'

'No, you're too distracting. Go upstairs, please.'

She stares at him, the phone suspended in the air by her ear. 'Fine.' She backs away slowly, her eyes darting back and forth from me to her dad. I smile at her – trying to break the tension between them. Finally, she smiles back.

'Scrooge,' she says, sticking her tongue out at him. He laughs.

'You're doing fabulous,' she shouts as she runs up the stairs. I chuckle.

She's just the best.

'Okay,' Michael says, walking past me. 'Maybe we can try some with you on the stool?'

'Sure.'

He picks up the stool and carries it into the centre of the white space. But as I lean on the edge of the seat, he lowers his camera, no longer engrossed in checking the images he has taken so far. Instead, he is looking at me, his eyes searching my face.

Shivers run through me. Goosebumps travel up my arms and across my chest as he watches me, and in the absence of Orla, the quiet of the room is all-consuming. It's just him and me. Nothing else. No sound. No movement. Nothing.

Just us.

'Okay, so why don't you just sit however you would sit, and we can see what looks good.'

I nod, slowly, my skin still tingling, and push myself back on to the stool. I cross my legs.

'Mm. You look a bit uncomfortable,' he says.

'Sorry –'

'No, don't be sorry.' He moves towards me, inching closer. 'This is the first time you've been photographed, right?'

'Yeah . . .'

'Didn't your parents ever take photos of you when you were younger?'

I blink slowly. 'I . . . They weren't those kinds of parents. And I never knew my dad . . . So . . .'

'I'm so sorry, Lily.' He holds the camera to his chest. 'When was the last time you saw your mum?'

I sniff. 'I was ten.'

'Well, maybe you'll see her again one day.'

'No.' I shake my head. 'She left. She doesn't care about me. Nobody cares about me really.'

'We do.'

I meet his eye. He said the words so quickly, so openly, like it is nothing at all to admit to caring about someone.

'Really?'

'Yes,' he nods. 'You know if you ever feel lonely, you can come to me, right? Even if Orla isn't here.'

I shift on the stool and glance down at the floor. 'Wouldn't Orla find that weird?'

'We wouldn't have to tell her . . . If you're ever lonely or worried – I can take care of you. Okay?' He moves closer again and his blue eyes make my stomach flip.

'Okay,' I whisper.

'Now,' Michael says, lifting his camera, his eyes not leaving my face. 'How would you sit, if you were at home, completely on your own? What would make you feel most yourself? Most safe?'

My body moves automatically, my limbs taking over as they adjust to their familiar position, the one I have adopted ever since I was little. My feet rise to rest on the stool, my legs tight against my chest, and I wrap my arms around my shins. Resting my face sideways on my knees, I inhale deeply, and look back at him.

Click.

'Good,' he says.

He takes another few steps forward, until he is standing directly in front of me. Close enough to touch.

'Here, just one second . . .'

My stomach flutters as he lifts his hand, reaching out to push a strand of hair from my face. He tucks it behind my ear.

'Perfect,' he whispers.

My breath is shallow and rapid as he moves away, stepping out of the lights and into position.

'Stay right there,' he says.

I stare down the camera, knowing that as he looks through the viewfinder, he is staring straight back at me.

19. Ava

The alarm is high-pitched and echoes around the expansive hallway. Orla dashes over to a keypad on the wall and taps in a code. The house falls into silence.

My eyes wander around the house as Orla takes off her coat and shoes, putting them away in a hidden cupboard to my right. Brilliant white light pours down into the hallway through the glass lantern. The staircase is iron, sleek and beautiful. The floor is tiled like a chessboard, and the doors are black and heavy, the walls stark and white. I glance to my left through an open door – an office panelled entirely in dark wood; an imposing desk set in the middle of the space.

'Would you like a drink?' Orla asks, gesturing to the back of the hallway to a set of double doors. 'Dad shouldn't be long.'

'Just a soft drink would be lovely.'

'This way.'

She walks towards the double doors and I trail behind her, taking in each of the rooms I pass.

'What a lovely place to grow up,' I say.

'Yeah, I guess. It was better when we all lived here.'

'What's down there?' I ask as I come to a standstill in front of an open door, a set of stone stairs leading straight down, into darkness.

'Oh. That's Dad's studio. And the darkroom.'

She carries on walking and I force my feet to follow, but my eyes linger on those stairs.

His studio and his darkroom.

His space.

We step through the double doors and my eyes widen at the large open living space. To the left there is a large kitchen: the cabinets a deep navy, and the island is topped with gleaming white quartz. In the centre of the room is a long dining table, plush velvet chairs set around it, and on the right are three forest-green sofas, all facing a massive television mounted above a wide fireplace. The floor is freshly polished: gleaming mahogany parquet.

Mine and Will's flat shimmers before my eyes. The damp that we've put off fixing. The furniture we've put off replacing. The three rooms that make up our daily life. Has Michael ever lived like most other people? Or has he always lived like this?

Orla pulls open the door of the large fridge and it swings open. 'We have juice, Coke, water –'

'Just some water would be great.'

She fills a glass from the fridge and then moves around the island to hand it to me.

'Thanks.' I sip, swallowing loudly. 'So, do you know what they'll have you doing tomorrow –'

A loud buzzing noise interrupts me, and Orla looks down at her phone.

'Do you mind if I answer this?' she says, biting her lip. 'It's a boy from my school.'

'No, of course not. I'll just wait for your dad.'

She nods and runs out of the room, her 'Hello?' echoing in the hall, followed by footsteps running quickly up the stairs. A door slams.

I am alone. Alone in Michael Osborne's house.

My eyes are automatically drawn to the end of the island where the knife block is sitting, innocuous – an innocent, everyday household item. A shining metal cube, knives placed magnetically around the outside, blades exposed. I've seen these knives before. But in the photograph, the metal was not shiny and reflective, but crusted in dark-red blood. And there, on the block, is the gap – the gap where the largest of the set would normally be placed. But now it'll be in an evidence bag, locked away in a police station. Returned to him once Lily is sentenced.

Buzz.

My hands fly upwards at the sudden noise. But it's just my phone, the vibration loud against the file in my bag.

Marissa.

I should answer it. She'll know I've left court – and we always answer. Never screen.

'Hi, love,' I say, my voice high and unnatural.

'Hey, you all right?'

'I'm good – you?'

I keep my eyes fixed on the hallway as Marissa talks, watching the door, listening intently for the sounds of Michael's return.

'. . . You at home?'

I close my eyes and chew on the inside of my cheek.

'No, I . . . I had a girl for work experience, I've just dropped her back at her house.'

'Oh, that's cool,' she says, her voice lifting. 'If she wants to spend more time at court, I'm happy to have her. Why don't you give her my email address?'

Shit. Marissa loves offering work experience; she often has law students shadowing her, her enthusiasm rubbing off on them, their interest and passion growing before everyone's eyes. But Marissa can't have Orla. She'll know who she is. She'll know I'm up to something. And she'll want to know why.

'Yeah . . . of course. I will. But she's at a solicitor's firm, being with me was just for the day.'

'Oh, that's a shame. Would be good for her to see both sides, you know? Prosecution and defence.'

'I'll definitely ask her.' My cheeks flush hot, the lie burning.

'Okay . . . well, I just wanted to see where you are tomorrow. Which court are you in?'

I clear my throat. 'Southwark. You?'

'Ooh, I'm at Inner London. Lunch?'

'Lunch sounds great. I'll see you tomorrow.'

'Bye, Ava.'

I let out a slow exhale. I hate lying to Marissa. And the lies I've told her in the past, the absence of the truth about my past, have never seemed like a betrayal. I've kept my silence for good reason. But now, it feels wrong. I'm actively hiding something from her. And from Will. Even George, who knows everything about me. The most important people in my life. My whole world would crumble without them. And instead of trusting them I'm . . . I'm here.

I lift my gaze, my body trembling as my eyes dart around the trappings of Michael's luxury home. Everything I'm doing is wrong. I'm breaking the rules of my job, I'm breaking the trust of my relationships . . . But for the right reasons. Does that make what I'm doing right? Or is it all tainted?

I shake my head, my jaw clenching resolutely. What I'm doing is a means to an end. And that end is exposing Michael Osborne.

Peering out into the hallway, my eyes are drawn back to the door that leads down to the basement. I pause to listen for sounds of a car on the drive or footsteps coming down the stairs.

Nothing.

I creep through the double door and back into the entrance hall, stopping outside the door to his studio. The stairs descend steeply downwards, silence emanating upwards. I glance back at the front door.

Nothing.

Before I can consider what I'm doing, I rush forward, holding on to the black handrail that is fixed to the wall, my feet moving quickly.

At the bottom, a large space reveals itself – his studio. Prints of his photographs are hanging from the dark walls, but the back wall is white – a stool placed in the centre of the floor – surrounded by equipment and lighting.

I lower myself off the last deep step and the back of my neck tingles, like someone is watching me. I swing around. But no one is there. I am alone.

In the left-hand corner there is a closed door – that must be the darkroom. The space where his vision develops, his ideas becoming a reality in the absence of light. I cross the space to look inside, but my eyes are drawn to an artist's desk to the right of the door and a thick pile of photographs scattered on its surface.

The top photograph shows a model – lithe and beguiling, her long arms propped up just so on her bent knee, her lips gently parted, her features captured in technicolour. I move it aside and there are more of the same. The same model, expensive handbag clutched in her hand, swinging forward, the energy of the movement captured by the camera. Then another one, this time just of her face, her bold eyes, and red lips.

I stack the photos back on top of each other, but the corner of a black-and-white photograph protrudes from the other pictures, highlighted by its monochromatic tones. I tug on the corner, releasing it from the bottom of the pile.

But this photo is not like the others.

It's Lily.

She is sitting on the stool, her knees tucked up to her chest, her head resting sideways against the tops of her knees. The photograph is so close to her face, cropped in tightly, intimately. She looks so vulnerable. So young.

I pull another photo from the bottom of the pile. It is her again. But in this one she is laughing, happy. Her hand raised to her chest, her fingers entwined in the chain of her necklace. But her eyes aren't focused on the camera. They are beaming at the person behind it. Sparkling.

'Hi.'

I jump, my nerves screaming at the sound of his voice. I spin around and he is standing in the doorway, one hand placed on the frame.

'Oh, hi,' I say. 'Sorry, you scared me.'

He walks towards me with a hesitant smile. 'Did Orla show you down here?'

'No, she had a phone call from a friend but she told me your studio was down here. Sorry, if I —'

'No, it's fine.' He smiles.

I turn my back on him to face the desk again, a lump in the back of my throat. My foot kicks against something under the desk and I wince, pain ringing through my toes. I glance down: the object I kicked is a safe, shining and silver.

'These photos are beautiful.'

I stare ahead as he moves closer towards me, his footsteps reverberating on the concrete floor. He places his hand on my shoulder. I want to run, to shrink away from him. But I can't. So instead, I turn my face towards him, and he leans in, wincing slightly as he kisses my cheek. I hold my breath, forcing myself not to flinch. Acid stings the back of my throat.

'Are you still in pain?'

133

'The recovery is slower than I'd like.' He shrugs his shoulders, then smiles. 'Anyway . . . How did today go?'

'It was great,' I say. 'Orla was fantastic. A real joy. You . . . you should be proud.'

'Thank you. I am.' His gaze veers away from my face and lands on the desk behind me. 'Ah . . . The photos of Lily.'

'I didn't mean to pry —'

'No, it's fine, really. I just . . .' He picks up the photo, the one of her laughing happily, and stares down at it. 'I can't believe that this is the same girl. This is the girl who attacked me. I mean — look at her.' He turns the photo around, showing it to me.

'She looks so happy.'

'She was . . . I offered to photograph her and she loved it. She and Orla had so much fun. I . . .'

His voice cracks and he holds his shaking fingers up to shield his eyes.

'Michael? Are you okay?' I whisper.

He lowers his hand — his eyes are shining with tears, even in the low light. 'I just wish I'd maybe done things differently,' he mutters. 'I mean . . . what if I made her think that I liked her in . . . that way, you know? I was just being kind. But she was so deprived of kindness — of good, honest kindness from a grown-up — that everything I did to try to help her, to make her feel welcome here, she took the wrong way. Maybe if I had acted differently, it wouldn't have happened.'

'Maybe. But . . . you can't think like that.'

He shrugs. 'No, I guess not. She reacted in a way I never could have predicted.'

'You must have been scared.'

'Terrified. I wasn't sure anyone would arrive in time. But . . . soon it'll all be over. She'll be sentenced and hopefully we can all move on.'

I nod, forcing a small, understanding smile.

But my insides are quaking, my mind racing as it tries to process his words. He seems so sincere, so concerned. Not driven by anger but overwhelmed with sadness. What if . . . What if he really did just try to be kind to her? What if she really is as broken as everyone thinks and her temper took over, pushing her to do something that most of us could never even imagine?

'I should go, really,' I say.

'You can't stay? Dinner?'

'No, I really should go. It's the last day of a trial tomorrow, so I need to go over everything, double-check my closing speech –'

'Quite the wonder woman, aren't you?'

I smile. 'Well . . . I try.'

He follows me out of the basement and waits at the front door as I climb back into my car. But as I reverse, watching him as he waves, a sudden surge of emotion swells up and over my head, and tears fill my eyes.

What if Lily doesn't need saving at all?

20. Ava

The rain is pelting against the windscreen. I stare through it, my eyes drifting in and out of focus, the house blurring then distorting back into a pin-sharp image.

The anniversary is always bad. The day that Dad and I left home, and he never came back again. I spent all day at court, and lunch with Marissa, thinking about seeing Mum, anxiety filling me up, as if I was empty, devoid of any emotion other than fearful anticipation. But still. I have to come. Even just for a few minutes.

'Mum, it's me,' I call out as I open the door, slicking off the rain from the sleeves of my trench coat.

I step into the narrow hallway – there is music coming from the living room. I walk cautiously towards the door to my right, following the sound, my hand outstretched –

'Belle?'

My head snaps towards the kitchen, shocked by the sound of my old name.

She hasn't called me that for years. I'm Ava. I've been Ava for longer than I ever was Belle.

Belle is gone.

'Mum?'

I walk towards the kitchen but falter as I enter, my feet fixed to the floor.

She is sitting at the kitchen table, a small glass of clear liquid in her hand. And scattered across the table are old photographs. Even from here I can see our faces.

Me, smiling. My mum – healthy, her face fuller, her eyes bright.

And Dad.

'Hi Mum,' I whisper.

She looks up from the table. Her eyes are red and swollen, her face damp with tears.

'Oh, Mum.' I rush forward, making my way to her in just a few steps, and wrap my arms around her shoulders. She clings to me, shaking, and I lean my head on top of hers as she rocks forward, her body juddering up and down as she sobs.

'It's okay, Mum.'

I move to stand in front of her and she hugs my hips, her face sideways against my stomach, clinging to me. We stay like that for a few minutes, me slowly stroking her hair, hushing her, telling her that everything is fine.

She suddenly lets go of me and places her hands on my waist. Looking up at me, she sniffs loudly and reaches for a tissue from her cardigan pocket.

'Sorry, Belle. Sit down.' She pats the chair next to her.

I fold myself into the chair, pulling my sleeves down low over my fingers, bending them at the knuckle to grip the edge.

'Old habits die hard, eh?'

'Pardon?' I say.

'Your sleeves. You used to do that when you were a teenager. Remember? When –'

'I don't want to talk about that.' I release my grip and the fabric slides back up my arm, the scarred skin tingling.

'Sorry, Belle.'

'Please stop –'

I pause. I want to tell her not to call me that name. But today, it might be too much.

'Please stop apologizing,' I say. 'How are you?' I place my hand on top of hers. They are cold.

She doesn't respond.

I clear my throat. 'What's in the glass?'

'Vodka.'

'Mum, don't you think it's a bit early to be on the spirits?'

'Don't push me. Not today, Belle.' She looks at me straight on, challenging me to keep questioning her.

I stare at her for a moment, my mouth slightly open, but I say nothing. My eyes swim around the room, unable to look at her, unwilling to look at what's lying on the table. I can't look at those photographs. I can't look at our life before, our family before everything fell apart – a mirror, cracking under the pressure of one swift kick, breaking into a million fragments. No matter how hard we tried, we could never put it back together. We didn't even have all the pieces. Not without Dad.

'You can't even look at him, can you?'

My lip trembles. Her tone has changed. I turn back to her and she is watching me, her eyes dark and unpredictable.

'What do you mean?'

'Don't play stupid, Belle, we both know you're not. You can't even look at photographs of your dad, can you?'

'Mum, leave it. Please –'

'No, I won't leave it. You should look at him.' Her fingers scramble on the table, her nails scratching at the wood as she picks up a photograph and thrusts it into my face. 'Look at him!'

'Mum, leave me alone,' I snap. But I focus on the picture just centimetres from my nose. It's me and Dad on a beach, barefoot, white sand beneath us, blue sky above. The summer I was thirteen. We're both laughing. I'm looking straight into the camera, my glasses falling down my nose, my face round and creased with joy, my hand waving at Mum taking the photo. And Dad is looking at me. Beaming. He was always so proud.

I grab her wrist and push her hand away. She reaches for the glass, throwing her head back to tip the remaining vodka into her mouth, swallowing with a loud gulp.

'Why are you like this? I've come here to see you, to make sure you're okay, but you can never just be happy to see me. Be pleased that I'm here –'

'Happy to see you? On today of all days?' she shouts, seething. She pushes her chair back and stands above me, her fingertips still holding the empty glass.

'Mum, put that down –'

'Why would I be happy to see you? None of this would have happened if it wasn't for you. None of this –'

'I'm leaving,' I say, standing up quickly and stalking towards the door.

Why do I keep doing this to myself? I can't help her. I can't save her. She can barely stand the sight of me. No matter how hard I try, she's never going to let me back in. We can't go back to how we were.

I need to get out of here.

But before I can step out of the kitchen, she has pushed past me, her arm holding the door frame, blocking my exit.

'Mum.' I glare at her. 'Move.'

'No.'

'Move!' Hot, angry tears prick the corners of my eyes.

'If it wasn't for you, I would still have your dad here with me. I lost everything. My husband, my home. All because of you. You pushed him to a point where he did something so out of character, so violent! If it wasn't for you, he wouldn't be locked away and I wouldn't be alone –'

'Mum, please just move out my way!'

'I even lost you! You've made yourself as different as you possibly can from my little girl. I can even see it in your face when I call you "Belle". You hate it.'

'I changed my name, Mum –'

'I didn't want you to do that, remember? I agreed because you and your dad thought it was for the best. But you were my baby, that was the name I gave you. Anabelle was my girl –'

'But she's gone!' I shout. 'She died! She might as well have never existed!'

Mum stops in her tracks, her mouth hanging open, and her grip loosens on the glass. I watch as it falls from her fingers, and it drops as if in slow motion, suspended momentarily in the air, until it suddenly hits the floor and smashes at our feet.

'I'm not that little girl any more, Mum,' I say, my voice low. 'And I know that you want me to go back to how I was before, because then you can pretend that it never happened. But it did. And it changed me. It changed you, too.' I blink rapidly and tears fall from my eyes. But I don't wipe them away. 'I . . . I know part of you wishes that I had just stayed quiet. You think that if I had just stayed quiet then we would still be a family and Dad would still be here.'

'That isn't true –'

'It is, though,' I whisper, looking her dead in the eye. 'You said it yourself. If it wasn't for me, Dad would still be here. And . . . that's true. But stop searching for Belle. She's not coming back.'

She stares at me, her mouth poised to retaliate, but she stays silent. I step over the splinters of glass and move past her, my boots crunching in fragments that have buried themselves in the carpet of the hallway. Glancing over my shoulder, I look for her one last time, searching for just a brief glimmer of my mother. But she has already turned away.

21. Ava

My eyes dance over Lily's previous convictions, worry worming its way around my stomach as I take in entry after entry.

Assault Occasioning Actual Bodily Harm
Common Assault
Breach of Community Sentence
Possession of Controlled Substance – Class C
Assault Occasioning Actual Bodily Harm

In only a matter of days, Judge Gilbert is going to have these convictions before him, armed with the details of what Lily did to Michael. And all he will see when he looks at her is a violent, troubled child. A child who has left him with only one option: custody.

Maybe that's what she needs.

'How long does Judge Alexander usually take to come back?' the defence barrister next to me asks.

'Depends.'

She sighs, but I glance away from her as my phone lights up, silently indicating an incoming message.

One message: Michaela.

I snatch a sideways glance at the defence, but she has gone back to staring at her laptop, her gaze narrowed as she clicks through her emails.

Tingles spread from my neck down to the base of my spine as I open the message, the hairs standing on edge.

Ava . . . I want to see you again. Tonight? X

My thumbs hover over the screen as my mind races. I can't see him again tonight – George is coming for dinner with me and Will. And I can't cancel, I can't just make up plans again. What if Will suspects something is wrong? My eyes widen as I scroll upwards, taking in the string of messages – the short, coy exchanges; the barely veiled flirtation. If he ever looked at these, he would think the worst. And how could I explain it to him? How could I make him understand?

I can't do tonight. But I can meet after work . . . Just for an hour. 5pm? x

As soon as the message has sent, I tap out and swipe my finger across the name. An icon of a bin appears, and I hit it.

The messages disappear.

My phone lights up again.

What a shame . . . would have loved to see you. I'm at home now but am heading out at 5:30 with Orla. Sunday evening? I'll be in London but we could meet at the hotel? I've been thinking about you X

He's going out with Orla? But she told me that she's with her mum for the rest of the week . . .

I quickly type a response, breathing purposefully as I try to push down the feeling of nausea that is tingling in the back of my throat.

Send.

Sounds great. Speak to you soon x

I lift the sleeve of my gown to cover my mouth as nausea washes over me.

Why am I doing this? What on earth do I think I can achieve? I can't prove what he did to me – it's too late for that. And Lily . . .

Maybe she's guilty after all.

But where is he going at 5:30? Who is he seeing?

My eyes shift to the clock that hangs above the judge's bench: 4:15.

If the judge comes back now, he can sentence this defendant in less than fifteen minutes, and I'll have enough time to get to Michael's house. I need to follow him: the urge is there, deep in my gut. I need to know why he lied. Just one last time and then I'll leave this alone. I'll cut all ties and let go of him – once and for all.

Just one more time.

My knee bounces up and down, hitting against the steering wheel as I stare across the road at Michael's house.

I glance at the clock in the centre console.

It's 5:36 p.m.

Where is he?

It took twenty minutes for the judge to return. As soon as he sentenced the defendant – eighteen months in custody – and left the court, I ran to the CPS room. Ripping my wig from my head, I hurriedly placed it in its box, closing the metal clasp before pulling off my gown and shoving it into its bag. I shouted goodbye at the court staff, my heels clicking across the tiled, cavernous entrance hall of the court.

Did he already leave? Did I miss him?

A light turns on in the entrance hall – shining out through the glass arch above the front door. I lean forwards, my face almost pressed up against the window, my fingers pushing so hard against the glass the tips are bright white.

The door opens.

There he is.

I reach for the handle, readying myself to follow him. But he doesn't walk down the drive. Instead, he goes to his car – a large black four-by-four, its windows darkened – and climbs inside. The engine growls and he drives forward, bearing right on to the road.

I need to know where he's going. Just one more glance through a peephole into his life; one more glimmer of innocence and I'll leave him alone.

He drives fast. I follow closely, making sure no one comes between his car and mine. I pull down the sun-visor to hide my face from his view in the rear view mirror. How will I explain it if he sees me? What am I doing? I should turn around and go home –

No.

Keep going.

I focus on his licence plate – reading the letters over and over again in my mind.

05B 0RN3 . . . 05B 0RN3 . . . 05B 0RN3.

His left indicator flashes orange, and he turns slowly. I squint at the sign on the corner: Malthouse Road. It's a residential street, lined with semi-detached houses that all look the same. Red brick, a garage fixed on either side, a paved driveway. He pulls over, coming to a standstill outside a house, his indicator light still pulsing rhythmically.

I continue driving, turning my face away as I pass his car, and pull across an empty drive further up the road. I quickly turn around, craning over my shoulder to stare at his car.

He is still sitting in the driver's seat, his eyes veering away from the house he has parked in front of, firmly focused instead on a cul-de-sac off Malthouse Road. I peer down it: at the end there is a small island dotted with tall trees huddled closely together, encircled by houses. The road sign is on the corner, a streetlamp looming above it, a camera fixed on top of the light, its lens trained down the street.

I strain my eyes, trying to pick out the letters on the road sign, but I can't make them out. I've parked too far away. I reach for my phone and open the camera then zoom in, watching as the image enlarges.

Franklin Walk.

No . . . Surely not.

Franklin Walk.

Is he meeting Lily? Is Franklin House down that road?

I sit back in my seat, my eyes burning into Michael's image in the rear-view mirror. He is still staring deep into the cul-de-sac, not looking away, even for a second.

The sound of a door slamming rings out on the peaceful road. Michael sits up, inching closer towards the window. But I can't see what he can see – the angle is wrong.

Is it her?

I inhale deeply, trying to calm my racing heart, but my breath catches in my throat as a blonde head bounces into view.

Lily.

She is scowling, glancing briefly over her shoulder before stopping where the cul-de-sac meets Malthouse Road. She reaches into her jacket pocket and retrieves headphones which she pushes into her ears, one after the other, her expression still set in an angry frown. Tapping on her phone, scrolling, she scuffs her feet against the tarmac of the pavement, her chunky lace-up boots marked with dirt and wear.

Is she waiting for him? Are they meeting?

I turn my gaze back to the rear-view mirror. Back to Michael.

He is staring, his eyes never leaving her face.

Surely if she was expecting him, she would be looking for him, or his car? She would have noticed him sitting at the end of the road. But nothing has alerted her to his presence. She is completely unaware, wrapped up in her own world, her own thoughts, oblivious to the man sitting mere feet away from her. Watching. Waiting.

She turns right, her head down as she looks at her feet striking the pavement, her hands in her pockets, her stride long and fast.

He waits until she is halfway down the road then gets out of his car, slowly closing the door, pushing it shut so quietly that it barely clicks. He reaches back and pulls the hood of his jacket low over his head. And he starts to walk, matching her footsteps, pace by pace, keeping his distance.

He isn't here to meet her at all.

He's here to follow her.

I wrap my fingers around the steering wheel and squeeze. I watch as both their backs retreat further and further away: her far in the distance, Michael stalking her silently. My hands are clammy against the leather. I lift my fingers to my mouth and chew the skin around my thumb, wincing as a loose piece tears away. I lift it to my mouth. Taste blood.

What should I do? Why is he following her? What is he planning?

I need to do something.

Do something.

I grab my phone and push the door open. As I clamber out, I close it as silently as I can, mimicking Michael's actions from moments ago. I go round to the back of the car and open the boot, retrieving a large scarf from my bag which I wrap around my neck and halfway up my face, covering my mouth and the lower part of my nose. I riffle through the contents of my car, searching for a hooded jacket or a hat, but there isn't anything.

I'll just need to stay out of sight.

He mustn't see me.

I peer around the car, scanning the road. I can't see Lily any more, but Michael is waiting on the corner at the far end. Has he lost her? Has she stopped? I stand completely still, fear stirring in my chest as I imagine him turning back, racing towards me –

He turns left and moves out of sight.

I exhale, slam the boot shut, and run. As I approach the end of the road, I decelerate, my run slowing down to a brisk walk. I peer around the corner.

It's a high street. The road is adorned with small shops, cafes, a few restaurants. It's fairly busy, the last traffic of the day as shops approach closing time. I scan the people that are strolling on the pavement, my eyes searching for Michael's hooded figure.

But I can't find him. Where is he?

Shit.

My eye is drawn to the end of the road, to bright blonde hair. Lily is coming out of the shop at the very end of the high street, the last shop of the parade, carrying a bottle of Coke and a packet of crisps.

But where's Michael?

I step under the canopy of the cafe next to me and stand next to the board with hand-painted lettering setting out the menu. But my eyes frantically search the various faces, search-ing for Michael –

'Do you fancy anything, love?' a voice calls out.

A woman is looking at me, taking a momentary break from cleaning a table as she waits for my answer.

'Um . . . I'm still looking. Thanks.'

'Just give me a shout if you need any help.'

'Okay, thanks.'

I look back down at the board, waiting for her to stop

watching me. She carries the now loaded tray back into the cafe, smiling briefly as she passes.

My eyes return to searching the pavements, scanning each face –

There he is.

He's crossed the road, standing under the plastic shelter of a bus stop, a few metres beyond where Lily is opening her packet of crisps. He's leaning against the back of the shelter casually, one leg lifted, foot against the wall, his phone cradled in his hands at waist height as if he's reading a message or looking at a website. But still, he's watching her.

Lily turns left and walks away from the shop, settling back into her fast rhythm. And as before, Michael waits a few moments, then follows. But he stays on the opposite side of the road, trailing a short distance behind her.

I begin to walk, cautiously, keeping close to the frontage of the shops. As I reach the far end of the parade, the number of people is dissipating, and suddenly I am out in the open.

Lily glances over her shoulder and I freeze. But her gaze is fixed on the road, and she dashes out in front of a car which blares its horn at her, long and loud. She reaches the opposite pavement and continues walking, then turns the corner off the high street. I walk quickly, desperate to catch up, and hide in the shadow of the phone box that sits on the corner. But I stare in horror at Lily's back and the long, empty road. No shops. Houses far away in the distance. Just a few passing cars.

Michael is so close to her now. So close that if he wanted to, he could reach out and touch her. Reach out and grab her.

Hands over my mouth. Strong arms pushing down. Legs kicking. Blue eyes. Dress ripping. Hands on my thighs. Pressure. Fear. Stillness.

She gasps in shock as he grasps her shoulder, her crisps scattering on to the ground. My hand dips into my pocket and I pull out my phone, my fingers shaking.

She stares up at him, her eyes wide in bewilderment.

He is facing her now, blocking her path. But to anyone passing at speed in their car, they might look like father and daughter. Or even a couple. A rebellious young girl and her older boyfriend.

Opening the camera, I tap on VIDEO and press the large red circle which begins to pulse, a timer ticking in the top right corner, counting up the seconds. I move closer, inching forward with my hand lifted, trying to move the camera into position. Michael glances over his shoulder. I wheel around and dash back behind the phone box, my heart hammering against my ribcage, my pulse pounding at the front of my skull.

After a few moments I walk carefully out from behind the phone box and aim my phone directly at them.

He isn't holding her any more. He isn't restraining her. But she's looking up at him as he speaks to her, unblinking, her face pale. He looks over his shoulder, his eyes searching the opposite pavement for anyone who might see them. I watch him, trying to focus every ounce of my energy on listening carefully, to pick out one word, anything. But I can't hear him. His voice is low, his mouth moving rapidly.

She begins to nod, the up-and-down movement of her head getting faster and faster. He moves around her, circling, and she follows his movements, turning with him until her back is to me and he is facing the camera. He places his hand on her shoulder and says one word. And now that I have a clear view, my skin turns cold as I make out his statement, his firm command.

'Understand?'

She nods again and he lets go of her shoulder. She stays frozen to the spot, her face crumpled with emotion as he walks away.

Directly towards me.

I rush backwards, stumbling over my own feet as I turn around the corner and throw myself into the old phone box. Lowering my head, I turn my back as he stalks past. After a few seconds I peer out through the dirty glass and watch his back as he retraces his route down the high street.

My hands tremble as I push open the door and step out. Walking slowly towards Lily, tears prick in the corner of my eyes as she shifts back into sight.

She's crouched down, her head buried in her knees. She gasps and looks up at the sky, smearing tears and snot across her face with the back of her sleeve. Inhaling deeply, she stands up before shaking out her hands and retrieving a cigarette from her pocket which she places between her lips. The lighter sparks. The cigarette looks so strange between her fingers: like a child playing at being grown-up, pretending to smoke with a pencil. But as she breathes in, long and slow, blowing smoke back out into the air, her head tipped backwards towards the sky, the fear and sadness in her expression slowly falls away. She is blank – a shell.

Anger bubbles away inside me, my body shaking from the sheer compulsion to chase after him. To make him pay.

I was right. I knew there must be something more.

Why would he track her down, follow her, if what happened was as innocent as he claims? What does he think she might say? And why now, when she has already pleaded and we're only a week away from the sentencing?

I narrow my eyes, waiting for Lily to move. Why did she choose to walk this way? She can't have come out just to go to the shop or she would have turned back and taken the same route home. But she didn't. She crossed from one pavement to the other and turned on to this empty strip of causeway, nothing but a straight dark river of road.

And Michael was ready. He was already waiting for her on the other side.

He knew she was going to cross.

It can't just be coincidence . . . He knows her routine; he knew she was going to come this way.

He's followed her before.

She's standing completely still, her only movements the rhythmic drag of her lips on her cigarette, the exhalation of smoke, the tap of ash on to the pavement. Her eyes are round and staring, the skin under the bottom row of eyelashes stained with thick mascara.

I push back the sleeve of my jacket and the blouse underneath to look at my watch. It's nearly six. Will gets home between seven and half past and I want to be home before him. I don't want to make up an excuse that court ran late. I don't want to lie to him more than I already have.

I turn away but can't help glancing backwards at the sound of her footsteps as she finishes her cigarette at last and starts to stomp away.

Where is she going?

I surge forward, following her again. Matching my footsteps with each of hers. Music is blaring out of her headphones again – a fast, hammering rhythm over long, drawn out bass. She walks on and on, never glancing over her shoulder to check he isn't there. For years after what Michael did, into adulthood and beyond, I felt sick at the thought of walking anywhere alone. I was constantly checking over my shoulder, moving around a room so that my back was against the wall, still flinching at loud noises or the touch of unexpected hands. But just ten minutes after being followed – she is walking onwards, no sign of fear or emotion.

A shiver runs over me.

She's given up.

I remember that feeling too. But mine didn't mutate into a lack of fear. Instead, it lashed out in reckless anger, a wild absence of restraint. There was nothing worth fighting for any more – the worst had already happened.

She stops suddenly outside a short row of terraced houses. I step backwards, hiding behind the fence that runs around its perimeter. The walls of the house on the end are graffitied. Glass litters the ground. But loud music is pulsating from inside.

She takes her headphones out and pushes them into her pocket along with her phone and rushes up the path to the front door of the second house in. Hammering on it with a clenched fist, she steps back. Waits.

I hold my breath as I watch her, praying that she isn't let inside.

But the door swings open.

She's gone.

Is this the place Marissa was talking about? Is this where she gets her drugs?

Footsteps thud behind me and I drop my head, shielding my face as a man passes me, his hood lowered. He walks up the path, just like Lily did, and knocks on the door. I back away, taking one final look at the house, the sky behind it an ominous grey, and my stomach sinks, a stone tossed into the sea.

I lift my head at the sound of Will's key being pushed into the lock. I tap on my phone, pausing the video, and Lily's wide-eyed face freezes on the screen.

'Hi, gorgeous,' Will calls out.

I lock my phone and toss it aside on the sofa, my attention turning to Will. His tie is loose around his neck, the top few buttons of his white shirt undone. His collar is askew, revealing his collarbone, the curve of his shoulder. My stomach flips. Still now, after all these years, he gives me butterflies. I rush towards him and wrap my hands around his neck, standing on my tiptoes to kiss him.

He beams. 'Did you miss me?'

I nod, my chest tightening with guilt, but my eyes are drawn to movement just behind him. George is lingering in the corridor, looking down at his feet, scuffing one against the carpet.

'Oh, hi, George,' I say, stifling a laugh.

He glances up, his mouth a lopsided smile. 'Don't mind me – never want to interrupt you two lovebirds.'

'Oh shh,' I say, holding out my arms.

He steps forward, hugging me tightly. 'You two make me sick,' he whispers.

'I know . . . Me too.'

He steps away, smiling widely. George was so happy for me when I met Will. He spent years telling me that I should let someone in. *You'll want someone to spend your life with*, he said. *Trust me.* But I resisted, insisting that I would always be alone, that letting someone into my mind, into my heart, was not an option. The thought of somebody touching me made me sick. So, the night I introduced him to Will, something in his face shifted as he took in the sight of us holding hands, Will's hand at the base of my spine, my soft smile as Will kissed my forehead. He told me afterwards that it was relief. He didn't want me to be alone. He wanted me to know love.

'Come in, come in,' I say. 'When have I ever had to ask you twice?'

George steps into the flat, and I shut the door. As I turn around, my breath becomes shaky as I'm confronted with the sight of George and Will standing side by side: the pillars that hold up my life. How swiftly they could come tumbling down if they knew the truth.

'I'll just quickly get out of this suit and then let's go – we still thinking the Old Bengal?' Will says.

I shrug. 'I'm happy with anything.'

'Old Bengal sounds great,' George says.

'Cool. Two minutes.'

Will disappears into our bedroom, winking at me before closing the door.

George leans on the back of the sofa, arms crossed, watching me.

Please . . . please don't ask me about Michael or the case.

'Did you see my mum on the anniversary?' I ask quickly.

He looks at the floor and shakes his head. 'No . . . I knocked but she wouldn't answer. I just left flowers on the doorstep.'

'We got into a massive argument.'

He sighs. 'I keep hoping it'll get better between you . . .'

'I'm not sure it ever will. She resents me too much.'

My eyes sting and I blink rapidly, forcing the emotion back down, deep inside me.

'I'm sorry, Ava . . . Did you . . .' George lowers his voice and glances at my closed bedroom door. 'Did you tell Caroline that you couldn't do that sentencing?'

I nod quickly. 'Yes.'

'Was she okay? Did she ask questions?'

'No, nothing. She was fine, I just said I had to have the day off.'

He nods and smiles. 'Well, that's a relief.'

I grip my hands behind my back, my fingers clammy. 'I know.'

'Now you never have to think about him again.'

'You never have to think about who again?' Will asks, stepping out of our room and back into the lounge. He walks towards me, straightening his T-shirt, carrying with him the scent of freshly sprayed cologne.

'Oh, you know that defence solicitor who I can't stand?'

'Ben?'

'Yes. He's left law.'

He chuckles. 'Good riddance, right?'

I smile, my stomach sinking. 'Right.'

George catches my eye over Will's shoulder, his eyebrows raised, surprised at the speed of my invention.

'Ready?' I ask, looking away from George and back at Will.

'Let's go, I'm starving.' He squeezes my waist and then leads the way out of the flat. George follows and I close the door behind us.

I release the handle, the metal slick with my sweat.

22. Lily

One week before the attack

I push my way outside and step back out into the world. The sky is covered over with heavy dark clouds, not a single star visible. But the air feels fresh and welcome, so different to that house and its creeping claustrophobia.

I know I shouldn't go there. I know that. It feels wrong. I feel dirty. But I need it. Just for a moment, for everything to stop. My thoughts, my memories, the overwhelming anxiety of night after night in the home, day after day at the school where everyone except Orla treats me as if I have a virus. As if my reputation is catching.

I shake my head and start to walk.

Straight home, straight up to my room. Straight to bed.

The road is empty, stretching out before me.

I inhale deeply, leaning my head back to look up at the dark sky. There is a break in the clouds and a single star breaks through the darkness. I smile.

But my smile quickly falls away at the sound of a car behind me – a low rumble. I swallow, my throat tight. It isn't flying past me as it should be, but instead it's creeping forwards, slowly closing the gap between us.

I quicken my pace, but it's starting to move closer, so close that soon it will pull up beside me.

My fists clench, ready to run.

'Lily?'

I stop at the sound of my name spoken by a familiar voice.

'Lily, what are you doing here?'

He emerges from behind the car, his face sending a buzz of energy rushing through me.

Michael.

It is him. I knew I recognized that voice.

'H-Hi,' I stammer.

'Are you okay?'

I nod, crossing my arms as he walks closer and steps on to the pavement beside me. 'I'm just walking home.'

'Here, let me give you a lift.'

'No, it's fine – it's not far.'

'It's late and you shouldn't be alone. Come on.'

'Are you sure?'

'Get in the car.'

My breath catches at his change of tone, stern and commanding. I nod and climb into the passenger seat. But he doesn't say anything. He is silent, my movements punctuated only by the sound of the rumbling engine.

I plug in my seatbelt and stare straight ahead, waiting for him to accelerate away. But he doesn't. I can feel his eyes on my face, watching me closely.

'Lily.'

'Yes?'

'Were you in there?' He cocks his head backwards.

'I –'

'Please, don't lie to me. You can tell me the truth.'

I look back out through the windscreen, avoiding his gaze. I nod.

'Have you taken something?'

I don't respond. I just continue to stare, watching the clouds as they move across the sky.

'Lily, you aren't in trouble. I won't be angry, I just need to know if you've taken something bad.'

I shake my head.

'You haven't taken something?'

'No, I have,' I mutter. 'But not anything bad.'

'What have you taken?'

'Benzodiazepine,' I whisper.

'Benzodiazepine . . . Why?'

I tear my eyes away from the clouds, away from the silence, and force myself to focus on Michael. Focus on this man who has been nothing but kind and good to me. The man whose ocean-eyed gaze gives me butterflies.

'Because I . . . I –'

'Why didn't you come to me?'

His eyebrows are raised, his gaze tinged with sadness, as if I have hurt him.

'I'm sorry, I –'

'You don't have to be alone, Lily,' he says. His hand rests on top of mine. I look down at it, drinking in the sight of his fingers closed around mine. 'You don't have to be alone. If you ever feel lonely, or need to get out of the home, you do not need to go to that place. You do not need to take anything. I never want you to feel alone or that you have nowhere to go. You're such a bright, beautiful girl – you don't need any of this. And I told you before – you can always come to me. Even if Orla isn't there. I'll keep you safe.'

I nod.

He smiles at me and lets go of my hand to grip the wheel.

My fingers feel cold, empty now, but I replay his words as he drops me back at home. As I climb into bed. As I turn off the light and settle my head on to the pillow.

He called me bright.

He called me beautiful.

23. Ava

I stand outside her door, my hand raised, fingers curled into a fist but unable to knock.

Why am I hesitating? Why am I so scared? I need to do this. Somebody needs to see this video. Somebody needs to know that he stopped her in the street, that he followed her. And I trust Marissa. She's my best friend . . . She'll know what to do. I don't even have to tell her the whole truth – I just need to show her the video.

I tap my knuckles on the door and wait.

'Just one second, Ava,' Marissa calls out.

The sound of her shuffling about inside the flat travels through the thin door.

'Hi, love,' Marissa says as the door swings open, looking so different to her court glamour self in tracksuit bottoms and T-shirt. 'Come in.'

I step inside. But the inside of her flat – its large, pale blue sofa, plush cushions and throws, and soft lighting – doesn't calm me like usual. The anxiety lingers, a lump at the back of my throat that I can't swallow down.

'I really don't want to disturb you – I know you work in the evenings.'

'No worries,' she says as she sits in the corner of the sofa, patting the seat next to her. 'It's good to have a break.'

'What've you got tomorrow?' I sit down next to her, tucking my foot underneath me.

'Same as today – private client, drink driving. Definitely

going to lose that one . . . How about you? Where were you today?'

'Isleworth. Just pleas and hearings . . .' My words trail away and I untuck my foot, placing both feet squarely on the floor.

Marissa moves closer, her mouth downturned. 'Ava, what's going on? What did you want to talk to me about?'

I lick my lips then press them together. 'I need to show you something.'

'Show me something?'

I nod and lean forward to retrieve my phone from my bag. I cradle it in my hands, a bomb ready to detonate.

'Yesterday evening after court, I went to . . . to meet a friend for a coffee. But as I was leaving, I saw something. And I've thought about it all night, and I just –'

'Ava, what –'

'I have to tell you.'

'So, tell me.'

'I saw Michael Osborne, the victim in that stabbing case, talking to your client.'

Her face drops, her inquisitive smile falling away. 'Talking to Lily?'

'Yes. But it . . . it looked like he was threatening her.'

'Threatening her? How?'

'I filmed it.' I unlock my phone and the video is there waiting, paused. 'Here,' I say, handing it to her.

She taps the screen then quickly clicks the button on the side, the volume turned all the way up.

The video jolts into life. But I don't watch it again. I watched it so many times last night, the screen lighting up my face next to Will in the dark. Marissa's face is screwed up in concentration, her eyes narrowed. The video ends abruptly but she presses play again, this time holding it to her ear, eyes closed, listening intently.

The sound stops and she lowers it away from her ear. She hands it back to me, shaking her head.

'What the hell do you want me to do with this?'

'What . . . what do you mean? Look at it again, he –'

'All that video shows is my client breaching her conditions by talking to the victim.'

'No, but look, he approached her –'

'The video doesn't show that. It shows them talking – the only word I can make out is him saying "understand?" For all anyone watching this knows, she approached him and he's telling her to leave him alone.'

'Marissa, just watch it again –'

'How do you even know that *he* approached her?'

'I . . . I don't, but –'

'Look, I appreciate you bringing this to me. I really do. But this video can't help Lily. At all. She's pleaded guilty. There's only a week until sentencing. All this video will do is get her into more trouble. And she doesn't need that. So . . . as far as we're concerned, I haven't seen this.'

'Marissa, let me –'

'Ava . . . why were you there?'

I falter and heat rises up the back of my neck as she watches me, her eyes full of unfamiliar accusation.

'Pardon?'

'Why were you there?'

'I told you, I was seeing a friend, and then I –'

'That's near where Lily lives. Why were you there?'

'Marissa, I don't know what to say. I was there and I saw them –'

'No. I don't believe that. There's something going on here. Something's wrong that you're not telling me – you've been weird about this case, you've asked questions that you've never asked about any case we've ever worked on together.

And now, you appear with evidence that proves nothing, and want me to . . . to do what exactly?'

She falls silent, watching me expectantly.

'Listen. If I tell you —'

I stop speaking, my words dying on my lips. If I tell her the truth about everything, I'll be placing her in an impossible situation – to keep my past, and what I've done, a secret, she'll have to lie. To the court, to everyone. She'll have to break every rule that barristers are taught to obey. And once I tell her, I won't be able to take it back.

'I just want you to speak to Lily. Please. Just speak to her and try, just one more time, to get her to tell the truth.'

'What truth, Ava? She's guilty. She was covered in blood; her prints were on the knife!'

'Please, just speak —'

'Fine. I'll speak to her.'

'Thank you.' I nod decisively and then stand, backing towards the door. 'I'll let you get on.'

She nods, leaning forwards, her arms resting on her legs, staring at the carpet.

'Ava?' she says, as I open the door.

I turn back to look at her.

'We've always been friends. We've always trusted each other, in our friendship, at work. But you're keeping something from me. And I don't like it.'

'I'm sorry. I . . . I hope that one day you'll understand.'

'Ava —'

I step out into the corridor and close the door behind me.

'Ava?'

Will's voice, tinged with concern, calls out from the sofa as I step inside our flat.

'I'm sorry I'm late again,' I say, avoiding his eyes as I step out of my heels and pull on my slippers which are lying by the front door. 'Marissa wanted to chat about a case she's doing and it went on a while.'

'Is everything okay?' He sits up, placing the book he is reading on his lap, face down.

'Yes. Everything's fine.'

'Are you sure?'

'Yes,' I say, finally meeting his questioning gaze. 'Why the questions?'

'It's just . . . Please don't take this the wrong way, I know you work hard and it's important to you but . . . You've been a bit strange this week.'

'Strange?' I say, moving to stand in front of the sofa.

'Yeah. Not quite yourself.'

'I promise, I'm fine.' I place my hands on his knees and lean forward to kiss him. He lifts his hands to my face, his lips soft, his touch wanting more. But there is something between us, something unfamiliar and uncomfortable. He knows something is wrong. And I can feel him watching me all the time, his mind whirring as he tries to understand.

I kiss him firmly, one more time, and then lean away.

He sighs. 'I don't know if you've forgotten but I'm going away tomorrow . . .'

I blink slowly. Guilt seeps into my stomach.

'It's okay . . .' he says. 'I know you've been busy.'

'I'm sorry. I've been so preoccupied with work and . . . I completely forgot.'

'Seriously, Ava. It's fine.'

'You're back on Tuesday, right?'

'Wednesday.'

'How are you feeling about it?' I step forward, so that I'm standing between his legs. 'It's a big potential client, right?'

'Our biggest yet – if we secure them.'

'You will. I know you will.'

He smiles, and as he wraps his hands around the back of my thighs, the tension that has been lingering in the air between us fades.

I can breathe again.

For now.

'I think I'm going to go for a run. And then shall we get a takeaway?'

'Okay,' he says. But there are still questions in his eyes.

I get changed and leave the flat, flashing a big smile at Will as I close the door. I push my headphones deep inside my ears and press play, willing the familiar music to empty my mind. I focus on the path that runs through the park, the trees overshadowed by the tall building behind them, the faces that pass me. But their features keep morphing into someone else's. Wide, scared eyes. School uniform and a bottle of Coke. Blonde.

Lily.

24. Ava

I step beyond the railings and walk up the path to the house, stopping at the door.

My eyes close and I picture Will – his final backwards glance as he left the flat for his trip this morning, his suitcase dragging behind him. What would he think of me being here? Would he be disappointed in me? Confused? Proud?

I blink his face away and wrap my jacket around me, pulling the low hood further down my forehead. I glance down at the envelope which I turn in my hands, watching as the smooth white paper flips over and over, its plain appearance hiding the enormity of its contents. If I could let Lily know that there's someone out there who understands, maybe she would speak. Maybe she'd stop being silent. And she wouldn't know it was me. But she needs to read it. She needs to know she isn't alone.

A corner slices into my finger and I wince, lifting it to my mouth as a pinprick of blood appears on the surface of my skin, near the nailbed.

My hand trembles as I raise it, but I curl it into a fist and pound on the door.

I listen for footsteps but all I can hear is music and the murmur of voices. I slam my fist against the wood again.

Nothing. Maybe you have to call … maybe they only answer if they know someone is coming –

The door jolts, the chain snapping into place, opening the door only an inch.

'What do you need?' a voice growls through the gap.

'I-I just need you to give this letter to Lily Hawthorne. Do you know her?' I mutter.

He sniffs loudly. 'Lily isn't here.'

'If I could just leave it here –'

'Who are you?'

'A friend.'

The pair of eyes close lazily, a blink in slow motion.

'I'm not taking anything from no stranger. Find her yourself –'

'Wait!'

The door slams shut.

'Hello?' I call out.

Nothing.

I back slowly away, pausing to look up at the house, harsh and cold against the blue sky.

This was wrong. I never should have come here –

The sound of footsteps on loose shingle is heading towards me, thudding quickly from the side of the house. I turn away, shielding my face, but catch a brief glimpse of the person rounding the corner.

Blonde hair. Small. Young.

Lily.

And she's walking towards me, her eyes narrowed.

I turn away, striding down the path and back on to the road, my pace quick but calm. No matter what I do, I can't run. If I run, she'll know this was no accident. She'll know I was here for her.

'Hey!'

I try to ignore the sound of her feet thundering on the pavement behind me. Don't look back, just keep going, she can't prove it was me, she can't prove I was here –

She darts around me, and I come to a halt as she blocks my path.

'I thought it was you –'

I pause, my eyes searching her face, feigning confusion.

'I'm sorry?'

'You,' she says, pushing her hair out of her eyes, her chest heaving up and down. 'You were the prosecutor. For my hearing –'

'I'm sorry, I see a lot of faces in my job, I didn't recognize you.'

'So why did you walk away when you saw me?'

'I didn't see you.' I straighten my back, standing tall above her, my eyebrow arched. 'I'm looking for a friend. He called me but he isn't in there. Now I've got to go and look for him . . .' I move past her, my heart racing, but pause to look at her over my shoulder. 'And you shouldn't be here. Leave, before I call Detective Hewitt.'

My feet start to move beneath me, and I focus straight ahead, concentrating on the grey of the pavement, on the markings of chewing gum, the empty bottles littered on the side –

'Did he send you here?' she says, appearing beside me. She grabs my arm.

'Excuse me?'

'Did he send you here? Did you follow me?'

'I don't know what you're talking about and I need you to let go of my arm.'

'No, tell me why he sent you here!'

'Lily, let go of me now –' I try to pull away, but she grabs hold of my collar.

'I did what I was meant to do,' she shouts. 'I just want to be left alone. Leave me alone!'

She lets go and suddenly I am falling, my hands grappling the air, as if in slow motion.

My chin slams on to the concrete. The pain vibrates in my head, my jaw searing with pain.

'Oh shit. Oh shit,' she cries. Her image wavers before my eyes. 'I'm sorry, I didn't mean to. I didn't mean to hurt you, I just –'

Brakes shriek on the road, like nails on a chalkboard. I sit up and turn my head, my hand cupped to my chin. A car has stopped beside us, the driver gawping at us through their open window.

'Are you okay?' they call out. 'Do you want me to call the police?'

'I –'

'No,' I say, pushing myself to my feet. Lily stops speaking, her eyes fixed on me, her lips parted. 'It's just my little sister. Don't worry.'

'Are you sure? You look hurt –'

'No, really, I'm fine. Seriously.'

'Okay.' They wind up their window, their eyes darting from me to Lily and back again, before accelerating away.

I lower my hand from my face. Blood has pooled in my palm, my fingers dripping.

'I –'

'Don't say anything. Just leave.'

'But I –'

'Seriously, Lily. I need to go and look for my friend.'

She steps away, her eyes lowered to the ground, fixed on the white envelope lying on the ground. I bend down and pick it up, my vision swimming.

'I won't say anything,' I say as I straighten up. 'I think you've got enough to handle at your sentencing without another assault charge.'

I stare at her, just for a moment, then turn away, and her footsteps echo as she runs in the opposite direction.

Keep moving: one foot after the other.

Don't focus on the pain.

Focus on the pavement.

Focus on the sky.

My grip crumples the envelope in my hand, now stained with blood.

Don't think about what's inside.

I lift my scarf around my neck as I turn on to the high street. There's a bin on the corner, next to the phone box. I open the envelope, removing the note inside. Tossing the envelope into the bin, I open the letter. My eyes dance over the words on the page.

Lily,

You don't know me, but I know who you are. I know that you've pleaded guilty for stabbing a man called Michael Osborne. But I also know what he is. When I was fourteen years old, Michael Osborne raped me and got away with it. If there's another reason why you attacked him, if you were trying to protect yourself, then there are people who will believe you. There are people who can help you and keep you safe. Please don't stay quiet. Not for him. You have a voice . . . Use it.

A friend

I shake my head and tears fill my eyes.

No matter what I do, no matter how I try to help her, it all goes wrong. It falls apart or drifts away, like sand disappearing through my fingers. I grip the top of the page and then pull swiftly, the letter tearing down the middle. I place the two halves together and tear again. Then again. Over and over until nothing is left of my story but red and white pieces of paper, thrown away, like they never mattered at all.

25. Lily

The night of the attack

'Lily,' a voice says. I can't open my eyes, and the sound is morphing, my name sounding alien, as if it doesn't belong to me.

'Lily.'

A hand shakes my shoulder. My eyes fly open, but my sight is blurry, the face that is hanging above me not coming into focus.

'What are these?'

They're holding something in their hand.

It rattles – the sound so familiar.

My pills.

The world finally becomes clear and Kacey's sneering face is looming over mine, her long fingers wrapped around the small bottle.

'Benzodiazepines. Pretty sure you don't have a prescription for these.'

I sit up, my head swimming. 'Give them to me, Kacey.' I reach out, but my hand moves slowly, and she quickly steps out of reach, laughing.

'Oh, you are groggy. You're going to have to move a bit quicker than that.'

My temper flares, a hot spike at the back of my head, fiery fingers spreading towards my temples.

'Give them to me,' I say, my voice getting louder as I stand up. 'Right now.'

'I knew you were taking drugs. I just knew it –'

I hold out my hand but she steps backwards again, out of reach, dangling them above her head.

'Kacey, seriously, please just give them back to me –'

'I mean, we all knew you would do this –'

The heat in my head is searing forwards, streaking down my cheeks and across my forehead.

'Kacey, give them to me now –'

'Like mother, like daughter, right?'

Rage descends, blinding me. My arms reach out and I run forwards, planting both hands squarely in Kacey's chest. She flies backwards and hits the wall with a loud, sickening thud.

Icy chills run down my spine as my anger falls away.

'I . . . I'm sorry,' I whisper. 'Kacey? Kacey . . .'

She groans loudly as she tries to sit up. Her hand reaches around the back of her head and her fingers emerge, painted red.

'Anne!' she bellows.

'Kacey, please –'

'Anne!' she screams again.

'Shit,' I whisper.

'What's all that noise?' Anne's voice calls out. She's coming up the stairs, her feet thudding on each step.

'Shit.'

I dash around my bed and run to my window. I grip the wooden frame and push upwards.

The ground outside rises up to meet me, the concrete floor a deep, dark pool.

Not too far to fall.

I inhale deeply and sit on the ledge.

'Lily!' Anne's voice calls out as she bursts into my room.

I jump.

My feet land on the hard ground, a stab of pain jolting upwards through my knees, and I rock forward on to my hands.

'Lily!'

I glance up, and Anne is looking down at me, her face red and fixed with a furious, disbelieving scowl.

Run.

I clamber up, momentum driving me forwards.

Keep going.

'Lily!' Voices call out into the night.

Don't stop.

'Lily, get back here now!'

Run.

Will someone come looking for me?

Will they call the police?

I keep running, my breath loud in my ears, my knees aching, hands stinging. My breath is shallow and dizziness washes over me. I stop and crouch down, my head lolling between my knees. But there's no sound of footsteps running up behind me. No more shouts of my name ringing up into the night. It's just me.

Alone.

I breathe in slowly through my nose as I try to push down the queasiness that is rising from my stomach and into my throat. After a few more breaths, it subsides, and I push myself to my feet.

I walk and I walk and I walk. I know that eventually I will have to go back and apologize. Explain. Face the police, if they are there. But not now. I rock my head back and look up at the ink-black sky. It's dotted with only a few stars, as if stars are a rarity, as if there aren't millions out there, hiding in plain sight.

Slowly, the houses change. The terraces give way to detached houses, and detached houses give way to houses so big that I could never even have imagined them. Not until Phil and Mum showed me. Houses like Orla's and Michael's. Houses that were meant for fairy tales.

I stop and look around, taking in my surroundings.

I'm so close to Meadow Gardens. But . . . Orla isn't there. She's with her mum.

I never want you to feel alone or that you have nowhere to go. I'll keep you safe.

That's what he said. And he meant it . . . I know he did.

I look up at the sky again. The stars shine.

Yes. Michael will help me.

I nod and turn on to Hillgate Avenue. Turning left on to Hillgate Road, I walk to the very end, then turn right on to Meadow Gardens.

Number 13.

I knock on the door.

'Lily?' he says, as he opens the door. He's wearing joggers and an oversized T-shirt, the neckline wonky, as if he's pulled it on in a hurry.

'Sorry, were you sleeping?'

'No, no – I was just watching TV in bed. Are you . . . are you okay?'

My face crumples and tears sting my eyes then fall down my face as I try to blink them away.

'Oh, Lily, what's happened?'

'I did something bad,' I whisper.

'Something bad?'

I nod, gulping air.

'What did you –'

He looks down at his phone, which is in his hand, the screen lighting up.

'It's Anne,' he mutters.

'Oh Michael, please –'

He holds up a finger and lifts the phone to his ear.

'Hello?' he says, looking away from me.

I watch him, trying to read his expression as he listens to

Anne, her fast words murmuring out of the receiver and then stopping.

He's going to tell her where I am – I'm not ready, I just need a bit more time –

'No, she isn't here, Anne,' he says, glancing at me. Anne's voice continues and I stare, mouth open in disbelief. 'I wish I could help,' he continues. 'I'll let you know if she comes here though. Okay . . . Goodnight.'

He ends the phone call.

'Michael . . . thank you.' I knew he would take care of me. I knew I could trust him.

'You must be freezing. Come in, come in.' He places his hand on my back, in between my shoulder blades, steering me through the door – I shiver.

We are inside. Alone.

He pulls me to him, his arms hugging me tightly to his chest. My fingers grip the back of his T-shirt, and I breathe in the scent of his aftershave. He smells like apples.

'Lily?'

'Yes?' I whisper, looking up at him.

'Don't tell Orla.'

'I . . . I won't –'

'Anne said you hurt one of the other girls and then ran away?'

I hesitate then nod. I don't want to lie to him. Not when he's shown me such kindness, such protection. 'Kacey. She took my pills and wouldn't give them back, I just . . . I lost my temper. I didn't mean to.'

'You're going to have to learn to control that temper, Lily.'

'I know.' I sniff, trying to focus on the feeling of his arms still wrapped around me. I peer up at him, and he gazes down, his eyes full of care.

'It's only going to hurt you in the end.'

26. Ava

The grazed skin on my chin stings. I press the icepack against it, wincing, and meet my own eye in the mirror. This should never have happened – I was foolish going there. Reckless. But I really believed that my note might help her see a way out, help her understand that no matter what Michael has told her, she can tell the truth. That she might –

Knock, knock.

I place the icepack in the sink and walk out of the bathroom, pausing to look at the front door from my living room, my wet hand gripping the sofa.

'Ava, I can hear you in there. Will you open the door, please?'

George?

I shuffle forward and look through the peephole. George is on the other side, staring directly at me even though he can't see me, one greying eyebrow raised. I open the door and his eyes widen as they dart to my face, to the row of small cuts that decorate my chin, the bruises dappling my jawline.

'What on earth has happened to you?' he says.

'What are you doing here?'

'I asked my question first.'

I turn back into my flat and wave over my shoulder, gesturing for him to come in.

'Ava?'

'I tripped on my way into the kitchen and hit my chin on the counter.' I roll my eyes as I look back at him. 'So stupid.'

'It looks sore. Are you sure you're okay?'

'Yes, I'm fine.' I sit down on the sofa but George remains standing, staring down at me, his face full of concern. I pull a cushion on to my lap and thread my fingers through the tasselled edge. 'Really, George. It's just superficial and the bruises will fade soon.'

'It won't look great for the next time you see Michael Osborne.'

My hands freeze.

'What did you say?'

'You heard me,' he mutters.

I shake my head slowly. 'I don't know what you're talking about –'

'Are you going to lie right to my face?'

I stare down at my feet. 'How did you find out?'

'How did I find out?' he barks. 'You're breaking every rule there is and you're concerned with how I found out?'

He pauses, waiting for me to say something. I clench my jaw, my mouth set in a stubborn line.

'Fine,' he says, crossing his arms. 'I had a coffee with an ex-colleague this morning. And he asked me if I knew that my ex-defendant was the victim of a stabbing. I said I did but I thought I'd check if you'd dropped the case like you said you would. But surprise, surprise – whose name is still listed as prosecuting counsel? Ava Knight.'

He lifts his hands, palm up to the ceiling, as if asking a question. My eyes dart away.

'Well?' he says, his voice a low growl, brimming with impatience. 'I've told my side of the story, now you tell yours. What the hell are you doing?'

'I . . . I want to help her –'

'Help her? Help her how?'

'George, please,' I whisper, finally meeting his furious stare. 'Please just let me tell you.'

He nods and sits down next to me, leaning forward, his elbows propped on his knees, his chin resting on his knuckles.

'I'm sure that there is more to this than anyone is saying. This can't be as simple as a teenage obsession getting out of hand –'

'Ava –'

'It isn't –'

'Ava, listen,' he says, reaching across to hold on to my hands. 'I know you hate him for what he did to you. And you have every right. But it's clouding your judgement.'

'George, I –'

'You need to let go of this.'

'I can't. I have to try to help her.'

'Has it even crossed your mind that she pleaded guilty because *she is*? All the evidence points in that direction – her prints on the knife, the blood –'

'But all the evidence *doesn't* point in that direction. I've been doing some digging and –'

'No, Ava – stop! If you've done something . . . if you've been trying to investigate, looking where you're not supposed to, I really don't want to know. I don't want to know how far you've gone or what rules or – God forbid – laws, you have broken. I don't want to be backed into a corner and have to choose between telling the truth or protecting you.'

He stands and stalks towards the door, throwing his hands up in exasperation. But as he opens it, he pauses to glance back at me over his shoulder.

'If this goes wrong, if you push this too far, you could lose everything. And I won't be able to help you. All I want to do is help you, Ava.'

'I know,' I whisper.

He sighs. 'Very well.' He steps out into the hallway and closes the door.

I lift my hand to my chin and press my knuckles into the blue and purple bruises on my jaw, focusing on the keen sting. Anything but the disappointment in George's face.

I have to keep going – I can't stop now. There's only a matter of days left. And then it will be too late.

But right now, I can still do something . . . Tomorrow is Sunday – I'm meeting Michael at The Osborne. I can feel I'm getting close – inching close enough that I no longer see the monster, and instead see the man. But I need more. I need to see behind the façade.

I need to get into his suite.

27. Ava

'Welcome to The Osborne.'

I step forward, smiling widely. 'Delilah, is it?'

Her eyes widen, her red smile tinging with surprise. 'Yes, it is.'

'Sorry, you might not remember me. I'm Ava – I met Mr Osborne the other night.'

'Ah yes, for dinner.'

'Yes.' I lean in, lowering my voice. 'I'm meeting him again but he told me to go up to his suite.'

Her expression clouds over, turning serious all in an instant. 'I'm sorry, but Mr Osborne hasn't arrived yet. If I could just ask you to wait –'

I glance over my shoulder, feigning paranoia. 'He specifically told me not to wait in the lobby.' I look back at her and speak in whispers. 'If I can speak to you woman to woman, I know he wouldn't like me sharing this but – we're not meant to be seeing each other . . .'

Her eyes travel down to my chin, to the fresh cut and bruises barely covered by make-up. 'Oh, I see –'

'Yes, so he wanted me to go straight up. Just . . . to be safe. But I lost my key-card. I didn't want to worry him.' I hold up my phone. 'I can call him and tell him that you don't –'

'No, no –' she says, holding up her manicured hand, 'don't do that. It's fine. I understand the need for discretion.'

I smile innocently, lips firmly shut. She swipes a key-card and slides it across the counter.

'Thank you.'

'Not a problem. Enjoy your stay.'

I lift the key off the counter and turn away without a word, staring down at the black rectangular piece of plastic in my hands.

The key to his suite.

I can't believe it worked.

I push the button to call the lift and one opens automatically, a loud ding ringing out through reception.

I hold out my finger and press again, lighting the number nine in red.

The lift travels up, floor by floor.

I did what I was meant to do.

Lily's voice rings in my ears.

I just want to be left alone.

I shake my head but see Michael's stormy eyes, his hand on her shoulder.

Understand?

The lift comes to an abrupt stop.

'Floor nine,' the automated voice says.

I step out into the corridor. There is only one door, straight ahead, and the room name, which hangs to the left of the wall in shining chrome, glimmers faintly in the low light of the corridor.

The Osborne Suite.

My hands tremble as I hold the key-card against the rectangular reader and watch as the red light turns to green.

Click.

What if she made a mistake? What if he's already here?

'Michael?' I call out as the door swings open. I wait, every muscle in my body tensing as it anticipates him appearing from nowhere, emerging from one of the doors.

Nothing.

Taking a few steps forward, my heels click against the dark parquet floor, my breath fast and shallow in my chest. A short corridor opens on to a central foyer, a grand table in its centre decorated with a large vase filled with white roses, and three further rooms.

The utter silence of the suite consumes me. I have the same feeling as I did in his studio – as if I have stepped inside a secret part of him, inside his mind. But everything is telling me to run, my nerves screaming. He could be here any second and I could be in danger. I have no idea what he might do –

Hands. Mouth. Arms. Legs. Eyes. Dress. Hands. Thighs. Pressure. Fear. Stillness.

I swing around, racing away from the foyer and back towards the door that leads to the safety of the hotel corridor. But my hand, which was reaching for the door handle, freezes in mid-air.

I did what I was meant to do . . . I just want to be left alone.

In her anger, her blind rage, Lily unwillingly spilled a drop of the truth. I can't leave. Not now.

Goosebumps prickle on the back of my neck and I peer over my shoulder to stare back at the three rooms. Turning away from the exit, I walk slowly towards the first, the door on the left. I bite down on my lip and hold out my hand, fingers shaking.

I rush forward, a surge of adrenalin buzzing through me, and burst into a large living room. A navy velvet sofa faces the floor-to-ceiling glass window and two charcoal armchairs sit opposite. Bookshelves line the far wall and there is a fireplace on the wall to my right, a love-seat angled just so in front of it. The fire is lit, crackling and sparking in the grate.

But the room is empty.

I turn away and approach the next door.

Behind it is the bedroom.

'Michael?'

Silence.

I move to the final door. It opens slowly and I step inside. Another living space, again with rows of bookshelves, but this one has a desk littered with papers, a large leather wingback chair. An oversized cream rug, dappled with blacks and greys, is lying in the centre of the room, two small sofas facing each other on either side.

I sift through the papers, my eyes scanning the documents, but they are business plans, a proposal for funding another hotel.

Rushing back to the bedroom, I hesitate for a moment at the threshold of the door, before propelling myself inside. A queen-sized bed is on the right side facing the view. The river beyond the glass sparkles in the slowly setting sun and I walk past the bed, its sheets unmade and rumpled, a leather holdall lying open on top. A monochromatic marble en suite is cordoned off from the rest of the room by nothing more than a wall of glass. A large free-standing bathtub with chrome clawed feet looks out on to the curving bend of the river and a monsoon shower is hanging behind a clear screen, the walls ornamentally dressed in black squares of slate.

I approach the bed slowly, as I would if there were someone sleeping within its pure-white sheets, the wooden floor creaking slightly in response to my movements.

He could be here at any moment.

I reach out and trace my fingers along the pillows. He slept here. How often does he stay here? Maybe when he doesn't have Orla. Or maybe he sleeps here when he isn't alone . . . But the other side of the bed looks undisturbed, the pillows still crisp and unwrinkled.

I peer inside the holdall, but it is empty except for a folded T-shirt and socks.

The top drawer of the bedside table is empty as well. I pull open the bottom one, my movements becoming more frantic, but it is the same: nothing inside it except a hairdryer.

Moving around the bed, I quickly open the drawers on the other side.

Nothing.

I shove the drawers closed, and they slam, rattling angrily.

My eyes scan the room, darting towards the empty hallway, before landing on a door to the left of the bed. I didn't notice it at first glance, built into a recess. I rush over and fling it open.

The lights inside turn on automatically, revealing a wood-panelled walk-in wardrobe. Each deep-mahogany-stained wall is lined with hanging space and drawers, accented with handles of antique brass.

I turn to leave, my eyes dancing around the space one last time –

In the far left-hand corner, partially hidden by a few long coats, is a small, low cupboard.

I lean out into the bedroom and peer again into the foyer, my skin tingling as I stare at the closed door. Stepping quickly back into the wardrobe, I throw myself on to my knees. Is this what I think it is?

Yes. The safe.

The small black box sits innocuously in the cupboard, yet as I stare at it, it feels as though it is staring straight back at me. Challenging. *You'll never know what's inside me.*

I move my face closer, and press 'enter'.

Four dashes light up, flash momentarily, and then disappear.

Four digits. I need four digits.

But what would Michael have as a code –

Orla's smiling face appears before my eyes, her gesturing me into the house before running over to the keypad by the door. I screw my eyes shut and focus, forcing myself to imagine, to remember, her fingers over the keys, the pattern mapped out by her movements.

My eyes open, and I inhale deeply. It might not even be the same code as their house, but I have no other clues. And people are creatures of habit, using the same password again and again. I hold out a trembling finger.

Zero –

Bleep.

Four –

Bleep.

One –

Bleep.

One –

The safe buzzes loudly, the screen flashing red. I tug at the handle but it won't move.

Closing my eyes, I watch again as Orla moves her hands over the keys. Straight to the bottom: that's definitely a zero. Then to the second row, to the left – a four. Then the top row. But I can't imagine where she put her fingers next. Was it two and then one? Or three? Or –

No . . .

It was one and then two.

Are you December? I asked her in the car. *Yes, the fourth*, she smiled.

Zero – four – one – two.

Four, twelve.

Orla's birthday.

I quickly press the buttons again, holding my breath as I push the final number.

The screen flashes green.

I exhale, turn the lever, and the door opens.

The safe has two shelves. The lower one is empty but on the top sit two boxes, side by side – one, a deep green, the

184

other, maroon. I quickly pull them out and snap them open. Watches: expensive ones.

I peer in. Is there really nothing else?

I run my fingers around the edges of the safe.

Nothing.

I was so sure . . .

As I rummage one last time, my finger catches on a small lip on the bottom shelf. There is a gap – a thin space between the shelf and the actual base of the safe. I dig my nails inside as far as I can, and they catch on something that has been pushed into the crevice. I scratch, my fingers white with pressure, and finally the very tips of my fingers grip on. Pulling gently, a thin brown envelope, the size of a standard piece of paper, appears from underneath.

It trembles in my shaking hands. He hid this – purposefully.

I unfold the flap of the envelope, which has not been sealed down, and slide my fingers inside. There are papers but they're thick, not like documents, like . . . photographs. I grip the edges and give them one swift tug. But as they slide out of the envelope, I gasp, falling backwards, the sheets flying everywhere.

They are photos of Lily.

But not like the ones that were taken in the studio. And not photos that he has taken from online. They are photos that he has taken without her knowing. There's one outside what looks like a school, a small smile on her face. Another of her stepping out of Franklin House. On the high street, a lit cigarette poised between her lips. Coming out of the drugs-house, her hood pulled up.

But . . . Orla is in some of these pictures. They aren't recent, they're from before. Before the attack.

He was following her before.

I pull out my phone and open the camera. I take each

photo and click quickly, capturing the image before turning to the next.

Click, click, click –

My phone vibrates. I cry out and clamp my hand over my mouth, as a photo drops to the floor.

It's him.

Are you on your way? I've just got back to the hotel. Remember the suite is on the 9th floor. See you soon x

'Fuck!'

I throw myself forwards on to all fours. Scrambling for the photos, I wiggle them back into the envelope and slide it back into the hidden compartment, my hands shaking. I scan the floor, just to make sure –

'Shit!'

One photo is peeking out from where it has slid underneath the fitted wardrobe. My fingers grasp the corner and pull, my breathing frantic. But I can't grip it, it's stuck on something underneath, and my fingertips are sweaty and slick.

'Come on!'

Finally it comes free and I slide it into the envelope and back into the gap under the lower shelf, then slam the safe door shut. I scramble up from the floor and run out of the wardrobe, pulling the door closed behind me, then dash out into the foyer and towards the door. I just need to make it outside to the corridor by the lift –

The lock of the door clicks.

He's here.

I spin in a circle as panic sends my mind into free-fall. Running to my left, I fly through the door and stand in front of the bookshelves. Inhaling deeply, trying to slow my breathing, I tuck my hair behind my ears and smooth down my dress, then pull a book from the shelf –

'Oh, hello.'

I look over my shoulder, pressing the open book to my chest.

'Hi,' I say, my voice low, my smile wide.

He stands in the doorway, one hand placed on the frame. But his brow is furrowed.

'Did someone let you in here?'

'No, I jemmied the lock with a credit card.' I laugh, my stomach turning. 'One of the girls at reception gave me a key. Sorry, I assumed that –'

'No, it's fine –'

'Please don't say anything to her. It wasn't her fault, I didn't want to be seen –'

'No, it's fine, really. It doesn't matter.' He coughs. 'Have you been here long?'

'Just a couple of minutes. You have a wonderful collection of books.'

He moves closer and places his hand on my shoulder. My body is repulsed, desperate to shrink away, but I can't. So instead, I smile, and he kisses my cheek.

'How are you?' he says.

'I'm well. How are you?'

'I've been busy.'

'Me too.' I allow my eyes to dance around the room then flicker back to him. 'How often do you stay here?'

'Sometimes it's much easier for me to stay here rather than commute back home. It was originally the Presidential suite but there's a penthouse, so I took this one for myself. Did you look at the other rooms?'

I shake my head.

'Come,' he says, gesturing, his fingers curling.

I walk past him and he places his hand on the small of my back, guiding me through the door to the bedroom.

I take a few quick steps away from him, exhaling as his hand falls away.

'Beautiful,' I murmur, unable to say anything else. 'I –' My words falter, stinging the end of my tongue, as his hands snake their way around my waist from behind, his hips pressing against me.

Hands over my mouth. Strong arms pushing me down. Kicking. Struggling. His blue eyes. My dress ripping. Hands on the inside of my thighs. Pressure. Fear. Stillness.

I freeze, stuck in place. I can't move. I can't do anything but feel his hands on me, his touch burning as if it is inside me, running through me. His lips are close to my neck, his fingers digging into my flesh, his breath hot on my skin. I'm going to scream, I need him to let go of me, please let go of me, don't touch me –

The sharp trill of a phone ringing bursts out into the air. He releases me and my lip trembles, my breathing shallow, my eyes glazing over with relief. I force my face into passivity as he appears in front of me, holding his phone up in apology.

'So sorry, I really have to answer this,' he says.

He strides out of the room, answering the phone with an authoritative utterance of his name. As he disappears around the corner, I stagger forward, my hand clamped to my mouth. My knees buckle and I crouch down, my hands digging into the wooden base of the bed, my neck flopping forward, forehead touching the duvet. But I lift my head abruptly, away from his sheets. They smell like him.

I blink rapidly and the room blurs.

I can't cry. If I cry, he'll know something is wrong.

But I can't let him touch me again. If he touches me again, I'll scream. Until now I've been able to control his touch – turn my cheek away from his lips, gently remove his hand from my waist. But this was different. This kind of touch – unyielding and insistent – has been a memory, a trauma, scars left across my skin, a dull, constant ache. But now it is burning. I am on fire.

I stride out into the corridor. He's in the living area, still talking, but his eyebrows raise as he sees me waiting.

'Sorry about that,' he says, emerging out into the hall as he tucks his mobile into his back pocket.

'It's okay. Michael, I . . . as lovely as this is, I'm starting to worry about how appropriate it is for me to be up here,' I whisper.

'Is there anything appropriate about us meeting at all?' he says, the corner of his mouth lifting.

He enjoys this part, I can tell. The knowledge that he is doing something wrong. The power of knowing that he could be caught.

'True,' I say, looking up at him through my eyelashes as he steps towards me. 'But this is a hotel. There're people everywhere. Cameras –'

'There are no cameras in this hotel,' he says with a smirk, coming to a standstill right in front of me. 'I'm the only one watching you.'

'Really?'

'My guests value their privacy.' His hands move to grip my waist, and every nerve in my body is screaming at me to run, to lash out, to fight him.

I need to leave, I need to leave, I need to leave.

'Well, so do I.' I step backwards. 'I shouldn't have come here. We've taken too many risks already . . . I should go.'

He sighs, looking up at the ceiling. 'I thought you were coming for a drink.'

'I know, and I wanted to, I really did, but now that you're here, and we're alone, I just . . . It's too risky . . . I'm sorry.'

I turn and walk towards the door, but he stays silent.

'Ava,' he calls out.

I look back at him. I'm just inches from the door. I'm so close –

'When can I see you again?'

'I'll let you know.'

He groans. 'Ava, you're killing me here.'

'Once she's been sentenced. Okay?'

'If you're worried about privacy, we can just go to my house.'

I nod. 'Next time.'

He inches closer, his hands reaching for me, but I smile and step sideways, out of his reach.

'Very well,' he says, moving past me to open the door. 'Allow me.'

I stare at his back, my eyes burning into the very spot where Lily stabbed him. And a thought appears in the forefront of my mind, suddenly, like dark thoughts sometimes do – bursting forwards uncontrollably: I wish she had killed him. I wish he was dead.

He mutters something, his back still turned, his words unclear.

'Pardon?' I say.

He turns slowly to face me, the door still closed, his fingers resting on the handle.

'Didn't you hear me?' he asks, smiling.

'No.'

'I said, it was fun while it lasted . . .'

There's a strange look in his eye. Empty: all the warmth rapidly draining away, leaving behind a shell.

'What was?' I ask, the words shaky.

'Playing with you . . .'

I frown as he pauses.

'. . . Anabelle.'

TWO

So full of artless jealousy is guilt.
It spills itself in fearing to be spilt.

Hamlet, Act 4, Scene 5

28. Lily

Ten minutes before the attack

'Do you want a drink, Lily? A hot one? Tea or hot chocolate? You must be freezing.'

I follow him to the back of the house, comfort easing over me – a warm blanket on a cold evening, rain on a window.

'Um . . . hot chocolate, please,' I say.

'Cool.' He gestures at the stools tucked under the island. 'Make yourself at home, sweetheart.'

I nod, my cheeks flushing with a sudden rush of heat. *Sweetheart.* I don't think anyone has ever called me that. Never Phil. Not even Mum.

I pull out one of the stools and climb up on to it. My legs dangle, my feet not reaching the footrest.

His back is to me as he moves to the fridge and retrieves the milk, then pours it into a saucepan before placing it on the hob. The gas clicks and a small flame appears. He is humming. Quietly, to himself – a song I don't recognize. I wonder what kind of music he likes. What he listens to when he's alone. What he thinks about . . . Does he ever think about me?

My face burns again, my stomach fluttering.

I stare at his back, watching his shoulders and the way they move under his thin T-shirt.

I'm so stupid. He's Orla's dad. He's a grown man – of course he thinks nothing of me except that I'm his daughter's friend. Why would he think anything of a scrawny, scruffy child who nobody wants?

'Here you go,' he says, turning around.

'Thank you,' I mutter, looking down at my lap.

'Lily, are you feeling sick? You're a bit flushed.'

'No. No, I'm fine.'

'Are you sure? You don't have a temperature, do you?'

'No. Really, I'm fine.'

Embarrassment pours down on me.

Flushed? A temperature?

He sees me as a child. A child, and nothing more.

I reach for the mug and wrap my fingers around it, lifting it to my lips.

'Be careful, it's hot,' he warns.

He turns back to pour his own and I roll my eyes. Does he think I haven't done worse than burn myself on a hot drink? Does he forget that I'm not one of the other girls, wrapped in cotton wool, kept safe from anything and everything? I've seen things – done things – that even he hasn't.

I'm not a child.

I haven't been a child for years.

'Perfect,' he says, clutching his own mug and taking a seat on the stool beside me. I tangle my fingers in my necklace and glance sideways at him. He looks so large on the stool compared to me – his feet touch the floor.

He raises the mug to his mouth –

'Careful,' I say. 'It's hot.'

A laugh bursts through his pursed lips. He looks at me sideways, and I smile, eyebrows raised.

'Okay, that was quite patronizing of me, wasn't it?' he says grinning.

'Well. Maybe.'

'I forget that . . .' His voice trails off and his eyes flicker away from me.

'You forget, what?'

He looks back at me, his face now serious. 'I forget that you're not like most fifteen-year-olds.'

I meet his eye. But he doesn't glance away. He holds my gaze, intense, his brow lowered, making his usually bright blue eyes dark. Brooding.

He smiles again and shakes his head. Sips, the steam from the hot chocolate rising up his face as he stares straight ahead.

I place my mug back on to the island, my forearms resting on the cool marble. He sips again, and a slurp as he inhales sends a quick smile across my face. But my smile disappears as he sets down his drink, his arm brushing against mine.

Is he going to move it? Has he even realized?

That feeling returns to my stomach. Flutters. Like swimming in the sea when you can't see the bottom. Adrenalin and curiosity and fear streaming together into something altogether unknown.

I tilt my head and my eyes slowly move up his arm, to his shoulder then to his face, which is still in profile.

My hand flinches. I move my fingers slowly, minuscule movement followed by minuscule movement until my little finger grazes his.

'Lily.'

He says my name as he slowly turns to look at me, his chin lifted. But it isn't a question. It's a statement. A warning?

I can't read him – I can't read his face or his voice.

But he hasn't moved away.

And I'm not a child any more.

29. Ava

'What did you call me?' I whisper.

'I called you by your name.' He moves towards me, his steps steady and deliberate. 'Did you really think I don't know who you are? You're Anabelle.'

He knows.

'I don't know what you're talking about,' I mutter. I reach for the door but his arm flies outwards, pushing it shut.

'What are you doing?' I whisper, my hand still clinging to the door handle. 'Let me leave.'

He smirks. 'I'm not going to hurt you, Anabelle.' He moves towards me and I shuffle backwards, my hands trembling. 'Belle? Would you prefer that? That's what they used to call you . . . I just want to talk.'

'That isn't my name. I don't know what you're talking about. I'm –'

'Ava Knight?' he scoffs. 'No. You aren't. I know who you are, so stop this "I don't know what you're talking about" act. You're Anabelle.' He moves again and I quickly step backwards, stumbling as my feet catch on the large rug. But still, he comes towards me. Relentless. One eyebrow raised as he looks me up and down. 'You've done a good job of making yourself . . . different. So different to what you looked like as a girl. And your personality . . . There was no fight in you then, was there? But there's plenty of fight in you now.'

I stand up straight, lifting my chin.

'Yes,' I say. 'There is. Now . . . Let me leave.'

'But you're impulsive,' he says, ignoring me. 'For someone

so intelligent, so measured in court, you're fuelled by emotion when it comes to me. Your anger has made you stupid. You know, I knew who you were almost straightaway . . . Did you really think I was going to let someone so easily into my life, into my home? A prosecutor, nonetheless? There are easy ways of finding out who someone really is. Especially when you have the one thing that most people want.'

'And what's that?'

He lifts his arms, his gaze darting around the room before returning to me. 'Power.'

Anger unfurls in my chest and my jaw clenches.

'Let me go or I'll call the police.'

'You'll call the police?' His eyes grow wide, mocking, his lips pushed into a pout. 'Really?'

I meet his eye, defiant. But there is a large vase in my peripheral vision, on the sideboard. It looks heavy.

'What will you say if you call the police, Belle? Because no matter what you say, I'll say that I entered into a relationship with the prosecutor of a case where I'm a victim and I know that was wrong, but I was just so besotted. Look at the messages. The phone calls. Her asking to see me. She came to my restaurant. She came to my hotel suite. But I didn't know that she was a girl from my past, clearly hell-bent on revenge.'

'They wouldn't –'

'What?' he interrupts. 'Believe me? Where's the lie, Belle?'

'Don't call me that –'

'Where's the lie, Anabelle?' His voice is raised, his eyes sparkling, a glint of temper shining through the smug exterior. 'Every word would be the truth.'

'You'll be highlighting that you were charged with rape –'

'The police already know about that. The CPS know about that – it's on my record. It isn't relevant because Lily is guilty. And I was acquitted. Remember?'

He falls silent, his eyes turning cold and empty as he stares at me.

This is the risk I took. I gambled with my life, with everything that I have, to try to prove what he really is. To try to help Lily. But all I did was give him power. The power to ruin my life all over again.

'What do you want?' I whisper.

'I want to know why you did this.'

'I . . .'

'Did you really do this because of her? Lily? Did she remind you of yourself?'

My eyes sting with tears and one falls down my cheek. I quickly brush it away.

'She should remind you of yourself. Because you're both liars.'

'I didn't lie,' I shout. 'You know what you did to me—'

'The DNA was contaminated. You lied, Belle.'

'You are sick.'

'Me? I'm the sick one?' His mouth twists into a smile, full of disgust. 'You're the one who's been skulking around, willing to do almost anything to prove that I'm some kind of monster. How far were you going to go to try to get close to me? Would you have fucked me, Belle?'

'Fuck you.' My hands clench into fists at my sides.

'Are you really going to risk everything you ever worked for, everything good in your life, for this one girl? A girl who will probably end up in prison at some point anyway. All because of me? Let justice run its course and move on with your life.'

'Move on with my life?'

His smile falls away like a mask, revealing his true identity underneath. Anger. Danger. A man who is willing to do anything.

'Yes,' he says. 'Or else, I'll take it all away. All of it. Everything that matters. I hoped that you would back off, that you would stop with this stupid game, a game that you simply can't win, but it was fun watching you try. It was fun watching you believe that you had the upper hand. But you've gone too far. I don't want to ruin your life, Belle. But I will. And if I tell the police, the CPS, everything that you've done – what do you think they'll believe? Your word or mine?'

My thoughts race, faster and faster, my mind desperately chasing after them as I try to form a response. But I can't see. Everything is blurred. There isn't a way out of this. If I don't do whatever it is that he wants, he can ruin my life all over again. But it won't be like last time. I'm not a child any more. I won't be able to run away and hide behind another name.

I close my eyes, inhaling deeply.

'What do you want me to do?' I whisper.

'Your job,' he says. 'That's all. I want you to forget this case just like you would any other. Stop digging around. Stop trying to give Lily a defence. She has no defence. You've created an entire persona for her in your mind that doesn't exist. She's a troubled girl who lost her temper. That's all she is. Once she's sentenced on Friday, I'll be gone – you never have to see me again. As far as you're concerned, I'll be a ghost.'

'You've always been a ghost. Since I was fourteen years old . . . You never left.'

'You've kept me in your life, not me.' He nods his head towards the door. 'Well?'

Rage tingles once more down my spine. I hate him. I will always hate him. He will always be a monster. I walked straight into his clutches, not even feeling his claws as they ensnared me.

I meet his gaze, my teeth grinding against each other, and nod.

He stands, shifting his weight from the door.

'See you soon, Belle. And don't try anything – I'll be watching.' He steps aside, the exit finally clear. 'Now get out.'

I walk forward slowly, my whole body trembling as I pass him and pull the door. But as my heels click across the parquet floor of the corridor, I start to run, my eyes fixed on the lift, my heart hammering, as if it's trying to burst free of my chest.

I press the button. It lights up but the doors remain closed. I press it again, over and over, my breathing frantic. Finally, they open and I thrust myself through the gap, and scramble to push the button for the ground floor. I watch the numbers tick slowly downward, taking me closer to escape.

'Ground floor,' the lift announces.

There are people waiting, their faces falling as they see me, averting their eyes from my distress. I stare down at the floor, not looking anyone in the eye as I cross reception, focusing only on the doors that will lead me out of this place. Away from him.

I step out into the warm night and inhale deeply, fresh air rushing into my lungs. A cry rises up from deep inside me but I clamp my hand to my mouth and walk quickly towards my car.

The engine growls as my foot slams down on the accelerator and I fly towards the traffic lights. But my vision blurs with tears. I stop the car, pulling over suddenly at the side of the road. A horn blares as a van swerves around me.

I gasp, my eyes darting to the rear-view mirror. My face is white, my eyes red and bloodshot. Tears sting my cheeks. I freeze for a moment, lost in the sight of my own horror.

You've kept me in your life, not me.

I slam myself back against the seat. My head throbs.

I'll take it all away. All of it. Everything that matters.

My knuckles turn white as I grip the steering wheel, tighter and tighter.

She should remind you of yourself. Because you're both liars.

No –

You know what you did to yourself. You lied, Belle.

Screams burst from my mouth. My fists pound the steering wheel and I scream again, over and over. Anger and frustration and overwhelming, blinding rage erupting out of me.

He's been playing with me – a cat playing with a mouse. My stomach rolls, nausea washing over me as I feel his hands on me again, his lips so close to my neck. His touch.

He knew. And he was torturing me. But I was so concerned with pursuing my prey that I didn't realize:

I was the one being hunted all along.

30. Ava

Goosebumps cover my bare arms, tingling in response to the sound of uneven footsteps creeping up behind me.

My fists tighten and my cheeks turn cold, the colour draining from my already pallid face.

I look over my shoulder quickly, expecting to see him there, his hands reaching for me. Ready to grab me. To hurt me.

But it's just a woman walking her dog, a large Labrador who is dragging her forwards as it tugs on the lead.

Shakily, I let my breath go.

'Sorry,' the woman says as I step sideways, flattening my back to the wall of the alley that runs alongside the court.

'No worries,' I say, breathless.

She continues down the alley and emerges where it meets the road, glancing back at me for a moment, a brief look of concern crossing her face before she is pulled away again.

I lean against the wall and look down at my shoes as I try to slow my pounding heart. But I'm unable to shake the fear that has been coursing through me since I left the hotel last night. All-consuming fear, just like before. The type of fear that has you crying out in your sleep; staring at inanimate objects, transforming them before your eyes until all you can see is someone standing there, watching you in the dark. Him. Standing over me, kneeling beside me, so close that I could hear him breathe.

I slept with the light on.

My head rocks back to rest against the rough brick, and I begin to count.

Count five things that you can see. Five things that are real. That's what George taught me to do years ago, when anxiety was rampaging through me, leaving no piece of me intact.

Five things that are real.

The orange early-morning sky is turning blue.

I move my head and it scrapes on the wall.

The court. Where I work. I'm going to work.

The sound of songbirds leaks into my mind.

Birds are singing. It's May – nearly summer.

I turn my head to look at the road. Cars are passing. People are getting coffee from the Italian cafe.

Lorenzo's: the cafe where I go to lunch with Marissa. Marissa is my friend.

I blink quickly as I watch the people outside the cafe. Sunlight is streaming into the alley. There's no need to be afraid. I'm safe. I'm –

My face falls into shadow. Someone is standing at the end of the alley, blocking the sun and my view of the road. I can no longer see Lorenzo's or the people. But the person is backlit, their face in darkness, their outline lit up like an apparition.

My heart begins racing again.

Think of five things –

'Can I speak to you?'

Lily?

She steps forward, out of the sun. Her blonde hair, her dark clothes, her croaky voice.

'Did you hear me?' she says, walking towards me. 'Can I speak to you for a minute?'

'I . . . I don't think we should talk –'

'But I just need to . . .' She stops a few feet away from me and scuffs her shoes on the concrete floor. 'I need to ask you something.'

I can't speak to her. I can't be seen with her. If Michael –

'Please?'

'Sorry, I need to go.' I step around her and then spin around, still walking backwards to the road, putting more and more distance between us. 'If you have questions you should speak to your solicitor. Or Marissa. I'm sure your solicitor will organize a conference for you –'

'But it isn't about the sentencing. It's about when you came to the house the other day.'

I freeze. I'm so close to the road the sun is warming my back. Should I just walk away?

'I, I haven't told anyone that I saw you there, by the way,' she says, holding out her hand. 'If that's what you're scared of.' She meets my eye, her expression open and sincere. So different to the frustration and outrage.

'No, not at all. It's just not usual for prosecutors to speak to the defendants.' I point backwards, over my shoulder. 'So, I should go.'

'But someone said there was a letter.'

Walk away. I need to leave. Right now.

'Someone inside said that a woman came to the door and asked for me to be given a letter. And when I spoke to you outside, you had a letter in your hand. I remember because it was on the floor and you picked it up and took it with you.'

'Lily, I don't know what you're talking about.'

'Yes, you do. You were there and you had a letter.'

'Lily –'

'Was the letter from Michael?'

I pause, taking in her confused face. 'What?'

'The letter. Was it from Michael?'

'No –'

'So, what was in it?'

204

I stay quiet, silenced by her questions that I'm unable to answer.

'What was in it? What did it say?'

'I didn't write it.'

'Who did?'

'Lily, I can't help you –'

'Help me?'

She falls still, staring.

'Were you trying to help me?' She blinks slowly. 'Could you help me?'

Her hands stretch out towards me: half raised in confusion, half asking for the one thing that has seemed out of reach: somebody who might save her.

But I can't. Not any more.

'I'm sorry. If you need help, if there's something you want to tell someone, you need to tell your barrister. Your solicitor. Anyone.'

She shakes her head, backing away. Her chin trembles, and the childlike innocence that was brimming over in her eyes just a moment ago drains away, leaving them dark and dull.

'Doesn't matter,' she mutters, her voice as lifeless as her gaze. 'I don't need help. Don't worry about it.'

'Lily –'

She runs past me, her shoulder knocking against mine, her face set.

She disappears and I stumble sideways, my back against the wall.

I can't help her.

I really want to. And I tried.

But I can't any more – not now that he knows, not now that he's watching me. Not with his threat hanging low and heavy, so close to my head, ready to break at any moment.

My mouth is dry, my head pounding.

Think about five things.
The sky –
Lily.
Five things that you can see.
The birds –
Michael.
Five things that are real.
Me –
Anabelle.

31. Ava

The court is silent. Morning light was streaming through the foyer, but the CPS room is windowless, the artificial lights garish and harsh. The space feels so small today. Close. Like the walls are moving towards me, inch by inch.

I spoke to Will late last night. I tried to summon enthusiasm for him, for how excited he was about his business trip and how well it was going. But he could tell something was wrong. *I'm just tired*, I told him. *Promise.*

I glance at the clock that hangs above my desk, but the hand isn't moving, and the short arm is hovering over the two. It's stopped. My fingers reach out and tap the screen on my phone. But instead of illuminating, it remains dark.

Shit. I didn't charge it.

Sighing, I plug it in and wait for it to light up, raking my fingers through my hair, which is hanging loose around my face.

'Ava.'

I gasp as I swing around in my seat. Standing in the doorway is Caroline, but her arms are folded, her expression so different to its usual warm openness.

'Caroline?' I say quietly as I stand, clasping my hands behind my back. 'Good morning. You're here early.'

She steps into the room but doesn't return my smile. Instead, she walks towards me, her face fixed and unreadable as she pulls out a chair from the desk beside mine.

'I think you should take a seat, Ava.'

My stomach tumbles, the hairs on my arms creeping upwards, as if a winter chill has swept through the room.

I sit back down. 'Is something wrong?'

'I tried to call you this morning, but your phone went straight to voicemail.'

'I forgot to charge it. I've just plugged it in.'

'Well . . . I didn't want to have this conversation here. I'd rather we were at the office, but as I couldn't get hold of you . . . Anyway, it doesn't matter now.' She sighs and looks away from me then rolls her head backwards, her neck clicking loudly.

'Caroline?'

'Ava, this morning the CCP called me about you.'

'The Chief Crown Prosecutor?'

'Yes.' She sighs. 'The victim in the Hawthorne case spoke to him. About you.'

I'll take it all away.

My throat tightens, and my chest is heavy, weighted, as if someone is pressing down on me, hands around my neck.

Everything. Everything that matters.

This can't be real.

'The victim in the Hawthorne –'

'Yes. Michael Osborne. Do you know who I'm talking about?'

'I . . .'

Why has he done this? I promised I would do what he wanted. What has he told them?

'I'm giving you a chance to be honest, Ava.'

My shoulders curl forwards, my body folding in on itself. She pauses, waiting for me to say something, but my mouth is dry, and I stare at her blankly.

Caroline shakes her head. 'Fine. He turned up at the office yesterday evening and insisted on speaking to the Chief Crown Prosecutor . . . He told him that since Lily Hawthorne pleaded, the two of you have been engaged in some sort of relationship. That you've been to his hotel, had dinner with him, been to his home –'

'Caroline, I –'

'I gave you a chance to tell your side,' she snaps. 'Just wait.'

I nod and freeze in my chair, every inch of me still and cold with fear.

'On its own, these would be a severe breach of the Code. You know that, Ava. But he also said that . . . he found out that you're actually a different person altogether. That you accused him of rape eighteen years ago but he was acquitted. And he believes that you got involved with him because of some desire for revenge.'

'I –'

'Well? Is it true?'

My mouth drops open, the words dying on my lips. Caroline raises her eyebrows, shock clouding her gaze.

'I was expecting you to deny it,' she mutters.

'Caroline, I know it looks bad, but this man isn't what he seems. I really think that Lily Hawthorne is a victim, just like I was, and she needs help –'

'That isn't your job, Ava. Your duty is as a prosecutor. You know what's right and what is wrong. You never should have done that hearing in the first place. As soon as you realized who the complainant was, you should have come forward and said you had to step away. Or you could have come to me straightaway afterwards. But you didn't. And not only that, you've also sought out revenge by infiltrating your way into this man's life!'

'But how was I meant to –'

'Ava, what he did or didn't do eighteen years ago has no bearing on your actions.' She pauses, looking away from me and down at her hands. 'Or the consequences.'

I inhale quickly, my arguments faltering as I wait for the consequences to fall: an executioner's blade, slicing through my life.

'You're suspended pending further investigation.'

I exhale slowly, my eyes shining with tears.

'Caroline . . . please. I love my job. You know how much I care about it, but I just wanted to help her –'

'Ava, I've always supported you. And I know how much your career means to you. That's why I was so shocked when I heard what you'd done. But that doesn't stop me from having to do this –'

'Please,' I say, my voice breaking as I sweep away a tear that has fallen down my cheek. 'I'm . . . I'm begging you. I don't know what I'll do without this job –'

'You should have thought of that before.' She sighs heavily, then looks away from me, down at the floor. 'I'm sorry, Ava. But there's nothing I can do.'

'M-maybe,' I stammer, my throat tightening, my voice high with desperation, 'if I could just speak to someone, or to the Chief, I could explain –'

'Ava, no. You know that won't work. We have to suspend you. You'll be able to put forward your side for the investigation.' Her eyes dart towards the door. 'You need to leave.'

I hang my head. I feel heavy, weighted, as if stones have been tied to my ankles, pulling me down.

But I did this to myself.

'I . . . I understand,' I whisper. 'I'm so sorry.'

She nods, then shakes her head, sighing loudly. 'Pack your things quickly. You should be gone before anyone else arrives.'

'Caroline . . . I really am sorry –'

'Just go please, Ava. HR will be in touch soon.'

I nod and stand. Tears are streaming from my eyes but I

let them fall as I tug my phone from its charger and hurriedly grab the few belongings that litter my desk, ramming them into my bag.

'Ava?'

I wipe my face with the back of my hand before turning to meet her disappointed gaze.

'Y-yes?'

'We'll also have to report this to the Bar Standards Board.'

I grimace as if she's punched me, even though I knew this would be coming.

I'll be disbarred. I'll never practise again.

Shock takes hold and I nod slowly as the emotions drain out of me, like blood escaping a wound. My lip trembles and I bite down on it hard.

Focus on the physical pain. Block out the emotion. Just like when I was a teenager. It's the only way to survive.

I lick my lips. Taste blood.

Glancing around the room one final time, I catch sight of my gown which is still hanging beside my desk. I pull it down, clenching the worn material, rough between my fingertips. I fold it carefully. Will I ever wear it again? Or is it over?

Everything I worked for. Gone.

I move past Caroline, my entire body trembling, then walk quickly out of the room and down the corridor to the entrance hall, my pace quickening until I am running towards the door, ignoring Stephen's familiar voice as he shouts goodbye, not knowing that he won't see me again.

I lift my hand to cover my mouth, forcing my cries to remain silent as I push my way through the door and into the blazing light, my breathing panicked and heavy –

But I come to a sudden halt on the steps.

There's a car parked across the road – a black four-by-four.

And through the darkened windows, the outline of a man, his head angled just so.

Michael.

Watching me.

I clench my jaw, suppressing my cries as hatred rolls through me, and meet his gaze as he shifts closer to the window, his face becoming clear beyond the glass.

My phone buzzes. It has lit up with Caroline's missed calls, but a new message has come through.

Michaela.

I warned you, Belle. I hope that conversation with Lily was worth it.

He raises an eyebrow, his head tilting to the side, his expression cold. The engine purrs and he breaks away, dismissing me as the car rolls down the road.

How did he see us? Did he follow her or me? Has he been watching me since the hotel? He told me that he would take everything away. Everything I've worked for. Everything that matters. And now he has.

Just like before.

32. Belle

Eighteen years earlier

My sobs stop suddenly at the sound of a knock on my door.

'Belle, love,' Dad says. 'Detective Cavanaugh is here to see you.'

I sit up quickly, wiping my face with the back of my hand. 'Come in,' I say, my voice hoarse.

The door swings open. 'Belle,' Detective Cavanaugh says, stepping into the room, Mum and Dad in the doorway behind him. 'I'm here to talk to you about what happened today at school.'

My lip wavers and I try to hold it in, but I can't. I collapse my head into my hands and burst into tears.

Everything is ruined. It's all over. I just want it to be over.

He rushes forward and sits next to me on the bed, hesitating, just for a moment, before wrapping his arm around my shoulders. I cry into his chest, and he hushes me gently. I peer through swollen eyes at the door and Mum and Dad are still standing there. Mum is crying, her fingers covering her mouth. Dad just looks helpless. He doesn't know what to do, how to fix this. I want to tell him that this isn't his fault. It just can't be fixed.

'Belle,' George says, after I fall silent. 'Can you tell me what happened?'

I pull away from him and sit up, tucking one foot underneath me.

'I-it was my first day back at school . . . I spoke to the

headteacher and then I went out on to the field to find my friends . . .'

I had searched the huddles of people for my closest friends. Rachel was sitting down on the grass, Dean's arms draped lazily around her shoulders. He whispered something in her ear and Rachel blushed, smiling down at her lap. Dean is so arrogant, full of charm and flattering words. But if you cross him, he can be unkind – cruel even. Martha and Holly were sitting on the bench, lost in quiet conversation, each of them occasionally sneaking glances at the lovebirds on the grass, then turning to look at each other. Holly giggled softly but Martha rolled her eyes. She's never liked Dean either.

And then there was Finn. He was sitting on the other side of the bench, paying no attention to anyone else, happy in his own world, as usual. He was reading. I smiled as his curly dark hair fell over his eyebrows and into his eyes, a frown settling over his tanned face as he raised a hand to shield his green eyes from the sun. He's grown bigger over the summer – the scrawny, gangly limbs have gone. He's broader now. Handsome.

'Belle!' Holly shrieked as she caught sight of me. She untangled her legs from the bench and flew towards me, flinging her arms around my neck.

I hugged her tightly but looked over her shoulder, searching for Finn. He was lingering behind the others but as I met his gaze, he smiled. My stomach flipped.

'Let go of her, Holly,' Rachel said, her voice equal parts joking and stern.

Holly released me and Rachel stepped forward with a knowing look in her eye, letting go of Dean's hands to hold her arms out towards me. 'I'm so glad you're back,' she whispered in my ear as her arms wrapped tightly around my neck. 'I really missed you.'

'Me too,' I said.

'Are you feeling . . . okay?'

'Yeah. I'm just glad to be back.'

'God, I'd give anything to be off for months,' Dean laughed, flopping his arm on Rachel's shoulder as she stepped backwards. But she didn't let go of my hand.

'Don't be a twat, Dean.' Finn jostled him with his elbow. His voice was light-hearted but his eyes were cold. Finn has always tolerated Dean, nothing more. They couldn't be more different. Finn's kindness to Dean's mean. Finn's quiet to Dean's loud mouth. Finn's humble nature to Dean's arrogance. Finn smiled again as he moved towards me, his serious face evaporating.

'Hi, Finn,' I said, looking up at him as he stepped into my space. He's tall – much taller than I remembered. I only come up to his shoulder now. He extended his arms and I moved into them, my hands interlocking around his waist, my head resting against his chest.

'I missed you, Belle.'

'Did you really?' I whispered, tilting my head upwards to look at him, my heart pounding.

'Did he?' Dean said, laughing. 'He hasn't stopped talking about you, Belle.'

Finn grinned, shaking his head, his cheeks blushing. 'Of course I did. How could I not miss that face?' He raised his hands to squeeze my round cheeks. I've always hated them but he says that they're cute. Each palm covered one side of my face, his fingers in my hair, and he squeezed, beaming.

My stomach, full of butterflies, tumbled. His hands were on my face. Soon they wouldn't be on my face, but around my neck, across my mouth, his voice whispering at me to be quiet, telling me not to scream, just lie there and be still –

'Belle?'

Finn was staring down at me, worried, his hands not on my cheeks but hanging down by his sides.

'Is something wrong? Don't you feel well?'

'No, I . . . I just felt a bit dizzy for a second. I'm fine now.' I forced a smile but stumbled backwards away from him.

'Fully recovered from your illness, hey, Belle?'

I froze as an arm hooked around my neck, a chest pressing into my back.

'James, let her go,' Rachel said with worried eyes. 'She . . . she doesn't like stuff like that.'

James. Dean's best friend.

'Doesn't she?' he said, his mouth close to my ear, his breath hot on my cheek.

'Let go,' I said, my voice shaking as I thrust my shoulders upwards, panic rising in my chest.

'God, you need to chill out. You've become so serious.' His arm moved from around my neck, but he carried on standing behind me, his hands roughly gripping my shoulders. 'Anyone would think you'd gone to a nunnery while you were away.'

'She's been ill, James,' Finn said, glaring. He moved towards James, their heads close to each other, like animals preparing to fight.

'Has she, though?' James said. 'That's what her parents told everyone, but I've heard different.'

'James, just fuck off,' Rachel said, her face flushing.

'Well, not just me. The whole world.' He let go of my shoulders and pulled off his rucksack. My heart raced, pumping harder and harder as he delved into his bag. He pulled out a pile of papers. Licking his fingers, he slid the top page off the pile and held it in front of me.

'Wh-where did you get that?'

It was a photograph of me leaving court. But my identity wasn't meant to be reported. I was told I'd be protected.

The paper spun as I read the words plastered across the picture.

THE GIRL WHO CRIED RAPE

'Why don't you tell your friends where you've been, Belle?' James said, his face cracked in half with a giant grin, revelling in the attention.

Other people were moving closer to our group, awkward smiles adorning their faces, curious to know what James was shouting about. They were all staring at me. Enjoying the spectacle.

'Let's see, mate,' Dean shouted, letting go of Rachel's hand. He strode towards us and snatched the paper from James's hands.

My feet were fixed firmly to the ground, rooting me to the spot as Dean scanned the page, his mouth dropping open.

'Belle, what's going on?' Martha said. 'Dean, what is it?'

I glared at Rachel.

'Dean, stop it –' she shouted, grabbing his arm, but he dodged her grip and swung around, arms held out to the side, like a showman, ready to entertain.

'Well, it looks like Belle wasn't really off because she was sick. She was off because she fucked some guy and said that he raped her.'

'What?' Holly said. 'Dean, don't be a prick –'

'Look!' He held the piece of paper out in front of his chest and I reeled – my entire body plummeting downwards, but there was no hole for me to disappear into, nowhere for me to go. Instead, I was frozen, unable to move – legs locked in position, fists clenched.

'It's all over the internet,' James said. 'I saw this and printed it off – thought you might want it.'

'Oh Belle, you're famous,' Dean shouted. He sneered, circling, coming to a standstill behind me.

His arm snaked its way around my shoulders.

'Get off of her, Dean,' Finn shouted.

'Oh mate, you must be so disappointed. Belle, I always thought you'd have your first time with Finny-boy but looks like teenagers aren't so much your thing.'

'Leave me alone,' I said, my teeth gritted.

'Unless Finn has already had his turn?' He pushed my hair away from my neck, leaning close to whisper into my ear. 'Do we all get a go?'

'Dean!' Rachel cried. 'Please, that's enough!'

'Get off me!' I said through barely parted lips, my voice low.

'Although the poor guy said that it wasn't him at all. Did you just make it up, Belle? Did you want some attention? God, how fucking desperate –'

'I said get the fuck off me!'

I gripped his arms and threw myself backwards, using all of my strength and weight to send us both tumbling to the ground. The papers flew out of his hands, soaring above our heads as we fell, the black and white words like birds circling violently. I scrambled off him, breathless, anger blurring my vision.

I launched myself, screaming – all the way from the pit of my stomach. He reached his arms up to cover his face as I lashed out at him, fists and feet flying, over and over again.

'Belle, stop,' Rachel sobbed, her eyes wide with shock.

Finn rushed forward and tore me away, forcing my arms to my sides, hands tight around my wrists, as he tried to pull me into his chest. But I struggled, the cuts on my arms burning, tears streaming down my face.

'Belle, calm down, it's okay –'

'Don't touch me!' I screamed.

He released his grip and backed away, his eyes shining with tears. 'Belle, I –'

'You crazy bitch!' Dean shouted, as a group of boys pulled him to his feet, his pale cheeks burning. He lifted his hand to his nose, his eyes round in shock at the sight of blood. My heart soared with satisfaction. I hurt him. And he deserved it.

A strange silence fell over the field. I turned slowly, my eyes darting around the crowd of shocked faces, searching for my friends. My chest heaved up and down as I tried to catch my breath, but panic washed over me as I found Rachel, Holly and Martha in the crowd. They were all staring, all watching me aghast, as if I was some kind of monster. As if they didn't recognize me at all.

I stop speaking and look up at Detective Cavanaugh.

'I'm so sorry that happened, Belle,' he says gravely.

'But how,' Mum says, her voice seething, her features contorted into a snarl, 'how has this happened? She was supposed to be protected!'

'I know this must be very difficult for all of you –'

'Everyone knows what happened,' Dad interrupts. 'Every single child at that school, every parent –'

'Dad, please stop –'

'Every fucking stranger on the street –'

'Stop it!' I scream.

They stop, shocked by my desperate cry.

'Anabelle –'

'No, Mum! Stop it, both of you!' I stand. 'Just get out, please. I want to talk to Detective Cavanaugh alone.'

'Belle, I don't think –'

'Dad, please!'

They glance at each other, Dad tilting his head just so in a silent question, Mum shaking hers.

'Fine,' Dad says. 'We'll be downstairs.'

They back away slowly and then turn to leave, passing through the door which stays open.

I sit back down and sniff awkwardly, my face hot with tears. 'I'm sorry,' I whisper.

'Don't be,' Detective Cavanaugh says. 'None of this is your fault.'

'Do you . . .' I sigh. 'Do you think you'll be able to find out who did this?'

He shifts on the bed, turning towards me. 'We have a cyber-crime team who are going to try to find out who leaked your identity. They'll do everything they can.'

I nod, biting the inside of my bottom lip. 'Do you think it was him?'

'I don't think so, Belle. He was acquitted. Why would he want to draw further attention towards the case?'

'I don't know . . . To make me look like even more of a liar?'

'I really don't think it was him.'

I shrug and we fall into silence. I can feel his eyes on my face, watching me as I pick at my fingernails, tearing at the loose skin around my nailbed.

'Everything is fucked. I'm going to lose my friends. Mum and Dad . . . I don't know if our family will ever be the same . . . I have nobody any more.'

'You have me,' he says, squeezing my arm.

'No, I don't. You're just doing your job. I don't expect you to care about me.'

'But I do, Anabelle. If you ever need me – for help, for someone to talk to – I'm here. Okay?'

I glance up, meeting his kind gaze. I lean against him, and

he hugs me to him. I bite down on my lip. I don't want to cry. Not now. Not again.

'I'll speak to you again soon, okay?' he says, standing. 'You can reach out to me whenever you want.'

I nod. 'Thank you.'

He smiles one last time and then leaves, and I listen to his footsteps as he goes down the stairs. I stand quickly and tip-toe out of my room and down the corridor. Mum and Dad will be waiting, ready to ask him questions. I stop at the top and peer through the bannister. I can just make them out in the hallway, huddled together by the front door.

'What's happened to PC Hart?' Dad asks, his arm around Mum's waist.

Detective Cavanaugh sighs. 'PC Hart was formally investigated for his mishandling of the DNA evidence, and he's been placed on performance measures.'

'He hasn't been fired?'

'No, Mr King.'

'Why not?' Mum says, her voice shrill.

'You know how sorry I am for what happened to Belle. But people do make mistakes. And yes, it was a devastating mistake for your family, but we can't be sure what the outcome of the trial would have been. And the proper procedures have been followed in the handling of PC Hart's employment.'

My breaths are stuck in my chest, my lungs feeling as if they are too full, almost ready to explode.

'What do we do about Belle?' Mum whispers, wiping her eyes. 'What do we do about our little girl? She's just a child. And she's so lost. She's so different to before. Sad. And so, so angry.'

'Penny, we're just going to have to talk to her, comfort her, make sure she knows that we're here and that we love her,' Dad says. 'We'll give her some time. But eventually she's going to have to face it. She's going to have to go back to school, back to her friends who will be there for her, no matter what she thinks . . . She can do it. I know she won't want to, but she can.'

No.

I can't go back. Not ever. It will never be the same. Nothing will ever go back to the way it was. No one will ever forget. Nobody at the school. Not my friends. Not me.

And if I can't forget, then what's the point? In anything?

My eyes dance over the three of them, gathered in the narrow hallway. I look at Detective Cavanaugh with his sympathetic gaze and offer of friendship. I wish that he could help me. But it's too late. I take in Mum and Dad one last time: their heads huddled together, their sorrow-painted faces. They'll be sad, I know. But together they'll survive.

I back away from the bannister and dash quickly to the bathroom.

Lock the door.

I turn on the bath taps, both hot and cold, sending water pummelling against the ceramic. The sound is like rain on a window, a storm billowing outside.

I open the cabinet above the sink, repeating the stages of my daily routine.

Reflection. Cupboard. Sleeves. Razor.

But this time my routine will have a different ending.

I place the razor in the basin and step into the bath, fully clothed. Removing my glasses, rolling up my sleeves, I allow the world to blur. Pick up the razor. As I lower myself into the lukewarm water, my teeth chatter.

I'm sorry, Mum and Dad. I know how much you wanted for me. I know you thought you could fix this. Fix me.

I close my eyes and hold my breath –

33. Ava

People spill out of court, some running quickly as they try to squeeze lunch into the hour break, others leaning against the brick façade, lighting a cigarette. Barristers still in their wigs and gowns, their brows furrowed, idly chatting. The world feels unstable, and I am untethered. No longer held down to my life by gravity, but floating aimlessly above it, skimming the surface.

I shift in the driver's seat and look down at my phone, the messages between George and me, still open on the dull screen. I couldn't face calling him or breaking the news in person – his disappointment would be too much to bear.

I've been suspended. Michael found out who
I was and told work everything. You were
right. I'm sorry . . . I've let you down x

> I'm so sorry, Ava. I know you just
> wanted to help her. x

Everything I did was for nothing.
I still didn't help her.

> You did everything you could.
> There's nothing more you can do.

My eyes are set on the tall double doors, watching as each person comes bolting through them, scanning for Marissa's face.

Finally, she emerges. She is flustered, her hair flying into her eyes as she crosses the road. Her usually sunny face is clouded over. I flash the headlights: once, then twice. She

223

nods, spotting me. I stare straight out of the windscreen as she opens the passenger door and climbs in. My hands wring the steering wheel – I can feel her eyes on my face but I'm unable to look her way. I've been so desperate to speak to her, but now that she's here, it's as if I'm fixed in place.

'Ava, what's going on?'

I look at her out of the corner of my eye. My mouth wavers, but I still can't speak. I don't know how to begin.

'I went looking for you. You were on the list for Court Four but your name was crossed out. And I went to see Caroline to ask where you were and she said that I should speak to you, that she couldn't say.'

I hold my breath as sobs rush to the surface, vibrating just under my skin. I cover my mouth with my hand – I don't want to cry. If I cry, I won't know how to stop.

'Ava, seriously – you're scaring me.'

'I . . .' I let out a shaky breath, trying to regain composure. 'I've been s-suspended.'

Her mouth drops open, her already large eyes growing into round orbs shiny with shock. 'Suspended?'

I nod. But I can't hold it in any longer. I rock forward, my forehead on the steering wheel, and cry. 'I'm so stupid,' I whisper.

'What have you done?' she asks. 'Is this something to do with Lily's case?'

I lean back, my head resting against the seat, and close my eyes. 'You said that you knew something was wrong.'

'Yes, but . . . what?'

I close my eyes which flutter rapidly, my lip still trembling. 'I know Michael Osborne. I shouldn't have done the case.'

She frowns. 'Okay . . . But you just did the plea. I know you shouldn't have, but surely you haven't been suspended just for that?'

'No. Not just that. I . . . I've been meeting up with him, trying to prove that he did something to Lily.'

'But . . . why? How do you know him?'

I meet her eye. She pauses, not understanding. But then her face darkens. I can see it there, in her eyes: realization.

'Did he hurt you?'

'When I was fourteen, I went to a party. At the house of a girl in my year. Loads of people were there and I felt uncomfortable . . . I hated things like that, but my mum encouraged me to go. I decided I wanted to leave so I walked home. It wasn't a long walk and it wasn't that late. But . . . I got to the riverside and . . . There's this place where the river runs parallel to the railway line and in between there's trees and bushes. And he just came out of nowhere. Dragged me off the riverside and into the cover. He . . . he raped me. I walked home. Told my parents. And we went straight to the police. But he was acquitted.'

She reaches across the gearstick and hugs me tightly, her head on my shoulder, my arms still dangling limply at my sides. 'Ava, I'm so sorry. You should have told me –'

'How? How could I have told you? I wanted to help you, help Lily, and I tried, but telling you this would have put you in an awful position –'

'No, I mean when we first met. During all the years that we've been friends. You could have told me.'

'I've never told anyone. Not since we moved away and changed our names. The only people who know are the people who knew me before. And now you.'

'Changed your name? Your name isn't Ava Knight?'

'It *is*. But it wasn't . . . not then. It was Anabelle King. My identity got leaked and everything fell apart. I lost my friends, my dad . . .' I can't say what happened to Dad, although she'll find out if she thinks to go looking. All it would take is a search of my old name, and what he did will appear. 'My dad . . . left. So, Mum and I moved away and changed our names.'

'I don't mean this critically but . . . how do you know it was him?'

'I identified him. And there was DNA.'

'DNA?'

'On my clothes.'

She shakes her head. 'How the hell was he acquitted?'

'It was mishandled by a police officer. The judge made it inadmissible and without it the jury didn't believe me.'

'Ava, I —'

'It's okay. I . . . I'm so sorry. I don't know what I was thinking. I just saw his name in the file and . . . I'm sorry.'

She sighs. 'I'm sorry too. I wish I had known.' She strokes the back of my hand and chews on her lip. 'What has Will said?'

'He doesn't know yet. He's away with work, I . . . I don't know how I'm going to tell him.'

I wipe my face and black smudges of mascara coat the back of my hand.

'Marissa . . . There's some stuff that I've found —'

'No, Ava,' she says. She holds her hand out but her kind, sad smile is still there.

'But I think that it could help —'

'Ava,' she interrupts, her tone suddenly stern. 'Don't.'

'But he —'

'Ava!' she shouts. 'Please, stop. You've been suspended. Do you really want to drag me into this too? I can't know anything. I won't be able to use any of it. I'd have to disclose to the court where I got it from, and it will all collapse.'

'But what if Lily —'

'I spoke to Lily this morning about whether Michael had approached her and she wouldn't say a thing. She just wants it to all be over – she's never going to give me a defence. And I can't force her to change her plea, no matter what you think actually happened. Just ... I'm sorry for what you went through. I really am. And you're still my best friend – I love you. But until this case is over, we probably shouldn't speak.'

I turn away from her, resting my head backwards against the seat to look up at the grey roof of the car.

'I understand,' I whisper, closing my eyes. 'I . . . I'm sorry.'

'I know. I just think it's what's for the best right now.'

I nod again.

'Bye, Ava.'

'Bye.'

She gets out and closes the door, then runs across the road and back inside the court, her head hanging low.

I squeeze my eyes shut, desperate to quiet the noise inside my mind, the million voices bouncing around, trying to make sense of everything that has happened. Everything I have done.

Sadness simmers under the surface, but Marissa and George's words repeat in my mind, a broken record player, humming deep down. And as I listen, the sadness is drowned out by a growing anger.

You've done enough. You did what you could. There's nothing more you can do.

Are they right?

Have I done enough?

There's less than three days until Lily's sentencing. Only a matter of days before her life is never the same, while Michael's remains unchanged. Like always.

Yet while Michael thinks he holds all the power, what he's overlooked is what happens when you take everything away from a person: you transform them into someone else.

Someone who has nothing to lose.

34. Ava

'Hello?'

I smile widely at the young woman who opens the door, her hair tied up in a messy bun, the shouts of children leaking out of the house.

'Hi. I was wondering if I could speak to Lily?'

'Lily Hawthorne?'

'Yes.'

She frowns. 'Who are you?'

'I'm Miss King.'

'Sorry, I still don't know who –'

'I'm a teacher from Lily's school. I arranged with her to meet her here – she was anxious at school about what might happen if her sentencing goes the way she fears.'

'She didn't say anything about a teacher –'

'Ah. Well, we've tried reaching her but couldn't. Could I speak to her?'

'She isn't here . . .' She pauses, looking me up and down. 'Sorry, could I see some identification?'

'Not to worry if she's not here. I'll see her tomorrow at school. Thank you'

I turn quickly and walk away, the woman's eyes on my back. I don't look back, my heart thudding away, waiting for a shout of my name, or a call to stop. But finally, the door slams.

Lily isn't there . . . In a couple of hours it'll be her curfew. But if she isn't here, and she has nowhere else to go, there's only one place she could be.

*

My fingers cling on to the railings, the rusted metal rough on my skin. Heavy clouds have darkened the sky, blocking out the late afternoon sun which occasionally breaks through in streams that fall on my skin. But I'm still cold and empty, filled with nothing but anger – pure and undiluted.

Anger at myself.

Anger at him.

I cross the path littered with glass and grime, my gaze fixed to the door. But I don't approach it – instead I move around the house, past the graffitied wall, my shoes scraping across the dirty shingle, until I reach the back corner. I slowly peer around, holding my breath –

No one is outside.

But the music sounds louder here, the tinny melody clear, where from the front of the building it was muffled, consumed by the bass.

I move down the wall, keeping my back close to the brick.

There's a window, low down, its glass shattered, and the music is vibrating out through the open frame.

Inside, the room is empty except for the large speaker and a man, shirtless, passed out on a threadbare sofa. Graffiti covers the walls. Needles lie abandoned by his feet.

I shiver. Lily is here alone. She's just a child.

No child deserves this life.

I push myself up on the window ledge and drag myself through the hole, wincing as glass pierces my hand. I fall on to the floor with a loud thud. But the man on the sofa doesn't stir.

Blood trickles down my palm and on to my fingers before dripping to the floor.

I wince.

Find Lily. Help Lily. That's all I'm here for.

I walk out of the room and move slowly through the darkness of the hallway towards the front of the house. Peering into a room, the one you can see from the road with its curtains always drawn, I scan the faces of the people inside: some sitting on a pile of blankets, and a woman passed out on the lone armchair.

She isn't here.

'Are you looking for someone?'

I spin round.

A man is sitting down on the stairs behind me, leaning against the wall, his legs tucked up, feet against the rotting spindles. His eyes are round, his pupils dilated.

'I –'

'Did you wanna score?'

'I'm actually looking . . . for my sister.'

'Your sister?'

I nod, holding his confronting stare.

'Who's your sister?'

'Her name is Lily.'

He frowns.

She isn't here. How am I going to find her? And if she isn't here, then where is she? Is she in another house, just like this one? Is she going to miss her curfew –

'Lily doesn't have a sister.'

I blink at him. 'You know Lily?'

He nods. 'We all do. A lot of us knew her mum. Try to look after her as best we can.'

'Is she here?'

'I saw her not that long ago. But . . . who are you?'

'A friend.'

He scans me, his forehead creased with lines. 'Are you police?'

'No.' I shake my head. 'I just need to speak to her.'

'It's just . . . you look strait-laced. Like you've never put a foot out of line – stands out in a place like this.'

Sadness flurries down on me like snow. 'You'd be surprised,' I mutter.

He looks me up and down again, and I hold my breath as his face contorts, his expressions changing from moment to moment.

'She's usually upstairs. In the room at the back.' He lifts his chin, nodding his head up the staircase.

I smile gratefully. 'Thank you.'

'No worries,' he says, smiling back at me, warm and genuine.

He moves his leg and gestures at me to pass. I climb the stairs, my eyes fixed on the open doorway.

I stop at the entrance, my eyes adjusting to the dim light that lies beyond. The windows on this side of the building are all boarded up and only thin streams of sun are managing to filter through the gaps: fingers of light reaching into the darkness.

But I can't see her. The room is empty.

Unless . . .

I quickly step inside, turning to face the left-hand corner of the room – the corner most shrouded in shadows.

'Lily?'

There she is, sitting down, back against the wall, knees tucked in tightly to her chest. She lifts her head, her face a mask of confusion.

'Hello?'

I move closer to her, removing my hood.

She rolls her eyes and rests her head down again. 'What are you doing here?' she mumbles.

'I . . . I want to help you.'

She scoffs, her mouth tearing into a wide smile, a smile that holds back every other emotion.

'You said you can't help me.'

'And I couldn't. But I can now.'

'What's changed?' she retorts with a frown.

I point to the spot beside her. 'May I sit down?'

'Do whatever you want.'

I crouch down and then rock back to sit beside her, glancing at the wall before placing my back against the greying concrete.

She says nothing. And neither do I. For a minute or so we sit in silence, her eyes closed, head turned away from me, pretending I don't exist, while I watch her, trying to figure out how best to explain.

'I lost my job,' I whisper.

She turns her head to look at me, her face resting sideways on her knees.

'Why?'

I sigh. 'I'm about to tell you something about me. Something that hardly anyone in the world knows. And I hope that when I tell you, you'll see that I've wanted to help you all along. I tried to help you.'

She doesn't say anything but is staring at me. Waiting.

'I lost my job because . . . When I was younger, around the same age as you, I was walking home from a party when I was attacked. A man in a mask grabbed me. And he . . . raped me.'

Her mouth falls open, her face contorting with disbelief.

'The case went to trial, but in the end, the most important piece of evidence couldn't be used, and the jury found him not guilty. It changed everything about my life. Everything about me. I changed my name. I . . . I lost my dad. And . . . my mother can't even stand to be around me.'

She nods. She understands. Of course she does.

'I lost my job because . . . the man who raped me was the complainant in one of my cases. And instead of doing what I was meant to do, I found ways into his life. I was trying to prove what he was. But he knew me – he knew all along.'

She is shaking her head, and tears fall from her lashes and on to the tops of her cheeks.

'You mean . . .'

'Michael Osborne. Yes.'

'That was you?'

'You . . .' I frown, my eyebrows stitching together. 'You knew?'

'Orla . . . his daughter mentioned it once. She told me that he wasn't found guilty and I didn't believe he could have done something like that . . .'

'Do you believe it now?' I ask.

'I . . .' She glances away and begins picking at her nails. 'You lost your job because of him?'

She didn't answer the question . . . But I need to do this carefully. I need to help her trust me. If she even can trust anyone any more.

'He told them,' I say. 'I don't know if he did it just to punish me or because he saw us talking outside court the other day.'

'I . . . I'm sorry,' she whispers. She tucks her chin to her chest, her forehead on her knees, hiding her face. But her shoulders are moving up and down, her cries silent but clear.

I hold out my hand, hesitating for a second before placing it on her shoulder. She flinches.

'I'm not telling you this to make you feel guilty. It isn't your fault. I'm telling you this because I was selfish and I did it for myself, but I *was* trying to help you too. Everything pointed to you being guilty, but I just couldn't let go of what I know he is. And I found –'

'You found something?' she interrupts, lifting her head suddenly.

'I found some photos of you. Loads of them hidden in a safe in his hotel.'

'Photos? He took photos of me in his studio –'

'No, not those ones. I've seen those as well but they're at his house. These ones were –'

'Wait –' She holds out her hand. 'You've been to his house?'

'Yes.'

'Have you met Orla?'

'Yes. She talked about you.'

She inhales quickly – a sharp intake of breath. 'What did she say?'

'She said . . . she told me what a good friend you were.'

Her lip trembles and another tear falls from her eye to join the pool collecting at her Cupid's bow.

'But the photos I found . . .' I pull my phone out of my pocket and open the gallery. I hold out the screen and swipe across, showing her photo after candid photo. 'He was following you. Look.'

She reaches for the phone slowly and peers at the screen, her eyes narrowing. She pauses, taking in a photo of her outside school, her arm linked with Orla's.

'But . . . these are from before.'

'Yes. Before the attack. He was following you.'

She stares down at my phone disbelievingly. 'One night I was here and he drove past me as I was leaving. I thought it was coincidence but –'

'No, Lily. He was following you. Waiting. He never cared about you – he was taking advantage. He wanted to take advantage of how vulnerable you are. If you tell me what happened, I'll help you. We can speak to Marissa; she can get the judge to retract your plea. If he tried to do something to you, or hurt you –'

'He didn't do to me what he did to you.'

'He didn't?'

I wait, watching her closely as she wrings her hands, her mouth twisting as she tries not to cry.

'But he tried,' she whispers.

Her breath shudders out of her as she lets the truth escape – the truth that she has been keeping inside her, finally set free.

'Okay,' I say, my voice shaking, 'we need to speak to Marissa and you can change your plea to not guilty. You can go to trial and speak out against him. I know it's scary, but he only has the power to keep you silent because he makes you believe he has the power. But once you realize that he is nothing but a man – a flawed, weak man – he can't silence you.'

'But I can't,' she says, turning sideways to face me, her face long and drawn in distress. 'You don't understand –'

'Yes! Go to trial and you can claim self-defence. Claim self-defence and then the prosecution have to *prove* that –'

'But that isn't the truth!'

'Why are you protecting him?'

'If I claimed self-defence, I'd be lying.'

'But why? Did you mean to hurt him?'

'No!'

'Then, why?'

'Because it wasn't me at all!'

An eerie quiet descends and the clouds move across the sun, plunging us into darkness.

'Who was it?' I whisper, watching her closely as she shields her face from me with both hands.

'She panicked. She was just trying to help me!'

'Who?'

'If I tell you, you have to promise not to –'

'Who was it, Lily? Tell me. It's okay.'

She slowly drags her hands down her face, her mouth and nose still covered, her eyes staring out at me, scared and wild.

'It was Orla.'

THREE

We each begin in innocence. We all become guilty.

Leonard F. Peltier

35. Lily

The attack

He leans forward quickly, his hands reaching up to my face.

His lips are on mine.

A kiss.

He's kissing me.

But his lips aren't soft like I imagined. Not like when I kissed Jamie at my last home, sitting on his bed, the curtains closed. No ... Michael's lips are dry. Hard. His kiss forceful.

I pull away, but his hands are still gripping my face, and his breath is hot on my mouth.

'Michael –'

'It's okay,' he whispers.

'No, I ... I don't want to.' I push on the island and my stool spins away. But as I slide off the seat, he reaches for me, now standing, and pushes me against the island, the corner digging into my spine.

His hands are on me. His mouth on mine. I clamp my lips together, moving my face to the side, but he buries his head in my neck, his breathing heavy.

'Michael, stop –'

'It's okay,' he mutters as his hands move down and fiddle with my buttons. 'I've seen how you look at me. And you're so beautiful, you're so special –'

'But I don't want to,' I cry, pressing my hands to his chest and pushing. But he is too heavy, too strong.

'Just keep still. It's okay. We won't tell anybody.'

I freeze, paralysed, a black curtain falling before my eyes as he tugs at the waistline of my jeans.

Please.

Not like this.

He pulls down my jeans and his hands creep up my top.

No.

He grabs my shoulders, his hands tight, and he starts to push me downwards, to the floor. My arms flail as I try to hold on to the island and they knock against the knife block, blades scattering, sliding across the wood towards the door. The room above me spins.

His weight is on top of me. My arms pinned to my sides.

Just lie still, Lily.

Close your eyes.

Count.

It will be over soon.

One.

No.

Two –

'Dad?'

Orla?

Her whisper came from the hallway.

She is there, standing at the open double doors, her face white, her eyes wide with shock as they scan the room – us on the floor, the knives at her feet.

But he hasn't heard her.

I can't speak. My words won't come to me.

But help me, Orla.

Please.

She is stuck to the spot, tears streaming down her face, unable to move. Unable to do anything.

I close my eyes.

And for a moment, everything falls silent. No noise. I block out everything, even the sound of his uneven breathing, his whisper of my name, over and over. *Lily, Lily, Lily –*

'Dad, stop it!'

Her scream echoes around the kitchen and he throws himself off me.

'Orla?' His face is white, his movements frantic as he pulls up his bottoms. 'What are you doing here?'

I roll on to my side and slowly push myself up to my feet. My body feels weak, as if all my energy has been drained away.

'What am I doing here?' Orla cries. 'What am I doing here? What are you doing to Lily?'

'Sweetheart,' he staggers towards her but she backs away, her back slamming against the wall. 'I'm so sorry that you had to see that but . . . Lily and I –'

'You what?'

'We like each other, sweetheart. Isn't that right, Lily?'

'It didn't look like she liked it – you were holding her down!'

'Tell her, Lily,' he says. He stares at me, his face twisted into a kind expression, the depths of his eyes still cold and empty.

I shake my head.

'You're lying!' Orla shouts at him.

'I-I just want to leave –'

I walk quickly towards the doors, but Michael runs around me, blocking my way.

'Let me go,' I cry.

'Dad, let her go!'

'I just want to make sure you're not going to tell people any lies,' he whispers.

'Let me go!'

My temper flares and I push out with both hands. He stumbles to one side and I try to run past him. He grabs me and I scream as his arms wrap around me, his chest pressed to my back.

'Get back here, you little bitch –'

'Dad, let her go!'

'Now, listen to me,' he says, his voice low and hot in my ear, his fingers tangled in my necklace which is cutting into my skin, firm against my windpipe. 'You're not going to say a word –'

'Leave her alone!' Orla shouts.

I start to nod, anything to be able to leave, to get out of here –

'Leave her alone!'

A scream, guttural and pain-fuelled, suddenly rings in my ears. Michael releases me and falls to the ground with a heavy thud. My necklace snaps.

I wheel around.

There is red everywhere.

Blood. Is that blood?

Michael is rolling around on the floor, his face contorted, his mouth torn in an agonized grimace.

'Michael?' I whisper, crouching down next to him. Blood is spilling out on to the floor from somewhere on his back; his breathing is so loud, so fast. My necklace is tangled in his fingers, clenched tightly in his fist.

I look up and Orla is standing above us, unblinking, a knife in her hands.

It drops to the floor.

'Orla?'

'I . . . I don't know . . .' she stammers. 'I didn't know what to do –'

I scramble to my knees, leaning forward over Michael. His

teeth are gritted together, his arm wrapped around his front to reach for the wound on the other side of his back.

My hands are shaking violently, my fingers dripping with thick, crimson blood. It's so dark. There's so much of it.

'Orla, get a towel or something, press it to his back.'

She doesn't move. She is simply staring down at her dad, trembling.

'Orla!'

She jumps at my shout and then runs around the island, pulling open a cupboard and grabbing a towel. She kneels next to him and pushes it into his back.

He screams, all the way from inside, a broken howl.

I place my hand down on the floor next to me, but something slips beneath my fingers.

The knife.

I grip the handle and move it aside.

'Lily,' Orla whispers. 'You . . . you need to leave –'

'I can't just leave you here.'

'Yes, you have to,' she whispers. 'I'll call an ambulance now, but you can't be here when they come.'

'I –'

'Lily, you weren't meant to be here in the first place. And you're already in trouble. Please, just go.'

'But what will you say –'

'Go!' she screams.

I push myself off the floor and stand, my feet moving quickly backwards towards the door, taking in the scene one final time: Orla kneeling over Michael, blood pumping out on to the floor.

And then I run.

36. Ava

The name, just a whisper, rings through the room, echoing like a shout.

'Orla stabbed her dad?' I ask. My mind has emptied, rendering me incapable of processing what she has said.

'Yes,' she whispers. 'I-I shouldn't have told you.' She pushes herself to her feet but I scramble up after her, reaching for her arm.

'Lily, wait, it's okay –'

'No, no, I shouldn't have told you. If he finds out –'

'It's okay. It's okay.' I hold her by the shoulders and finally she meets my eye. 'Just breathe. Look, do it with me –'

I inhale deeply and then let it go. She tries to copy me but her exhale rattles, choked.

'Again.'

She closes her eyes. Breathes in – and then out.

'Okay,' I whisper. 'Do you want to sit down?'

She shakes her head, wringing her hands.

'That's fine, we'll stand. I just want to ask some questions. I need to understand.'

She nods. Her gaze is almost pleading, desperate for comfort, for the answers that she cannot give herself.

'The evidence said that you were on your own with Michael. Was Orla actually there the whole time?'

'No. I knew that she was at her mum's that night, but Michael had told me I could go there whenever I wanted. That he wanted to look after me. He told me not to tell Orla that I was there but . . . I thought Franklin House might call her to find out if I was with her and she'd be worried. So, I messaged her saying that I was in trouble and had gone to her dad's house.'

'Did she message back?'

'No. Nothing.'

'When did she get there?'

'It was when he was . . .' Her eyes glaze over. 'When he was —'

'You don't have to say it. It's okay.'

She nods gratefully, a faint cry muffled through her closed lips.

The knife. Orla's fingerprints must have been on it. But Michael's would have been as well. It's their home – their prints would have been easily dismissed, but Lily's . . . Lily's would only do one thing – point towards her guilt.

'How did your prints get on the knife?'

She gasps, a deep, panicked inhale. 'I touched it. It was right next to me and I picked it up and threw it aside. I didn't think about it!'

I step forwards, closing the space between us, and tentatively place my arms around her. She flinches again, her whole body tense, but then she begins to cry – huge, overwhelmed sobs. 'It's okay,' I whisper, hushing her gently. I say it over and over again, until she falls still.

'I'm sorry,' she whispers, sniffing.

'Please – don't say that.'

She stares down at the floor, and she suddenly looks so much like a child. Her hands clasped in front of her chest, her ankles rolling outwards, ripped jeans and baby-faced. Just like any teenager. But so vulnerable. So broken.

'When did the police arrive? How long had it been since you left the house?'

'I don't know. No more than an hour.'

She raises her hand to her mouth and chews at her ragged nails, the black polish chipped to halfway down.

'Was there anything else, anything you can think of that could help you?'

'When you said you found something – before you told me about the photos – I thought you meant . . .' She sighs. 'H-he has my necklace.'

'Your necklace?'

'Yes.' Her fingers trace her collarbone, her eyes unfocused. 'Orla gave me a necklace . . . but he pulled it off.'

There was no mention of a necklace in the evidence. No trace of it at all. Just like when my bracelet was lost. We had assumed that it was just lost at the scene but . . . what if he took it?

'He must have hidden it,' I say.

She nods, her gaze still fixed on a distant memory.

'You went no comment in your interview. Why?'

'The lawyer told me to go no comment until they disclosed what evidence they had. So I did. I thought once they heard from Orla, it would be fine.' She rolls her eyes, shaking her head. 'I'm so fucking stupid.'

'You're not –'

'I am. I really believed that it was going to be okay. That it was just a mistake. But then they told me that Michael had said I had tried to kiss him and he'd pushed me away. And that he said he was going to call Anne and that's when I stabbed him. They said that Michael was in the house on his own. That no one else was there when the ambulance arrived. And that's when I knew.'

'He sent Orla home.'

She nods. 'He was never going to let her say a word. If it came out that she had done it then people would want to

246

know why. And as far as the police know, Orla was at her mum's that night.'

'Do you think her mum knows?'

'No. She wouldn't lie for Michael. She doesn't know that Orla left in the first place.'

'Did Orla sneak out?'

'Yes. And her mum goes out a lot, she has a new boy-friend. She left and got back without her mum ever knowing.'

She falls quiet with a small shrug and a glance over her shoulder, towards the door.

I'm losing her. It's there in her face – she's shutting down. Soon she won't want to talk any more. She'll leave.

'You should have said something in your interview. You need to do something, Lily,' I say. 'You can't just admit guilt for something you didn't do.'

'I can't do that to Orla.'

'Orla is letting you take the blame!'

'Do you think she has a choice?' she says pointedly. 'Really?'

I balk at her pointed expression – her blunt ability to see past all the complex layers of life to the harsh reality. Of course, Orla doesn't have a choice. Michael controls every-thing, he makes sure that everything always goes his way. That people succumb to his will, even strangers. By any means. And she is his daughter. How many children would speak out against their own father?

'I called her. Begged her to tell the truth but she said that she can't. And then Michael followed me, threatened me. He told me to leave Orla alone. Then he changed her number.'

That's what I saw when I followed him. His stern, cold face is so clear in my mind, his 'understand?' so crisp it's as if he's here this second, muttering it in my ear.

'You can tell the truth,' I say firmly. 'You need to tell the truth. If you say what really happened, they'll have to question Michael and Orla.'

She takes a few steps backwards, shaking her head. 'He said that even if I tell the truth, he has people who can make it go away.'

'People?' I move towards her.

'Yes . . . Police. He even said . . .'

'What did he say?'

'He said that he's done it before.'

My skin prickles. Everything I knew about what happened to me – the trial accidentally slipping through our fingers – shifts.

'Done it before?'

She nods. 'That's what he said. Do you think he meant you?'

'I . . . I don't know.'

'Maybe he was just trying to scare me.'

I grimace but try to morph my face into a reassuring smile. 'Maybe . . .'

The clouds shift again and sun filters once more into the dank room. I glance at my watch.

'Lily, you need to go home – your curfew.'

'What time is it?'

'Half six. I can take you.'

'I like the walk,' she says.

'Are you sure? I don't mind.'

'Thanks. I'm sure.'

'Please think about what I've said,' I say. 'Here . . .' I delve into my bag and pull out my pen and notebook. I scribble down my phone number and then tear it out, pressing the scrap into her hand. 'I can help you. And Marissa can help you. You can't just give up.'

'Who would believe me? All the evidence is there. And I know how they see me . . . This is easier.' She shrugs, smiling sadly. 'Don't you get it? I'm exhausted. I just want this to be over. My guilty plea means I'll spend however long in a young offenders and then it'll be over –'

'*Over*? What happens in two days will affect the rest of your life. Having a stabbing on your record will never be over –'

'But if I change my plea, I'll have to wait months and months for a trial. And then I'll have to stand there and listen while people call me a liar. I'll have to listen as people say that he never touched me, that it was *my* fault, that I forced myself on him. And I'll make Orla choose between lying or going against her dad. And we both know what will happen.' She shakes her head firmly, her eyes hard and resolute. 'I can't do it.'

'Lily –'

'Thank you for trying to help me. Really. I'm sorry that you've lost so much. And I'm sorry that it was such a waste.'

And with that, her dismissal hanging in the air, she leaves, her feet dragging across the concrete floor, her head hanging low.

I crouch back down as my legs weaken, and my chin falls forward against my chest. I thought that once I knew the truth, I could convince her to speak up. But I haven't. And . . .

I don't blame her.

If I could have spared myself everything that happened by staying silent, would I? I could have avoided the trauma of being called a liar, the questions in court, watching as he was acquitted, the names, the fights, losing all of my friends, my family, myself, the guilt . . . I've seen countless trials collapse before my eyes and the victims who choose not to give evidence, who change their story days later, saying they were confused or he didn't mean it . . . It happens all the time.

People choose, or are forced, to let a part of them die with the truth. Maybe, if I had known how it would end, I would have chosen differently.

But then what is the point of any of this? What is the point of justice? Why should the victim stay silent and let monsters – people like Michael Osborne – get away with it?

He did this to me. *He* did this to Lily.

We weren't to blame. Not me. Not her.

Him.

He has people who can make it go away. He's done it before.

PC Hart. My clothes being contaminated. The evidence being inadmissible.

What if it wasn't a mistake at all?

This question swirls around my mind the whole drive home. I try to find my way through, but it is like quicksand pulling me under, and I'm unable to move. The more I struggle against it, the faster I sink.

Exhaustion makes every movement heavy as I climb the stairs to the flat. My eyes are heavy, my legs filled with lead. The door swings open and relief washes over me as it closes again, locking behind me.

Home.

Safe.

But tingles of fear creep up my arms – there are footsteps in the bedroom.

I press my back to the door.

My hand reaches sideways and I wrap my fingers around the handle, readying myself to run.

The bedroom door opens –

'Hello, gorgeous.'

I burst into tears as his face appears.

Will.

He's home.

37. Ava

I finish speaking and everything falls quiet. The only noise is the sound of the rain thrumming down on the pavement outside and quiet, faraway thunder. The storm came on quickly. Will's face is still, a small wrinkle appearing on the bridge of his nose, his frown creating lines in his face that aren't usually there, his laughter lines disappearing.

'Will,' I whisper. 'Say something.'

He looks down, his teeth scratching at his bottom lip, his head tilted slightly to the side. It's as if he's biding his time, thinking through what he's going to say. How to respond to an entire history he didn't know I had.

'Please –'

'When will you know if they're letting you go completely?' he asks, not quite meeting my eye, his gaze fixed on something just past my shoulder.

'I'm not sure. They haven't said. They've just said there's an investigation. But . . .'

'But?'

'I don't think I'll be allowed back. I don't think I'll be allowed to practise again. The Bar Standards Board –'

'You think they'll disbar you?'

I nod, chewing on the inside of my cheek. 'I think so. I can't see them letting me carry on.'

He expels his breath in a gentle huff and rocks his head back, his face turned up to the ceiling. He closes his eyes, that line still there, creasing his forehead. He looks so sad. So hurt. I didn't mean to hurt him. I never wanted him to have to deal with any of this.

I did it for myself. Because I felt compelled to do something.

So selfish. I'm so selfish.

'Will, I'm sorry. I'm sorry that I kept it a secret. I should have told you what happened to me, I just –'

'You think I'm upset about that?' he asks, his eyes now fixed on me, anger seeping into his irises.

'I –'

'I'm not angry you didn't tell me about what that animal did to you. I'm not surprised that you felt more comfortable acting like it had never happened. I'm so sorry, Ava.'

He lifts his hand to my face, but then flinches, retracting his fingers like I have burned him.

'I'm angry that when he came back into your life, you lied to me. All those nights on your phone, those times when you were out late at work or out for dinner with Marissa – you were with him. And you lied to me so easily. As if it was nothing.'

'How could I tell you? How was I supposed to tell you that I was doing something so crazy? You would have –'

'You don't trust me.' Will says the words so simply, a blanket statement, but his face is full of shock. As if he has just realized the true extent of my betrayal. 'You didn't tell me,' he continues, 'because you didn't trust me to stay.'

'No,' I say, reaching for his hand, but he pulls it away, his gaze turning dark. 'I wanted to tell you, I did, but I was scared that it would change the way you thought about me –'

'Why would it?' he shouts. 'I love you, Ava. All I've ever done is try to show you how much I love you. We've built a life together. I've tried to support you with work, with your mum . . . I adore you. I always have, ever since the first time

I saw you. We're supposed to be getting married.' He throws his hands up. 'I don't actually know anything about you. Do I?'

'You do –'

'No. I don't. I didn't know why your relationship with your mum was so bad. You told me she blamed you for your dad leaving, but you . . . you let me believe that your dad just left! But he's in prison!'

'I . . . I'm sorry,' I cry.

'What happened? What did he do? He's been in there for years . . . there's only so many offences that . . .' His eyes widen, his mouth dropping open. He's realized. 'Did he kill someone?'

My breath catches in my chest. It's been eighteen years, but I'm reminded of that day every time I hear the rush of a train; the loud warning signal blaring. Dad's eyes appear in my mind, his face changing, his usually calm exterior being consumed by anger.

'Ava! Is he in prison for murder?'

I lift my chin and then nod, my head heavy.

'It . . . it was an accident.'

He inhales sharply. 'Who was it?'

My lip trembles. He had a family. A wife. A young baby.

'PC Hart,' I whisper, a pounding heat beginning to burn my temples. 'The police officer who contaminated the DNA evidence.'

'What did he do? How did it happen?'

'I don't want to talk about Dad now, please, we need to talk about us –'

'I need to know, Ava!'

'I can't talk about it –'

'Apparently you can't talk to me about anything,' he shouts. 'I know nothing about you. I don't know you at all!'

'That isn't true,' I shake my head, tears streaming down my face.

'If your dad's released, what were you going to tell me then?'

'I –'

'More lies! You would have told me more lies!'

His voice breaks and he hangs his head, his chest heaving. In all our years together, Will's anger has never been directed my way. His frustration, maybe, but never his anger. That is an emotion he saves for other people.

'Did he touch you?'

I stare at him through tears, his face blurred. 'What?'

'This time, now – did he touch you?'

'Will –'

'Fuck.' He grimaces, his mouth trembling. 'He didn't –'

'No.'

He looks up at me, heartbreak in his gaze. 'How far would you have gone? If he didn't find out?'

'No further, I –'

'Really?'

'I promise. I felt sick being around him, but I just . . . I thought I was doing the right thing.'

'I mean . . . what other secrets are you keeping from me?'

My mouth falls open, but I say nothing.

He looks at me with sudden disdain. He sniffs again then pinches the bridge of his nose, rubbing his eyes. He stands then nods his head assertively, just once.

He's made a decision.

'Ava –'

I rush to my feet. 'No, please don't –'

'I think I'm going to go and stay with Jamal for a bit.'

'Will –'

'No,' he says, throwing my hand off his arm. 'I need space. I need to process what . . . what you've done.'

'Please don't leave me –'

I reach for him and he tries to back away, but I throw myself on to his chest, my tears seeping into his T-shirt. His arms hang loosely at his sides.

'Ava, let go of me.'

My sobs grow louder at his toneless command, his quiet anger. He reaches around his back and unclasps my fingers, removing my arms from around his waist. Walking quickly into the bedroom, he comes straight back out, the bag from his trip not yet unpacked. He strides to the door and I follow behind him helplessly, my eyes pleading, begging for him to change his mind. To stay with me.

'When will I see you again?' I cry as he steps outside.

'Ava, don't make this harder, please –'

'But I love you.'

He pauses, his fingers clutching the handle, his eyes fixed on me. But he simply shakes his head and closes the door.

38. Ava

My fingers are laced together, my palms clammy from the sweltering heat of the visitors' hall.

I need to speak to someone – and there's only one person left who will listen.

Dad.

The prison is near Oxford – an old Victorian building, the central watch tower looming over the nearby houses. Mum and I used to come together, but after a while she stopped, choosing to come on her own, or not at all.

He has people who make it go away. Police. He said he's done it before.

We've always believed it was a mistake: an unforgivable and preventable mistake, but a mistake nonetheless. Human error.

But did Hart do it on purpose? Did he know what would happen?

Did he care?

A door behind me creaks open and men begin to file in. I sit up, my neck stretching as I search for his face. I smile as I see him, and he spots me, smiling back. He looks better than last time; he's put on weight, his face fuller.

I stand up, glancing at the guard standing near our table, who nods quickly. Holding out my arms, I step into his hug, my head pressed sideways against his chest, like always. In his arms, I am safe. A little girl again.

'Hi, Dad,' I breathe.

'Hello, darling,' he says.

We separate and sit either side of the table that has been reserved for our visit.

'You don't normally visit on Thursdays,' he says.

'I know. I called first thing and they said there was space.'

'I'm glad. It's so good to see your face.'

'Yours too.' I sniff as I feel tears coming, like water filling a well all the way to the brim.

'How are you?' he asks, his eyes peering into mine. 'How's Will?'

Will. I haven't been able to get his face out of my mind, his anger and disappointment. I lay in bed last night, staring at his side, wondering if he'll ever fill the space again, my body aching with missing him. Is he going to come back? Or will I have to miss him forever?

'I . . . he's fine, Dad.'

'How's your mum?' he continues, although I can see in his face that he doesn't believe me.

'She's . . . the same, Dad. It's not great between us.'

He clears his throat, his eyes shining.

'I'm sorry, Dad.'

'It's okay, darling.'

'No . . . I'm sorry for everything.' My voice wavers and he glances quickly at the guard before reaching for my hand.

'Please, don't get upset. You know I can't see you upset, Ava.'

'I know. But . . . so much has happened since I last saw you and it's made me realize that . . .'

He frowns. 'Made you realize what?'

'Maybe it would have been better if I'd just stayed quiet –'

'What?' His face screws up, bewildered. 'No. Never. You told the truth and that's all you could do.'

'But you're here because of me –'

'Stop that. Now.'

I flinch, my tears stopping, shocked by his change in tone. 'Never say that,' he whispers. 'Never.'

The day PC Hart was killed feels like a fever dream – the colours too bright, the memory at times too vivid and then disappearing to nothing.

We were on the way home from a meeting at my new school, the one I was going to after my old school had become unbearable. After I'd . . . after I'd tried to kill myself. We'd met with the counsellor and the headmistress – the only two people at the school who were told what had happened. Dad had taken me on the train instead of driving – he wanted to show me that my friends could still come and see me at our new house, it was only a short journey away, I didn't have to lose them all. Not if I didn't want to.

But that's when we saw him. The train came to a stop at Shire Green, an almost unused station in a tiny village, the stop before ours – and there he was. PC Hart. Getting off the train and coming to a halt on the empty platform, smiling down at his phone. Dressed in his uniform. Going about his usual life as if nothing had happened. We were changing our entire lives, but he –

There were no repercussions. None. He hadn't even lost his job.

A loud bleeping noise filled the carriage, warning us that the doors would soon close, and my heart hammered away, keeping its fast rhythm.

'Belle,' Dad said. There was a strange lilt to his voice, a warning.

'It's Ava now, Dad. Remember?' I said, my voice shaking.

His face reflected mine – rapidly brewing anger. And then . . .

The sound of the doors bleeping shut. Dad running through the gap. Me, panicked, following behind him. Dad shouting. Struggle. The fast train approaching, the one that doesn't stop. A scream. My cries. Dad! What have you done?

A loud clang echoes around the visitors' hall.

I jump and look over my shoulder to where a guard has closed the gate that leads out to the wings. I blink myself back into the present, away from the blazing sunshine of the platform, and back to the stark fluorescence of the prison.

'Dad, it's just . . .' I lick my lips, sniffing loudly, my throat tight with emotion. 'If I hadn't said anything, none of this would have happened. Mum would be fine. We all would have stayed together. I wouldn't have had our names plastered everywhere. I'd still be Anabelle King. And you . . . you wouldn't be in here.'

'I'm here, Ava, because of a choice I made. What happened to you was horrific – and just because he was acquitted, that doesn't mean that you should have stayed quiet. '

'Mum blames me –'

'Your mother is wrong.'

'She wishes I'd stayed quiet. What good came from me telling the truth?' I say, frustration bursting out of me in a shout. A man at the table next to us, sitting across the table from a woman, his wife, turns to glare at me. Dad raises a gentle finger to his lips.

'Sorry . . .' I sigh. 'Nothing good ever came from it. He got away with what he did. Nothing about his life changed. The only effect the truth had was ripping our family to pieces.'

'Ava, you've worked your whole adult life to become a prosecutor because you believe in the exact opposite of what you're saying. You were a victim. And you believe that victims should be heard. Don't you?'

I nod, biting down on my lip.

'So, what's going on?'

Staring down at the table, I take in the scratches and etchings of names on its surface, the evidence of countless people who have sat in this hall, visiting or being visited, unable to comprehend how they ever ended up here.

'I've seen him,' I whisper.

'Seen him? Seen who?'

I bite down on my lip to stop myself from crying.

'Michael Osborne.'

He gasps, a slight intake of breath. 'What do you mean, you've seen him?'

'I . . . Dad, I've ruined everything.'

'I don't understand.'

The story spills out of me, every detail, every message, every glance and soul-crushing touch. I scratch at the table as I speak, every so often glancing up at him. He sits silently, listening carefully as I explain, his expression fixed in place.

I stop – there is no more story to tell. But he doesn't say anything. He just stares at me blankly.

'Dad . . . Say something.'

'I . . .' He clasps his hand in front of his face, his mouth resting against his thumb. 'I can't believe you did that.'

'I know, but this girl –'

'I understand why you did it. I do, I really do. But I can't believe you did.'

'She . . . she also told me that her necklace snapped off, but the police never found it or mentioned it in evidence. She thinks he has it.' I press my lips together, watching as Dad's eyes narrow. 'What if he took my bracelet? What if he has them hidden away like . . . like –'

'Keepsakes.' Dad's lip curls.

'What if what he told Lily is true? What if this is bigger

260

than just him? He said that he has police who can help him. He said he's done it before. We've always thought that the mistake with my dress was just human error, but –'

'Ava, you know how manipulative Michael Osborne is.' He raises an eyebrow. 'He's clearly trying to manipulate her into sticking with her guilty plea.'

'But what if Hart contaminated the evidence on purpose? What if?'

He rubs his lips with his knuckles, deep in thought. 'Well . . . If he did, he paid for it dearly. And so did I.'

I nod slowly and wipe away a tear. Even if Hart was helping Michael, even if it was all part of a plan – he didn't deserve to die.

Dad sighs. 'When is she being sentenced?'

'Tomorrow. After that she can't change her plea . . . it'll be too late.'

'And you can't convince her to tell the truth?'

'She's adamant. She wants it to be over.'

He sits back in his chair, rolling his neck in a wide circle before lifting both hands, palms up.

'Well, there's nothing you can do, then.'

'But what if I –'

An incredulous look flickers on Dad's face. 'No, Ava.'

'Listen –'

'Ava, I can see what you want to do. I know you. Even after all these years apart, all the time I've spent in here, I know you, deep down. You're an incredible person and you worked so hard to achieve what you have after so much trauma, but . . . you're still so angry. And because of that you've let him ruin your life again.' He shakes his head. 'Don't do anything stupid: you know he's a dangerous man. And I almost lost you once – if anything was to happen to you –'

'Dad, I –'

'What do you think revenge is going to achieve? Look at where we are. Look at me. I've been here for eighteen years. And you know I don't blame you – it was my decision – but what life have I had?' He stabs his finger pointedly on the table. 'That's where revenge got us.'

'But . . . this isn't about revenge.'

He sighs, his face awash with sadness. 'Then what is this about?'

I pause, my nails finishing the letters that I have been scratching into the wood. My initials.

A.K.

'Justice.'

39. Ava

His headlights turn on, the beams flooding down the drive to the road.

I slump down in the driver's seat. He accelerates quickly, turns left on to the road and disappears into the distance.

Avoiding my reflection in the window, I climb out of my car, closing the door gently. I can't stop to think about what I'm going to do. I just need to get inside.

It's his home – his sanctuary. And home is the one place where people truly let down their guard. We see it all the time in criminal cases – people's comfort gives them a sense of security. Their judgement lapses. And if he can hide photos of her in his hotel room, I need to know what he has hiding in his home. What if there's proof that could help Lily? Something that could finally convince her to break her silence.

And what if there's something inside that could help me? What if I could prove that all those years ago, I wasn't lying? A guilty man walked away and has lived among us, silently stalking, all too ready to pounce when he holds the power – and nobody believed me.

I dash across the road. My body feels strange, like I am not in it – as though I am watching another woman who looks just like me, about to do this dangerous, illegal act. I'm hovering just above myself, a spectator to what I am about to do. But I could stop myself, if I really wanted to. Dad would tell me to stop. So would George. And Will.

But I don't want to.

I reach the top of the drive and squeeze through the small gap between the wall and the planter. I scramble around, feeling for the key . . . She definitely got it from here. Where is —

My fingers clasp around the damp metal. I straighten up, squinting at it, and smile as it sparkles in the refracted light from the porch.

Thank you, Orla.

Pushing the key into the lock, I hold my breath — waiting for the loud blare of the alarm.

It sounds, calling out to alert listeners to an intruder's presence. I rush across to the panel, my fingers tingling.

Zero —

Four—

One —

Two.

The house is shrouded in an abrupt silence.

I don't know how long he'll be gone. I waited and waited, hoping that he would leave. My eyes wander up the long staircase, scanning the closed doors in the hallway. But the door in the furthest corner of the hall pulls my gaze. His studio.

There was a safe down there.

I look down the steep stairs, the dark opening like a wide-open mouth, ready to consume me. I place one foot on the first step, then the next step down, then another, slowly lowering myself into the void.

It's pitch-black down here, so dark that I can barely see my hand in front of my face. I pull off my rucksack and reach inside, then pull out the torch.

Its narrow beam wavers in my shaking hand.

The safe was under his desk.

I walk quickly over and crouch down, shining the torch at

the safe door. But this isn't like the safe at the hotel – an electronic lock and keypad. This has a dial and a hundred lines around the outside, each minuscule etch of the wheel signifying a new possibility of combinations.

What if it isn't the same?

I reach out and grip the dial, turning it quickly through the numbers.

Zero. Four. One. Two.

I pull the handle.

It doesn't open.

Shit.

What else would he use?

What else would a man like Michael Osborne use?

His date of birth?

No.

I close my eyes.

Think. I just need to think.

As much as I don't want to, I know this man. Not the details of his life, the intricacies of his day to day, but him. I know who he is, deep down. And what he is. He is only about himself: a narcissist, to the very bone.

His hotel. The Osborne Suite. His numberplate: 05B 0RN3.

I reach out and slowly click around the numbers, focusing intently as I count through the alphabet.

O . . . 15.

S . . . 19.

B . . . 2.

O . . . 15.

R . . . 18.

N . . . 14.

E . . . 5.

Click.

I grip the handle again and twist –

The door jolts open.

I'm barely breathing, my head pounding at the temples as I peer inside the large metal box.

Stacked one on top of the other, are plain-brown manilla files. Some thicker than others. I pull out the one on top and flick through the contents. It looks like bills for the restaurant, payslips.

I place it on the floor beside me and retrieve the next file down. But as I focus the light on the cover, the beam shines across two letters on the card, imprinted in black marker.

A. K.

My initials.

The skin on the back of my neck prickles, and my teeth begin to chatter, as though I've been plunged into icy water, unable to find my footing.

I slowly open the file.

My breath catches at the picture on the first page.

Our messages. The messages I sent him and he sent back. He's printed them, made copies.

The next document is my entry on the Barristers' Register. My photo, my qualifications.

And then, newspaper clippings. My teeth grind against each other as I look at the headlines from all those years ago. *The Girl Who Cried Rape. Young Photographer of the Year Acquitted. Son of Jeremiah Osborne, Michael Osborne, Falsely Accused. The Daughter Who Lied, The Father Who Killed?* It tore my life apart to read these, my heart breaking under the weight of my shame and he –

He kept them. Like a record of achievement.

I push the papers back into the file and return it to the safe.

Does Lily have a file too?

Reaching for the next file down, I aim the light at the

cover, searching for a name or initials. And there they are again: thick, black letters.

G. C.

I frown, rubbing my lips together as I flip open the file. This one is stuffed full of documents.

I scan the front page: another photo.

But the faces staring up at me . . . don't make sense.

I lift it up, raising it close to my face, the paper shaking violently.

In the photograph is a young boy standing on a rugby field: dark hair, the same mole on his cheek. *Michael.* He can't be more than ten.

But crouching down next to him, his arm around Michael's shoulders, his face not wrinkled with age, his hair not grey, but blond . . .

George.

G. C.

George Cavanaugh.

40. Lily

Now

Ava's words haven't left my mind. They've been playing on an endless loop, repeating again and again. Sometimes, a mocking taunt; other times, a rallying cheer.

You can't give up.

I've tried to shut it out but as soon as my brain stops buzzing, her whisper is there again. But I need to ignore her. The sentencing is tomorrow and then it will be over.

Having a stabbing on your record will never be over.

I shake my head, pressing my fists into my eyes. My head is throbbing.

'Lily?' My name is followed by a gentle knock.

'Come in.'

The door opens and Anne's concerned face appears. 'Are you okay in here, love?'

I nod. 'I've just got a headache.'

'Well, try and get some sleep. Maybe an early night tonight?'

'Okay. I will.'

She smiles and then closes the door, her footsteps retreating down the corridor.

I lie back on my bed, lifting my phone above my face.

Her message is there, still on the screen, the unknown number at the top.

I'm so sorry. I hope you can forgive me one day. I didn't want to. O x

Orla. From a new number.

And my response:

> I know. It's okay. It's not too late to help me xxx

Nausea sloshed in my stomach as soon as I sent it. He told me not to speak to her again. He warned me.

What would Michael say if he found out? What would he do?

I trace my hand over the words in her message – her apology crying out through the screen. But I've never blamed her. I've always known that she had no choice. She'll never be able to tell the truth, though. He won't allow that. And who would believe us? Two teenage girls suddenly coming up with a defence?

But she's the best friend I've ever had. If she hadn't been there . . .

Her message is everything. A simple text – but an act of rebellion.

My phone vibrates.

It's her number flashing in the centre . . . She's calling me.

'Orla?'

She doesn't answer. But the line is open, the sound of breathing rustling in the receiver.

'Orla? Are you there?'

A pause.

'Come to the window.'

My stomach drops. The voice isn't her soft, well-spoken lilt. It's deep, a sinister growl.

'M-Michael?'

'Come to the window.'

I stand, the phone pressed to my ear, my breath shallow. I pull my curtain open, just the tiniest bit, and peek out through the gap to the road below.

His car is there, parked on Malthouse Road, directly opposite. And he is facing the house.

'I can see you,' he says.

I close the curtain, shaking my head quickly from side to side.

'Come outside.'

'I . . . I can't,' I stammer.

'Why not? Just quickly come outside – no one will notice, I'll meet you around the corner.'

'What do you want? And why have you got Orla's phone?'

He sighs. 'I thought we agreed that you wouldn't speak to Orla again?'

'We didn't agree that. We never agreed anything –'

'Lily – calm down.'

'No! Why have you got her phone?'

'She's got another new one now. She knows she shouldn't have messaged you. She won't contact you again. And you're not going to try to reach her either, are you, Lily?'

I stay silent and close my eyes. His breathing rattles.

'Lily? There's nothing anyone can help you with. That's what we agreed – this is what's best for everyone, right? And do you really want to ruin Orla's life? Besides . . . no one will believe you. So don't be foolish now. You'll be a good girl, now – right?'

You can't give up.

There it is again: Ava's voice in my ear. No longer a whisper. Now, a command: a war-cry.

'No,' I mutter.

'What did you say?'

'I said, no!'

I stab my finger at the screen, ending the phone call. Closing my eyes, I remain at the window, my knees locked, the muscles in my legs tremoring.

I listen. And after a few minutes, the car rolls away, the engine loud on the quiet street.

I can't give up. Not now.

Never again.

I reach across my bed and pull open the bedside drawer. The scrap of paper is lying there, staring up at me. With shaking hands, I tap the number into my phone and scroll through my address book.

The dial-tone rings but there's no answer.

'Hi, you've reached the voicemail of Ava Knight. I can't come to the phone right now but please leave a message and I'll get back to you. Thanks. Bye.'

I wait for the beep, a lump at the back of my throat.

Beep.

'Hi . . . Ava, it's Lily. You said I could call you and I . . . I wanted to tell you that . . .'

I inhale deeply – after this, there's no going back.

'I want to change my plea.' My teeth chatter as emotion overwhelms me, sudden tears streaming down my face. 'I'm going to contact my solicitor now . . . I want to tell the truth. I just hope it's not too late.'

I look out of the window at the night sky, teeming with stars.

'I hope that they'll believe me.'

41. Ava

My phone vibrates in the bottom of my bag, long and low. A voicemail. But I can't tear my eyes away from the photo lying innocently on the floor, the image searing itself into my mind.

Michael and George?

Even if I tell the truth, he has people who can make it go away.

People?

Police. He even said he's done it before.

I cry out and the photo drops to the floor, the weight of the revelation too heavy to hold on to.

It wasn't PC Hart. It was never him. He was manipulated, along with the rest of us. George must have contaminated my dress before it was given to PC Hart to process for testing.

It was George.

It was George all along. And an innocent man was blamed in his place. An innocent man was killed.

My stomach turns violently, and acid stings the back of my throat. I clamp my hands across my mouth, my eyes burning as I blink rapidly up at the grey ceiling.

No. This can't be real. That can't be George, not my George, the man who has been in my life all these years, helping me, supporting me, giving me advice. My oldest friend. It can't be him. It can't have been him.

The file is still balanced on my knees. I take a breath and look down at the papers. Just like my file, there's messages, but this isn't just a couple of pages. There are hundreds of messages, emails – all printed out, sorted in date order. I quickly rifle through the pages.

The air leaves my lungs as if someone has punched me. There are messages here all the way back to the trial. All from an unknown number: a burner phone. Short sentences, just a few words at the most. Updates.

> It's done.
> Evidence sent.
> Report filed.

They were in communication the whole time. George helped him. He made sure Michael went free. And Michael has kept the evidence. George can't ever say anything against Michael because if he does, Michael has the power to drag George down with him.

He said it himself: the one thing that everybody wants is power. And locked away in this safe, he has it hidden away in files. Secrets give him power. They give him control.

Heat runs up my spine, flushing my whole body with a burning anger. My hands start to tremble, my eyes blurring as shock takes over.

George's smiling face appears, his arms around me as he pulls me into a hug, his gruff voice telling me that he's never been so proud.

He was never my friend.

I bite down on my lip as hot tears run down my cheeks.

If this goes wrong, if you push this too far, you could lose everything. And I won't be able to help you.

George tried to deter me from looking further into what happened to Lily. He tried to convince me that she was guilty, that I was letting my hatred for Michael contaminate my perspective. Did he help Michael this time too? Is that why he was so insistent?

The case against Lily flips through my mind, the evidence appearing, slide after slide after slide.

The phone records.

The phone call.

There was a phone call to an unknown number just fifteen minutes before the police were called. What if . . . what if they called George? While Michael was lying bleeding on the floor, a stab wound to his back, who was it who decided to send Orla back to her mum's house? Who was it who conjured the plan to blame Lily? It can't have been Michael alone . . . What if they called George and asked for help?

The truth is blinding, a bright white spotlight illuminating the dark. George helped him before, and he helped him again. Two innocent girls' lives left in tatters, and all this time he was helping him –

A loud slam echoes down the stairs.

My body roots me to the spot. I grip the torch, my knuckles turning white, the beam bouncing around the ceiling and the walls. I quickly click the button and the torch goes out, plunging me into darkness.

His voice is echoing around the hall, his words unclear.

He's talking to someone.

Is someone with him?

My ears strain, desperate to hear another voice. But there is nothing – just his mutters, then pauses before he mutters again. He's on the phone.

My hands scramble with the papers, hurriedly placing them back inside the file. I clutch it to my chest and close the door of the safe, holding my breath as I turn the handle and the lock snaps into place.

I stand, the muscles in my legs burning, tightening, readying me to run. But run where? Where can I go?

Michael's voice is getting louder, his words clearer, and one word floats down the stairs, decipherable from the rest.

Lily.

Slowly, I tiptoe across the floor, moving closer to the bottom of the stairs. I clamp my hand across my mouth, my breath hot and shaky against my fingers.

'Something's happened, something has changed –'

Silence.

'No! She isn't listening any more. And when I asked her if she was going to be a good girl, she said no.'

Silence as he listens.

'Stop saying it's going to be okay You don't know that, George.'

I gasp. Why is George doing this? Why is he protecting a man like Michael?

'Okay . . . Okay. Bye.'

A shadow appears on the stairs. Footsteps.

My feet frantically move backwards, my eyes darting about in the dark, searching for a place to hide.

The darkroom.

I open the door, throw myself inside and push it to, but it doesn't close completely.

A sliver of light shines into my hiding place and his feet thud around the studio. I hold my breath. Each of his steps sounds as if it's right next to me, his breathing as if it's in my ear, rustling my hair.

I jump as something loud bangs, like he's dropped something or placed something heavy on the floor. Moving forward, I peer through the gap, frowning. He has rolled up the white screen that creates his studio space. Behind the screen is a wall of large, wide cupboards. And one is open. But the panel at the back of it has been taken out and placed on the floor, revealing a cavity behind.

He is looking at his phone, his thumb pushing down on the top – turning it off. He then reaches into the wall, his arm disappearing downwards and returning empty, like a magic trick. He replaces the panel. Closes the cupboard.

He glances over his shoulder towards the darkroom.

I back away quickly, my hands reaching sideways to prevent myself from colliding with anything. I grab on to something – feels like a bench – and move around it, crouching down quickly.

Footsteps.

My breathing sounds so loud, he's going to hear me, he's going to find me –

I press my hand to my mouth again, holding my breath. But my teeth begin to chatter.

More footsteps. The click of a light switch. Darkness.

The rhythmic thud, thud, thud as he climbs the stairs again.

I stay in the dark, alone, small whimpers escaping my lips as fear floods through me. I rise to my feet but the black mass before my eyes spins, exploding with bright spots of colour.

How am I going to get out of here?

The basement isn't too far from the front door. As long as he's upstairs or in the back when I emerge out into the hall, I should be able to leave without him realizing.

George's file is still pressed against my chest, my arms bending the pristine documents. Could I take it with me? I can't use it to prove anything but . . . I could use it to get George to tell the truth. I could use it for the very purpose Michael created it in the first place: blackmail. I could turn his own weapons against him.

I open the door and step out of the darkroom. Clicking the torch on, I turn towards the stairs, but my eyes are drawn to the white wall.

I need to leave . . . But I can't. He hid his burner phone inside that wall. What else could be in there, secreted away, waiting to be found?

I stare back at the door, my body torn in two directions. But I rush forward, my feet carrying me towards the white wall.

I set George's file on the floor. Opening the cupboard, I crouch down and reach to the back. Running my hand along the edge of the back panel, I feel for something to grip onto. Finally, in the top right-hand corner, it is there, a slight indent, rough and worn. I slide my finger into it, wincing as my nail is pressed between the panel and the wall, and pull forward. It comes away, revealing the true wall behind.

I place it down on the floor carefully, quietly, leaning the top edge against the adjacent cupboard.

My hands are damp, fear seeping from my skin as I reach down into the cavity. I close my hand around something rectangular, plastic – the phone. I pull it out and place it quietly on the floor, glancing quickly at the stairs, my heart hammering in my chest.

Hurry.

Returning to the cupboard, I push myself forward, my shoulder wedging into the space inside. There's something there, just out of reach. I grit my teeth, growling with frustration as my arm scrapes on the boarding, and stretch.

'Come on,' I whisper.

My fingers finally clasp around a file. No – an envelope. I pull it out and place it on the floor before scrambling around inside again, my movements becoming more frantic. He could come back down here at any moment. I graze something else, something round, medium sized. A box.

Setting it down on the floor next to the envelope, I gaze down at my two discoveries. An envelope. And a box.

My hand reaches for the envelope first.

Is it more photos of Lily? Messages? Threats?

I pull out the sheets slowly, and the top of a head appears, blonde hair sliding out from the white envelope. But my breath catches in my throat as the picture fully emerges, her face becoming clear.

It isn't Lily. I don't recognize this girl at all. Her uniform is different – navy blue and white. Her skin is tanned, olive. She is smiling, completely unaware that she is being photographed.

The next photo is another girl. Red hair. Pale skin. Green eyes.

The next is brunette, tight curls, dark skin.

The next –

And then –

Girl after girl after girl. All teenagers. All young and naive and blind. Are these girls he's approached already? That he plans on approaching? Or does he just watch? He took photos of Lily months before he assaulted her. These are his preparatory acts – the warm-up before he takes the next step.

Hands over my mouth. Strong arms pushing down. Legs kicking. Blue eyes. Dress ripping. Hands on my thighs. Pressure. Fear. Stillness.

Tears sting my cheeks, but I clamp my teeth together. How many girls has he done this to? How many girls have been transformed into victims because he was acquitted?

I draw in a juddering breath and turn back to the photos. At the bottom of the pile is a folded piece of paper, worn and faded with age. Different to the other photographs. I open it slowly, bracing myself for another innocent face.

I drop the paper, and my mouth stretches open in a shocked silent howl.

It's me.

Fourteen-year-old Anabelle King. Hair still blonde and

long, glasses, full cheeks, black school skirt and white shirt, blazer dangling at my side, walking home from school along the riverside. Still naive. Still innocent.

Realization ploughs into me, a speeding train out of nowhere. What he did to me wasn't random. It wasn't an attack of impulse like we always believed. It was premeditated. He'd followed me. He'd chosen me . . . just like the others.

My eyes slowly, fearfully, shift to the round box. I reach out, my hand trembling violently, and pull off the lid.

It can't be.

Inside, is Lily's necklace. Shiny and new. The silver still sparkles, her birthstone green in the light of my torch. But next to it, dull with age . . . is my bracelet. I hold it up to my face. Yes – there it is – the engraving on the inside of the metal.

My bracelet. He's had it all these years. He's kept it, like some sick fucking medal: evidence of what he did – an award for what he got away with. But my bracelet and Lily's necklace aren't alone. Nestled in the box is a hairclip – a slide dotted with fake pearls. A school prefect badge. A flower.

What can I do? Someone needs to see this; I need to do something. Here, laid out at my feet, is the proof I've needed all these years –

'Hello?'

My head snaps towards the entrance. His shadow is there again, falling down the stairs. I hold my breath.

Silence.

'I know you're down there.'

42. Ava

He's coming.

Stay still. Quiet. He doesn't really know there's anyone down here.

I hold my breath, completely exposed.

Just stay completely still.

He thuds down on to the first step.

Hide.

Adrenalin zings through me and my body takes over, my mind falling quiet and empty. I don't have time to put this all away. My hands reach for the box and the photographs, and I run to the opposite wall where a long work bench is covered in equipment. I crouch down behind it, squeezing myself into a gap behind a tall spotlight.

The quiet shivers over me, my body flinching at the only sound – his footsteps on the stairs.

His feet appear first, then his legs, his torso. And suddenly he is in full view, standing on the bottom step, illuminated by the light spilling down from the hallway. A click sounds and I am no longer hidden by the dark of the windowless room. My shoulders curl forwards, my chest pressed against my knees as I make myself as small as possible.

But he isn't even looking this way. His eyes are fixed on the other side of the room, his intense stare set on the scattering of papers on the floor.

He strides across, his paces long and purposeful, his fingers in tight fists. He crouches down, his back to me, and his hands hover above the papers, not touching anything. Just staring.

Soon he will move. He'll find me.

I can't stay here.

I slowly turn my head. It isn't too far to the stairs – I could creep across slowly . . . or just make a run for it.

Glancing back at him, my mouth falls open. He is holding the burner phone which is now lit up. What is he doing? Is he calling the police?

'George, you need to come to my house, right now,' he whispers. My heart sinks. 'I think she's here . . .'

My eyes grow round, my ears straining – but I can't make out what George is saying in response; all that echoes out of the phone is a faint low rumble.

'What do you mean, who? I mean Anabelle.'

Another pause. My hands are shaking, my legs screaming, begging me to move.

'I didn't realize until after I got off the phone with you, but when I came home the alarm didn't go off. And I always set it. And . . . there's stuff in the basement . . . I think she's down here with me . . . Yes! Right now.'

Another pause, George's voice louder this time, his words still inaudible. Michael stands and revolves, scanning the room. Every minute movement of my body feels as if it could give me away, my shallow, silent breaths sounding like gasps, vibrating in my ears.

Please. Please don't see me.

His gaze floats over me, his head snapping to the half-open door of the darkroom.

He smirks, his eyes still cold, the phone dropping to hang down by his side, George's voice still echoing out. He moves across the space, each foot carefully placed, quiet. He stretches out his hand, setting his feet wide so that he is blocking the exit, and pushes open the door.

I stand, rising slowly, inch by inch.

One step forward, heel to toe, slowly –

His head snaps towards me.

Run.

I stumble forwards, my feet flying underneath me.

'You fucking bitch!'

His shout echoes around the room as I reach the bottom step, and he chases, his footsteps like approaching thunder.

I scream, terror shuddering through me, my hands clawing up the stairs.

Fingers grab my ankle and my feet are swept from beneath me. My arms flail outwards, the box and photos flying into the air, and I collide with the floor, my nails scratching at the stone as I try to cling on.

'No!' I cry, as he tugs me down the stairs, my chin smashing into the steps.

I flip my body over, kicking wildly. His face is below me, his eyes seething.

I thrash about, desperate for him to let go. For just a second, he loses his grip, and I thrust my legs outwards, hitting him squarely in the chest.

He tumbles backwards, landing in a crumpled heap at the bottom, groaning. I scramble to my feet, blood dripping from my chin. Pelting up the stairs, I finally reach the door and slam it closed behind me, then dash across the hall to the front door.

It won't open.

It's locked. He's locked it from the inside.

I pull and pull on the handle, a scream bursting through my gritted teeth.

He's coming up the stairs, moaning loudly in pain.

I clap my hands over my ears, my head shaking. Running across the hall, past the basement, I hurl myself through the double doors and into the kitchen.

I scan the room, searching for a hiding place –

An open toolbox, lying on the floor by the island, a hammer discarded on the counter.

Grab it.

I snatch it up and run around the island to the tall cupboard at the end. There's just a mop, bucket and broom inside. I slide in and crouch down, curling my fingers around the edge of the door to pull it closed.

The door of the basement bursts open.

I squeeze my eyes shut, my hands pulled in tightly to my chest, the hammer cold against my face.

For a moment there is silence. I can imagine him, standing in the hall, thinking, trying to decide which way I would run.

A shiver courses down my spine: footsteps. Moving closer.

I hold my breath.

He's coming into the kitchen.

One step. Another. Slow. Purposeful.

He is circling the island.

Tears creep out between my lashes and slide down my face.

Has he noticed that the hammer is missing?

I open my eyes and stare into the dark. My muscles are rigid, fear locking me into place. Sweat slick on my forehead.

I can't hear anything. Has he gone?

Listen.

Nothing.

He's gone –

Light bursts in and Michael's silhouette looms above me.

'No!' I scream.

He lunges quickly and grabs hold of my wrists, forcing them against my chest. I manically try to push the hammer away from myself, but he is too strong. He yanks me out of the cupboard and drags me to the floor.

'Let go of me!'

I kick frantically and he loses his grip. I flip over, struggling to find my feet, and stagger forwards, running towards the hallway, my hand still curled around the hammer.

'Help!' I scream as he ploughs into me from behind, throwing me to the floor.

He grabs my shoulder and flips me on to my back.

Hands over my mouth. Legs kicking. Blue eyes. Dress ripping. Thighs. Pressure. Fear. Stillness.

Please, no. Please.

He straddles my waist, forcing my hands down either side of me. I struggle, thrashing my arms and legs, but he doesn't let go – he bashes my fist against the tiled floor, over and over, until my fingers open and the hammer skids away.

'Please, let go of me,' I cry, as his face moves closer to mine.

'You couldn't just fucking leave it alone. Could you?'

'Please –'

'Could you!' he yells. His breath is hot on my face, his hands moving away from my arms and up to my shoulders. 'Just like when you were younger – you couldn't keep your fucking mouth shut.'

Horror engulfs me as his face transforms. His mouth is curled, his eyes manic, consumed with rage. And his hands don't move to cover my mouth. They slide to my neck. His fingers wrap around my throat.

'No!' I cry.

Squeeze.

No.

'Michael,' I gasp, scratching at his neck.

His grip tightens. His face is red, his eyes round and unblinking. He is staring at the space just above me – he isn't looking at me at all.

I can't breathe.

Please.

No.

I gasp, desperate for oxygen, my fists pummelling, pounding into his back, my legs kicking.

I can't breathe.

Please.

Faces flash before my eyes.

Mum. Dad. Marissa. Will.

I need to see them again. I don't want to die.

My arms feel weak, my punches feeble.

His hands begin to shake, and he pushes, his weight bearing down. My head is screaming, the pressure unbearable.

I search desperately for air, my hands reaching sideways for something, anything.

My vision blurs.

The back of my hand knocks against something hard.

The hammer.

My fingers curl around the handle.

'Michael,' I croak.

He lowers his head to meet my eye.

My arm moves without thought. Just instinct. Again, and again.

I don't want to die.

He slumps to the side, falling on to his back.

I gulp for air and toss the hammer aside, my vision wavering.

I can't see – everything is black, the world fading away.

But I can hear him. His low moans of pain, his fast, shallow breathing.

My eyes flutter closed.

Silence.

43. Belle

Eighteen years earlier

I'm alive.

I repeat the words in my mind as I lie with my head in Mum's lap, my feet on Dad's. Mum's fingers comb through my hair, her soft touch comforting and warm, the rhythmic movement making my eyes flutter closed. Dad chuckles at something on the television, glancing across at me and Mum to see if we're following along. I smile.

I'm alive, I repeat again, just like the therapist told me to. Think of three things that make you happy to be alive, she said. Do it every day. It doesn't have to be anything big. Just three things.

I'm alive.

'Mum,' I say. 'Dad . . .'

Mum's fingers stop moving. I crane my neck back to look up at her.

'What is it, Belle?' Mum says, her fingers light on my forehead.

'I wanted to speak to you and Dad about something.'

Dad reaches forward to pick up the remote which is lying on his footrest, and clicks off the television. I push myself on to my elbows, suddenly aware of the eerie quiet in the room, that ominous feeling that hovers when something is about to be said. Something important.

I sit up, my hands cradled in my lap, my fingers pulling at the edges of my frayed sleeves. 'I hope you know how much

286

I appreciate what you're doing for me. Moving out of this house, moving our entire lives for me . . . I just . . . Thank you.'

When I got out of hospital, after I'd been home for a week or so, they asked me if I wanted to move away. Grandma had said that we could live there until they sold the house and bought one near her. They wanted me to get back to school. They wanted me to have some normality. I could still see my friends if I wanted to, we would only be moving an hour away. Dad even offered to take me on the train so I could see how easily my friends could visit me. But they didn't want me to go back to my old school if I didn't want to. They didn't want me to feel trapped. *We don't want to lose you*, they had whispered.

'Of course, darling,' Dad says. 'We'd do anything for you.'

'Anything,' Mum repeats, squeezing my hand.

'Well . . .' I breathe in deeply, trying to draw bravery into my lungs. 'You know when George visited me yesterday . . .'

They weren't going to like this. Dad might be okay, but Mum . . . Still, it's for the best, I know it is. I trust George.

The first time he visited me, when I was still in hospital, I was shocked. I hadn't expected it. My cheeks flushed as he stood over my bed, taking in my bandaged arms, my sunken cheeks. But now he visits at least once a week. He's become my friend, just like he promised.

'How's everything going?' he asked me yesterday, settling himself into the armchair.

I tucked my feet underneath me on the sofa, holding a cushion close to my chest. 'I'm okay . . . I had another session with the therapist today.'

'Do you want to chat about it?'

I shrugged. 'We were just talking about the move.'

'How are you feeling about it?' He leaned forward, his forearms resting on his knees.

'Okay, I guess. I just . . .'

'What is it?'

'I just don't know if it will change anything . . . will it really be that different? I'll still be the same person. It still happened to me. And what if all the kids at that school know who I am?'

'Well, you can't change what you look like –'

'I want to dye my hair black,' I interrupted.

'Ah. Well, yes, of course, I guess you *can* change what you look like, but . . . there is something else I wanted to talk to you about. There's something else you could do if you really wanted to start afresh.'

'What?'

'You could change your name.'

I frowned, but tingles of anticipation ran up my arms. 'My name?'

He stood up and crossed the living room quickly to sit down beside me on the sofa. 'The photo of you has been taken down but your name is out there now. Always. That can't be taken back. It won't go away. And you could change your name so easily. It's not just about hiding who you are, it's about starting again. Don't you think you deserve to start again?'

'Yes . . .'

'Moving away won't be enough, Anabelle. If you really want to start again –'

'That feels so big.'

He nods, his kind smile appearing. 'Of course, it's a big step, and it would have to be your choice, but I believe that the best thing you could do for yourself would be to change your name, change your hair if you want to –'

I laugh, tears filling my eyes.

'– and be someone new. You don't have to be the person who went through all of that. Not if you don't want to be . . .' He reached out and held my hand. 'Do you want to be Anabelle King?'

The Girl Who Cried Rape.

I shook my head.

'So, who do you want to be?'

'Somebody else,' I whispered, gripping his fingers tightly. 'Anybody else.'

I blink myself back into the room, my eyes darting between Mum and Dad's expectant faces. I don't know how to ask them. How do I –

'I think I should change my name,' I blurt out.

A strange sort of silence consumes us. Dad stares at me but Mum's eyes flicker across to him and back again several times before she finally turns back to me with a frown.

'Change your name?' she asks.

'My name is out there now,' I say, repeating George's words. 'Always. That won't go away –'

'But your name is who you are,' Mum says, shaking her head, her grip tight around my fingers.

'Does it have to be?'

'You can't just –'

I turn to Dad, staring at him, pleading.

'It might be a way . . .' Dad interrupts, pinching the bridge of his nose as tears shine in his eyes. He sighs. 'It could help her begin to let go of what's happened. And does it really matter, Penny? It's just a name.'

'You don't want to be Anabelle King any more?' Mum asks, her lip trembling.

'I wish I could be,' I whisper. 'But she's now just the girl who lied. The girl who accused an innocent man. That's how people think of her. I don't want to be her any more.'

Mum and Dad stare at each other, speaking their familiar silent language. A small shrug from Dad, a widening of eyes from Mum. A small nod.

'What name?' Dad asks.

My mouth breaks into a smile, happy and wide. 'I thought maybe, Knight, as a second name?'

'My maiden name,' Mum says.

'Yes.'

Dad curls his arm around my shoulders and rests his head on top of mine. 'You could use another name beginning with A? That way your initials would be the same.'

I nod. 'I thought the same. And I like Ava . . . Ava?'

Dad tilts his head, and Mum smiles, her eyes still sad.

'If that's what you want,' she whispers.

I nod again, the name poised on my lips: the girl I have become.

'Ava Knight.'

Yes. That's who I am.

Anabelle King is gone.

44. Ava

My mouth gasps for air, my lungs screaming.

I'm alive.

I clutch my neck, grappling at my bare skin as if his hands are still there, phantom fingers crushing the air from my throat. But they are gone.

I open my eyes slowly and turn my head.

Michael is lying beside me, his head in a dark pool of blood.

He's completely still. Unmoving. Eyes round and open, not blinking. No flutters.

I stretch out my hand and rest it in front of his mouth.

He isn't breathing.

'Michael?' My mouth moves in the shape of his name, but no sound emerges. I grit my teeth as pain vibrates through me, my throat burning, ears ringing.

I reach out again, hesitating for a moment before I grab his wrist. His arm is heavy, a dead weight as I lift it – I let go and it flops to the floor with a solemn thud.

'Michael?'

I lift his wrist again, pressing my index and middle finger downwards, feeling for a pulse.

But there isn't anything. No gentle thud, thud, thud.

Nothing.

I push myself away, scramble backwards across the floor and come to a sudden stop as my back slams into the wall. He is lying there, completely still. Lifeless. And dead – because of me.

But I didn't mean to. I was defending myself – if I didn't do it, he would have killed me. It would have been me, lying there instead.

My eyes dart across the scene, taking in each forensic detail.

The hammer discarded by Michael's side. The photographs flung across the floor. The box – his keepsakes, upturned.

Clamping my hand across my mouth, I stare at his body. They're going to think I murdered him. It won't take long for them to find out our history, to discover that I was recently suspended, that I manipulated my way into his life. And I broke into his house. This will look like revenge or an outburst of rage, an uncontrolled act – nothing more.

Panic takes hold of me, wrapping tightly around my shoulders, which fold over as I curl into myself. I can't breathe.

Knock, knock, knock.

My gravelly, frantic inhales are interrupted by a soft tap – like fingers on glass.

Fear strikes and I freeze, my mouth trembling.

There's someone knocking on the glass window that falls ceiling to floor on the right-hand side of the front door.

I lift my chin, shivering, and look.

George?

'Ava?' he says, his face white. His eyes dart over the chaos of the hallway, finally landing on Michael's body and the floor around him, swimming in blood. 'Ava . . . what have you done?'

'He . . .' I cough. 'He tried to kill me.'

He pauses, his face unchanging. 'I can't hear you,' he says. 'Move closer.'

I drag myself across the floor. Stopping beside the office, I look up at the window.

'Open the door, Ava!'

'The door is locked,' I croak. 'He locked it from the inside . . .'

'What's happened to your voice?'

I shake my head and glare at him, my eyes piercing his through the glass. 'Why are you here, George?'

His mouth drops open slightly. I thought I could read him like a book, but all these years of knowing him, trusting him, have been a lie.

'I . . . I heard –'

'I know that you were on the phone to him.' I wince, clasping my hand to the base of my throat. 'I know everything.'

He blinks rapidly, his forehead creasing as he frowns. 'I heard on the phone . . . I heard him shout and . . . I heard you scream. Muffled voices and then . . . nothing. I thought he'd killed you.'

'You didn't come here for me. You came here for him. Because he asked you to.' I rock my head backwards and rest it against the wall. Inside, I am seething, sick at the sight of him. I want to throw myself at the glass, kicking and screaming. But my body is trembling, too weak for the strength of my rage. My eyes sweep over the house: the curved iron staircase, the chandelier, the glass lantern filtering moonlight down, bathing Michael in an eerie white light.

'How do you know him?'

'He . . .' George shakes his head, his mouth contorted.

'George, I heard everything!' I say, desperate to shout, my throat searing with pain. 'I heard you talking. He has files in the basement with all your messages, all the way back to the trial! Just tell me the truth!'

My head spins.

George sighs and crouches down to meet my eye. 'His father was my best friend when Michael was little –'

'How could you do that?' My whisper transforms into a hoarse shout, a strangled shriek. I move forward, wincing, so that I'm kneeling in front of the window. 'Is that why you became my friend? Is that why you stayed in my life all these years? To keep an eye on me? To make sure I didn't do anything stupid?'

'No, I stayed in your life because I care about you! I've only ever cared about you. I've spent the past two decades trying to help you –'

'You helped me to lessen your guilt.' Tears stream down my face and run into my mouth. I taste blood. 'You ruined my life to save his.'

'His father was my best friend growing up. We hadn't seen each other in a while, not since Michael was little, but he asked me for help when Michael was arrested and I –'

'You helped them! You helped him get away with it. You . . .'

Moving away won't be enough, Anabelle. You don't have to be the person who went through that. Do you want to be Anabelle King?

I blink rapidly as the memory slots into place.

'You even convinced me to change my name . . .'

But it wasn't the attack itself that led to me changing my whole identity. It was everyone knowing who I was. *The Girl Who Cried Rape.* My name being released, when that was never supposed to happen.

I stare at him, my mouth hanging open. 'It was you . . . you leaked my identity, didn't you? You told the world who I was and then convinced me that the only way to move on was to change my name. It was in Michael's interests for me to disappear forever. So, you made it happen!'

'No, I –'

'And my dress – the DNA evidence. You let Sam Hart take the blame. It's your fault he's dead!'

'My fault?' He sneers, his features distorting into an expression I haven't seen on his face before. 'That was your fault – you and your dad. He's dead because of you –'

'He's dead because you chose to help Michael!'

'And Ava, I've helped you too. Don't forget how much I've helped you –'

'You betrayed me!' I slam my fist sideways against the window, blood smearing down the glass. He doesn't respond but stares at me blankly. 'And even after his dad died, you kept on helping him. You helped him hide what he did to Lily. How many crimes have you helped him cover up?'

'Ava . . .'

'How many?'

He moves closer to the window, reaching his hands up but pulling them away before he touches the glass. Always thinking of evidence. Fingerprints.

'I can explain everything to you later, and I promise I will, but you need to listen to me. I can help you . . . We can make all of this go away. Okay?'

'George, this isn't contaminating evidence or manipulating teenage girls into silence – this is a body! The scene of a death. You can't just make this disappear.'

'I can . . . I promise you that I can. Just let me help you.'

How many times has Michael asked him for help? How many times has Michael reached out to him, desperate – *I've done something terrible. Help me, George.*

'Don't do anything stupid, Ava. I can help you get rid of all of this. We can hide what you've done and just –'

'Just what? Just make it all disappear?'

'I'm trying to help you –'

'You're not. You're trying to save yourself!'

My eyes veer over the evidence scattered across the floor. If George helps me cover this up, all the evidence against them will be hidden too. Everything I've done will be for nothing. And as soon as it becomes clear that Michael is gone, won't the glare of suspicion turn my way? Even if George manages to smear someone else with the stain of guilt . . . who? Who will be found guilty in my place?

I can't spend the rest of my life looking over my shoulder. Wondering. I can't be indebted to George. And I can't be silenced by Michael. Not again.

'You deserve punishment just as much as he did,' I whisper.

'Ava . . .'

I grip the doorway of the office and stand, my whole body trembling violently. My teeth are chattering, my vision swimming. I walk, doubled over, back to my phone, but my eyes are drawn to the mirror that hangs on the wall above the sideboard. My neck is already bruised. The centre of my chin has a deep gash and blood has trickled down my neck. My lip is cut open and swollen.

I lean on the wall beside the door to the basement and slump back down to the floor, reaching for my phone.

'Ava,' George says, his voice muffled. He moves closer to the glass. 'What are you doing?'

I need to do this. Anything but the suffocating silence of another secret.

I tap in my password again, blood smearing on the screen.

'Ava, don't you fucking dare! Don't be stupid.'

I tap three times. 9 9 9.

'Ava, you're going to be charged and spend the rest of your life in prison.'

I close my eyes, blocking him out.

Wait. Listen to the ring.

Don't be afraid.

'They're not going to believe you!' he shouts. 'Ava!'

'Emergency. Which service?' a voice says.

I pull the phone away from my ear, my finger poised above the screen, ready to hang up. George's mouth is hanging open, his eyes round as he watches me.

'Put the phone down,' he says, his voice low and threatening. Just like Michael's.

No more silence.

'Ambulance,' I whisper, closing my eyes. 'And police.'

'Ava!'

'Putting you through now.'

The line clicks and ringing starts again.

I open my eyes.

George is gone. Vanished. As if he was never here.

45. Ava

A siren screams and blue lights bounce up the driveway then illuminate the hallway, throwing a haunting light over the devastation of the evening.

'They're here,' I say.

'Are they at the door, Ava?' the emergency services handler asks. She has remained so calm, her voice never wavering throughout the conversation, through my one-word answers and explanations, no hesitations or uncertain, fearful pauses, not even when she asked me what happened. *Self-defence*, I whispered. Are they okay? she responded. *No. Dead.*

'Yes,' I say, breathless. 'They're at the door. Police.'

'The ambulance is pulling in now as well, okay?'

'Yes,' I whisper again, but a sharp pain stabs the back of my throat.

I hold my trembling fingers, covered in his dry blood, up to my mouth as coughs overcome me, and I'm unable to breathe through the dry, hacking barks. I gag.

'Ava, are you okay?'

I gasp, trying to force oxygen down into my lungs. My head is pounding, my vision blurring. Bile forces its way up my throat, my own body choking me.

'Ava, if you feel like you're going to pass out or be sick, I need you to lie down and roll on to your side, okay?'

I slide my shoulders, which are propped up against the wall next to the basement door, down to the floor, and slowly turn, groaning.

'Ava, they're at the door now,' her calm voice says, rising

up from where the phone has been discarded next to me. 'The police will use force to get in, okay, so don't be shocked by the sound. They know you're there, and they're going to count down. Should be any second.'

I nod to nobody.

There are voices outside, footsteps on the porch.

'Three –' somebody shouts.

'Two –' My body tenses.

One –'

A thundering bang bounces around the walls of the hallway. Then another. And finally, cool air rushes in, tingling against my face.

I squint into the ambulance headlights that are shining through the open door, lighting up the darkness.

Feet move towards me, legs bending down to crouch at my side.

'Ava?' a voice says gently.

'Hmm,' I croak. I try to turn to look up at them, but their hands grip my shoulder.

'No, don't move – they're bringing the stretcher now.'

More footsteps vibrate on the floor, and a voice from outside: 'Careful where you're treading.'

That's the police. They'll be standing outside, waiting for their turn to enter, ready to preserve the evidence: the blood trailing from the basement into the kitchen, the documents and photographs flung around the kitchen. His body, lying there – dead eyes staring up at the blank ceiling. The evidence tells the story. But what will it say to them? Will they be able to read it and see the truth? Or will it lie?

There is muttering between the man at my side and a woman, but I can't make out what they're saying. Their words seem unintelligible, as if their syllables are being slowed down and then rapidly sped up.

'Okay, Ava, my name is Hannah,' the new voice says from behind me. 'We're going to roll you on to this stretcher. We're also going to put you into a head immobilizer, it's like a neck brace.'

What has he done to me?

'Now, listen, I don't want you to worry, the brace is a precaution as there seems to be quite significant injury to your throat. We want to make sure that we don't cause any further damage. Okay?'

I make a small noise to let them know I've heard them. That I understand.

'On three,' she says. 'One, two, three.'

Strong hands roll me on to the tight fabric of the stretcher and strap me into the immobilizer. I can't move my head at all, my neck is firmly held in place, and I blink up through tears at Hannah's face as she directs her partner through the hallway, occasionally glancing down at me with a reassuring smile.

They manoeuvre me out of the house and into the night. There are voices, lots of them, but I can't see anything. I want to shout out to the police: look in the basement, look in the walls, look for George Cavanaugh, it was self-defence, he was going to kill me.

The night sky, scattered with stars, gazes down at me, and tears sting my bloody face as I am pulled back into the past once more. The night it happened. But then the stars disappear and the sky is replaced by the white curved ceiling of the ambulance. The stretcher is locked into place, but the lights are too bright, too white. I blink and colours burst in the space behind my eyes.

'Ava,' a deep, raspy tone says. A face appears above me, dark eyes and bright white teeth, a body clothed in a jumper and jeans, not the dark blue uniforms of the ambulance crew.

'My name is DC Farrah. The paramedics are going to take you to hospital, but I need to place you under arrest before you go. Do you understand?'

I blink.

'Ava Knight, you are under arrest on suspicion of murder. You do not have to say anything, but it may harm your defence if you do not mention . . .'

His words fade into oblivion. All I can hear is my breaths as they rattle up into the air.

'Ava, I have to ask you – do you have any comment?'

I stare blankly.

'No . . . okay,' he says, looking away from me and at the paramedics. 'You can take her.'

He walks away, moving out of my vision. A hand touches my arm.

'It won't be long, Ava,' Hannah says, placing an oxygen mask over my mouth and nose. 'We'll be at the hospital soon.'

I blink again, and she nods, as if she understands me.

Closing my eyes, I try to focus on the feeling of Hannah's hands as she takes my blood pressure, concentrate on her voice as she talks me through what she is doing. But my mind drags me back to the house, Michael's weight on top of me, his hands bearing down, second by infinite second.

I don't want to die.

And I didn't. I'm alive.

But at what cost? For me to spend the rest of my life behind bars?

It can't have been for nothing.

And what about George? Where has he gone? Will they believe me if I tell them what he did? Will he get away with it forever?

You know I'm always here for you, right? George's voice whispers in my ear.

Why did he do this to me? I trusted him. I let him into my life, blindly.

I am wheeled out of the ambulance and into the hospital. The next few hours are a flurry of blurred movement, hospital ceilings rushing above me, the sound of voices discussing me, fingers touching, painkillers. Questions. And only blinks in response from me. One for yes; two for no. They've told me not to speak. Not for now.

'You should try to get some sleep,' the consultant says as she places my notes back into the holder that hangs at the edge of the bed. 'I know it's uncomfortable in the brace, but . . . try.'

She leaves, closing the door behind her. The only sounds are the low buzz of the air-conditioning, and the machines whirring and clicking as they monitor my heart. My airflow. There are no other patients – I've been left in a room on my own.

My body feels like it's buzzing, my muscles all tense, my legs ready to run, my fists clenched at my sides, ready to fight.

But the mumbled sound of my name draws my attention to the glass window that looks on to the rest of the ward just visible in my peripheral vision.

It's the consultant, her arms folded across her chest. My fingers tingle, my rapid breathing sending waves of pain down my ribcage, as the person she is talking to comes into focus. The black and white uniform is clear, the handcuffs hanging from his belt, a baton in the holster at his side. A policeman.

The consultant nods at him and walks away, stalking down the corridor. But he stays, turning briefly to peer in at me through the glass before he sits down in a chair directly beside the door.

Not just a policeman.

My guard.

46. Ava

'Ava?'

Mum's soft whisper is close to my ear, her hands stroking my hair.

I'm dreaming. I am home, and Mum is taking care of me, comforting me. It is the past. I am Anabelle. But . . . she didn't call me Anabelle, she called me –

'Ava?' she says again, but louder, and accompanied by the steady beep of a heart monitor.

I'm not at home. I'm in hospital.

I'm under arrest for murdering Michael Osborne.

My arms flail outwards as my eyes fly open, panic throwing itself around my insides, like a bird trapped in a cage, searching for a way out.

'Shh, Ava, it's okay, it's okay – look at me.'

I gasp, a juddering inhale, and focus on Mum's face, hovering over mine. Her sad eyes. Full of kindness. Love.

'Mum?' I whisper.

'Shh, darling. Here, they told me that if you wanted to speak you should use this.' She hands me the whiteboard that I discarded on the floor beside the bed – a way for me to communicate, to prevent me from speaking.

My face crumples, tears squeezing out of the corners of my eyes, and I toss the whiteboard aside again.

'I'm sorry,' I say, my voice hoarse, barely a whisper.

'Don't apologize to me, sweetheart. I'm sorry –'

I shake my head. 'No, Mum. Please . . .'

She straightens her back, taking hold of my hand, her

fingers rubbing my knuckles. She sniffs. 'They . . . they haven't told me what happened. They just told me that you've been arrested for . . . for murder? Michael Osborne? What happened?'

'I . . . I was trying to help a girl he'd attacked. I broke into his house but he . . . he tried to kill me.'

'So you defended yourself?'

I nod.

'How did you even find him? How did this happen?'

'I . . . I can't explain now,' I gasp, my breaths shallow. 'I . . . I'm sorry.'

She hangs her head, her chin to her chest, a low sob shuddering out from deep within her. 'I can't do this again, Ava. We're just about to get Dad back, he's up for parole so soon and now . . . I can't lose you in the same way. I can't do it.'

I release a breath and stare at her through blurred vision. I'm going to break her all over again. So close to the return of her missing puzzle piece . . . and I rip out her heart.

'Ava, listen to me,' she says, leaning forward, her face close to mine. 'No matter what happens, if you're charged . . . you fight. Okay? Don't go down without a fight.'

I blink up at her, unsure what to say. Unable to speak.

'Promise me,' she says.

'I . . . I promise.'

'You promise that you'll fight? You'll stand up for yourself?'

I take in the look in her eyes, so different to the dull veneer I've become used to, now dark and insistent. I grit my teeth and exhale.

'I'll fight.'

My heavy eyes flutter to a close, the weight of exhaustion too much to resist, but within a split fraction of a second, they fly open again, my body alerting me to a non-existent, deadly danger. A shadowy figure, hovering above the bed, my movements restrained by the brace, its hands reaching for my throat.

I turn my eyes to the window again. Mum is gone, but the police officer is still sitting outside – he is looking downwards, his neck tilted forward. Maybe he's looking at his phone, reading messages or watching something, anything to keep himself awake.

I scan the corridor through blurred vision.

Have they got through to him yet?

As Mum was leaving, a nurse asked if there was anyone else who they should call. I blinked, once, and wrote down a phone number. And a name.

Will.

Mum said that she had tried to reach him already but hadn't been able to get through. The nurse said she would keep trying. But she didn't come back. She took down his details and left – not returning to inform me that he knew where I was and had been told what had happened. Nothing.

'Ava?'

Will. Will's voice on the other side of the glass.

'Ava!'

I blink rapidly, the muscles in my neck screaming as I try to see him. I can hear his voice, full of panic, but I can't see him. Where is –

Suddenly he appears, racing down the corridor. He flies to the ward desk, his hands gripping the edge of the counter, nurses looking up from their stations and wheeling around at the sound of his urgent voice.

'It isn't visiting hours, sir –'

'I got a phone call – my fiancée is here –'

'Slow down, please,' the matron says. 'Who is your fiancée?'

'Ava Knight.'

She glances towards my room, her expression shifting. But Will doesn't look behind him; he hasn't noticed that I'm here, just beyond the glass.

'I need to speak to you privately first, please ... what's your name?'

'Will Holmes. Somebody called me, and told me she was here –'

'If we could just go to a private room and I can explain –'

'Is she dead? Fuck, is she dead?'

'No, sir, but I need you to –'

The police officer stands. 'Sir, please calm down and listen.'

Will spins around, his eyes widening at the sight of a policeman, his face grey with fear. But suddenly, he falls still, frozen, his eyes fixed on the window.

'Ava?'

He rushes towards my room – I lift my hand, which sends pain across my ribcage to the centre of my chest. I'm desperate to touch him, to hold his hand, but his path is blocked.

'Will, I'm going to ask you one more time,' the police officer says, standing in front of the door. 'As the nurse has said, there is a situation that needs to be explained and we need you to come with us.'

'I tried to tell you on the phone,' the nurse says, nodding. 'But you hung up too quickly. I did try to call you back –'

'I wanted to get here,' Will says, his voice shaking. 'She needs me ... Has her mum been told? Or George?'

'Her mum has already been here. Please – just come with us to the family room, and we can explain.'

He looks at me again, chewing his lip. 'Okay,' he whispers.

They turn and walk away, Will craning over his shoulder.

My eyes flicker to the ceiling, and I concentrate on the pattern of panels. But fear takes hold, like water filling the room, lapping over my head. Drowning in panic.

'Will,' I whisper, no louder than a breath.

I close my eyes. He'll be back soon. I just need to see him, just for a moment. I don't want to be alone.

Please.

Please come back.

'Ava?'

Fingers grip mine and Will is beside me. His other hand moves to gently stroke my hair, tears filling his eyes as he takes in my injuries: my brown irises consumed by a red, vampiric gaze; my purple neck; my bruised, torn lip.

There is movement behind Will's shoulder. The police officer is standing only a few feet away, watching us intently. The nurse is by his side, but her back is turned, her hands clasped at her waist, looking down at her feet.

'They've told me I can't stay long,' Will whispers, tracing the shape of my face, scrunching up his nose as tears trickle into the line of his Cupid's bow.

'I –'

'She shouldn't speak,' the nurse interrupts. 'You shouldn't speak, Ava. Not until we're sure it won't cause damage.'

My chin shakes as I move my gaze to the whiteboard on the chair beside my bed. Will leans across and passes it to me. My hands feel weak, and I'm barely able to hold the pen, my words appearing in a childlike scrawl, the letters wonky and mismatched.

I'm sorry.

'No, I'm sorry,' he says. 'I shouldn't have left you.'

I curl my fingers inwards in a weak fist, and smear my apology away, replacing it with new words.

It's not your fault. I love you.

'I love you.' He sniffs, his face crumpling. 'What has he done to you?'

I remove the writing again. Scrawl out a few more stilted sentences, my heart aching for him.

I'm okay. I promise. Don't be sad.

There's a sudden knock at the door and Will looks over his shoulder, then hangs his head. The police officer who placed me under arrest is standing outside, staring in.

'Will, you need to go now, okay?' the police officer by my bed says. 'Once she's in custody, we can get her a phone call.'

Will nods, his focus moving to the nurse, who smiles kindly at him. 'You'll call me if anything happens?'

'Of course, but she's stable. We're just trying to manage her pain.'

'Okay . . .' He brings my hand to his mouth and presses his lips to my palm. 'Rest,' he whispers. 'And don't be afraid. I'll come and get you when they let you go,' he whispers.

My lip trembles. One more sentence.

They might not let me go.

'No,' he whispers firmly. 'You'll be home soon.' He nods, certain, but I can see it there in his eyes: worry. Fear. What if they don't? What if the police don't believe me?

He leans forward and kisses me gently. I inhale deeply, even though it sends agony rippling through me – he smells like home. Like coffee in bed, bleary-eyed. Like pancakes on Sunday mornings and *The Office* on Friday nights. Movies on Mondays. The closing of a laptop and the whisper to come to bed. Like sleep in strong arms. Will isn't just 'like' home. He *is* home.

'I love you.'

He walks slowly backwards, his arm outstretched, then lets go of my hand. He walks quickly out of the room, clearing his throat as he concentrates on his feet, looking at me one final time.

My eyes screw shut, my mouth opening in a silent cry. But I'm unable to wipe my tears or cover my face. I'm unable to do any of the things I would usually do to hide my emotion. It's just there for everyone to see. Exposed and raw. But truthful.

I sniff, blinking rapidly as the door creaks open again and the other police officer enters and strides over to my bed.

'Ava, I don't know if you remember me. I'm DC Farrah,' he says. 'I know you need rest, but this won't take long. Is that okay?'

I blink at him.

'As you're aware, you were arrested on suspicion of murder on the basis of what you had relayed to the emergency services handler.'

I blink again, frowning.

'However . . .' He pauses, glancing at the nurse.

I blink again.

'Mr Osborne is in hospital receiving treatment. He's in intensive care.'

His words are like shouts lost on the wind, the weather turning them faint and unclear.

'He –'

'Ava, the board,' the nurse says from the corner of the room.

I grab the pen, ink staining my fingers as I turn it the right way around and hurriedly stamp out my question.

He isn't dead?

'No,' DC Farrah says. 'When you checked him, his pulse must have been very faint, he was barely breathing. He's unconscious. But he's alive. So, I have to further arrest you.

You're under arrest on suspicion of attempted murder. You do not have to say anything but . . .'

His voice disintegrates, my mind unable to decipher what this means. For him. Or for me.

When he wakes up . . .

What will he say?

47. Ava

I've never been in the cell of a police station. Even when I was a pupil and defence work was chambers' bread and butter. But as a prosecutor there's so much that is avoided. We hover above the dark parts of the criminal justice system, but now I am here: on the other side of the thin veil that obscures the light from the dark.

And Michael Osborne is alive.

The three nights in hospital burgeoned with loneliness and the prospect of the police interview played on my mind, swirling through my thoughts and dreams. I could go no comment, I thought. That's every suspect's right. But I know what no comment represents. I know what the police would hear if I said those words, what the prosecutor would subconsciously think when they opened the file and turned to the summary of the interview. *Guilty*. And if I'm charged and this goes to a trial, I'll need to defend myself, but the jury will be told that they can infer whatever they like from my silence. And the inference is always guilt. The inference is always that the defendant stayed quiet to give them time to construct a fabricated version of events.

So, when I was finally brought into the interview room, I told the truth. I told the truth as a DC Young and DC Farrah asked me question after question, hour after hour. I need to give myself a chance, I need to make sure that they see the truth. I need them to see me for what I am: a victim.

The cell door clangs open, creaking on its hinges.

I glance up. DC Young is standing there, her expression

unreadable. My fingers squeak against the styrofoam cup, the dark tea inside still steaming. As soon as the officer handed it to me, Will's face appeared in my mind, his bemused smile as he sloshes more and more milk into my favourite mug, shaking his head and laughing as he hands me my pale, sweet tea – just as I like it. This tea is strong and bitter, a strong and bitter reminder that I am not at home – I might not ever go home. I could go from here to prison. Then from prison to court and eventually back again. And however Will feels towards me now, his strange combination of love and anger and regrets, would eventually begin to fade. He would move on. He would deserve to move on.

'You can come with me,' DC Young says.

'Can I bring this with me?' I whisper, looking down at my tea.

She shakes her head. 'I'd leave it there.'

I stand slowly, my hands trembling as I place the cup on the floor, the droplets of tea sloshing out of the cup and on to my skin, scalding.

DC Young steps aside and I move past her, out of the cell and into the corridor beyond, the floor cold under my bare feet. The cell door stays open behind us. Is she bringing me back here? Is that why she told me to leave my tea there? Or is it because they're letting me go home? Maybe they're releasing me on bail. If I'm charged, will I stay here over night, ready for court tomorrow morning? Or will they take me to prison first? In court, the defendants appear in the cells, as if by magic: my mind has compartmentalized how the system works – I don't focus on where they have been or how they got there. I didn't want to be reminded of what Dad had gone through. I had a job to do, so I did it. But all defendants have been where I am now. Scared. Afraid of what might happen to them, to their family and loved ones.

Rehearsing their truth, or their lie, over and over again in their minds, desperate to commit it to memory so that it might be believed.

DC Young walks away from the cell and I trail behind her, my eyes burning into her back, desperate to impart an outcome from the way she is moving, her expression. But she is blank.

We approach the front desk, where the custody sergeant is sitting. It's the same man who booked me in, and he looks at me expectantly. He's ready.

'Ava Knight.'

'Yes,' I whisper.

He looks away from me and back to the screen on his left. 'Right, you know how this goes.'

I nod.

'Ava Knight, you are being charged with the offences of Attempted Murder and Grievous Bodily Harm with Intent. Do you have anything to say in response to these charges?'

I take a few short breaths, my bottom lip trembling, mouth gulping, a fish out of water.

'I–I'm being charged?'

DC Young shifts her weight from one foot to the other beside me. 'Ava –'

'But what about him? What about what he did to me? I was defending myself –'

'Ava, you need to calm down.'

'But this isn't right!' My fragile voice breaks. 'I . . . I don't understand.'

'Ava,' the custody sergeant says, ploughing onwards, 'you are also being remanded to custody until your appearance at the magistrates' court as there are substantial grounds for believing that you would interfere with the witness or otherwise obstruct the course of justice.'

I stare down at the floor, my body tingling with anxiety before turning numb.

'What about the girls?' I ask, although my voice sounds strange and empty. 'What about all the evidence of what he's done?'

'We can't discuss that further. It's under investigation.' DC Young cocks her head back to the corridor that leads to the cells.

'Wait, please . . . What about Lily? She was meant to be sentenced on Friday. Did she change her plea?'

She sighs, glancing at the custody sergeant who continues to stare at the screen of his computer. 'The court allowed her to retract her plea. She's pleaded not guilty.'

'Really?'

'Yes . . .' She places her hand on my shoulder. 'Ready?'

I nod slowly, then follow her back to the cell.

They're investigating Michael. And Lily . . . she changed her plea. So she'll have told them the truth about what happened. He's pushed me down – ensnared by his story – but I can feel him there, just beyond my grip. And the first chance I get, I'll pull him down with me.

Somewhere – in hospital, at home – Michael Osborne has given his own side of the story. But his story has distorted everything – the truth of my injuries, his hands around my neck; he has corrupted the tale that should have been told by the evidence scattered throughout his house. His story will be one where I was filled with rage and revenge. He was just trying to keep me away from him: his hands at my neck were to keep me at arm's length until he finally succumbed to the blows of the hammer.

And like before, it will be my version of the truth against his.

Except this time, it will be me who is locked behind the glass.

48. Lily

'Crown Prosecution Service barrister Ava Knight has been charged with the attempted murder of photographer and head of the Osborne empire, Michael Osborne. She has been remanded into custody. No further details surrounding the incident have been disclosed by police.'

I jab my finger at the remote and the television turns black. The room falls silent, all conversation suddenly stopping. The dark screen blurs in and out of focus, bursts of colour dappling my vision as I blink robotically.

'Was that the man?' Kacey asks, her ongoing resentment of me momentarily replaced by curiosity. 'Oi, Lily, was that the man? Did someone else try to kill him? Poor man can't catch a break –'

'Everyone out,' Anne says as she marches into the living room from the office, followed quickly by Eleanor.

Why is Eleanor here?

'But wait, Michael Osborne – isn't that the man?'

'Kacey, leave it alone,' Anne says as she points towards the door that leads to the hallway, her arm fully extended. 'Out. All of you.'

Kacey gets up from the sofa, rolling her eyes, and the others follow, all of them trailing one by one out of the door. Eleanor and Anne approach where I'm sitting in the large red armchair, my legs curled underneath me.

'What's going on? Do you know what's going on? That barrister I told you about, the one who tried to help me, she's been –'

'No, we don't know anything, Lily,' Eleanor says. 'But the police called. Anne let me know so I came over straightaway.'

'The police?' I whisper, fear trickling down me like icy raindrops. 'Was it about my change of plea?'

'They want us to bring you to the station,' Anne says.

'What for?'

'They want to interview you about what that man did to you.'

I frown, trying to understand. 'But . . . won't that just be my defence at the trial?'

'I don't know. They said they would explain once we get there. But you're not in trouble.'

I turn my face towards the window and close my eyes as the sun – which is shining, dappled by the trees – warms my face. 'Will you come with me?' I whisper.

'Of course, sweetheart,' Eleanor says. She hugs me tightly, and I rest my chin on her shoulder and sigh.

'Eleanor?' I whisper into her hair.

'Yes, darling?'

'Can you . . .' I close my eyes and a tear squeezes out from between my lashes. 'Can you not call me sweetheart?'

DC Hewitt greets us at the main entrance. But he looks different. He isn't staring at me with a glare of suspicion like usual – his eyes look kind today.

'Good morning, Lily,' he says.

'Hi.'

'Good morning, Detective,' Eleanor says, holding out one hand to shake his, the other resting on my shoulder.

'Thank you for coming,' he says.

We both nod, unsure what to say.

He leads us to a room. But it isn't what I was expecting. It isn't the small sterile box where I was interviewed when I was arrested. It isn't even similar. This room is painted blue, a sofa and armchairs in the centre, scattered with cushions, slightly threadbare. A lady is sitting in one of the armchairs, and she stands, smiling.

'Hi, Lily,' she says. 'I'm Detective Schofield. But please, call me Kathryn.'

'Hi,' I whisper, my voice fading away, like somebody has turned my volume down. I stand immoveable in the centre of the room, waiting for someone to tell us what to do.

'Good morning,' Eleanor says, her voice loud in the cosy space.

'Please, take a seat,' Kathryn says.

'And me?' Eleanor asks, pointing at her chest.

'Yes, please,' DC Hewitt says. 'We have some things to discuss with you both.'

I move slowly across the room to the sofa and sit down, pulling one of the cushions on to my lap.

'Would either of you like some water?' Kathryn asks, as she folds herself elegantly into one of the armchairs.

'No, thank you,' I say quietly, my eyes flickering up to the camera that is mounted above her head.

DC Hewitt sits down in the other armchair, but he is propped right on the edge, leaning forward on his knees, his palms together, like he's praying.

'Now, you might have heard in the news today, that Michael Osborne was hospitalized, and somebody has been charged with attempted murder.'

My eyes glaze over. Should I tell them? Should I tell them that I know Ava? That she tried to help me . . . Do they already know? Will it get her in even more trouble?

'I –'

'Lily, before you say anything, we want to have a chat with

you in a bit where you can tell us anything that you want to tell us, but for now we just need to explain, okay?'

'O-okay.'

'During the investigation into what happened to Michael, other evidence has come to light which affects the case against you.'

I throw a sideways glance at Eleanor.

'A witness also gave evidence about what happened the night of the incident.'

Orla.

My heart soars but I pull it back, restraining hope.

'The charge against you is being withdrawn.'

I stare blankly at DC Hewitt. I can feel Eleanor's eyes on my face but I can't do anything. I can't move or blink or think.

'Withdrawn?' Eleanor says, her voice dulled with disbelief. 'As in . . . dropped?'

He nods. 'Yes.'

'Oh, Lily,' Eleanor whispers. I turn my head to look at her, my mouth agape, and she smiles at me with misty eyes. Emotion rushes over me in a giant wave, knocking my composure off its feet, and I rock sideways, collapsing my head on to her chest, my fingers raking at her loose T-shirt as relieved sobs take over. She strokes my hair, hushing me gently.

'It's okay, Lily,' she whispers. 'It's okay. You're safe now.'

Eventually the crying subsides, and I wipe my face with the back of my hand.

'I'm sorry,' I whisper, turning to face DC Hewitt and Kathryn.

'It's fine, Lily,' DC Hewitt says.

'Yes, please don't apologize,' Kathryn says. 'We know it's a lot to take in.'

'Now,' DC Hewitt says. 'I know you must feel very

overwhelmed, so we can arrange for you to come back and talk to us another day –'

'No, no,' I sniff, straightening my back. 'I want to do it now . . . If that's okay.'

'Are you sure?'

'Yes.'

'Okay. Well, as your social worker, Eleanor can stay in here with you while we chat – is that okay?'

I glance at Eleanor who smiles reassuringly.

'Yes,' I whisper.

'And Lily, if you'd rather I didn't stay in here, there's someone else who can come and chat to you with Detective Schofield.'

'No, no. It's fine. I . . . I know you.'

He nods with a small, surprised smile.

'Okay . . . you ready to begin?'

'Y-yes.'

There is a click and my eyes dart back to the camera. The light on top is now red.

'Now, I see that you've noticed the cameras already. There's the one right above my head,' Kathryn points to the one suspended above her, 'and there's also one directly behind you on the wall.'

I turn. There, trained on us, is another camera.

'The cameras are to give us a permanent record of the interview. Do you understand?'

'Yes,' I whisper.

'Okay. Before we begin, I just need to confirm that if I ask you a question you don't understand, then you should say so. And if you don't know the answer, then you should tell me that you don't know, okay? And if you think that I've misunderstood something that you've told me, then you need to tell me that too. Don't be afraid to tell me.'

'Okay,' I say.

'And I know you're not a little child, but we still need to have a chat about one more thing: the difference between telling the truth and telling a lie. Can you explain the difference to me?'

'Yes,' I say, wiping a stray tear from my cheek. 'Um . . . If I tell the truth about something, then I'm telling you what really happened. But if I lie, then I'm not telling you what actually happened. I . . . I'm trying to hide something from you.'

'Okay, good. And what do you think the consequences of telling a lie are?'

I pause. There could be a million different consequences of lying. And a million different reasons for doing so. You can lie to protect someone. You can lie to save someone. And sometimes the truth is just too hard.

'If you lie, you could get somebody into trouble.'

'Okay. Thank you.' She crosses one leg over the other. 'Now . . . you recently changed your plea for Grievous Bodily Harm with Intent from guilty to not guilty. In your application you put forward a detailed account of what happened that night. Can you tell me what happened now?'

I glance down, taking in the fabric of the cushion, the way it weaves itself together, its infinite number of threads.

I inhale deeply, meet Kathryn's eye, and start to speak.

Maybe her mum won't answer. Maybe they'll just ignore us.

Maybe she won't want to see me.

The door to the house suddenly swings open and Orla's mum is there, her dark hair, not in glamorous curls like usual, but instead in a messy bun on top of her head, her face red and patchy. Her eyes widen as Eleanor's mouth moves, but I can't hear what they're saying. But then her gaze darts towards the car.

I open the passenger door and step out.

Finally, Eleanor turns away from the house and makes her way back to the car.

'Is everything okay?' I ask.

'She's said you can go in and see her.'

I smile, my face breaking in two, tears already springing from my eyes. 'Is Orla in trouble with the police for what she did?'

'No, she's not. They believe that she was defending you. That it isn't in the public interest to prosecute her.'

My eyes close with relief. She saved me.

'But, darling,' Eleanor continues, 'Orla's probably very torn that she told the truth about what happened. No matter what he's done to you or to anyone else, he's still her dad.'

I nod.

We walk together, through the gate and down the front path, but I stop before I reach the porch. What am I going to say to her?

'It's okay, Lily,' Orla's mum says, holding her hand out, her fingers curling towards her palms, back and forth. I step forward and she opens her arms, sweeping me into a tight hug.

'I'm so sorry,' she whispers, her voice choked.

'It's not your fault.'

'I swear, I didn't know.'

'I'm okay. I promise.'

She lets go of me and steps backwards, her cheeks flushed, her eyes red.

'You're a strong girl, Lily,' she says, her words replacing the warmth of her embrace.

I am strong.

Not pretty. Not beautiful or special or different.

Strong.

'Thank you,' I whisper.

We climb the stairs together, one step at a time, towards Orla's bedroom. The door is closed.

'Darling, someone's here to see you,' Orla's mum says through the door.

'I don't want to see anyone, Mum.'

My heart leaps at the sound of her voice. I just want to see her. I want to rid the last image I had of her from my mind, her scared face, telling me to run.

'But . . . it's Lily.'

There is a pause and then the door opens slightly. Orla peeks through the narrow gap, her eyes growing round in disbelief as they lock on to my face.

'Lily?'

She lets go of the door and it swings slowly towards her, her mouth dropping open.

For a moment, we both stand there, staring at each other, neither of us knowing what to do. But then, in a sudden rush of movement, I dart towards her, my arms flinging around her neck.

'Thank you,' I whisper.

'I'm so sorry,' she cries. 'I'm so sorry –'

I hold her by the shoulders, lowering my head to look into her downcast eyes. They are red, like her mum's, the skin around them puffy, as if she hasn't stopped crying.

'It's okay. I know you didn't have a choice. And they've let me go because of you. It's all going to be okay –'

'But . . . but . . . I hate him.' She pauses, taking a ragged, uncontrolled breath. 'I didn't realize, I never thought he would hurt anyone. Even when I found out about the rape trial, I just didn't believe that it could be true –'

'None of us did, darling,' her mum says from where she is

standing on the stairs, her face overcome with emotion. 'It's not your fault.'

'But I didn't tell the truth from the beginning. I didn't know what to do.'

'It's okay,' I whisper. 'It's okay, Orla.'

And just like I did only an hour ago, my face pressed into Eleanor's body, Orla buries her head in my shoulder and cries, her entire body shaking, her voice choked. And remembering the comfort of Eleanor's touch, I stroke her hair, tell her it's going to be okay.

'Thank you, Orla. Thank you, thank you, thank you.' I squeeze my eyes closed, resting my head against hers.

'But it's all my fault,' she says. 'If I hadn't been friends with you, none of this would have happened.'

'If we hadn't been friends, I don't know where I'd be. I just know that I would be alone,' I whisper. 'You're my best friend . . . You saved me.'

And she did. In more ways than one.

I'm free.

But . . . Ava.

What will happen to Ava?

FOUR

And poise the cause in justice' equal scales,
Whose beam stands sure, whose rightful cause prevails.

King Henry VI Part II, Act 2, Scene 1

49. Ava

Six months later

The door from the cells into the courtroom opens and I step inside the dock. I've travelled from my cell in prison to the cell downstairs in the bowels of the Old Bailey, to this final cell. A glass box – a fishbowl – spectators gawping in. Over the months, I've slowly acclimatized to the prison cell, the routine – it feels like a waiting room. Or at least that's what I've convinced myself. It's just a waiting room. It isn't permanent.

But I'm not sure I'll ever get used to the view of the courtroom from the dock. The perspective is wrong, the entire courtroom before me rather than behind me. Backs turned away.

I sit, and a security guard closes the door and takes her seat beside me. I look down at my hands, not wanting to look through the glass to my past life. My nails are bitten down, short and ragged. Last night, a nail on my left hand tore down so low it bled, leaving the bed exposed and raw. I press on it and wince.

I look up as somebody knocks on the glass.

'Good morning, Ava,' Helena says.

Helena Atwell QC – my defence barrister. One of the most respected criminal defence barristers of the whole Bar. She fights cases tooth and claw. Her name is always associated with cases involving violence against women. If anyone can help me, it's her.

'Good morning,' I say.

'Feeling all right?'

'I . . . Yes, I'm fine.'

'Okay, good,' she says, her voice always warm and low. 'Any questions? I know I don't really need to ask you, but –'

'Actually, I was wondering . . . I haven't heard from the officer in charge of the other investigation in a while and . . . Have you heard anything? Do you know if they've found George Cavanaugh?'

'I . . .' She sighs. 'As far as I'm aware, they're still looking for him. They've put calls out saying he's needed for questioning about a historical sex offence but . . . nothing. He's disappeared.'

My head drops forward and I stare at the rough carpet that lines the dock. I sigh then glance back up at her. 'Sorry for asking that, I just –'

'I understand . . . We'll be starting very shortly.' She throws me a small smile but as she does so, her eyes veer to the side, up to the public gallery. 'Ah . . . it looks like your family is here.'

She walks away and I lean forward, my fingers pressed against the glass as I peer up at the public gallery which hangs suspended above the courtroom. Will is sitting down, his face creased with worry. Beside him, her face drawn, is Mum. She turns to speak to the person sliding into the seat next to her who suddenly appears in view. My eyes grow round as I take in his face, so alien out here, in the real world after so many long years.

Dad.

My mouth wavers, trembling as I fight back tears.

He was released last month. And after all this time, all these years of waiting for him to come back to us, I wasn't there. I was locked away. And even though Mum has been visiting me, he didn't come with her after his release. Mum said he couldn't face seeing me in prison, not after all the years he had spent there himself.

I tear my eyes away. I can't focus on them – every time I do, I am reminded that I might not see them again, not out here in the real world. Not for a long time. Maybe never.

'Can I just quickly speak to her?'

My head snaps forwards at the sound of Marissa's voice. She's standing close to Helena, fully robed, her wig dangling from her fingers. They're from the same chambers; Helena even mentored Marissa during her pupillage. She has visited me in prison every week, never missing a visit – just like Will. The two of them a lifeline in the dark.

'Go on then,' Helena says, her head jerking towards the dock. 'But be quick.'

'Thank you,' Marissa says, already striding towards me.

I stand, moving towards a thin gap in the glass.

'Are you okay?' Marissa asks in a low whisper.

'Yes.' I nod, holding her warm brown gaze.

'I'm going to be in Court Three doing that trial I told you about, but I'll keep checking in with Helena, okay?'

'The armed robbery trial? Is the QC okay? I hope he –'

'Ava! We're not talking about my trial right now. Are you serious?' She snorts and I smile. It feels good to smile. To hear someone I love, laugh. 'Anyway,' she continues, her mouth settling again into a stern line, 'just try not to worry about any of the legal stuff – Helena is incredible. You just need to focus on your evidence.'

'I know.'

'Marissa,' Helena calls. We both glance towards her and she directs her gaze to the large clock which hangs above the judge's bench.

Marissa sighs. 'I have to go. But I'll be back, okay?'

'Okay.'

'And I'll be here for the verdict. I promise.'

I nod, inching my finger into the gap between the panes of glass. Marissa looks slowly at my hand, her eyes brimming with tears, and does the same, the very tip of her finger touching mine.

'I'll see you soon,' she says, and walks away, whispering thanks to Helena.

'Goodbye,' I whisper.

I step backwards quickly, the backs of my knees hitting the plastic chair, and sit with a thump. I stare down at my trembling hands, inhaling deeply, but my entire body feels as if it's shaking deep within me – tremors: a volcano of emotions, ready to explode.

'Court rise,' the clerk calls, and I stand quickly, instincts kicking in.

The judge enters from a door behind the judicial bench. He lowers his head as he takes his seat, and my chin automatically tilts downwards.

'Good morning,' he says, his voice amplified through the speakers in the dock. 'Are we ready to empanel the jury?' he asks his clerk.

'Yes, My Lord.'

'Very well.'

She nods and crosses the room, exiting through a door to the side, next to the jury's benches. We wait, just a few moments, and then she returns, holding the door open for a large mass of people who gather in front of the dock, their eyes sliding to look through the glass. Some of them glance away from me quickly, but others stare, drinking in my image.

The clerk is holding a deck of cards – names she will call until twelve are selected.

'Jasmine Bughari.'

An older lady, probably in her mid-sixties, steps forward.

'Keira Hawton.'

A middle-aged woman this time, dressed smartly, her hands tugging at the hem of her blazer.

'Bruce Pine.'

A man, probably in his late twenties, steps forward.

The clerk continues calling out names, and I wait, my eyes fixed on each person as they shuffle along the jurors' bench and take their seats.

Twelve jurors. Seven women. Five men. Slightly skewed towards an older generation. The people who will decide my fate: guilty or not guilty. Acquittal or conviction. Freedom . . . or year after year in prison.

The clerk steps forward and asks each of them to take the oath.

I swear that I will faithfully try the defendant and give a true verdict according to the evidence.

Their voices blur. I've heard the oath so many times, trial after trial. But so much of the outcome is based upon the composition of those twelve people. On the balance of age, sex, culture, area . . . They will think that they're basing their decision on the evidence alone. But everything they have ever experienced, their journey through the world, through life, will have an influence on how they interpret the evidence. On how they perceive Michael. On how they judge me.

After the last one – an older man with square-framed glasses, a pen already poised in his hand – the court takes a momentary pause. A breath before we begin. Some of the jurors sit back in their seats, arms crossed, waiting, while others lean forward, their eyes dancing from me to the judge to the barristers and then back to me again, in anticipation.

'Members of the jury, thank you for being here to carry out your civic duty.'

He leans forward, his eyes glancing over the three people sitting near each other in the public gallery before returning to the jury. The three have flip notebooks and pens in their hands. Reporters.

'I know that you will have heard about this case in the media,' he says, 'and you will have heard of other investigations that are still ongoing. However, whilst you are considering this case, I must ask that you do not discuss the evidence with anyone else, including each other, until you are adjourned for your deliberation, and that you please ignore anything you hear in the news, written in newspapers or on social networks. Only consider the evidence that you see and hear during the course of this trial. Being a member of a jury is a vital part of our criminal justice system, and justice could not be done without you, so I thank you. Sincerely.'

He pauses for a moment, then removes his glasses, placing them on the bench in front of him, and sits back in his chair.

'Mr Burton,' he says with a slight inclination of his head towards the prosecution barrister who stands with a grand flourish of his silk gown.

'Good morning, ladies and gentlemen of the jury. I am Alan Burton QC and I appear on behalf of the Crown in this case. You will hear a great deal of evidence over the course of the coming days, but at the heart of this case are two people: Michael Osborne and Ava Knight. And whilst you will hear arguments to the contrary, I am sure that it will become as clear to you as it is to me, that there is only one victim in this case, and that victim is Michael Osborne.'

I inhale deeply, readying myself – bracing for the onslaught.

So, it begins.

50. Ava

'The Crown calls Michael Osborne.'

The door next to the jurors' bench opens and Michael appears, following behind the usher. He is wearing a tailored dark grey suit, a black tie, his stubble, perfectly groomed. A long, fading scar running down his face from his temple. His expression, innocent, naive – as if he doesn't understand how he ended up here.

He is the consummate performer.

And now is his time to bask in the spotlight.

He steps up on to the stand and clears his throat – forced, false nervousness.

I grit my teeth.

'Good morning, Mr Osborne,' Burton says. 'Thank you so much for taking the time to be here to give evidence today.'

'Of course,' he says, his voice gruff. He coughs again.

'Could you please state your name for the court?'

'I'm Michael Osborne.' He locks his hands behind his back.

'What do you do for a living, Mr Osborne?'

'I'm a photographer, but I also run the Osborne Corporation.'

'The international brand of hotels?'

'That's correct, yes.'

Burton places his pen down on his notebook. 'Mr Osborne, it's correct, isn't it, that when you were twenty-five you were accused of rape?'

'Yes, that's correct,' he says, answering without hesitation.

'What was the outcome of that trial, Mr Osborne?' Burton has lowered his voice, purposefully. My eyes dart to the jury: some of them are already leaning in. Hooked.

'I was acquitted.'

'You were acquitted.' Burton pauses, meeting the eyes of the jurors, allowing the point to land. 'When did you first meet the defendant?'

Michael's eyes veer towards the dock for the first time. But his expression doesn't change. It remains passive, neutral, as if he has no emotion towards me whatsoever. 'I saw her at court – she was the prosecutor for a hearing where I was the victim of a stabbing –'

Helena stands to her feet. 'My Lord, that charge has been discontinued and the use of the word victim is misleading.'

The judge nods. 'Mr Burton, please move on.'

'Mr Osborne, you were the complainant in a stabbing case, and while that charge has been discontinued, Ava Knight was the prosecutor, correct?'

'Yes.'

'After the hearing, did you see her again?'

'Yes.'

'When?'

His hands appear, no longer behind his back, moving as he speaks. 'I was at a cafe down the road from my house. I saw her through the glass and I recognized her, so I said hello.'

'What did Ava Knight say to you about why she was at that cafe?'

'She said she had a friend who lived nearby.'

'What happened next?'

'I asked her if she wanted to have a coffee, and she said yes. So we had a coffee together. Chatted for about fifteen minutes and then she left.'

'Was that the last time you saw her?'

He shakes his head. 'Uh, no. She had offered to have my daughter for work experience. I gave her my card and she messaged me –'

'The same day?'

'No, the next day. Sunday.'

Burton turns towards the jury. 'My Lord, members of the jury, the messages between Mr Osborne and Ava Knight are behind tab one.' He angles himself slightly back towards Michael. 'What did her message say?'

'She told me that she could have my daughter for a day of shadowing on the Tuesday. I said that was great and that's all I thought of it. But then she messaged again and said that she had enjoyed speaking to me and she'd like to see me again.'

'That's the message on page two of the bundle, is that correct?'

'Yes.'

'What did you say?'

'I invited her for dinner.' He shrugs casually, his characteristic charm radiating from him. 'She's an attractive woman, we got on well, she had told me at the cafe that she didn't have a partner . . .' He meets my eye. 'I was excited to see her again.'

My gaze darts up to the gallery, to Will. But he isn't looking at Michael. Or at me. His head is hanging, his knuckles pressed against his lips. Guilt somersaults in my stomach.

'When did you go for dinner?' Burton continues.

'Monday evening. She came to the restaurant at The Osborne.' He nods. 'We had a good time.'

'You said that she offered to have your daughter for work experience. Did that happen?'

'Yes, on the Tuesday. And I actually saw her again that

day – she dropped my daughter off at the house and Orla invited her inside.'

'Where were you at this point?'

'I was out. But I got home soon after.'

'Where was Ava Knight when you got home?'

'She was downstairs in the basement. My photography studio.'

'Was your daughter with her?'

'No. She was on her own.'

'What was she doing down there?'

'She said that Orla'd got a phone call and had left her in the kitchen. And she wanted to see the studio.'

'What did you think about that?'

He frowns, his brow furrowed. 'I thought it was a bit strange, but after she explained, I didn't think on it.'

'And what happened then?'

'She told me she had to leave. That was it.'

'Was that the last time you saw her prior to the twenty-seventh of May?'

'No, she came to the hotel.'

'What time did you meet at the hotel?'

'That was the strange thing,' he says, his voice going up at the end of the phrase like he's asking a question. 'I had told her that she should go straight up to the room and I would meet her outside, but when I arrived, she wasn't waiting even though I was late. I just assumed that she was running late too, but when I let myself into my suite, she was already inside.'

'She was inside the suite?'

'Yes.'

'How did she explain that?'

'She said that she'd misunderstood and asked the receptionist for a key. She had assumed that that's what I meant.'

'Did you believe her?' Burton says, imbuing his voice with shock.

'After that night I started to suspect that she wasn't who she said she was.'

'Who did you think she might be?'

'I thought she might be Anabelle King –' he pauses, '– the girl who accused me of rape.'

'What made you think that?'

'Just how suspiciously she was acting. It was eerie. I couldn't understand it. But then it just briefly crossed my mind, just one of those thoughts, and I dismissed it, I thought I was being crazy, but then I started to look at her. Really look at her.'

'How did you confirm who she was?'

'She doesn't have social media any more, but I found an old account. Went through some of the photos and . . . there was a photo of her and her mum. I recognized her straightaway.'

Hatred swells inside me. The truth of what happened merges so seamlessly with his lies. He knew who I was because of George. He had known, from the very beginning. From the moment he saw me at that cafe. He knew.

'You recognized Ava Knight's mother?'

'Yes. I recognized her as the mother of the girl who had accused me of rape. I realized she was the same person.'

'Did you confront Ava Knight?'

'No.' He shakes his head assertively, as if confronting me would be completely out of his nature. 'I didn't see the need to confront her directly. I don't know what that would have achieved. But I did what I thought was right – I went to the Crown Prosecution Service and told them everything.'

'Why did you think that Ava Knight had infiltrated your life in that way?'

337

He turns his head away from Burton, angling his face towards the jury.

'Revenge.'

'Revenge,' Burton repeats back at him, before pausing dramatically.

I shake my head. Dig my nails into the palm of my hand.

'Now, Mr Osborne, I want you to take us through what happened on the night of the twenty-seventh of May.'

Here we go. I've read his statement, I know what he's going to say, but I still can't bear to watch. I can't bear to hear him say it. It comes so easy to him: to stand up there, in front of a judge and jury, under oath, and lie.

'I left the house at around nine in the evening –'

'Where were you going?'

'I just popped down to the high street to go to the corner shop. I was gone no more than twenty-five minutes.'

'What happened when you got back to the house?'

'I was on the phone –'

'Now Mr Osborne, we should clarify at this stage that the phone you were on is part of an ongoing investigation that the police are conducting, is that correct?'

'Yes, that's correct.'

'You were speaking to someone?'

'Yes, an old friend.'

My toes curl. *George.*

'When you got into the house, what did you do?'

'Well, at first I didn't think there was anything strange. I was on the phone so wasn't really concentrating. But after I ended the phone call, I realized that the alarm didn't go off.'

'How were you sure that you set the alarm before you left?'

'Because I always do. Without fail. So, I knew that somebody was in the house.'

'And what did you think when you realized that?'

'My first thought was of her.'

'Who?'

He turns towards the dock, briefly glancing at me before lowering his gaze. 'Ava Knight.'

'And how did that make you feel?'

'I was scared. I was worried that she would hurt me if she could.'

'Why did you think that?'

'Because of how much she'd risked just to get close to me.' His voice is rising, filled with emotion. 'She'd lost her job because of what she'd done. She's so sure that I'm the person who assaulted her all those years ago, even though I was found to be innocent, and I'm so sorry that any woman has to go through that, but she was clearly filled with so much hatred towards me. And that made me scared.'

'Once you realized there was somebody in your house, and you suspected that it might be Ava Knight, what did you do?'

'I went down to the basement.'

'What did you see in the basement?'

I lean forward, inching closer to the glass. What is he going to say now? The prosecution are trying to protect him from the inevitable questions that will be asked during cross-examination. But is he going to try and explain away everything that I found in the basement? Or will he stay quiet?

'There were documents and other things on the floor.'

'What were they?'

He clears his throat, his eyes darting momentarily towards me. 'As much as I'd like to assist, I don't think I can answer questions about those things as they're under investigation.'

A thrill of satisfaction sings through me, loud and in

harmony. He's refused to answer. Which he's perfectly entitled to do – he doesn't have to answer any questions that could result in self-incrimination. But that will be ringing alarm bells for the jury. If he's innocent, if the whispers about him aren't real, why won't he answer the question?

'Mr Osborne, let's return then to the basement. What happened once you were down there?'

'She ran at me out of nowhere.'

'Where did she run?'

'She ran to me, pushed me out of the way, and then ran to the stairs.'

'What did you do?'

'I ran after her.'

'Why?'

'Because she'd broken into my house – I wanted to call the police and stop her from leaving.'

'What happened when you ran after her?'

'She slipped on the stairs and hit her chin. I called out to her but she turned and kicked me down the stairs.'

Burton pauses, then raises his glass of water to his lips. He sips, returns the glass to the bench and turns back to Michael, his expression serious and considered.

'Mr Osborne, in her police interview, the defendant stated that the front door was locked with a key from the inside. So she couldn't get out the front door. Is that correct?'

'Yes. I always double lock my door that way.'

'Why?'

'For the same reason I always set my alarm: security.'

Burton nods. 'So,' he says. 'She's kicked you down the stairs. What happened after that?'

'I got up after a minute or so. Because the door was locked, I knew she'd be somewhere in the house. There was blood on the stairs from where she'd hit her chin, and there were a few drops in the hall on the way into the kitchen.'

'What did you notice once you got to the kitchen?'

'I had left my toolbox in the kitchen. I'd been doing some DIY earlier that day. And I noticed straightaway that the hammer was missing.'

'How did you feel when you noticed that?'

Michael shakes his head, lowers his gaze. 'I was terrified. A woman who lied her way to get into my life, who clearly hates me, had broken into my house and had armed herself. It was terrifying.'

'What did you do after that?'

'I didn't have time to do anything. She ran at me and struck me on my jaw.'

'Members of the jury,' Burton says, 'if you turn to page twenty-three, behind tab two, you will see photographs of the first injury suffered by Mr Osborne. My Lord, this is agreed evidence.'

'Yes,' the judge says, turning the pages of his file. 'Thank you, Mr Burton.'

'Of course, My Lord,' Mr Burton says. 'Mr Osborne, after the defendant struck you on the face, what happened?'

'It . . . I couldn't see, I couldn't think, I just knew that I had to try to stop her from hitting me again.'

'What did you do to try and prevent that?'

His eyes dart in my direction then over to the jury. 'You can't see how much smaller she is from in the dock, but I'm quite a lot larger than Ava, so I grabbed on to her arm and tried to pull her away from me but we both fell to the ground. She was madly waving the hammer around, kicking and screaming, trying to hit me, so I held the arm that was holding the hammer with one hand, and used the other to try and get her to stop. I . . .' He pauses and clears his throat. 'I didn't realize that it was on her throat.' He looks up, his eyes shining with tears in the light. 'I didn't want to harm her, I just wanted to stop her from trying to kill me.'

My teeth grind against each other, my stomach turning.

'What happened then?'

'She started making a choking noise, spluttering, so I let go of her. I was so shocked and faint, and . . . she rolled away from me. I remember thinking that she was going to leave. But then . . . that's when she hit me again.'

'How many times did she hit you?'

'Three more times.'

'The injuries are on pages twenty-four to twenty-six of the bundle,' Burton says, nodding encouragingly at the jury. 'Can you describe what she did after that?'

'No,' Michael says, his voice low, his shoulders folding forwards as if he is shrinking. 'I don't remember anything else. The next thing I can recall is waking up in the intensive care unit.'

'Thank you, Mr Osborne,' Burton says. 'My Lord, I'm mindful of the time – now may be a good time to –'

'Yes, I agree,' the judge says, nodding. 'Thank you, Mr Burton.' He swings his chair to face the jury and pushes his glasses to the end of his nose. 'Mr Osborne, thank you for your evidence so far. If you could please return at two p.m.'

'Of course,' he says, bowing his head.

He steps down from the witness box and follows the usher towards the door, past the benches and the jurors. But as he comes face to face with the dock, his back to everybody else, his eyes fixing me in place – he raises an eyebrow, his eyes glinting.

51. Ava

'The defence calls Ava Knight.'

I've been anticipating this for six days – the moment they will call me to give evidence. The jury have seen expert medical evidence, police evidence, photos and documents and messages. But our stories – his lie and my truth – are so deeply interconnected, so entwined, that it will all come down to this: my telling of the story against his. Helena gave everything to cross-examination, barraging him with questions about his version of events, his initial naivety, the case against Lily, the items in his basement. But he was there without hesitation, an answer ready. A natural. A fine balance between charm and nerves.

But it's my story to tell. And yet now that it's here, I can't move. My legs feel weak, as if they won't bear my weight. The security guard who has been sitting beside me throughout the trial has already opened the door of the dock and is waiting, watching me expectantly. I stand and quickly smooth down my black dress. My favourite. The one I used to wear for all my big trials, the career-defining trials. But I am no longer Ava Knight, prosecuting barrister. I'm the defendant.

I'm just Ava.

Let that be enough.

Clasping my fingers together in front of me, I step up on to the stand, my eyes quickly moving to Will in the gallery. He nods at me then raises his hands to his mouth, chewing the nail of his index finger. Mum is beside him. Her face is sallow but her eyes are wild, more alive, more fuelled by emotion than I've seen in years. But she isn't looking at me. Her head is angled towards the other side of the gallery. Her eyes are burning into Michael.

My stomach turns. If I'm found guilty, I'm not sure she'll ever recover.

'Good morning, Ms Knight,' the judge says.

'Good morning, My Lord,' I say, returning my gaze to the bench and bowing my head forward instinctively.

I turn to face forward, keeping my eyes lowered. I mustn't look up at the gallery.

'Do you wish to swear on a holy book or say the affirmation?'

'The affirmation, please.'

She steps away to retrieve the card, but I could say it by heart. The promise that I will tell the truth. But my eyes veer to the twelve faces staring at me, my mind taking in each of their faces. Will they pity me once they hear my story? Will they see me as a victim? Or will their hive mind swing the other way towards judgement and scrutiny? *I would never have done that. She wanted to kill him. She went too far.*

The usher returns and holds the card in front of me.

'I do solemnly, sincerely and truly declare and affirm that the evidence I shall give shall be the truth, the whole truth, and nothing but the truth.'

The card disappears, the usher stepping away.

I lift my head, but my eyes flicker upwards to the gallery.

And Michael Osborne is staring straight back. Just like he did then. His gaze still unflinching.

'Ms Knight,' Helena says, her voice distant, my name losing its meaning as Michael fixes me in his binding stare. He shakes his head.

I blink rapidly, breaking the connection between us, and turn to Helena.

'Can you please confirm your name for the court?'

I take a deep breath, readying myself.

It's finally time.

'My name is Ava Knight.'

'Thank you, Ms Knight. No further questions from me, My Lord.'

Helena takes her seat, sweeping her robe backwards. She takes off her glasses and places them next to her open file, her pen pressing into a clean page in her blue notebook, sneaking sideways glances at the prosecutor who is standing, his silk robes pristine.

My stomach drops. As he rises to his feet, I am falling, plummeting through the floor. I can't do this. I'm not ready. Answering Helena's questions was fine, telling my story was fine, but . . . Cross-examination is a different story: a battle to protect the truth from being buried by smart questions and lies.

'Ms Knight, I'm going to ask you some further questions,' Burton says, his voice smooth, his accent plummy and full. Everyone at the criminal bar knows who he is. He's swift with his questioning, bombarding defendants with a barrage of statements that leaves them breathless and confused. Helena did well at covering the less appetizing parts of my evidence, shielding me from the questions that will arise. But they will arise, nonetheless. And in the hands of the prosecution, they take on a different colour – they will block my path to the light, keeping me in the dark.

My hands are damp, nerves seeping out of the skin at the back of my neck, my breath uneven.

Are you lying, Belle?

No. I'm not that little girl any more. And I know what happened. I know what is real and what's a creation. And they have to prove that I wanted to kill Michael. I don't have to prove anything.

'Ms Knight, can you tell the members of the jury what you do for a living?' He pauses, holding up a hand. 'Apologies – I misspoke. Tell the jury what you used to do for a living.'

I shake my head, refusing to bite. 'I've already answered these questions.'

'You were a prosecutor, correct?'

'I was a barrister working in house for the Crown Prosecution Service.'

'A barrister. How long were you practising for?'

'I'd been practising for nearly ten years.'

'And have you always prosecuted?'

'Yes, except for a short time as a pupil.'

'Ms Knight, what does the Code for Crown Prosecutors state about prosecuting a case where someone involved, a victim or a defendant, is known to the prosecutor?'

I lick my lips, holding his steely eye contact. 'It's not meant to be done.'

'What should a prosecutor do in that position?'

'As soon as it comes to their attention, they should flag to someone that they're unable to prosecute the case.'

'And I imagine this is because of perceived bias?'

'Yes, that's correct.'

'But you didn't do what you were meant to, did you, Ms Knight?'

My fingers grip the glass that sits on the stand, and I lift it to my lips. 'No, I did not.' I sip, my mouth becoming dry as soon as I swallow. Sip again.

'You knew straightaway who Mr Osborne was, but you didn't step away from the case.'

'I did the plea hearing, yes.'

'Yes, you did the plea hearing. But not only that, you then carried out specific actions to manoeuvre your way into Michael's life.'

'I didn't believe that the child in that case was pleading guilty out of choice. And I was right – she changed her plea and the case was dropped –'

'You followed him to a cafe, you went to his house, you spent a day with his daughter, you went to his restaurant and up to his hotel room. You're telling me that this was just for Child H?'

'Yes.'

'Ms Knight, I think it's clear to everyone in this courtroom that you infiltrated your way into Michael's life for one reason alone. You wanted revenge, didn't you?'

'Not revenge, no.'

He picks up the pen that is balanced on the ledge of the lectern and strikes a line through the top of his page. The first line of questioning – complete.

'Ms Knight, you said in your evidence that Mr Osborne knew who you were from the very beginning. But that isn't correct, is it?'

'It is correct,' I say, trying to maintain composure, my hands clammy behind my back. 'It's the truth. He knew who I was from that first meeting at the café.'

'That's simply a lie, Ms Knight. Why are you lying?'

'I'm not lying. And he confronted me in the hotel suite, and like I said before, his precise words were, "It's been fun playing with you, Anabelle." He wanted to see how far I would go.'

'Ms Knight, he did not know who you were until after the night in the suite, and as soon as he knew, he told the CPS. Correct?'

'No. With all due respect, Mr Burton, that isn't correct. And it isn't me who's lying.'

He sighs dramatically, lifting his glass, his gulp loud in the concentrated quiet of the courtroom.

'Ms Knight, I want to take you back eighteen years – to the day that Mr Osborne was acquitted of the accusation of rape that you levied against him.'

I wait for the question.

'That must have been devastating for you, as a fourteen-year-old girl.'

'It was.'

'And unfortunately, as the jury have already heard, your identity was leaked which must have made the situation far worse for you. Correct?'

'I think that any fourteen-year-old would struggle to cope with that situation.'

'This led to you moving home, moving school and changing your name.'

'Yes.'

'And your father went to prison, didn't he?'

My eyes dart up to the public gallery. Dad is staring down at his feet, his head hanging. 'I don't see why my father is relevant.'

'It's relevant and has been allowed into evidence, Ms Knight, because it goes towards your intent. Your entire life fell apart and you blamed everything that happened to you on Mr Osborne being acquitted, didn't you?'

'I . . .'

Stop. Breathe.

He's doing his job, that's all he's doing. Rising to his questions will only do one thing – chip away at my defence, chip away at the doubt that would lead them to acquit. He wants me to appear temper-driven, reactive. He's firming up

Michael's case: he was defending himself and I'm still that traumatized teenager, hell-bent on revenge.

'My life would have been difficult no matter the outcome of that trial. I was raped and had to live with that.'

'You hated him for what someone else did to you.'

'I hated him for what he did to me.'

'You do hate him?'

'Any person, unless they've been manipulated into thinking otherwise, should hate the person who did something like that to them. It's a normal human response. That doesn't mean I'm here because I was seeking revenge. I'm here because he tried to kill me and I defended myself.'

'So even though he was acquitted, by a jury of men and women just like this one . . .' He turns towards the jury, meeting individual pairs of eyes, allowing silence to fill the room. '. . . you still blamed Michael for what happened to you, didn't you?'

'He was acquitted because evidence was contaminated –'

'Now, Ms Knight –'

'And it was contaminated on purpose.'

'That hasn't been proven, Ms Knight – you're simply speculating.'

'No, it hasn't been proven . . . Yet.'

Burton's head snaps towards the judge. 'My Lord, the defendant is speculating –'

'Well then, you may wish to change your line of questioning, Mr Burton,' the judge says.

My face remains impassive, patiently waiting for him to continue, but inside, that familiar thrill of satisfaction is bounding through me, unencumbered.

Burton looks up at the judge for a moment, then nods, twirling his pen quickly across his fingers, and strikes another line across the page.

'The night of the twenty-seventh of May of this year, we've already heard that you broke into Michael's house using the spare key and you turned off the alarm.'

'That's right.'

'And you were in the basement when Michael got home.'

'Yes.'

'You came out of the basement and went to the front door.'

'Yes. It was locked.'

'And then, the evidence indicates that you then went directly to the kitchen.'

'That's correct.'

'Why the kitchen?'

I blink, pausing, my mind trying to see a few steps ahead, a game of chess, moving pawns and queens.

'I'm not sure I understand the question.'

He smiles. 'Why did you choose to go to the kitchen rather than the office which is directly by the front door?'

'I –'

'Or there's also a formal living room, directly opposite, isn't there?'

'I don't know about that.'

'So . . . why the kitchen?'

'I was looking for somewhere to hide.'

'Were you? Or were you looking for a weapon?'

'No.' I shake my head, my fingers tangling together behind my back. 'I was looking for somewhere to hide.'

'But you said in evidence that you armed yourself *before* you hid?'

I lick my lips. My mouth is so dry, the skin in the corners cracking sideways.

'You said you "saw the toolbox, grabbed the hammer, and then hid in the tall cupboard". Is that correct?'

I gulp at the water. 'That's correct. But –'

'So you did go to the kitchen because you wanted to arm yourself.'

'No, I went to the kitchen because it was the first place I thought of to hide and when I got there, I saw the hammer and took it. I was scared.'

'Were you scared? Or were you angry?'

'I was scared. I knew that he wanted to hurt me.'

'But why? Mr Osborne has no history of violence. No convictions or accusations of assault –'

'He raped me –'

'He was acquitted. Is the truth really, that you broke into his house looking for something that might bring you your much-desired revenge?'

'No –'

'And when Mr Osborne got home, you realized that you were in a position to get rid of him completely and frame it as self-defence?'

'No, that isn't what happened. He tried to kill me, you saw the injuries –'

'You struck him four times in total. Correct?'

I hold my breath then lick my lips as I slowly exhale. 'Yes.'

'Now you know very well, Ms Knight, as an ex-prosecutor, that you can use force to protect yourself, but the force has to be reasonable. Surely, you must agree that striking some-one with a hammer once is an extreme act to take, but multiple times? Surely that's intentional?'

'No. I couldn't breathe. He was going to kill me. I just swung.'

'He was trying to protect himself against you, wasn't he?'

'No.'

'You kicked him down the basement stairs, and when he came upstairs into his own kitchen, you attacked him –'

'No, that isn't how it happened.'

'You both fell to the floor, and he pushed his hand on your throat to try to stop you from hitting him again –'

'No.' Tears prick the corners of my eyes. 'That's a lie.'

'Well, what isn't a lie is that you initially believed that you had killed Michael, correct?'

I sniff, quickly wiping away a tear. 'Yes.'

'When did you realize that he was still alive?'

'When DC Farrah came to the hospital and told me that he was receiving treatment.'

'Until that moment, you believed that you had killed this man who you have so hated for most of your life, and you knew that you could claim self-defence and would have no one to dispute your version of events.'

'No. That isn't what happ –'

'So you created a version of what took place that would allow you to claim self-defence, didn't you?'

'No –'

'What really happened, Ms Knight, is that you tried to murder Mr Osborne in cold blood, and he tried to defend himself.'

'I . . .'

My eyes dance around the courtroom, over the jury and up to the gallery where Mum and Will are both leaning forward, their faces long and drained. Tears are flooding Mum's cheeks and Will's brow is low, his mouth downturned. But Dad is sitting back in his seat, his eyes focused up at the ornate ceiling, unable to even watch. I blink and look away from them, but my gaze lands on Michael – blood thirsty and leering down at me from above.

'I . . . I made many mistakes. I've been suspended from the job that I love. A job that I worked tirelessly to be able to do. I should never have gone inside that house. I should never have crossed lines to try to prove that Michael Osborne is what I know he is. But I did. And I can't change that. But I –'

'Ms Knight –'

'My Lord,' Helena says, standing quickly. 'The Crown is preventing the defendant from giving evidence.'

'Let the defendant finish, Mr Burton.' He looks at me over his glasses. 'Continue, Ms Knight.'

'I can't change the things that I did wrong. But he locked me inside the house – there's evidence of that. He chased me out of the basement – and there's evidence of that. He dragged me out of the cupboard where I was hiding and . . . he tried to kill me. You've seen my injuries.' I lift my chin and look Burton square in the eye. 'I'm not a prosecutor any more. And I probably won't ever be a barrister again, but I know that what I did was self-defence. I did what any person would have done in that moment. And I won't let you, or that man, ever put words in my mouth again. I didn't want to kill him. What I did wasn't to hurt him. It was to save myself.'

I clench my jaw, refusing to look away from his authoritative gaze, even though my eyes are clouding over with angry, frustrated tears. Mr Burton studies me then looks down at his notes. He needs to be careful. Push me any further and the jury might start to pity me. They may start to be convinced of my role as the victim.

'No further questions, My Lord,' he says, taking his seat.

'Any re-examination?'

'No, My Lord,' Helena says.

I let out the breath that was trapped at the back of my throat and look up at the gallery. Mum holds a hand out towards me, the other shaking over her trembling mouth, and Will nods, his eyes full of love. Pride. Dad is still staring upward, his expression unmoving.

I quickly avert my gaze, not allowing my eyes to drift to the other side. I will never look at Michael again.

The judge finishes speaking, and I step down from the stand, briefly looking at the jury as I pass them. Some avoid my eye, but others meet it, looking at me as one might an animal in a zoo, unsure whether to greet me with horror or pity.

I step back into the glass cage, a strange kind of relief after the barrage of questioning. I don't know what will happen, I can't even bring myself to think about what the jury are going to do, how their deliberations might fall into place . . . But I did everything I could. I told them my story.

They will be given legal directions by the judge, guidance on how they should consider the evidence, the burden of proof, how they have to be sure that I meant to kill Michael for them to convict – anything less than sure is simply not enough. But what it always comes down to in the end is belief.

Who will they believe?

52. Ava

'The jury are back.'

I sit up quickly, my back aching from the hard bench, and stare at the guard through the bars of the gate.

'What?'

'They're back.'

'With a verdict? Or a question?'

She pauses, blinking, and then pulls the gate open. 'Verdict.'

'Already?'

She nods and then cocks her head sideways – it's time.

I stand, pressing the tips of my fingers into my palms as I try to quell the anxiety that is swelling in my chest. I follow her out of the cell and along the meandering tight corridors then up into the stairwell. We climb. And with each step, I feel as if I'm climbing towards my downfall.

Did I make a huge mistake? Was this all for nothing? What if I'm found guilty and the investigations into Michael go nowhere? What if the new evidence isn't enough for his acquittal to be overturned . . . will the other girls lose their courage?

What if this is the ending to the story? Me locked away and Michael free?

They only retired this morning . . . It's only been five hours. Five hours of sitting in my cell, remembering everything I said, every word of evidence, the photographs of my injuries, the expert, the stone-faced prosecutor and Michael's brutal stare as he watched every moment. It has felt like an eternity. But it isn't a long time for a jury to deliberate. It isn't a long time for them to already be returning with a verdict. When I prosecuted, if the jury came back quickly the corners of my lips would curl upwards, my stomach fluttering in anticipation. The quicker the return, the more likely a conviction. That's the pattern. The rhythm of justice that runs through you when your life is in court, day after day of acquittal and conviction, innocent and guilty.

We stop outside the locked door to the courtroom. I turn my face into a shaft of sunlight that is filtering through the arched barred windows that line the stairs. I lean sideways and peer up at the cold blue sky. Somewhere directly above me, on top of the vast dome of the Old Bailey, is Lady Justice, gilded: arms extended, balancing the scales. I close my eyes, and hope: let today – let this time – be the day her scales tip in my favour.

The jury file in.

They each take up their seat, the one they've been sitting in for the duration of the trial. Some of their gazes veer towards me, and others look stoically ahead.

I lean forward, my face close to the glass, and look up at the gallery, refusing to even see Michael. Instead, I focus on the people who matter. Marissa is there, just like she promised she would be, her face calm but her hand clutching Will's, her knee bouncing up and down. Will's face is drained of colour. He meets my eye with a hopeful smile but my heart deflates, shrinks – I'm going to lose him. Forever.

I tear my eyes away from his, unable to bear the warmth of his dark eyes for another moment. Mum is staring down at her lap, not looking at anyone, not Will or Dad. Cocooning herself in her own little world, protecting herself from this familiar brand of horror. But for the first time, Dad looks directly at me. Is he angry with me? Disappointed? He warned me not to be reckless. He told me what could happen. I press my fingertips to the glass.

'Ava Knight,' the clerk calls. 'Can you please stand.'

I rise to my feet, my knees shaking.

'Can the foreman please stand,' the clerk calls.

A man – the one with dark hair speckled with grey and glasses – stands.

'Have you come to a verdict upon which you are all agreed?' the clerk asks.

'We have,' says the foreman.

A lump blocks my throat and a crack in my breath fills the moment of silence.

'And what is your verdict?'

The foreman looks up from the floor, chin raised.

Please. Please believe me.

I inhale –

'Not guilty.'

My mouth drops open. I blink slowly, the court swimming around me as I shift into a new reality. Will is smiling, almost laughing with tearful, overwhelmed relief. Marissa's hand is raised to her mouth, her eyes screwed shut, then she reaches out to Will and they hug, rocking side to side. Mum's head is buried in Dad's chest, his arm gripping her back as his face breaks with emotion.

And I finally allow myself to look at him.

Michael.

His face has fallen and he meets my eye. His gaze burns, his mouth turning downwards into an ugly scowl. He is consumed by hate. By the absolute need for control. For power. And I was too. But the stark difference between us is suddenly clear: he has millions, the mansion in the suburbs, the fancy cars, and yet my family are here, supporting me, loving me, even in the worst, most unthinkable circumstances. And Michael . . .

He is alone.

I walk out of the courtroom doors into the vast grand hall. My eyes rise upwards to the dome and are drawn to the inscription above me.

Poise the cause in justice' equal scales.

'Ava!' Will's voice echoes out and suddenly I am in his arms. His hands gripping my face, his mouth on mine, his wild, relieved breaths against my neck. I inhale him, tears burning my face. I'm home. Finally.

He lets go of me, his hand on the small of my back, and I pull Mum – who is standing hesitantly back – into a tight hug.

'I'm so proud of you,' she whispers. 'I'm so sorry you couldn't come to me.'

'No, Mum,' I say, looking her straight in the eye. 'Don't apologize. It wasn't your fault. No matter what. Never.'

She nods, her mouth trembling. 'Oh, my girl.'

I hug her again, but as I open my eyes, Dad's face, patiently waiting, shifts into focus. Stepping towards him, I hesitate, uncertain.

'Come here, sweetheart.' He folds me against his chest, like always, my head pressed sideways, his heartbeat loud in my ear.

'I'm sorry,' I whisper.

He holds me tighter, his arms pulling me close. But he doesn't say anything. He just holds me silently, his quiet tears falling on to the top of my forehead.

'Let's get you home,' Will says.

We walk down the stairs, passing barristers in their wigs and gowns, flustered clerks, and defendants, their heads hanging low. And finally, we emerge.

I breathe in. Fresh, cold winter air. A bright blue sky.

Free.

'We'll let you go home,' Dad says. 'You must be exhausted.'

'But I want to spend some time with you –'

'Darling, it's okay,' Mum whispers. 'Go home and rest. We'll see you soon.'

'Tomorrow?'

She nods, a quiet smile. 'Tomorrow.'

I rush towards them, pulling them both into a final hug.

'I love you both. So much.'

'We love you too, Ava,' Mum whispers.

'Always,' Dad says. 'No matter what.'

They move away and then Will takes my hand, and we walk together to the car. My senses are in overdrive – it's only been six months, but my mind frantically tries to take everything in. The sound of the wind rushing down the long road. Traffic. Strange faces passing by. Will's fingers wrapped around mine.

We climb inside the car and I stare, shellshocked, out of the window.

'Will, I –'

'We don't need to talk about anything now,' Will says, his fingers curling around mine. 'I don't care about anything except that you're safe and you're home with me. I missed you so much.'

I nod through teary eyes, and he smiles. He kisses the back of my hand and then releases it and starts the engine. He manoeuvres the car out of the car park and on to the road, and as we turn, the dome of the court comes into view above the surrounding buildings, before quickly disappearing as we drive away.

53. Ava

One year later

I place the newspaper in front of Will, open on the page with my photograph, my face open but serious, the headline bold across the double-spread.

SHATTER THE SILENCE

'Ava,' he whispers. 'This is amazing!'

I beam at him, watching as he lifts his coffee to his lips and continues to stare at my photograph. I spike pancake onto my fork and push it into my mouth, chewing happily, my heart swelling with pride.

'Can I read it out loud?' he asks, tearing his gaze away from the page as he pushes his glasses up his nose.

'Sure.' Nerves flutter in my stomach.

'You may not recognize her face,' he begins, 'but this time last year, it is almost guaranteed that you had heard her name. Ava Knight, now thirty-three, was a barrister for the Crown Prosecution Service, when she came across the man who raped her when she was only fourteen. He was acquitted. You will know his name, too. Michael Osborne. Their shared history is a long and complex one: Ava took justice into her own hands in her attempt to protect another young girl, and in doing so she uncovered a number of victims who had been silenced, convinced that, if they came forward, they would never be believed. But last year, Osborne was finally convicted for a slew of sexual offences. This included the most recent of cases, the attempted rape of a fifteen-year-old known only as Girl H, and five other counts of sexual offences and grooming. He was also convicted of the historic rape of Ava: he was recharged after new and compelling evidence was brought to light after eighteen years of being hidden. He has been sentenced to life imprisonment and will serve at least twenty-two years in prison before he's considered for release.'

I take another bite of my breakfast and watch Will as he reads, his voice sparkling with emotion. My eyes glaze over as I listen to my story, told by somebody else.

'. . . another victim of this case was Police Constable Samuel Hart . . .' Will's voice trails away. 'Sorry . . . I'll skip this bit.'

'No, you can read it,' I whisper. 'It's okay.'

He clears his throat. 'PC Hart was blamed for key evidence in the original rape trial being ruled as inadmissible – with this evidence, a jury would have been far more likely to convict Osborne all those years ago. In a cruel twist of fate, Ava Knight and her father crossed paths with PC Hart some weeks after Osborne's acquittal and an altercation led to PC Hart being pushed in front of a fast-moving train. Ava Knight's father spent eighteen years in prison but has since been released.'

My toes curl against the floor, and I stare down at my plate and let Will's voice wash over me.

'. . . in the shadows there was potentially another character at play: George Cavanaugh. Cavanaugh was the officer in charge of the rape case when Ava was fourteen. The police were keen to question him in relation to the offences committed by Osborne but have been unable to locate him and the search has been suspended.

'"I think he could still be found," said Ava. "A person can't hide forever. If anyone has seen him, or think they know where he might be, then they need to come forward. He needs to be questioned about his involvement."'

Will looks up from the paper, smiling at me sadly. I spike another bite of pancake, the fork screeching against the china.

'But Ava Knight is a force that cannot be stopped,' Will continues, his sad smile transforming into a proud beam. 'After being disbarred for her actions in bringing Michael to justice, she has turned to another vocation in her effort to protect other women and girls from being silenced. "Shatter the Silence is a charity that I've set up to support victims of sexual or violent offending," Ava told us. "It's a charity that will allow victims to speak openly and anonymously if they so wish and receive the support that they need as they go through the criminal justice system. People from the charity will be there to help them with every step, every word, along the way. And hopefully, we can help change society so that the balance of power can tip towards the victims of this type of crime, rather than be so firmly in the clutches of the perpetrators. The phoneline is open, twenty-four hours a day, every day of the year. We're here. We're listening. And we can help you speak."'

Will lets go of the corner of the paper and it flutters back on to the table.

'What do you think?'

He looks across at me, beaming. 'It's amazing,' he says, lifting my hand to his lips and pressing a kiss into the knuckles where my engagement and wedding rings sit happily together. I smile. We got married a few months ago, at the beginning of the summer, with just our families and a small group of friends watching. It was perfect, intimate. It was just what we needed.

'The way they told your story was amazing,' he continues,

his wide smile still fixed, cheek to cheek. 'And you got the word out there about the charity. That kind of exposure . . . You'll help so many people.'

'I hope so.'

'We should go out for lunch later today. To celebrate.'

I nod. 'Sounds perfect.'

'Cool.' He stands and I smile up at him, happiness rising through me, a warming sun over the horizon. He leans down, cupping my chin in his hand, and kisses me. 'Shower time.'

I sigh, my eyes trailing after him, fixed on his broad back as he saunters towards the bedroom.

'Ava, your phone is ringing,' he calls out.

I push myself off the sofa and dash across the slippery wooden floor to the bedroom. Will reaches for my waist as he passes me on the way to the bathroom, and I giggle as I throw myself across the bed, reaching for my phone which is resting by my pillow.

No Caller ID.

I frown, pausing as I stare at the screen. I should answer it – it could be a journalist or someone from another studio.

'Hello?'

'Ava.'

I pause, my stomach dropping. That familiar tone, the signature crack: I could recognize his voice anywhere.

'George?'

The line crackles, his breath raspy as it echoes out of the speaker.

'How are you?'

A chill washes up and over me, like being plunged into ice-cold water. 'Are you really asking me how I am?'

'You keep on talking about me. I saw the wonderful article about you . . . You're doing such brilliant things, but I just wish you hadn't mentioned me.'

'George, where are you hiding? You know you can't hide forever –'

'Ava, I only want the best for you. Please don't force me to tell the truth. Because that's what I'll do if they find me.'

I frown, unease sending a shiver up my spine. 'What do you mean?'

'Do you really think that Michael is the only person I've ever lied for? The only person I've protected? I've spent years protecting you too.'

'I don't know what you're talking about –'

'I know what really happened that day. To Samuel Hart.'

My mind falls still and silent, emptying, as fear freezes me solid.

'What?'

'If you keep pushing people to continue searching, I'll make sure that everyone knows who you are once they find me.'

He falls silent and I wait – bracing myself.

'You killed a man,' he mutters. 'And you let your dad rot in prison in your place.'

That day feels like a fever dream – the colours too bright, the memory at times too vivid and then disappearing to nothing.

I chased Dad through the closing doors of the train. They slammed behind us and it pulled away, leaving us on the empty, quiet platform, nobody around except for us and Samuel Hart. He turned around suddenly, looking up from his phone, his eyes widening as he recognized my face.

'You're Samuel Hart, aren't you?' Dad said, circling him until Hart's back was to the tracks.

'I am,' he nodded.

My mouth trembled. 'Dad –'

'You must recognize my daughter, right?'

Hart's eyes darted towards me and then darted away, as if I would break if he even looked at me.

'Yes, of course I do. I . . . I'm so sorry,' he muttered. 'I don't know what happened. I'm always so careful with handling evidence. I swear I didn't do anything wrong –'

'How dare you say that to her face?' Dad moved towards him and I followed, scared of what he might do. 'How dare you say that when her whole life fell apart because of your mistake? That man got away with what he did because of you!'

Dad's shout echoed up into the sky. My stomach turned with unease as they stared at each other, Hart's mouth hanging open, unable to speak. I glanced away from them and into the distance, the tracks stretching out as far as I could see.

A train was coming. I'll get Dad to get on, I thought, and we can go home.

'I-I'm so sorry,' Hart stammered, his eyes finally fixing on me, full of tears. He met my gaze. 'I've felt so guilty. I just don't understand how it happened –'

'You should feel guilty –'

'Dad, please stop,' I shouted, lifting my hands to cover my ears.

'Do you know she tried to kill herself?'

Hart's eyes widened, his mouth hanging open.

'No . . . I'm so sorry.' He rushed towards me, just a few steps, but panic flooded through me at the sight of his outstretched hands.

'Don't touch me,' I cried, my mind racing, my body shaking with adrenalin.

Fight or flight, fight or flight, fight or flight.

The train blared its horn.

'But I'm so sorry,' he said, his hands gripping my arms. 'Please forgive me, it was just a mistake –'

'Hey, let go of her!' Dad gripped his shoulder.

'Don't touch me!'

Fight or flight.

I placed my hands on his chest and pushed.

Time seemed to slow down. Sam Hart stumbling backwards. The train approaching the platform at full pelt – a train that didn't stop at Shire Green. Dad shouting. My loud gasp as he fell off the edge. The sound as he hit the front of the train. The boom of the horn. Collapsing to my knees. My violent, heaving cries.

'Dad!' I screamed.

'What have you done?' he muttered, bewildered.

'I . . . I didn't mean to! He touched me, I just wanted him to get away –'

Dad crouched down beside me, his eyes darting around the empty platform, his breathing heavy. Footsteps sounded behind us and a man in a suit, briefcase dangling from his fingers, stared open-mouthed at the blood splattered on to the platform, the fast train slowing further up the tracks.

What happened? I saw you all struggling . . .' His words faded away, his colour draining. 'I'll call 999.'

I watched as he backed away, retreating from the scene. 'Oh my God –'

'Belle, listen –'

'I'm going to be arrested –'

'Shhh! Listen to me, we don't have long.'

'I killed him, I didn't mean to hurt him!'

'Belle, listen!' he shouted.

I stopped and stared at him, gasping for air, wide-eyed.

'When the police come and they ask you questions, you

have to say that it happened quickly, and you didn't see what happened, okay?'

'O-okay.'

'You say nothing else. Do you understand me? You stick to that story.'

'But what will you say?'

He didn't say anything, just looked at me with those warm, loving eyes. 'They know the connection between us. They're not going to just let this go. They're not going to believe he fell –'

'Dad –'

'I'll tell them it was my fault.'

'No! I'll tell them what happened. I'll tell them that I panicked, and I didn't mean to push him –'

'And have you arrested for manslaughter?'

'You can't, Dad! And what if there's a camera?'

'It's all the way down there, outside the ticket office. Remember when Finn was mugged? They couldn't make out a bloody thing.' I followed his eyes to the other end of the platform, to the small, unmanned office. 'Belle . . . Ava – you're my daughter. I would do anything for you. And you've been through so much already. I want you to have a life.'

'But you can't just take the blame –'

'I can if it comes to it. Promise me that you'll say you didn't see what happened, okay?'

'Dad, please –'

'*Promise me.*'

George coughs, his voice crackling through the phone, and I blink away the past, tears falling from my lashes and down my cheeks.

'George –'

How does he know? How does . . .

The camera. The police said that there was no CCTV. They said that the camera wasn't working – it had no footage of the event. But –

'Was there CCTV?' I whisper.

'There *was*. Until there wasn't. It was faraway but if you watched carefully . . .' He sighs exaggeratedly. 'It was around the station within minutes that the father of Anabelle King had killed Sam Hart. I offered straightaway to go to the station. It just didn't sound right to me . . . Your dad, a killer? Everything was so chaotic, I said I could get the tape from the camera. Nobody questioned it when I said that there was no footage, the camera had malfunctioned. Things like that happen all the time. And your dad was admitting to getting into a fight with him, so nobody questioned his story. But I know the truth.'

My hands are tingling, my chest slick with sweat. 'I –'

'I think your dad thought he might get off with a low manslaughter sentence, but who was going to believe that? Who would believe that he didn't mean to kill the man who was responsible for his daughter's rapist being acquitted?'

'George, listen –'

'No, you listen. You've always acted so innocent. And I kept your secret because I truly believed that you were an innocent child forced into a horrific situation. But I also know what you're capable of when backed into a corner. You've let people believe that the only thing you're guilty of is taking justice into your own hands. You convinced a jury that you're innocent. But all this talk of justice, and you've never been punished for what you did. And do you think if the truth came out about you killing Hart, people would still believe that you didn't mean to kill Michael?'

'But I didn't –'

'The police have let the search for me go. Just let it go, too. I kept quiet for all these years. Now it's your turn.'

'George –'

'Goodbye, Ava.'

The phone goes dead.

'Ava?'

I jump, spinning around to face the door. Will is standing in the corridor, a towel slung around his waist, water dripping from his hair on to his shoulders.

'Are you okay?' he asks, taking in my tear-strewn face. 'What's wrong?'

My brain stalls, a glitch as I try to process what to say, which lie to choose.

'No, nothing. It was just my dad. Telling me how proud he is.'

He places his hands on my hips, pulling me towards him. I turn into his neck, cowering away from the lie.

'We all love you so much,' he whispers. 'I'm proud of you too.'

'Thank you.'

'And I'm sure someone will come forward with information about George.'

I suppress a panicked inhale and swallow loudly. 'I . . . I don't know. Maybe not. And Michael is locked away, that's the most important thing. Maybe I just need to let it go.'

'Don't say that,' he says, placing a soft kiss on my collarbone. 'He's guilty. And he should be punished.'

My hands dig into Will's back, and I pull him closer, holding my breath, biting down hard on my bottom lip as realization hits.

I need to let George go. I need to let the fire that has been raging inside me, desperate for justice – for revenge – die out. For the sake of my family, for myself . . . I have to stop.

369

I don't have a choice. Dad took the blame for what happened to Samuel Hart for one reason only: love. His love for me was more important than his morals, his reputation, his principles. His freedom. If George proves what I did, it will all have been for nothing. His sacrifice – all those years in prison – his love, would be wasted. And it would destroy my family. Mum, Dad . . . Will. I'd lose them all over again.

'No, I think it's best for me to just move on,' I whisper, nodding up at Will decisively. 'He's taken up so much energy. So much emotion. I . . . I don't want to speak about him any more.'

He sighs. 'If it's what you need, of course I'll support you, but I –'

'Thank you.' I smile at him. 'I'm going to go and shower. Do you want to book somewhere for lunch? Surprise me.' I kiss him on the cheek and turn away, my eyes brimming with tears as I close the bathroom door.

My fingers grip the edge of the sink as I stare down into the basin, my chest heaving with panicked breaths.

I promised myself that I would do everything in my power to prevent this from happening. That I would help people who needed to speak. I would give them a voice. Will is right. George deserves to be punished for the part he played. But to protect myself – to protect my family – I must protect him.

I'll never say his name again.

I wipe my tears away then lift my head, meeting the gaze of my reflection as I set my lips into a stern line.

I choose silence.

Acknowledgements

Another book – my second out into the world and I still can't quite believe it. I must start by thanking my amazing publisher, Penguin Michael Joseph. I feel so lucky to be published by a team who not only are amazing at getting my books out into the world but are truly wonderful people. I don't know where I'd be without my amazing editor, Clio Cornish, who makes my books shine in a way I never could have anticipated. Thank you also to Vicky Photiou, Ella Watkins, Madeleine Woodfield, Louise Blakemore, Beatrix McIntyre and Sarah Bance. Thank you to Joe Mills and Lauren Wakefield for the incredible design for the cover – it is perfection.

Thank you to my wonderful agent Kate Burke who is always there to support me and my writing. You are an absolute star. Thanks to the rest of the incredible team at Blake Friedmann.

Thanks to my sister-in-law, Kathryn Middleton, for her advice on interviewing children and for taking my incessant questions with such patience.

Thanks to all of my friends and family in their continued support for my writing career. It means everything to me.

And finally, thank you to you, the reader. I would not be an author without readers who open the pages and immerse themselves into the world and characters I have created. So, thank you. I hope you enjoyed *Your Word or Mine*.

He just wanted a decent book to read ...

Not too much to ask, is it? It was in 1935 when Allen Lane, Managing Director of Bodley Head Publishers, stood on a platform at Exeter railway station looking for something good to read on his journey back to London. His choice was limited to popular magazines and poor-quality paperbacks – the same choice faced every day by the vast majority of readers, few of whom could afford hardbacks. Lane's disappointment and subsequent anger at the range of books generally available led him to found a company – and change the world.

'We believed in the existence in this country of a vast reading public for intelligent books at a low price, and staked everything on it'
Sir Allen Lane, 1902–1970, founder of Penguin Books

The quality paperback had arrived – and not just in bookshops. Lane was adamant that his Penguins should appear in chain stores and tobacconists, and should cost no more than a packet of cigarettes.

Reading habits (and cigarette prices) have changed since 1935, but Penguin still believes in publishing the best books for everybody to enjoy. We still believe that good design costs no more than bad design, and we still believe that quality books published passionately and responsibly make the world a better place.

So wherever you see the little bird – whether it's on a piece of prize-winning literary fiction or a celebrity autobiography, political tour de force or historical masterpiece, a serial-killer thriller, reference book, world classic or a piece of pure escapism – you can bet that it represents the very best that the genre has to offer.

Whatever you like to read – trust Penguin.